Following years of consultancy in civil engineering that have taken him through Europe, the Middle East and Asia, Barry Troy launches into a literary career with *Dirty Money*. He is currently working on his next book. He is married to artist Vera Bowe. Chris, their son, is a Molecular Biologist. They live in Dublin when they are not travelling.

GW00493624

# Dirty Money

*Barry Troy*

PIATKUS

*For Vera*

For more information on other books
published by Piatkus, visit our website at
www.piatkus.co.uk

Copyright © 2000 by Barry Troy

First published in Great Britain in 2000 by
Judy Piatkus (Publishers) Ltd of
5 Windmill Street, London W1T 2JA
email: info@piatkus.co.uk

This edition published in 2000

**The moral right of the author has been asserted**

*A catalogue record for this book is available from the British Library*

ISBN 0 7499 3230 9

Set in Times by
Action Publishing Technology, Gloucester

Printed and bound in Great Britain by
Mackays of Chatham plc, Chatham, Kent

# Chapter One

In a docklands pub at six in the morning you don't expect your past to rear up and hit you.

'Sweet Jesus!' Frankie Quinlan said, as I walked into the bar.

He backhanded a smear of froth from his lips.

'What's a clean-cut millionaire doing in squalor like this, early of a Monday morning?' he asked, grinning, shaking the hand I held out.

'How's it going, Frankie?' I said.

'Bit here, a bit there,' he said. 'Not as well as it's going for you with a tan like that. What're ya havin'?'

'Coffee,' I said, and watched his eyebrows go up.

'Coffee!' he said. 'Johnny Constantine having coffee! Go on, tell me the worst. You're waiting for a liver transplant.'

'New leaf,' I said. 'Getting old, getting sense.'

'In a pig's,' Frankie said.

He turned to Jody Dunphy.

'Coffee for my queer friend,' he said. 'And gimme another pint.'

Frankie's from my home town. We went to school together. Like most of our generation we make our living in Dublin.

'You been away?' he asked, as we waited for froth to subside.

'Middle East for a few weeks. Business. Couple of

1

weeks R and R in the Canaries to end with. How've you been keeping? Uncovered any more high crimes and misdemeanours?'

Frankie is one of the country's shrewdest investigative journalists, our number one dung bettle. Love him or hate him, you can't ignore him. When they dig up the bodies, Frankie's shovel is never far away. Lately he's been having field days.

His office is up the street from Dunphy's.

I was on the back leg of my morning jog – the master plan was to lose at least eight kilos by Christmas. I'd been running seven klicks a day in the Canaries and I'd vowed to keep it up. It was my first morning in Dublin in six weeks.

'We live in sloppy times,' Frankie said. 'Too many wealthy Celts all of a snap. Country isn't ready for that kinda thing. Rich are getting so they feel they were born to the purple, think they can get away with anything. You and I were taught in school our elders and betters knew best, could do no wrong. Now we know the kind of stuff they were getting away with all along. Like any farmyard, thaw comes and the old bullshit begins to poke through the snow. Too many instant millionaires in this country – they can't all have won the Lotto or figured out how to play the stock market. Hell, you ought to know, you're one of them.'

He grinned wickedly, waggled his bushy eyebrows, took a slug of his fresh pint.

Dunphy's pub has a licence to open early. Newspaper guys use it a lot. They rub shoulders with the night shifters, the minions of the moon. I guess Frankie gets some of his sleaze from the patrons. Most of the regulars don't look any too healthy – morally or physically. They're the usual operators of the parallel universe of night, kind that have to get back to their crypts before daylight catches them. One of these jogging mornings I'm going to look in Dunphy's mirror and I'll be the only one with a reflection.

'Hear who's talking!' I said. 'You're not doing so bad yourself. You must have the most syndicated nose in

Ireland, not to mention the brownest. As things stand, even a bishop can't get his oats these days without finding you up his arse.'

'And not before time,' Frankie said, leaning back, smiling ruefully.

'What's the latest?' I asked, cup almost to lip.

I was totally unprepared for his answer. He began looking shifty, like a guy who's been caught doing something he shouldn't.

'You obviously haven't heard,' he said, not looking at me, watching me in the mirror. 'Paddy Brett died last night.'

I froze solid. Paddy Brett was the nearest thing to a brother I ever had.

Frankie saw it in my face.

'Christ, Johnny,' he said. 'I'm sorry. I thought you of all people would know.'

Paddy Brett and I grew up together, reared by decent people in a back street terrace of two-up-two-downs in a small town that was Middle Earth to us. We were inseparable as kids, couldn't spit without each other, never went anywhere except as a team. I was an only child and used to get a kick when people took us for brothers – and we were, too, in all but name and closer than most brothers I've known.

'Tell me,' I said, and put down the cup. I had a sudden flash memory of daredevil blue eyes laughing at me.

'He was found dead in his car out by Bullock Harbour. Old guy walking the dog at two in the morning came on him. That's what I hear. We haven't run the story yet. Your friend and mine, Sergeant Tom Crotty, tells me it was murder – that was as far as he'd go. I'm really sorry, Johnny. I know you guys were close when we were kids.'

'Yeah,' I said. 'That we were.'

'Did you know he was down to appear as a witness in the McGregor Tribunal *and* the Harkness Inquiry? He was due before Judge Connolly in Dublin Castle week after next.'

3

Frankie left it hanging between us like Robert the Bruce's spider. Suddenly I didn't like Frankie anymore, didn't like that innocent look he floated. Frankie Quinlan might be from the old neighbourhood, but Paddy Brett was *family*.

'What're you getting at, Frankie?'

I felt cold inside and Frankie knew the mood had changed.

'Hold hard there, Johnny old son,' he said, raising open palms. 'No point in shooting the messenger. You know as well as I do Paddy Brett was one of the slickest financial guys in this man's town. We both know what that means. You remember that bank he started – North East Baltic? I've been digging into that off and on for a year now. I can't prove anything but I'll bet every penny you own that it has to be the original ram's horn. What the hell? The guy was right at the heart of the financial system. How many companies was Paddy a director of? Open the financial section of any paper these last few years and you could bet on finding good old Paddy Brett.'

That was true. I'd seen enough pictures of Paddy behind a carafe of something and a place card that announced to the world P. Brett was chairman of this or director of that. Usually he'd be staring out belligerently, as though the cameraman had shouted something nasty. Turn on television and up he'd pop, talking in those fancy clipped tones he'd adopted – kind of accent that would embarrass the folks at home, but one they'd be proud he had all the same. Usually he'd tell us of this or that industrial concern he was turning around, slimming down, rationalising, making leaner, fitter. Normally followed by shots of redundant workers coming through factory gates looking oddly down-sized, irrationally unhappy at being slim, lean, fit and showing no pride in fulfilling their director's obligations to the shareholders.

Times like that I used to wonder what kind of post-graduate courses he'd attended that had downloaded his

4

humanity, taken all the fun out of his face, put ice in those blue eyes. When I knew him he laughed a lot, but any time I've seen him on television he never even smiled – and more's the pity because he had a good smile, infectious, made you want to join in. He could have got away with twice as much if he'd smiled.

'How'd he die?' I asked.

'I don't know,' Frankie said, shaking shaggy curls. The man has a big head, bigger than most. 'Crotty wouldn't specify. Said they'd taken the body to the morgue in Malachy's to await the state pathologist. Now there's a man that never expected to be overworked when he applied for the job. I reckon our pathologist's been on telly more times than the Taoiseach. This country's gone to hell – too much *NYPD Blue* if you ask me.'

'Crotty say if he has any idea why it happened?'

'Too early. I reckon it has to be those tribunals of inquiry. There's far too much shit rising to the surface these days. The big names are beginning to bob up and if anyone had the dirt on those players it was Paddy Brett. How much you reckon he was worth?'

I could see the professional scab-lifter emerging from behind the old schoolmate and I didn't like it.

'No idea,' I said. 'We lost touch years ago. Went our separate ways.'

That was true. In the past twenty-five years we hadn't spoken to each other much, not more than six, maybe seven times, and even then not for long. Accidental meetings at venues of overlapping interest, seminars, the usual businessy things. Like the cowboys we adored when we were kids, we came to a fork in the trail, an 'adios amigo', and we lost the true language of blood brothers. That doesn't mean I've forgotten what he was to me, what we meant to each other.

'He married Joan Callaghan, didn't he? Now there was a cookie! You three used to be pretty thick, far as I remember,' Frankie said, wearing his sneaky look again.

'Yeah,' I said. 'We were neighbours.'

Other kids used to call us the Gang of Three, but we knew we were the Three Musketeers. For a split second in Dunphy's pub on the Dublin quays I looked down the tunnel of thirty years into two smoke-blackened young faces staring at me in white-eyed astonishment as the fire brigade's bell confirmed our November bonfire was out of control – time for all smart musketeers to be indoors.

They married when Paddy qualified. I was best man and there were no hard feelings – well, none that anyone could see. I even managed to kiss the bride on the day – but not on the lips. We knew that would have been pushing it too far. By then I'd started losing contact with them – I was at university in Cork, out of the frame.

'Funny the way things fall out,' Frankie said, shaking those Medusa curls. 'Guy as smart as Paddy Brett ending up dead at this hour of his life.'

There was no answer to that.

'What are ya having?' I asked.

He looked at me from under his eyebrows.

'Only if you're having something decent,' he said.

'Pint and a glass of Bushmills,' I said, and Jody Dunphy nodded from behind the taps.

'You ever hear of a thing called the Montego International Investment Fund?' Frankie Quinlan asked, not looking at me, reaching for his nearly empty glass.

He knocked back what was left of his drink. He drew his hand across his mouth and looked hard at me.

'What am I sayin'? You've probably got a couple a mill stashed away in it,' he said.

Investigative Journalist Quinlan was staring at me.

'Don't come the Ace Asshole with me, Frankie. I never heard of Montego whatever it was you said. Go dig the shit somewhere else.'

He grinned, waved his hand apologetically.

'Can't help it,' he said. 'Automatic with me. Even my wife won't answer questions any longer.'

Jody Dunphy put the drinks in front of us.
I picked up the whiskey and raised my glass.
'Paddy Brett,' I said.
Frankie Quinlan raised his pint solemnly.
'Old times and absent friends,' he said.

I left Dunphy's and walked by the glittering Liffey as it swirled silently and ran away to sea. A fine drizzle had started, as though I needed proof I was really back in Dublin. I paused on the bridge and watched the watery sun slither up the river, my mind full of a sunny day and two naked boys and one very naked girl leaping like wild monkeys from the old tree branch that leaned out over our Huck Finn's Mississippi, our piranha-infested Amazon, our White Nile. I found it difficult to come to terms with the news, to visualise the reality behind the words. It was like hearing the announcement of my own death.

I live the other side of the river from Dunphy's in a penthouse in the International Financial Services Centre area. I traded a rat-infested docklands site for it. I started jogging again but somehow my heart was no longer in it. I settled for a brisk walk that had me at my apartment block in ten minutes.

In my tracksuit I never take the lift. I run the sixteen stair flights and hit every step. I've been told it's great practice for skiing which I've promised myself I'll take up one of these winters.

A young unmarried mother – or single parent, I'm never sure which is correct – lives on the seventh floor in the apartment beneath mine. She runs a discreetly limited entertainment business. Can't say I blame her – got to admit it's better than exploitation by today's employers, beats the hell out of lonely evenings in grubby bedsits. Besides, government policy actively supports free market forces, encourages entrepreneurial talent in all spheres.

As she says herself, all she does is make ends meet. Who am I to criticise? She has it worked out nicely, down to a fine art, and only deals with four guys on a regular basis. One of her favourite throwaways is what's the good of a Financial Services Centre if you can't get serviced?

There's a workaholic young foreign-exchange guy who needs his tensions blown around six thirty on his way to gamble his clients' money on the latest Nikkei figures. Time's her own then until midday alternate days when she does a smoked salmon sandwich, glass of white wine and quick consultation for a forty-something barrister who legs it from the Four Courts – his other exercise.

Around teatime she's back in or on the sack with another early-morning starter who likes to get business and sex – in that order – out of the way before quality time with wife and kids. One of your modern caring men. About nine most evenings she rounds off the day with an older guy, chief executive – she calls him her after dinner stint. He needs a long time to get it together and it doesn't always happen – but when it does it's bonus night. She doesn't work weekends unless something's gone wrong, like a wheel coming off in her private financial arrangements.

She does all right and likes the idea of me upstairs as a kind of nominal protection. Which is OK with me as I've never had to get involved. On the odd occasion when she's had to broaden her commercial base, diversify, to meet some unanticipated financial emergency and it's gone a wee bit sour for her, banging the broom on the ceiling has proved enough to end the crisis.

She's a fine young woman and nice-looking with it – got a really neat, sexy figure. Takes great care of her four-year-old son, Sean. She likes to visit between projects and so far we've managed to keep it platonic.

That particular morning, when I reached her floor, Nikkei Man was leaving her apartment and crossing to the lift.

'Grand day,' says I, 'bit blowy out.'

I didn't catch his reply.

He decided not to loiter for the lift, opted for a head-down dash for the stairs. Magdalen – that's her real name, honest – stood in her half-open doorway in a beguiling chartreuse négligé. She grinned, winked, stuck her tongue out lasciviously.

'Welcome home, Johnny,' she sang out. 'You're looking great. See you later on.'

She shut the door on a harsh world before I could answer.

I climbed the last two flights to my floor.

Where I grew up folks never followed an unlocked-door policy, but they did the next best thing and kept a key on a string accessible through the letterbox. Times change and I was sorry I hadn't availed myself of Dunphy's lavatory by the time I got through my own security and made it to my bathroom.

I shaved carefully. In the mirror light I looked almost black from my travels, especially the last two weeks on the beach at El Cotillo in Fuertaventura with an old friend. We were at university together. Like myself, she did well in the property market of the early eighties. Now in her forties and with two failed relationships behind her and still warped by the trauma of having given up a baby for adoption in her teens, she's turned her back on love and plans a colony of like-minded, well-heeled people to look after one another through to the end. I was invited to join, but pleasant though our fortnight was – we even managed a spark from a past affair – I came away still convinced old ways are best, still hopeful after all those years.

I stood under the shower for a long while lost in thoughts of other days when Paddy Brett and Joan Callaghan were the whole of my waking world.

It really is true. You can't go home again.

I don't go in much for clothes – never did. Paddy Brett used to say I'd always be covered but never dressed. I reckon independence is all that's worth having – all the rest is window dressing.

9

I learned a long time ago that the one great thing money can buy is time – the leisure to do things that really matter to me. Only magpies collect for the sake of collecting.

That morning I settled for a blue sports shirt, dark cords and a blue-green jacket – Donegal all the way. The reddish brown shoes were bought in Bassano del Grappa en route to the Dolomites early that summer. Why Bassano? Because that particular woman didn't give me the old heave-ho until two days later and we were still in love – or whatever it was we were in – when she saw the shoes in a window in Bassano and said they were definitely me. She was a compulsive shopper.

Women nearly always pirouette and clap their hands at the sheer modernity of my kitchen. To be honest, I enjoy the design even if I never cook anything more complicated than bacon and eggs. That morning I started coffee before deciding to eat in the Mokha Coffee House in Dun Laoghaire, see if they knew anything of what had happened.

I slipped into a lightweight waterproof and closed the door behind me. I went through the locking sequence and, as always, was tempted to shout down the stairwell, 'Elvis is leaving the building.'

I took the lift to the basement car park.

Most overnight cars had left and been replaced by day-time parking when I eased my car up the ramp and out into the traffic that was building up to the morning rush hour. Once across the bridge the situation improved and got better as I turned against the flow and headed for Dun Laoghaire. An occasional lazy swipe of the wipers kept the windscreen clear of drizzle. To my left was a pleasantly misty view to Howth Head across a gunmetal sea – all in all a good morning to be alive and one that Paddy Brett would have given his eyeteeth to look at.

A stranger coming upon the Mokha Coffee House might think it as startling as finding a Kitty O'Shea pub in Petra. Its glass doors open into another world redolent of exotic spices. Music full of quarter tones and the jingle of belly-dancers is low but pervasive.

How Stanley Thornton, a neighbour's child from down home, born in the next lane but one from the gasworks, scion of a house of honest coke shovellers, could come to be living with Abdulmeguid – 'Guido' – Shulfan, an Arab of undisclosed nationality, in this extraordinary emporium in Ireland is a continuing mystery. A large picture window faces out to sea and gives the long tunnel of their café a magically unreal quality. When I'm there I sometimes feel I am looking across the Bosphorus.

The morning rush was over when I arrived. Shulfan was cleaning the Espresso machine with long languid swipes, a dreamy look on his swarthy face. When he saw me he dropped the cloth, took up a towel, then offered his hand across the counter, his face split in a hugely welcoming grin, his big brown eyes dancing.

'*Yonny! Salam 'alekum,*' he said.

'*Wa 'alekum es salam.*'

'*Ehlen wa sehlen.*'

'*Shlon kefek, kef halek.*'

'*El hamdu lillah.*'

'You've got me now, Guido,' I said. 'That's as far as I go.'

'It is much more than many,' he said, smiling. 'You look well – you have been travelling I see. You have looked into the sun.'

He went to the swing door of the kitchen and called out something in Arabic. In a moment an aproned Stanley Thornton came through, smiling, wiping his hands. Stan is a tall, thin man with an abstracted air that's given a certain gravitas by a tooth-brush moustache of uncommon bushiness. He's a cadaverous man, kind you'd expect to see in a green smock holding up his hands for a theatre sister to roll the gloves on or maybe he should be standing at a lectern tapping his baton for hush. I can never figure which of them is the feminine half of the relationship.

11

'Johnny, it's good to see you.' He took my hand warmly, held my elbow.

'How's it going, Stan,' I said.

'Have you had breakfast?'

'I decided on one of your Sunrise Omelettes,' I said, grinning, knowing how it pleases him when people remember what they've eaten in his restaurant.

He led me to a seat by the window, his arm loosely about my shoulder and left me to chat with Guido. Stan brought the tray himself and Guido retreated to look after the few other customers.

It was a great breakfast. Coffee with a hint of cardamum, flat Arab bread, an omelette with onion, tomato, sweet peppers, chopped herbs and a dusting of cayenne pepper. Stan sat with me, did all the talking, wanting me to concentrate on the food.

Stan left our neighbourhood at sixteen, ran away to sea when he realised his true nature and fell in love in and with Alexandria. All things Arabic fascinate him and he's quite an authority in his own right and always an interesting conversationalist. Once I'd finished eating he was like any Arab – he wanted the news, the latest from the Middle East. It wasn't long before we got around to Paddy Brett.

'I take it you've heard about Paddy Brett?' he asked.

'Yeah,' I said. 'I met Frankie Quinlan in Dunphy's on the quays and he told me.'

'How is Frankie?'

'Same old scab-lifter,' I said.

'Thought he might be,' Stan said. 'You and Paddy were very close.'

'That we were,' I said.

Stan nodded thoughtfully.

'When he was young he was very beautiful,' Stan said, suddenly, surprising me.

He looked at me and smiled sadly. I realised then the true difference between us. I poured coffee for both of us. Stan

12

held up a Turkish cigarette, a question in his raised eyebrow.

'Fire ahead,' I said. He lit the cigarette, blew a plume of smoke vertically from his outhurst lip.

'I saw Paddy in the Dun Laoghaire Shopping Centre a little while ago. I was surprised to see him pushing a trolley amongst housewives. I mean usually you see him on the telly reorganising the economy and all that sort of thing. I don't understand that kind of high finance but he always seemed to know what he was talking about. I don't think he saw me – if he did he didn't show it.' He smiled sadly at that as though it was something he was used to.

'He was found in Bullock Harbour I believe,' I said.

'That's right. That's what was on the early morning news. One of the guards involved was in here on his way off duty. He told me Paddy was found in his car. He drove a Lexus – that's a fine machine, very expensive. I saw him standing next to it in the car park of the shopping centre. He was having a ferocious row with his daughter.'

Stan laughed, stubbed out his cigarette. 'Paddy was hissing at her and she let fly. I heard her tell him to fuck off. Do you know his daughter? She's really beautiful. I'm told she may be getting a part in that new Neil Jordan film that's coming off. Mind you she ought to be good-looking with a mother like Joan Callaghan. You used to be friendly with her too, if I remember correctly. I saw her a while ago – she got very old-looking. I mean she can't be more than, what – forty-five?'

Forty-four on the seventeenth of May, I thought, and had a sudden flash memory of the window of Sullivan's jewellery store and the brooch it had taken seven months to save for.

'Might not have been one of her best days,' I said, loyally. 'I haven't seen her in over ten years would you believe!'

'Time flies,' Stan said. 'But she's a beautiful woman, the daughter, and quite a handful I'd say from what I overheard.

13

Paddy must be very wealthy. I think he lives out around Killiney – somewhere along the Vico Road I think.'

Guido joined us then and the talk turned to my travels and the state of business in the Middle East. Guido told of a boyhood in the desert and of how much times have changed, but I came away without knowing which desert he had been young in.

'It'll be a big funeral I suppose,' Stan said, returning to our earlier conversation. 'Way they usually write about him anyone would think the government might fall without him. He came a long way from where we started.'

'Didn't we all?' I said, and grinned at them.

'A man ends where he ends,' Guido said, and smiled his sad smile.


Ten to ten and the morning clearing, crisp and tangy, the sun making a brave attempt to air the streets. I left the car where it was and walked towards St Malachy's Hospital.

The grey sheen was gone from the sea – it had turned blue to mirror a better morning. White plumes from the Pigeon House smokestacks streamed east toward sparkling Howth.

A lazy, village air lay over the town's almost empty streets. Too close to breakfast and school time for women to be out shopping, it was mainly the cloggingly parked vans of delivery men and traders setting up for the day's business that were strewn about – not so much parked as abandoned. Neat pensioners with mirror-shined shoes walked sedately toward ten o'clock Mass, nodding to each other, doffing hats politely, surprised and happy to have made it through the night.

I strolled across the front parking lot of the hospital and went in by the main entrance. There was no one at Reception. I leaned on the high desk and looked out across the car park and watched a woman with an I-told-you-so expression drag a crying ten-year-old, his hand wrapped in bloody bandages, toward Casualty.

14

Behind me and a long way down a squeaky-lino corridor I could hear approaching footsteps and thought of Goon Shows Paddy Brett and I had listened to on the small radio his Aunt Lil, his godmother, gave him for his fourteenth birthday the year she won the hundred pounds in the crossword competition. Fabulous present. Paddy loved Aunt Lil.

I turned and was facing a red-haired dullard (great word of Paddy's) walking splay-footed at me. He was advertising acne full time. I reckoned I'd found the source of any cross-infection endemic in the hospital.

He walked behind the desk and looked sullenly at me.

'Yeah?' he said, or something close to that. He fished a pen from the ink-stained top pocket of a once-white coat as though about to do something – sign the Magna Carta, Proclamation of Independence, anything anyone might put in front of him.

'I'm looking for Sister Camilla,' I said.

He was scornful as he twirled the pen between thick fingers before taking a telephone from beneath the desk.

'Someone down here in the hall to see Sister Camilla,' he said, and hung up. A born communicator.

In a while I heard light footsteps squeak on the hall and the butterflies were loose in my stomach as I turned to face Sister Camilla. We hadn't met for some years. She's tall and graceful, and you take one look at that face, that figure, and especially what you can see of those legs, and you know it's just got to be some class of a joke and she's not really a nun – they've got her dressed like that for the film she's making.

She saw me and began to smile that great smile of hers and held out both her hands, leaning back. Margaret Hourican and I had been lovers once, about a thousand years ago, when the world was new and everything was possible. She was from the old neighbourhood, but younger than me. We didn't get to know each other until she came to Cork to do nursing.

Turned out she'd had a crush on me all through school and

I'd never known. She was my first real affair and I never told anyone about her, not even Paddy Brett. Sometimes, mostly when it's late and I'm in a time warp, I think that Margaret and Paddy and Joan Callaghan are the only people I've ever loved – then I usually pour another and forget about it.

'Johnny Constantine,' she called out, laughing, and it brought me back with the speed of light and the pain of youth to sand dunes and endless summer.

'How'rya Margo?' I said, and bent slightly to take the kiss that at the last moment missed my mouth.

When she qualified as a nurse the call became too much for her and she'd answered. In love, God is a terrible rival – there's no one to hate, no one to punch.

'Come on down here,' she said, not letting go of my hand, taking me in tow, and I went willingly, years falling from me.

We went into a small office where Margo asked a pleasant young woman cheerfully walloping a word processor to be kind enough to fetch us tea. She seemed pleased to abandon her task.

'Johnny Constantine,' Margo said again, smiling, studying me as we sat opposite each other, knees almost touching in the small boxroom. Her eyes held me as they always had, as they always will, and she looked about eight years younger than she had any right to. Outward warmth and internal tranquillity seemed to be her only cosmetics.

'You look good,' she said, 'the tan suits you. At least you seem to be taking care of yourself – as big as ever and twice as handsome.' She laughed, struck her knees with her palms. 'I see your name in the paper now and then. What is it you invented that they write about?'

'Nothing world shattering,' I said. 'Mainly gadgets for non-destructive testing of engineering materials. Nothing that would relieve the suffering of humanity.'

She smiled at that and I thought I detected a trace of a blush. It was why she'd left me, taking with her what I'd thought was my whole existence.

16

'If it makes money – and looking at you it obviously does – then it can be turned to a good purpose,' she said, and laughed.

'You're a true nun,' I said, 'money first.'

'It talks,' she said, 'but it can't pray.'

We were laughing when the girl returned with a tray of tea things and Margo stood to make room for her to set it down. The girl looked at the keyboard, then at Margo and decided it was time to leave.

'You look beautiful,' I said, and felt a dull ache.

'Why thank you, Johnny Constantine,' Margo said, tilting her head back. 'Last time a chap said that to me he was all of five years old.'

'You know about Paddy?' I asked.

'I was on duty when they brought him in,' she said. 'I should be gone to bed but I decided to wait for Joan, see if there's anything I can do. I got an awful shock when I saw who they had. I couldn't believe it. There he was, beautifully dressed and dead. As good-looking as ever, but dead. I was thinking of you only an hour ago and saying to myself it wouldn't be long before you'd be around. Mind you, I thought he got very old – he looks much older than you.'

'Hard to look your best in that condition,' I said. 'What happened to him?'

For an instant her eyes went official, but changed as she decided I was family, then hardened again as she spoke.

'He was cold-bloodedly murdered,' she said. 'He was hit on the back of the head – it fractured his skull, I'd say – then a polythene bag, kind used in a freezer, was put over his head and tied around his neck. It was viciously done.'

I was shocked.

'When did it happen?'

'I don't know,' Margo said. 'He was found around one o'clock this morning down in Bullock Harbour, in his car. I'm not sure exactly where. Mr Goulding found him. He's a retired schoolmaster – reason we know him here is he runs a painting class in Rehabilitation. Grand poor man in his

17

seventies – his wife died last year and he finds it very hard to sleep, goes walking with the dog late at night. He nearly had a seizure when he happened on it – the police brought him into us as well. I gave him something to help him sleep when they were taking him home. Pathologist is due this morning to complete his examination. From the feel of the body I'd say he'd been dead less than six hours when they brought him in.'

'What time did they arrive here?'

'Four.'

'Have you spoken to Joan?'

'Garda told me they went out to the house, but couldn't see her. She's not well I believe. They spoke to her son, young Patrick. He must be nineteen or twenty now – God, how time flies! He said they'd come in this morning to formally identify the body. When I rang at nine I spoke to Patrick – he sounds very nice, very mannerly. He said they'd be in around eleven when Joan had pulled herself together.'

Margo dropped her eyes, carefully picked specks of lint from her skirt before looking at me again.

'I don't know the story there, Johnny, but I don't think that's a happy house in spite of all the money. Father Mulhall knows them very well – Joan mainly – and I've heard him speak of them. I'm not that well acquainted with Joan – she's a few years ahead of me. I would have thought she'd have been down by now. The police usually insist unless the person is ill. All they told me is that she's under doctor's orders.'

'Probably in bits,' I said, but I was puzzled. It didn't sound like the Joan I'd known. 'Would it be possible to have a look at him for old times'?'

'Don't see why not,' Margo said, standing.

My squeaking plod echoed her light step as we made our way along grey lino between yellowing cream walls to a bare room that leaped into blinding white at her flick of a switch. He – what remained of him – lay on a stainless steel

18

gurney barely raising the snow-white sheet someone had
spent a long time ironing. Margo drew it back with a
gentle, apologetic movement, her face all sadness.

She was right – Paddy did look older than he should, and
death had made him smaller. Still good-looking, the waxen
face seemed sculpted, the lines more pronounced. I was
filled suddenly with a piercing grief and memories of all the
happy days we'd shared. I might have stood there for an
hour if Margo hadn't broken the silence.

'At least whoever did it left his face alone,' she said.

She put off the light and we returned along the corridors
not saying much. To keep my mind off those lifeless
features on that shining trolley I concentrated on the noise
we made on the lino and thought how I'd go mad if I had to
walk on that stuff every day of my working life.

In the last hallway I could see Reception and my acned
friend talking to a young woman who had her back to us.
She was tall and neatly proportioned with long shapely legs
and tightly dimpled haunches in a form-hugging dark-grey
suit. We were almost upon her before she became aware of
our approach and turned to face us.

Margo and I halted simultaneously – there was no
mistaking who she was. The best day Joan Callaghan ever
had she was no match in beauty for this girl who was so
clearly her daughter. Her face, tremulous and pale, looked
as though she'd been crying. She wore almost no make-up.
Margo moved toward her, arms reaching out.

'My dear, you must be Joan's daughter,' she said, taking
the girl's hands. 'I'm Margaret Hourican, I knew your
parents years ago.'

'I've heard them speak of you,' she said, smiling wanly.
'I'm Patricia.'

She had a lovely caressing voice, but its hoarseness may
have been from grief and tears.

Margo half-turned, pointed to me.

'This is Johnny Constantine, Patricia. He was your
parents' best man.'

19

'Oh I remember you,' Patricia said. 'You brought me those lovely things from Turkey when I was little and we were living in Dundrum. You were to be my godfather, but you were away in Russia or someplace and Mom wouldn't accept a proxy.'

'I was in Africa then,' I said. 'I'm sorry about your father.'

She bit her lower lip and inhaled deeply before turning back to Margo.

'I only heard in the last hour. Could I see him?'

'Of course you can, my dear,' Margo said. She turned to me. 'I'll talk to you later, Johnny.'

'Goodbye for now,' Patricia said to me, and followed Margo.

I turned on my heel and left, ignoring Acne Man as I passed his desk. I was about to cross the car park when I saw a vaguely familiar-looking young man stoop to assist a dark-suited woman from a Renault Clio. The woman turned and I recognised Joan Callaghan – but only just.

Her figure was trim, well groomed and she held herself erect, but her face was different. Even at that distance I knew it wasn't a night's grief I was looking at but years of strain, of bearing up, holding it together. I walked toward them.

The young man was Paddy Brett out and out, but more delicate of feature – more of Joan than of Paddy in him. He had hardly any of the hard, street-fighter's face I had known so well as a boy. His father's eyes – cool, hard bullets – watched my approach, weighed me to the gramme. Last time I'd seen him he'd been in a carrycot.

Joan saw me and I came on slowly to give her time to compose herself. She swayed, turned toward her son, leaned on his arm as her face crumpled. The young man turned wary, automatically squared up to me.

'Hello, Joan,' I said, feeling the hopeless inadequacy of the greeting.

'Hello, Johnny,' she managed, her lips pursed, her face

20

creasing into lines of premature age. The hand I clasped was cold, but not as icy as the cheek I kissed awkwardly.

'I'm sorry, Joan,' I mumbled, feeling foolish, but knowing there was nothing more to be said.

'I know, Johnny,' she said, nodding absently, looking beyond my shoulder as though she could see our young selves marching out into a brave new morning. She remembered her son and said, 'Have you ever met my son, Patrick?'

He had a good solid handshake and I told him I was sorry about his father. He smiled politely and muttered something about having heard his parents speak of me.

'I've just met Patricia,' I said, and waggled my thumb at the hospital entrance. 'She's inside with Margo Hourican.'

I stopped then, unable to think of anything else to say, held spellbound by old memories deep within those green eyes. I shook myself and added lamely, 'I'll be happy to help if there's anything I can do.'

Joan shivered, drew herself erect, ceased leaning on her son's arm and became resolute.

'Not right now, Johnny, thank you, not right away. But there is something, something I'd like to talk over with you. Maybe you could call up to the house later on today – if you could spare the time, if you wouldn't mind.'

Her eyes pleaded with me and I was oddly hurt that she felt she had to beg for my help, me of all people. Patrick looked startled and glanced quickly, reprovingly I thought, at his mother.

'Sure,' I said. 'Anytime. How would four o'clock suit?'

'Fine,' she said. 'I'll be expecting you.'

She pressed her cold cheek to mine before linking her son and walking toward the hospital. I wondered why she hadn't told me where they lived – I had never been in the house they'd moved to from Dundrum – but I smiled and waved encouragingly when she looked back from the door. I strolled pensively back toward my car.

Business was picking up and the streets weren't as

empty now. A good-looking twenty-something woman in a too-tight traffic warden suit that emphasised a fine bosom began rushing the writing of a ticket for the car next to mine as she realised I was about to deny her the first five-in-a-row of the day. She was a good loser and ruefully returned my smile as I drove out slowly toward Bullock Harbour a mile away, the improving day badly suited to my dark mood.

Normally even seagulls hardly stir at that time of day in Bullock Harbour, which is tiny and crowded with battered small boats and rusty old trawlers that look as if they have as little intention of ever putting to sea again as the pensioners who gaze wistfully down on them from the windows of the retirement home. But not so that morning.

Hip-tilted women conversed in groups as they jiggled pramfuls of screaming progeny and paid occasional attention to the unhurried activity within fluttering yellow plastic tape that was strung between the cranes, bollards, and railings cluttering the edge of the granite pier, managing to suggest the festive air of regatta. I parked well back and strolled past the women and small knots of old men. Above me the windows of the old folks' home were filled with interested faces.

Police cars were parked at odd angles and the centre of attraction was a grey Lexus. I counted seven gardai examining the ground minutely. In the centre of it all a big man watched everything and occasionally wrote in the notebook dangling from his hand.

I recognised Detective Sergeant Tom Crotty – he's a good guy, decent, but peculiar in his ways and a holy terror for women, chronic pole vaulter. A fellow county man, he was a handy hurler – damn near won an All Ireland medal on two occasions; certainly wasn't his fault we lost. We'd met again a few months before when my factory unit in the government-sponsored Industrial Enterprise Centre was raided and two of my staff injured in the attack.

'Mornin' Tom,' I said. 'How's she cuttin'?'

22

'Johnny boy,' he said, 'what are you doing here? Don't tell me Brett was your accountant too.'

'Nah,' I said. 'We were kids together, neighbour's children, same street, same school. Bit of a shock when I heard about it. Can you tell me anything?'

'Not much more than you'll read in the papers. Belted over the head and smothered with a plastic bag, end of story. Lousy business. Pathologist still to report.'

'When did it happen?'

'Have to wait on the report.'

That's what I like about Crotty – straight up, no bull. Knew I wasn't going to be telling anybody. I nodded toward the Lexus.

'That his car?'

'Yeah.'

'In the car when he was found?'

'Front passenger seat,' he said, laconically, not looking up from his writing.

'Happen here?'

'Dunno. Can't say, but my guess is it didn't.'

I mooched around and one or two of the gardai gave me a reproving look until Crotty answered their quizzical glances with a shake of his head. Apart from becoming a new focus of interest for the rubbernecks I achieved nothing. I waved to Crotty and he nodded as I eased my way back through the crowd to my car.

# Chapter Two

During his one and only visit to Dublin, Duk Song Kang, the Korean who has the South-East Asia distribution franchise for my inventions, told me the Vico Road reminded him of the Peak District in Hong Kong. Said it was where the snobs hang out and look down on the harbour and the rest of humanity – a perfect description of Killiney.

Who *does* live in those houses that could be leftover lots from *Citizen Kane*? A friend of mine claims most of them are descendants of Brits left stranded by the Easter Week Proclamation, high and dry and forever gazing out toward the Hub of Empire.

That afternoon I almost persuaded myself I could see the Welsh mountains across the twinkling expanse of bay as I rolled along that splendid road in the clear sunshine of a cloudless afternoon. Early for my appointment I eased back and let the car take me.

Killiney roads are country-narrow and demesne-secretive, the walls on either side high. This is where the rich hide and moan to friends how they're barely making ends meet – how taxation is killing them, wiping them out. Where wives with delicate hands give gushy weekend-supplement interviews on how they're cutting back, making do; how they no longer can afford to eat out and have to limit their dinner parties to twelve.

I figured there was something of a gulf between perception

and reality the moment I swung the car wide on the narrow road to negotiate the leaning granite piers that flanked the entrance to Paddy Brett's pot-holed drive. Slightly skewed, a black-marble plaque advised in faded letters that I was now entering upon the grounds of Windward. Wrought-iron gates, their ends buried in the mud, pleaded to be rehung or, at very least, painted. A team of gardeners would be needed to put a look on the grounds enclosed by six-foot high walls of mica-flecked granite. By the time the house came into view I'd decided my old friend, Paddy Brett, had died in debt and danger.

It was the kind of big house beloved of conservationists, deathwatch beetle and fungi of the genus *Merulius*. The external render had come away in leprous patches and the exposed yellow brickwork suggested advanced jaundice, galloping decay. The large forecourt was balding – more ponded clay than gravel – and grass advanced from the scraggy margins. Here and there a major weed had taken hold and been given its head to see what it could make of itself. Paint was called for – paint by the bucketful.

It was very quiet as I left the car and walked to the door. A bird chirruped, but immediately stopped, as though a mate had reminded it there was a death in the family. I tried the verdigris-encrusted bellpush and heard nothing. I passed the time counting the number of knots that had fallen from the flaking door. Half expecting it to come away in my hand, I lifted the large brass knocker and let it drop on the scarred timber, a dull sound that made me think of that murderous blow to Paddy's head and I shivered remembering Crotty's words – 'belted over the head, smothered with a plastic bag, end of story'.

I waited for what seemed a long while before deciding to take a peek round the back.

If the front could be considered overgrown, the side and rear were the last of County Dublin's rain forest – spear-carrying leprechauns could not be discounted. At the rear corner of the house I came upon a major collection of empty vodka bottles. All popular brands were represented, but there was a clear preference for Smirnoff.

Bare floorboards and an empty room lay behind the first window I came to. The second was a kind of white-walled pantry with cluttered shelves, but somehow I wouldn't care to be depending for survival on what they held.

A sixth sense made me pause and peer cautiously in the next window and I was glad of the intuition that made me hesitate as I am not by nature the Peeping Tom type.

They were at it hammer and tongs, *con brio*, like rattlers, her back against the wall, her legs around his waist, her dress to her armpits. His trousers were puddled about his feet, his tongue to the navel inside her, his clenched buttocks frantic as a trip hammer. I have an abiding memory of a mass of ringletted chestnut hair against the white wall behind her. I ducked back and retraced my steps before the jungle obliterated them.

This time I really used the door knocker. It took a while before he answered and I hoped he'd finished what he'd started and that his lovely companion had reached harbour also, as Mr Cleland so quaintly but aptly put it. He had the grace to be a little flushed, a mite breathless.

'Afternoon, Patrick,' I said gustily. 'Your mother home?'

'Hi, Mr Constantine,' he said, and threw wide the door. 'C'mon in. Mom's lying down, having her nap, but I'll get her for you.'

On home turf he was laid back, at least as relaxed as a nineteen-year-old can be when he's been interrupted at a critical juncture in his affairs. I'd misjudged him outside the hospital – he really was a very handsome young man with steady intelligent eyes that met mine calmly if not a tad sardonically.

Apart from the faintest smell of damp the hall was respectable enough. The room he ushered me into was bright and airy and suggested that most of their living was done there. The furniture was of pensionable age, saggy with the memory of bygone bottoms, but right for all that.

26

It was a clean well-lighted place as they say where I come from.

'I'll get Mom,' he said.

'Please don't disturb her,' I said. 'I really mean that – I don't mind waiting and I'd rather she had a rest. It's a tough time for her, for both of you.'

'Not as tough as you think,' he said, and took the wind out of my sails. 'Would you like a drink? There's whiskey or vodka.'

'Whiskey's fine,' I said, and eyed him warily, wondering what lay behind that laconic comment.

'Be a tick,' he said, and left the room.

The more I examined my surroundings the more I despaired of my friend's solvency. In one corner of an external wall the paper had started to curl and the floor beneath a sideboard of dubious provenance was rotted through. Gilt flaked from the frame of a large bevelled mirror that looked as though it had hosted the fly Olympics and the lathing showed in two areas of the ceiling. A pretty decent ormolu clock was stopped at three ten and was flanked by silver-framed photographs. There we were in one, Paddy and I, each with an arm about a radiant Joan Callaghan, and I could not remember when, or identify where, the photo had been taken. Christ, I thought, we really had looked cool!

'Weren't you the tearaways,' he said teasingly, coming through the doorway.

He carried two glasses the right colour for whiskey and she carried a small cut glass jug tinkling with ice as she glided into the room. She was beautiful as only the beautifully young can be, her wild chestnut hair a mass of fluffed out ringlets and clothes enhanced rather than reduced the sensual impact of her body.

For a guy short of twenty he was loaded with confidence and she wasn't far behind. Her smile was impish, a guess-what-we've-been-doing grin, a see-if-I-give-a-damn look in her eye.

'Candice Delamere, Mr John Constantine,' Patrick said, waving a glass-holding hand at each of us in turn and, I suspected, barely restraining a tarrraaa. He handed me a drink.

I did the easy thing and smiled affably at her, tried hard not to be patronising.

'Call me Johnny,' I said, and nodded to include him in the invitation.

'And you must call me Candy,' she gushed melodramatically, overdoing the Duchess of Malfi bit, pursing her bruised, bee-stung lips. 'Water, Johnny?'

As I held out my glass for her to pour I was reminded of altar-boy days. Her breasts nestled softly in her low-cut dress and quivered slightly as she moved. With a shock I realised I was envying the son as I had once envied the father.

She tripped lightly across and added about the same amount to Patrick's drink, looking him in the eye as she did so, running her tongue slowly and lasciviously across her upper lip, ignoring my presence. He grinned crookedly at her before turning to me.

'Cheers,' he said, and plopped into one of the sombre armchairs. 'Grab a pew before your feet go through the floor,' he said cheerfully.

Candy set the jug down on a fine dinner table and settled herself at its head – Queen Mab in a carver.

'Hear you and Dad used to be close when you were kids,' he said, and took a belt of whiskey without batting an eye. Times change, I thought – at his age his father and I were only experimenting with pints of stout.

'Regular David and Jonathan,' I said.

'How come I never met you until today?'

'Well, actually, you did,' I said, 'but you couldn't have been more than five or six months old. After that your father and I didn't move in the same circles.'

That made him scowl, seemed to sour his humour.

'My father didn't move in circles,' he said, 'he was in a fucking spiral, a tailspin.'

There was no answer to that so I didn't try one. I sipped whiskey and let sugar Candy cut the silence for me.

'I'll bet he was a beautiful baby,' she said, 'or maybe you're not a judge of babies, Johnny.'

'He was sweet,' I said, mainly to needle him. I didn't like his sulky behaviour.

'Who gives a shit?' he exploded.

'Now, now, lover, let's not get morose,' she began, but he cut across her savagely.

'Shut the fuck up. When I want your advice I'll fucking ask for it.'

'How many times must I tell you not to speak like that in polite company?' Joan Callaghan said, pushing in the door, not yet seeing me. 'Why, Johnny Constantine, I never heard you arrive – I must have fallen asleep again.'

She patted her hair absentmindedly, her smile a nervous tightness, her eyes not doing quite what she wanted them to do. Her son's face showed either a patronising sneer or a grimace of despair. There was a sense of *déjà vu* about the scene.

I went halfway to meet her and kissed her cheek. For someone just out of bed her face was cold. I've never been good at sympathising, just plain awkward. Lumpish, silent commiseration has always been my bag at wakes. I retreated to my chair and left her stranded in her own living room like someone who's just missed a train at a hamlet stop on a Hitchcock prairie. Her gaze lighted on my glass and immediately flicked to her son's.

'I think I'll have a drink too, Patrick dear,' she said, with a coyness that did not become her. From the hostility of his glance I realised my presence was being used to break a standing agreement and for a moment I thought he would refuse. After a brief, angry hesitation he left the room.

Candy Delamere said nothing, decided to sit this one out. She threw me an opaque glance that said she'd been down this road before and knew when silence was the better option. She began to suck her thumb.

29

'You must excuse the state of things, Johnny,' Joan began, waving her hand vaguely. 'Paddy bought Windward about twelve years ago as an investment. Paddy was great at investments – but it never struck him that we had to live in this investment. Twelve years now we've been camping here – there's no other word for it – waiting for the great financier to tell us we're moving to the next bloody investment. It needs an awful lot spent on it to make it any way comfortable or presentable. There isn't even central heating in the place.'

'At least we don't have to argue about things like that anymore,' Patrick said from the door, with a certain grim finality.

He carried a glass of clear liquid and I reckoned we'd just established who the Smirnoff-bottle collector was. It surprised me. I had never seen Joan drink anything stronger than lemonade. The hand that took the glass trembled and she seemed to leave us immediately as she went about the solitary business of steadying her nerves.

'Has Patricia arrived?' Joan asked, brightening, and I could see the blast of vodka had restored some confidence.

'She's not coming,' Patrick said, 'rang to say she was all tied up.'

Outside his mother's range of vision Candy Delamere made a face at him, put her hands behind her as though bound, thrust her hips back and forth and mimed ecstasy. When she stopped she grinned at me before settling down to stare sulkily at him. Unambiguously and with startling lewdness she gave head to her thumb.

Patrick grimaced wryly at her before turning back to his mother.

'She said she'll ring you later.'

'Patricia shares an apartment with a girl in the same class at university,' Joan said, and Candy began flicking her tongue wildly. 'Another one of Paddy's investments,' Joan added sarcastically, and took a lash of her drink.

Vodka was calming her, relaxing the elastic that had been wound tightly when she'd entered the room. Slowly, I was becoming used to the transformations in the face that had once been life itself to me. Her complexion had an unhealthy sheen and her make-up, the little there was of it, had that hit-and-miss quality you find with elderly ladies who refuse to acknowledge the need for spectacles.

Her hair was neat, but in an old-fashioned style I remember my mother favouring and her composure bespoke a woman who no longer cared what others thought, an elegantly offhand gone-to-seediness, sad in such a relatively young and still beautiful woman. Most of the tremble had gone from her hand, but she fiddled incessantly – now with her drink, rotating her glass on the occasional table beside her, now with the tassel of the torn cushion protruding from beneath her elbow.

I couldn't decide if it was my unaccustomed presence or that of Candy Delamere that fazed her, made her hesitate to speak her mind, to get around to the business she'd mentioned outside the hospital.

Suddenly, she seemed to pull herself together, reach some conclusion. Full of determination to assert, she faced her son and spoke with the deliberateness of someone trying desperately not to slur the words, to be in command.

'Would you very much mind, dear, if Johnny and I had a little chat about old times?'

The sentence was too long for her and before its end her confidence leaked out and turned to a sad pleading.

Patrick ceased being warily attentive, became slightly paler and clenched his teeth – Hollywood heroes of my youth were forever doing that in lieu of acting and I half hoped he'd crush the glass he held to complete the illusion. Candy Delamere stopped clowning and watched him carefully.

'You're going to ask him to do what we were talking about this morning, aren't you?' he said, through teeth that seemed to have become welded together beneath far from friendly eyes.

'No dear,' she said, and absently touched her hair again.

31

'I merely want to reminisce about old times, days when we were young and very happy.'

Her voice quavered off plaintively on a dying note that seemed a touch theatrical, but was consistent with the day's events, complemented the sombre mood I felt even if no one else seemed to feel it in that chilly room.

'I don't think you'd understand or even be interested in what concerned us when we were your age,' she added, saying it clearly, her unexpected verbal adroitness somehow establishing a moral bridgehead.

Having reached Smirnoff cruising altitude she'd levelled off, was on automatic pilot and beginning to cope. I wondered if vodka was the reason she hadn't gone with the police to identify the body in the small hours of the morning.

He fumed. He smouldered. I felt like telling him he looked beautiful when he was angry to see if there was a chance he could take a joke. His light of love seemed totally pissed off at his slow burn and grimaced prettily as she drew attention to herself by tapping an unbelievably long emerald fingernail on the table top.

I said nothing, just let silence waft over us like sea mist and waited for someone else – preferably Patrick – to become as fed up with amateur theatricals as I was. In the end he gave in, shot out of his chair, abruptly calling to Candy, 'Let's get the fuck out of here,' and ignored his mother's wince at the intemperance of his language.

Hand on heart, I'd never seen anyone flounce until that day. All previous efforts at the flounce paled into minor petulance, momentary irritation, by comparison with that high-rumped flick, that ballerina's goose step that brought Candy Delamere clear of the carver and halfway to the door in a trice.

'Byee,' she called musically, over her shoulder, and was gone. I had a feeling that a source of great warmth had been taken away. Patrick stormed after her.

'How I wish he wouldn't use that awful language,' Joan

32

said, seconds before her son attempted to take the front door off its hinges. The bang reverberated through the house, rattling casements.

'Even before Paddy moved out I kept asking him to be stricter with Patrick,' Joan continued, 'try to establish some parental control, behave like a father for a change. But no, neither of them ever listened to me. He'd put off speaking to the boy until he had a few jars on him and then it would end in a shouting match with me in the middle getting the blame. But what kind of a way is this to treat an old friend – your glass is empty.'

She grabbed it before I could decide if I wanted to take avoiding action and was at the door calling over her shoulder that she wouldn't be a tick.

Even I can figure how long it takes to pour yourself a lash of vodka, get it down, then pour two normal drinks – that was how long she was. If she'd been cruising before, she was floating serenely now, high on a Smirnoff thermal, reentry of the drinking module, not a care in the world – I wondered if she'd popped something for good measure.

Suddenly it came to me, I recognised my *déjà vu* – Katherine Hepburn in *Long Day's Journey Into Night*. Then I had second thoughts – maybe she was being Blanche Dubois. Unsure of where the conversation had been headed I stuck my nose in my glass and waited for her to get comfortable and continue.

'It's quite remarkable, you know,' she began, one hand back to patting her hair, the other unconsciously making wet circles with her glass. 'You've really changed very little in over twenty years. You've worn well, as my mother used to say, God rest her.'

She surprised me by blessing herself, a hasty sign of the cross – or maybe she was warding off the evil eye. I thought people had given up that sort of thing long ago.

As she spoke she stared at me, but I don't think she saw the man that sat in front of her. She was focused on the

33

past, on the magic threesome we'd once been, Paddy and
Joan and Johnny, a trio straight out of Enid Blyton she
seemed to think, and was to keep repeating while a late
afternoon of her tortuous meanderings wound into a long,
forgettable evening.

By turn she was maudlin, testy, spiteful – all in all not a
pretty sight or sound. But I didn't mind, just sat there,
knowing that people go a little mad when those they once
held dear die denying them apology or revenge.

Mainly she was angry, mad at her husband for leaving
without giving her the opportunity to retaliate, to say those
things she'd been saving to throw in his face the first
chance she got of him. She was lamenting the now-never-
to-be-enacted    scenarios    developed    in    the    pent-up
frustrations of a lonely bed: those one-liners Dorothy
Parker would have killed for and that would never now be
used: remembrance of chance gossip hurtfully overheard:
the pain of fatherless children slowly becoming unmanage-
able with the years and turning on her disdainfully as her
habit grew and bit deeply into their lives, twisting their
perception of the adult world: the pain when children
blamed her for cutting them off from the source of wealth
and the commonplace luxuries of their peers.

And overall the terrible dawning of an only chance
missed, the bitter realisation of what might, what should,
have been, the recollection of opportunity lost, of dreams
allowed to fade.

The jungle outside the rusting metal of the french
windows had vanished in darkness by the time she got
around to her reason for asking me to call.

'You know, Paddy always said you were the most street-
smart guy he ever knew – said that a lot of the things that
he took years to learn you knew when we were kids. Used
to say if you'd been born in Chicago you'da been a millionaire before you were out of your teens. Tough as old boots
and smart as a whippet – that's what he used to say of you.'

She smiled at something and looked at me in the

strangest way. I had the weirdest feeling she was going to suggest we try going to bed.

'Paddy had all the brains,' I said, playing for time, leery of this eulogising, growing more certain by the minute I was not going to like what was coming.

'Don't write yourself down,' she said, and I realised her unlovable simper probably seemed wondrously coquettish seen from her side. 'It isn't only Paddy who thought you smart – I do too. That's why I asked you here.'

She pulled herself together, sat higher in her chair and I braced myself mentally.

'Johnny,' she said, not without a certain dignity, 'I want you to help me find the money.'

Time, that scrawny old carrion eater, fluttered down and sat on the threadbare carpet between us.

'The money,' I said, my mouth suddenly very dry. 'What money?'

She lifted her glass to her lips a trifle jauntily, her little finger raised like a gun sight as she took aim at me over the rim.

'All the money,' she said, and smiled horribly.

# Chapter Three

When I was a kid, Granny lived with us in what nowadays is called an extended family – back then it was known as overcrowding – and she was a nasty domineering old woman who could never be satisfied. Compared to Gran, Paddy Brett used to say, Hitler was an amateur, but the moustache was better. She was full of pishogues, would threaten the evil eye on anyone who didn't agree with her, and revelled in bloodcurdling tales of ghosts, graves and banshees that to this day can send creepy things scurrying across my back.

Most potent of her omens was a tapping on the window – any storm or passing cat could warn of the imminence of a death in the general family and could shock our crowded kitchen into quaking silence. In school I knew instantly what the knocking on the gate in Macbeth really meant.

That October evening as I looked across the empty fire-place in Killiney at the woman I'd kissed and fondled when we were young – her eyes a trifle glazed now, not quite focused, but her earlier tremors gone off the Smirnoff scale – one of Granny's portents hit the window making us both sit up, almost, but not quite, causing Joan to spill her drink. We heard a plaintive squeal, a light scraping of beak or claw on glass and the feeble flutter of wings as some bird or spirit tried to break free, cast itself adrift. Crawlies shot across my shoulders and an image of a fourteen-year-old

Paddy Brett stared imploringly from some pain-filled, airless space.

'What money do you have in mind, Joan?' I asked, and settled back in the chair, moving my shoulders as though trying to make myself comfortable, but really masking my involuntary shiver.

'Paddy did well, Johnny,' she said, twirling her glass before sipping, concentrating on a spot somewhere behind my head or maybe just unable to focus. 'Made a lot of money, and I mean a big lot. Kind he used to call fuck-off money when he'd had a bit too much to drink and wanted to brag, make little of me, put me in my place, show me how dependent I was, how vulnerable he wanted me to feel. For a good while I couldn't figure it out. I kept wondering, asking him why, if he had that much money, he didn't do something about the house, buy a tin of paint now and then. He'd just sneer, say there was nothing wrong with it, tell me it was far from houses like it I was reared. As time passed, I began to realise there was something fishy about the money, something not quite above board. The money couldn't be shown.'

I should have anticipated it, should have known it was coming when she stood and began a demented pacing, but before I could stop her she was on her way with our glasses to Lake Smirnoff with an airy 'Won't be a jiff, freshen up these.'

I stood at the french windows and looked through my reflection at the darkening night and pondered what had failed these two beautiful people – the couple most likely to succeed. What cold subterranean currents had eroded caverns deep in their personalities, undermined all that had been between them in the anarchy of childhood when all the fools in town were on our side? And what had happened to the comrade I had dreamed dreams with? What had changed my Huckleberry Finn, my Aramis, my Zorro? What had turned the White Knight against his Lady?

Joan sidled into the room behind me and her pale reflec-

37

tion floated across the window pane superimposing itself on the fading tracery of an almost leafless tree that snared the brightening stars of evening. I turned and rejoined my past.

'I don't know where he had it or what he had it in,' Joan said, settling herself, at ease once more, the next twenty minutes secure in the glass in front of her as she tried to pretend this was social drinking and not the abatement of panic. 'All I'm sure of is there's a lot of it. Before he walked out and left us he'd sometimes boast when he was a bit pissed that it was in eight figures, said he'd earned it and that he'd be damned if the taxman was getting any of it.'

She sipped and some trickled down her chin but she didn't notice. Her speech had deteriorated over the afternoon and now she seemed to abandon all attempts at being ladylike and kept slurring her words, only occasionally pausing long enough to get it right or to go back over what even she realised was incomprehensible. Not to embarrass her I spoke slowly, kept her company so to speak.

'I know the National Lottery has kinda cheapened money, but eight figures is still an awful lot of bread. You sure it wasn't just the jar talking?'

'No, Johnny, I always knew when he was serious, when he really meant it. He might boast and brag in an empty way about who he knew, who he'd been drinking with – hear him tell it at times you'd think he'd just come from a boozing session with three or four cabinet ministers. But behind all the bragging when it came to money he was always serious. Money had become his god, his whole existence. Used to deliver po-faced lectures in his cups about it – tell me how it could buy everything; how everyone and everything had a price tag – a bottom line. Christ! How I hated the way he'd keep repeating that bottom-line bit.'

'You know, Joan, I don't recognise this man you're talking about,' I said.

I could have been cruel and said that neither did I know

the woman who spoke, that for me it was turning into a double wake and that I knew for sure now I was the last of the Three Musketeers.

'Johnny, the man you knew started to disappear about eighteen years ago.'

She sipped her drink and remained silent. Her lips kept moving, but it was a little while before she began to speak aloud again.

'He started buying property in the eighties, a lot of property – don't ask me where the money came from. He'd come home and ask me to sign deeds and stuff for things he was buying. Then, later on, I'd be signing again when he was selling – I never could keep up with it, but back then, even though we were fighting most of the time, I still trusted him, still thought home and kids meant something to him. How wrong can you be!'

Again she lapsed into silence, became morose, began moving her lips silently again. I could almost hear the ratchet as her mind slipped a cog or two – or maybe it was her teeth grinding. I said nothing, waited for her to pick it up once more.

'You haven't said if you're going to help,' she said, suddenly returning from whatever hell-hole her mind had fallen into. Once again she turned on that wheedling smile that snuffed out the girl I'd known and loved as she aimed her gaze at me and missed. They had become shades now, my Paddy and my Joan, but I was still their Orpheus, the one left behind.

'Goes without saying,' I said, and hoped my smile held more warmth than hers. 'Any ideas where I might start the search? Eight figure sums aren't all that difficult to hide if you're Paddy Brett. Do you have any of his records, papers? Did he keep stuff in the house?'

'There's his practice in Ballsbridge – Paddy Brett & Co. One of those renovated houses – he owns the building. He has three associate partners – I only know the oldest one, the one who joined him when he set up on his own that first time, man called Oliver Pettit. But that's all legitimate I'd say – probably worth a good few shillings but not the real story. He could have other offices for all I know – he always believed in keeping his eggs in as many baskets as possible.

'Then there's that kip of an office, the one he first opened – over O'Connor's bookshop in Glasbury Street. I always hated that place. Three rooms on the first floor, peeling wallpaper and that horrible brown lino you used to see everywhere thirty years ago. That's the place to start if I know Paddy. Place where no one knew what he was doing. No associates or partners to look over his shoulder, no one except that poor mad woman he took in when her father committed suicide after Paddy had ruined him. Christ! He used to have the cheek to say he was looking after her as part of his corporal works of mercy – Paddy Brett! After he'd ruined her father! Hah!

'There's always those computers of his – he hardly ever let that small one out of his sight. He brought that every-where with him. Young Patrick tried to see what was in it one night but he said there was a whole series of passwords or something needed before you could see what he kept there. I used to go through all his papers but, when he found out, he kept everything under lock and key. Not that it ever did me any good – I could never make head or tail of all that complicated paperwork he carried around.'

She grew silent once more, began to sway slightly from side to side.

'This money,' I said. 'When he talked about it, did you get the impression he already had it or was it something that was going to happen? Was it in cash, like in a bank or a building society? Did he ever go abroad or talk about going to places like the Channel Islands, Isle of Man, Virgin Islands, anywhere you remember?'

'Abroad!' Her snort was ugly, a grunt. 'Went through a phase when he had a permanent tan. Going through his pockets I'd find receipts, money in notes and coin from all

40

over. Florida, New York, Far East, Spanish resorts, Geneva, Rome, West Indies . . .'

Her face twisted into bitter recollection and there was a mean look in her eye as she continued.

'All the places we once said we'd go to when the kids were old enough. He was never short of excuses for junketing. Hear him tell it the Minister for Industry and Commerce couldn't use the toilet without the great Paddy Brett holding him out and wiping him afterwards. If it wasn't that, it was the economists' or the accountants' Passover, or the chamber pots of commerce dinner, or some deal that could only be concluded in a brothel in Hamburg or Bangkok or wherever men go to get whatever it is they want.'

Joan thought for a while. 'He was a director of a number of companies but there was one company that always struck me as being different. He didn't often mention it, but when he did I could see it had a special significance for him. That oily accountant friend of his, Bill Grattan, was also a director. It was called the Montego International something something – can't remember the rest of it.'

She lost her nose in her drink, then stared morosely into the cold fireplace. After a while she looked at me again, slightly bleary now.

'You cold? I should have got Patrick to light the fire before he went out. Don't know how many times I asked Paddy to put in gas fires. Bet that little blonde bitch has gas fires in her place. You got a mistress, Johnny? Probably two or three. Everyone's at it these days – you're entitled to your share. God how easy it is now! When we were kids mortal sins were mortal sins and no getting away from it – no getting away *with* it! Did you know I trapped Paddy?'

Her question came out of the blue.

Suddenly I did feel cold, felt I didn't want to listen to any more recriminations, but she was going to tell me things whether I liked it or not – she'd reached that point in her drinking where she was in a timeless zone.

41

'You know,' she mused crookedly, 'I was really unlucky back then. Two great young men to choose from and I picked the wrong one. An old aunt of mine used to say that you can have the first child whenever you like – all the rest take nine months. It's true – it's what I did. Paddy did the decent thing and married me when I let myself get pregnant. If Patricia hadn't such a look of him he would have got around to thinking she was your daughter.'

She laughed harshly. My glass was empty, but this time I pushed it firmly between my thigh and the chair arm.

'Speaking of Patricia,' I said, trying to distract, 'how close was she to her father? Would she know much about his business?'

'Paddy never let anyone know his business, and I mean anyone. But they got on together like bugs in a rug – when they weren't fighting like cat and dog. He treated her like one of his girlfriends.' Her face became ugly at some thought and a dribble formed on her chin – she brushed it away loosely with her hand.

'Did you know Paddy chased young girls? I mean really young – like sixteen, seventeen. Nearly what you'd call a paedophile. He shagged them as well, you know. There was nothing platonic about it. Helen Cronin down the road came to see me, threatened to get the police when she found out he was sleeping with her daughter who was in the same class as Patricia, when they were in transition year. Helen took her daughter out of the school. Paddy used to bring her to a hotel in Wicklow somewhere. There was a time back then when I thought he might be interfering with Patrica – there's a lot of it about. She and I had a terrible row over it. She's always sided with him – always knew who had the money, which side her bread was buttered on.'

Again she went silent, but her lips kept moving. In a while she began again, hoarser now.

'They're all at it these days – even the bloody bishops are screwing all round them. Christ, nothing Paddy Brett would do could surprise me. Do a cat going through a skylight, as

42

Kate Hartigan says. Once Patricia went to university she took to staying in town with him in that apartment of his in Donnybrook. I hated the thought of her being there with those sluts of his going in and out of the place. She got what she wanted, mind you. Got him to buy her that place on the quays. I suppose even he got embarrassed at having his daughter around while he was running his little three-ring sex circus.'

Joan was looking into the fireplace again. I was tired of this prolonged bitterness and wondered how I could extricate myself.

'Who's Kate Hartigan?' I asked, in an effort to get Joan out of Mr Bunyan's Slough of Despond and all unknowing took a left-hand turn in my destiny – such a simple question.

'Neighbour,' she said, after a long, lip-trembling pause, as though she had difficulty remembering the question. 'Lives up the road, huge house with green gates.' She waved vaguely with her free hand and drank from the other. 'Paddy straightened up her affairs for her when her husband shagged off with his secretary or someone. Girl only half his age – Kate I mean. Kate said Paddy was brilliant – screwed a massive settlement out of that bastard of a husband of hers. Wish to Christ I'd had someone like that when Paddy left me. Kate told me here one night that she fancied Paddy – she was pissed at the time, of course. Pissed when she was telling me I mean. Said she tried to seduce him once – that's a laugh. He can't have fancied her – she's thirty something, too old for him I'd say. It didn't take much coaxing to get Paddy Brett to drop his trousers!'

'And you don't think Patrica would know about his business affairs?' I asked the question as a distraction, to pass the time, no longer interested in the private life of Paddy or Joan, wishing only to be gone from there.

'Patricia knows more than is good for her,' she said, slurring her words, nodding, closing one eye, and I realised that she did it to focus and not for emphasis. Joan nodded

43

some more and slowly, so slowly I didn't realise for some moments what was happening, she shut the other eye and was asleep. Her face gradually relaxed and, for the first time since she had entered the room that afternoon, I was looking at Joan Callaghan – or at least someone I could say I'd once known.

'She's out now,' Patrick said, startling me. He'd come into the room as though Scottie had beamed him down. 'She'll be out for three or four hours. Nothing will wake her.'

He spoke softly, despairingly, all the smart shit gone out of him, and it made him seem comparatively human, vulnerably young. I wondered how long he'd been outside the door, then realised he probably did it often, had had to become an expert eavesdropper if he was to be any help to her.

He took up a tartan travelling rug – exposing a bad cigarette burn on the chair arm – and tucked it about her with infinite care as though wishing to repay her for all the kindnesses of childhood with one single gesture. Turning to me, erect and grave, his face purged of its earlier petulance, he was suddenly his father's son – not quite what could be called tough, but someone who could not be ignored for all that, a force of sorts that would insist on being reckoned with.

'Do you believe my mother?'

I was conscious of the formal seriousness of the question.

'About buried treasure? It sounds like an awful lot of bread,' I said warily, 'but your mom surely thinks he had it. What's your guess?'

'I really don't know,' he said, shaking his head and I believed him. 'My father was certainly smart enough and he was full of surprises, so I wouldn't put it past him.'

With that remark his young-turk mask slipped over his face and I knew I could really dislike his alter ego.

'There's money somewhere, that's for sure,' he went on. 'He was always able to come up with whatever he needed to buy cars, apartments, that sort of stuff, not to mention the women he paid and paid for. As to how much there is I have no idea – I suspect it's more likely to be thousands rather than millions. His practices ought to be good for a few grand.'

'Any idea where I might start looking?'

'If I had, what would be the point in her asking you?'

'Right,' I said, 'I know when I'm not wanted.'

I stood and began moving toward the door. 'Tell your mother I'll be in touch.'

'I didn't mean to be rude,' he said, quickly, apologetically. He smiled – a trifle sadly but a smile all the same. 'I'm a bit on edge. Mom and I aren't so sure where we go from here.'

'I understand,' I said, with more generosity than I felt.

He followed me out of the room and saw me to the front door. As I walked out into the night he nodded as though we were all talked out – which I certainly was. The door clicked shut as I reached my car.

'He's really a sweet person,' she said, scaring the daylights out of me, materialising at my elbow. Definitely another crew member of the *Enterprise*, Candy Delamere hovered beside me in the starlight and her delicate perfume descended on me like pollen.

'You and Patrick fly by night?' I asked, when I'd caught my breath.

Her whiter-than-white teeth glistened in the glimmer from the door's fanlight as she grinned and my eyes grew accustomed to the darkness.

'You don't look the type that scares easily,' she said. 'I didn't want you going away thinking he was a brat. It's just that he's overly clever and tries too hard to be a smart ass.'

'He succeeds,' I said, opening my car.

'He had nothing to do with his father's death,' she said suddenly, blurting it out as though answering an accusation. 'He was with me. We were in bed all evening and we weren't asleep.'

45

Her head was tilted back defiantly and I wished I had a friend as young and lovely and as quick to defend me.

'But you would say that, wouldn't you?' I said teasingly.

'Ask Julie Hartigan,' she snapped. 'She was with us.'

She spun on her heel and aimed for the rear of the house leaving me to write up the captain's log any way I wished. I shook my head and got in the car.

I mulled things over and let the engine warm up. I turned on the fan and waited for the heater to clear the windscreen. I shivered – it really had been cold in that room. I thought about the people I'd just left – wondered why no one had mentioned that Paddy Brett, husband and father, had been foully murdered; why no one had cast even a moment's thought, wasted a tittle of speculation, on who had killed him or why.

Conscious of the long afternoon of whiskey I drove down the overgrown drive carefully but even so managed to find four of the deeper potholes. On the last one, as the car jounced and scraped – I reckoned I'd done in the exhaust for sure – I swore and told myself that with a drive like that there was no way Paddy Brett had died and left an eight figure stash.

Next day I found the money, or rather it found me.

Eight fifteen the following morning I woke to the insistent bing-bonging of my front-door bell. I sat up too quickly and my head rolled under the bed. My second attempt got both arms into the dressing gown and, on the way to the door, I checked the level in the Jameson bottle. As I suspected – some bold lad had snuck in during the night and finished off about half of it. In the hall mirror I promised my guardian angel I'd give up solitary drinking no matter how low I felt.

In the door's fish-eye lens a distorted Magdalen stuck out her tongue and I threw open Château Despair to the public for another day.

'Christ! You look awful. Do you know it's after eight?'

46

She pushed past me in one of her diaphanous creations, my newspapers in her hand.

'That's all I needed,' I said, disgusted, closing the door behind her, 'some smart-arse hareem houri poking her tits in to tell me I've missed the best part of the day.'

'Whatja get up to last night then?' she asked, making straight for the kitchen, her favourite place. She tossed my *Irish Times* on the table and began filling a kettle.

'Wake,' I said.

'Course I'm awake,' she said, crossly, 'and a day's work done already. What you need is coffee.'

I let it go, didn't try to explain. Maggs began shuffling about purposefully, with great economy of movement, knowing where everything was because she'd put it there to begin with. Maggs adores my kitchen – claims she rather than me should have it – and gets this irrepressible urge about once a month to come up and clean it and reorganise my cupboards. I can never find half my Black & Decker tools after she's been.

I sat at the table, opened the paper, read the nothing new Beckett claims the sun has no alternative to shining on. Garda Siochana were continuing their inquiries into the death of well-known financial consultant, blah, blah, blah.

'Feel like a rasher and egg?' Maggs asked from the cooker, tapping the work top with a spatula.

I shook my head. 'I don't even look like a rasher and egg,' I said.

'Hah bloody hah.' The kettle began its whistle and Maggs blasted the top off my head with the coffee grinder.

'Do you fucking have to?' I shouted.

'I fucking do,' she roared back.

It was on the Business & Finance page. A brief history of his career, a list of his directorships, his rise and rise to prominence in the financial community. Fellow directors spoke of the loss to capitalism without once mentioning the word. Two government ministers lamented the gap created in the ranks of the captains of industry. Someone called him

47

a genuine Master of the Universe. A brief paragraph outlined the success of North East Baltic, the bank Paddy Brett and fellow director, Bill Grattan, had helped introduce to Ireland, together with its most successful product – pioneered by P. Brett – the Montego International Investment Fund. Paddy had been a real live Celtic Tiger tamer.

'God meant you to drink he'd have given you the head for it,' Magdalen said. 'You should eat something.'

'Coffee and toast'd be fine,' I said, folding the paper, putting it away.

Magdalen poured my coffee and pushed some buttered toast across to me. I added some marmalade and began to eat.

'What got you started last night?' she asked, settling opposite, pulling her see-through cobweb tight about her high nipples.

'Death of a friend,' I said, then, in the hope of a glimmer of sympathy, lugubriously added, 'a very old and dear friend.' I reckoned I'd got the tone right.

'Jesus! Men! Any excuse for a jar,' Maggs said.

'We grew up together,' I said defensively, and wondered why I should feel the need to justify myself. 'Spent the afternoon with his wife. She grew up with us too.'

I felt that should explain it, put things into proper perspective.

'Aha!' Maggs said.

'Howja mean "Aha"?' I snapped, irritated.

'You and she do it back then when you were kids doing all that growing up together?' she asked mockingly, and I gave her ten out of ten for perspicacity.

Maggs leaned back, smiling triumphantly, drawing her gown around her, making it even more transparent. Maggs has a lot of sex packed into her tight, lovely body.

'You sure you wouldn't like to slip into something more comfortable?' I asked savagely.

'Ooohhh!' Maggs said, queening it. 'We are upset this

morning. So you did do it last night. I believe that's the first thing widows want – check to see if it still works.'

'As a matter of fact – not that you'll believe me or that I give a damn whether you do or not – we didn't do anything.'

She leaned around the table, inspected my groin. 'You suffering from morning-after eroticism? I have an infallible cure – real holistic job.'

'Thanks but no thanks,' I said, then realised I was being nasty and ungrateful. 'But it is nice of you to offer.'

'One of these days,' Maggs said, smiling sweetly, shaking back a sleeve, pouring more coffee.

I stirred mine and waited. I wondered why Maggs had called so early, but decided to let her tell me in her own time. I didn't have long to wait.

'I wasn't aware you knew Dutch Gaffney,' she said.

'The critical essays or the poetry?' I asked.

She ignored that. 'He was here yesterday while you were out – him and Hocks Mackey.'

'You been reading Runyon again?'

Her gamine face was serious – what I could see of it over my Wedgwood as she held the cup to her lips with both hands, elbows propped on the table.

'You being straight up when you say you don't know them?' she asked, very quietly.

'Why do I get the feeling that what you are about to tell me is not good? Who the hell are they and how come you know them?'

'Dutch Gaffney is bad news – I mean seriously bad news. Like, "plagues-here" bad news. He runs a string of girls – mostly dependent, do anything for what they're on, what he started them on, what he keeps them on. He hooked my sister, Christine. He killed her. She was nineteen. He's evil, genuinely evil. I mean, me, I don't believe in God, but I believe in Dutch Gaffney. Dutch says jump, you jump. Girl don't do what Dutch says she loses her nipples, gets a bigger mouth.'

She nodded gravely, sipped some coffee.

'I was getting out of the lift, bringing Sean home from playschool, when I met them coming down the stairs from here. For a minute I thought you must be in cahoots with them. You can see how it figures. Dutch is a main dealer – hard to see how a guy can live as well as you do without being into something, know what I mean? But I've always figured you as being above board, too nice to be into that scene.'

'Well thanks for the vote,' I said. 'But how come if he killed your sister he's still walking around?'

'They couldn't pin it on him.'

'Then how do you know he had anything to do with your sister's death?'

'Dutch likes to boast. After all, that was why he killed her, wanted his girls to know what happens if they try to cut loose. Showed them what they were in for if they ran away.'

Magdalen was staring out the window, very pale now.

'Know what he did?'

She didn't look at me and I said nothing. She'd spoken so softly it seemed she hardly meant me to hear. Something in her profile warned me I would regret hearing what she was about to tell me.

'Christine got it together long enough to make her way to that rehabilitation place in the mountains. Saved up for it, was turning tricks on the side, not handing it over to Dutch. Christ, the other women told me afterwards she wanted out so bad she'd do anything, anything. The worst perverts in town whacked it to her. Jesus! Nineteen years old.'

Magdalen was crying, shaking her head.

'She was only there two days when Dutch found her. Just drove by, waited till she showed and flung her into the car. He took her way up into the mountains to this god-forsaken shack, out in the wilds of nowhere. Hut used by sheep farmers to keep stuff in – sheep dip, that kind of thing, I don't know. He tied her naked on the floor. Staked her down. Then he got a sow from somewhere and put it in with her. He left them there. Can you imagine – a girl out of her mind for a fix and a starving sow.'

Magdalen was sobbing hysterically and I put my arms around her. It took a time before she got control. In a while she pulled herself together.

'Police came for me ten days later to identify her. It was terrible. Only the upper part of her face was intact.'

Magdalen broke off sobbing.

I held her heaving shoulders and tried to remember the detail. I'd seen it in the papers, but I'd associated it with the drug culture, something that happened to other people.

Magdalen got up, pulled her gown around her, hugged herself.

'Afterwards I shared a flat with this girl. At the time I didn't know she was one of Dutch's girls – not until Dutch and Hocks came one night, beat her up.' Maggs stopped, closed her eyes, and I waited for her shivering to stop. Her eyes remained closed for a long while.

'They raped both of us,' she said, leaning back, staring up at the ceiling, biting her lip.

'Christ!' I said softly.

'No,' she said, sitting again, leaning her elbows on the table, giving me the hardest eye I've ever had. 'No, Johnny, not Christ – Dutch Gaffney and Hocks Mackey.'

She remained staring for several long moments before hissing at me passionately.

'Swear you don't know them. Christ, I almost passed out when I saw them. They wanted to know where you were. I told them I knew nothing about you. Now that they know where I live, now that they've seen Sean, I'm terrified. Swear you don't know them, Johnny.'

'I don't know them and I don't know why they should be calling here. I swear I have nothing to do with them or anyone like them. Do you want protection? I know good guys who do that kind of work and I can get them tax free.'

'No thanks,' she said. 'Long as you're not in with them

51

it's OK. I might take you up on it later though, but you need more than good guys for those two. You need the IRA, SAS, guys like that to deal with that pair. Anyway there's not a lot of point – they never give up if they decide to do you. With people like Dutch Gaffney you've got to terminate, there's no other way.'

'They give you any idea why they were looking for me?'

'No, they were just nasty, asked where you were. Made a few cracks about me and Sean. They seemed to assume I was your partner and I was too busy being scared to set them straight, too worried about what might happen to Sean. Hope you don't mind.'

I shook my head. 'I mean it about the security and I can get some really hard nails. Could be I need it anyway if they're looking for me.'

Maggs had recovered her cool and was smiling again. She reached across the table, patted the back of my hand.

'I'm real glad you have nothing to do with those bastards.'

I smiled into her young face and squeezed her hand. Her ice-cold fear was genuine and it was catching.

Washed, shaved, dressed, and the paper read from cover to cover, I sat in a favourite chair and looked out over the Liffey toward the Dublin mountains. Maggs had left after straightening out the kitchen one more time. I was wondering if I should have a word with Detective Sergeant Tom Crotty about her fears – he was the kind of man who'd enjoy mixing it with the likes of Gaffney and Mackey – when the phone rang.

'I need to talk to John Constantine.'

The woman's voice was high-pitched and shrill. She was shouting – the voice of someone who didn't use the phone often. I couldn't place it, but very few people call me John and no one I normally speak to would have said they *needed* to talk to me.

'Speaking,' I said, louder than usual.

'Johnny, this is Elizabeth Meagher.'

'Aunt Lil,' I said, and sank back in my chair.

I was suddenly, magically twelve again. Where I was reared the Meaghers were great people; the largest – and poorest – family in the street where I first saw the light. Josie Meagher married Tommy Brett and had five children of whom the youngest was Paddy. Her mother had borne thirteen and reared eleven.

Her sister, Lil, never married and was Paddy's godmother and favourite aunt – he genuinely adored the ground she walked on. Of their family Lil and Josie were the only ones to stay in Ireland – all the others ended in England, Canada or Australia. Lil, the youngest, had looked after her mother and her uncle – gassed at the Somme, for years he'd crouched with burbling lungs beside the kitchen range – and she'd taken over the old house when they died. Paddy and I had our tea there all the best days I can remember and she became my Aunt Lil too.

Ever since I'd seen Paddy Brett stretched out on that gurney I'd pushed the thought of Aunt Lil away from me. I couldn't handle it, knew I would not be able to tell her and, coward that I am, I hadn't even asked Joan if she'd told her. Now I tried to make amends.

'I can't tell you how sorry I am, Aunt Lil.'

'Sure don't I know that, boy,' she said. 'If you weren't, who would be?'

She was silent and I heard the clink of coins and knew she was calling from a public phone.

'What's the number on that phone?' I asked.

'What?' She was confused.

'The number, Aunt Lil. Tell me the number and when the money runs out hang up and I'll ring back.'

She understood, gave me the number and at that very instant was cut off. I waited a few seconds and rang back. the receiver was picked up, dropped, picked up again.

'God, but you were always the smart one, Johnny Constantine,' Aunt Lil said, a little breathlessly. 'But listen to me now, these phones cost a fortune. I have something for you. Paddy gave it to me to give to you and to no one else. I don't want to post it to you. I don't know what the funeral arrangements are but I'll be coming up by train – I have the free travel now you know – got it along with the old age pension. I can go anywhere in Ireland for free – now that I have little reason to travel. I can bring it with me when I go.'

'The funeral won't be for days,' I said. 'I'll come down to you. I think what you have could be important.'

'Oh, it is, Johnny, it is,' she said. 'Paddy said it was very important.'

'I'll be there in a couple of hours, Aunt Lil,' I said. 'Is that all right with you?'

'I'll have the kettle on,' she said, 'but mind yourself on the roads, the traffic is terrible these days.'

Going abroad I'd discontinued my answering service. I reinstated it now and, thinking of Aunt Lil, that face from the past, I headed for the door and the town that made my bones.

The Porsche flicked into the mirror about two hundred metres behind me as I slowed for the lights at Newlands Cross. One of those screaming red cars that everyone should own at least once in their lives and preferably in their twenties.

Made you think of top-down summers, blonde hair, wind-torn laughter as light as streaming chiffon. Like a cat at a door, the Porsche kept peeping out impatiently in my lane about twelve cars back as though waiting to make its bid for supremacy once the lights changed. I lost interest, fiddled with the stereo.

When it was still there ten kilometres later I began to wonder. It became distinctly odd once we hit the motorway and it still hung back – car like that can't resist overtaking no matter what its driver thinks. I eased back a shade on the pedal, but nothing happened to the elastic between us. I put the hammer down – no change.

I took the feeder for Kilcullen and at the top of the ramp I saw the Porsche's indicator come on as it followed. I parked outside the Hideout Pub and went in. I took my toasted cheese and coffee to a table and enjoyed them slowly, all the while accusing myself of watching too much television. Then I had a slash and went back to my car.

I almost made it to the end of the straight beyond Kilcullen before the red dot skipped into view again. Too much coincidence for one morning. I dropped to a sedate sixty and held it all the way to my home town. The Porsche might as well have been on the end of a tow bar.

It's no longer my town. Most of the people I knew have either left or gone the way of all flesh. It's good to see the young people well dressed and well fed. Buildings have been refurbished – not before time – and look like emigrants returned prosperous. Whole streets have disappeared under new development. Familiar alleys I once raced down ahead of marauding rival gangs now end in blank walls.

But the basic layout is much as it was and I entered the new down-town shopping centre at an easy pace, paid no attention to pursuing Porsches. In the supermarket I had them make up a hamper and had fun selecting smoked salmon, snipes of champagne, white wine, a little brandy – Aunt Lil loved a drop of brandy in champagne – brack, layer cake (she had a sweet tooth), biscuits, fruit, goat's cheese – dairy products gave her migraine – flowers.

I went into Charlie Holden's awful pub – The Classic Bar! – and ordered a pint. Neither of the two old men hanging over half-full glasses knew me and the barman was young and a stranger to me. I paid for the pint and knew they wondered what a guy like me was doing in Charlie's carrying roses and a basket of food – I couldn't have looked one bit like Red Riding Hood.

I abandoned the pint – I knew Charlie was too set in his ways to have done anything about improving the quality – and went through the door marked Gents. I followed the long corridor past the ripely smelling lavatory out into the lane behind the pub. This feature – the means to avoid wives and other restraining influences – is the only one that has ever endeared the Classic Bar to anyone.

Moving quickly through a series of small lanes I was soon sitting idly on a bench in the People's Park. After ten minutes I reckoned I'd shaken off pursuit unless my shadow had managed to get into a pram and arrange for a fourteen-year-old girl to push it. I made my way across the park and down Tinmen's Lane to the terrace of small houses as well remembered as my mother's face.

Aunt Lil loves her brasses, always did. You could direct folks to her house just by telling them it's the one with the shining knocker and they'd find it every time.

I passed my old home with only a glance. They're both dead these twelve years and all my fault. I bought them a car and Dad thought he was ready to drive. They'd be alive today if I'd left them alone, hadn't tried to act the big guy, insisted on buying them things they'd been happy without. I don't know who lives there now but I hope it's still a happy house.

She must have been standing behind the door waiting for my knock. She's a small woman and, as both my hands were full, she threw her arms about me and buried her face against my breast bone. She cried a fair bit. Kept waving her hands helplessly at me, kept repeating Paddy, Johnny, Joan – all sorts of bits and pieces of our childhood.

The house was astonishing. Outside it was exactly as I remembered it, but inside now it was huge by comparison with the house I'd known. When she calmed down, got control of herself, she told me what Paddy had done. He'd bought the house either side and knocked the three together to make her final home. It was the kind of pad the glossies adore writing up and the only anachronism in it was Aunt Lil.

She hammered the rose stems and dipped them in boiling water before arranging them in a vase. She put

56

away the food I'd brought but left the booze on the table. Two of her treasured Waterford cut glasses were set down reverently and drinks poured – champagne and a dash of brandy. All the while she talked of the old days, of Josie and Tommy Brett, of my parents and how I shouldn't go on blaming myself after all the years. It was almost an hour before she could bring herself around to what had her mind in turmoil.

'How did he die, Johnny? Tell me what happened.' She sprung it on me suddenly, those green eyes lancing into me, giving me no place to hide, no time to fabricate.

I told her the truth as I knew it and didn't try to gloss over any of the bad parts. People like Aunt Lil and my parents always wanted the truth no matter what hurt came with it. She studied me as I spoke, watched my eyes, and her expression never changed as I told her. Now and then her lips moved as she silently repeated what I said. When I was finished she covered her face with both hands for a long while.

'This man, this policeman you know, Sergeant Crotty, has he any idea who did this thing to Paddy?'

'No. He's only starting on the investigation. No one has any ideas yet.'

'How is Joan taking it? You needn't bother trying to keep anything from me. I know things weren't good between them – Paddy told me.'

'I don't think it's sunk in yet,' I said.

'And Patricia and Patrick?'

'It's a great shock to them but, again, they haven't had time to take it in.'

'Paddy was here on Saturday night,' she said, adding champagne to my glass, topping with brandy. 'He was very upset – that is he was trying to pretend he wasn't upset, but I could always read him like a book. He was so tired, exhausted really. He lay down on my bed for an hour so that he wouldn't fall asleep driving back. I wanted him to stay over but, as always, he wouldn't be told.'

57

We were in her kitchen and she got up now and put on the kettle, began laying cups and saucers, took the smoked salmon from the fridge and started slicing it into thin leaves.

'He arrived at one in the morning. I got a fright. I thought Joan or one of the kids had been in an accident. He was very agitated. Said he'd been trying to get in touch with you for weeks, but no one knew where you were or how to contact you.'

'I was in the Middle East and the Canaries,' I said. 'Got back Sunday night.'

'He said he was in important negotiations – something like that. I don't know. God, why couldn't he have stayed small and happy?' I had no answer for that – my mother once said the same to me. I remained silent as she cried uncontrollably.

She went to the sink for some tissues and looked out the window until her mood passed. Then she went to where tea-towels hung on a rack. She lifted a towel and a brown bubble envelope hung on a safety pin beneath it.

'Paddy said I was to give you this if anything happened to him. To give it to you and to no one else – not even to Joan. I thought that was very strange. More than that – he said to tell no one about it even when I'd given it to you. He scared me the way he talked, but he said it was only a precaution, a temporary measure until he had other arrangements made. He said he was scared of having a car accident that might prevent him completing what he had started. I didn't ask him why he felt he had to drive through the night, turn up at that ungodly hour of the morning with it.'

The envelope was half A4 size and quite light. It felt as though it contained a tape. I would have preferred not to let Aunt Lil see what was in it – the less she knew the less possible danger she would be in. But it would have upset her to be excluded so I unstuck it and tipped the contents on to the table. Three items fell out – an audio tape and two diskettes. Aunt Lil stared at me.

'What are those little ones, Johnny?' she asked.

'They're used in a computer,' I said. I picked up the tape. 'Do you have a tape deck?'

I was glad when she shook her head. I didn't want her to think I'd keep anything from her, but I wanted to hear it before she did, just in case. The less she knew the safer she would be. I put the stuff in the envelope and stuck down the flap.

'Will you have tea or wine with this?' Aunt Lil asked, putting a basket of brown bread and a dish of salty country butter in front of me. I thought of the drive home to Dublin and opted for tea.

Barely touching her food, picking a bit here and there as I ate, Aunt Lil slipped further and further back into the days of my childhood. I was surprised at how much I'd forgotten, astonished by the detail she remembered.

People I hadn't thought of in years came alive again. As she spoke, the significance of relationships I'd been too self-engrossed to notice or understand when they were happening suddenly clicked into place and explained things I'd never been able to fathom. We don't listen enough when we're young – but then maybe we're not meant to.

'It was such a shame the two of you lost touch with each other,' Aunt Lil said. 'God but the pair of you were hard nuts as children. Nothing too hot or too heavy for you. You know people still ask about you as though you were a Brett and not a Constantine. But sure it's the way of the world – there's a season in all things.'

On the second cup of tea she became wanly provocative, began asking if I had anyone steady, a serious girlfriend. Was there a possibility of wedding bells, a day out for her? I was glad of the chance to kid, to lighten the conversation.

'I'm at the stage where no one will have me,' I said.

'Deed you're not,' she said. 'You're a fine big lump of a catch for any girl and Paddy said you were a long way from being short of a shilling. We all thought yourself and the girl of the Houricans, young Margaret, were going to make a go of it. God, but wouldn't ye have made a lovely pair? Mind you, the children would have been giants.'

I stopped eating.

'How did you know about that?'

'Sure didn't the whole street know about it that time she went nursing in Cork. Wasn't her mother thrilled when she heard about the two of you taking up? She was terrified of those cute Cork fellas. It nearly broke her parents' hearts when she became a nun. Do you see her at all now?'

I told her about meeting Margo in St Malachy's Hospital, how well she looked, even told her that she'd asked after her – which was only half a lie as Margo would have if she'd thought of it and we'd had more time together.

'Isn't it strange?' Aunt Lil said, 'God, but the world's a small place.'

She poured tea and was silent for a while.

'Religion is a terrible curse,' Aunt Lil said suddenly, surprising me with the sentiment and the vehemence she put into it.

This from a woman I knew to be a daily communicant.

'How do you mean?' I asked, sensing something deep behind her remark.

Again she was silent and in a while her eyes filled with tears.

'I suppose it doesn't matter now, there's no one left to hurt. There's only me now. You see, Johnny, I need to say it out loud to someone, not have it forever running around in my brain.'

I reached across the table and laid my hand on hers. She covered it with her other hand.

'He was my son,' she said, 'Paddy was my son.'

'He always thought of you as a second mother,' I said, nodding encouragement, helpless to ease her pain.

'No,' she said. 'You're not understanding me at all. Paddy was my real son. I carried him. I had him. He was mine. Josie and I reared him between us.'

60

I stared at her, stared at the tear-stained face of one of the kindest people I have ever known.

'Did he know?' I had to ask.

She shook her head. 'I couldn't tell him,' she said. 'I couldn't do that to Josie's memory, she was such a good sister and such a good mother to my boy.'

She got up and plugged in the kettle, threw out the tea-leaves and stood by the sink.

'I was twenty,' she said softly, talking to the clouds racing eastward toward oncoming night that could be seen in the gap between the dark bulk of the gasometer and the grey lime-stone of St Patrick's Church at the end of her small garden. 'Josie was pregnant with a fifth child at the same time and both of us were out of our minds with worry. She knew who Paddy's father was, knew there was nothing could be done.'

The kettle whistled and she turned to making tea, set the pot on its stand and pulled the flower-embroidered cosy over it, smoothed it absentmindedly as though caressing a cat.

'Josie lost hers in the third month. Mrs McCurtin, the midwife, was looking after her at home and it was she who had the idea. We told no one about Josie's miscarriage and went on as though nothing had happened. My mother didn't even know until almost the end. Oh God, she was the most beautiful sister a girl ever had.'

I waited through her tears, enthralled, feeling I'd not appreciated how I'd been reared by Hittites or some such vanished race. How could all of this be happening without anyone knowing?

'Do you remember Father Winters in St Patrick's? You'd have been ten when he was shifted to Dublin.'

I nodded, vaguely remembering a tall authoritarian who used to come round the school looking for children with vocations for the religious life.

'No harm in telling you now – he was Paddy's father. He died two years ago in a hospice in Dublin. I didn't want anything from him. He was even more scared than I was –

he was only twenty-five and he'd been in religion since his people had shoved him into it at twelve. It's a terrible thing, religion. He was petrified I'd tell and that really disappointed me. He never understood I loved him. Poor boy didn't know the meaning of the word – never having had a kindness in twenty years. I only hope he didn't spend the rest of his days blaming himself.'

Aunt Lil was crying again, but I felt she'd found the telling helpful. Living alone as she did, and with all her close relatives gone or emigrated years ago, and now Paddy dead, her despair must have been total.

'Josie went to see him, talked to him in confession.' Aunt Lil smiled a trembling smile. 'That must have been some conversation – poor lad in his box suddenly being hauled over the coals. Josie must have been in some state as well 'cause she was a very shy person and it capped everything him being a priest. God, weren't we innocent in those days!

'Josie pulled the rug from under him and he organised a job for me in a convent near Limerick. I stayed there until I was due. Josie kept padding herself. When I knew I was ready I rang Joey Brett, the taxi man, Tommy's brother, and they both came and brought me home. It was a terrible drive, an awful night full of rain. We even had a puncture on the way – you never saw two fellas change a wheel so fast! God be with her, Mrs McCurtin delivered Paddy two hours after we got to Josie's – we'd have been lost without that good woman.'

Aunt Lil went to a drawer, hunted through it and came back to the table with a photograph. Tommy and Josie Brett stood with their backs to an Anglia, Josie held a baby in a christening shawl. A man I vaguely remembered as Paddy's uncle stood next to Tommy. Aunt Lil stood beside Josie, her face turned toward the infant, a wisp of stray hair blowing out and giving her a slightly startled appearance. They looked very young, Bonnie-and-Clydeish.

'That was taken the day of Paddy's christening. I was

godmother. His father baptised him – Josie insisted. So there you have it. And now he's gone too – it's a woeful thing to have your child die before you.'

Not knowing what to say, I said nothing. I went to her, knelt beside her and put my arms around her and she cried a long time. Now that I knew why, many things began to fall into place, small scenes from childhood suddenly stood out, took on new meanings. Again I marvelled at how blind we are as kids, how much we assume, take for granted.

'I hope they punish the bastards, Johnny,' she said, and somehow that word had a new meaning in her mouth.

# Chapter Four

There was a fifteen-pound parking ticket on the windscreen. I looked around at ticket-free cars whimsically abandoned in the square – all local registrations. Parking tickets were only on out-of-town cars. It was after five with plenty of light still in the day.

I spotted him watching me from behind a lamppost. Ostrich-like he was assuming that if his little pointed head couldn't be seen then the pear-shaped bulb of his brown-uniformed arse would be invisible. I marched across waving the parking ticket.

'Where does it say restricted parking?' I demanded.

His mirror glasses showed my distorted face. He needed a wash and a shave.

'Sign on the way into town says disc parking in operation.'

'Nice way to treat people doing business in town,' I said.

Over his left shoulder I saw the red Porsche neatly parked. The heavily tinted windscreen reflected the cloudy sky and gave no hint of anyone within.

'We were depending on cheap shits like you, town'd have been dead long ago.'

He sniffed, spat, swaggered away.

I threw up my hands in exaggerated frustration and walked back to my car. I was glad I'd used Aunt Lil's safety pin to hold the bubble envelope down the front of my trousers. I hadn't wanted to reappear from Tinmen's Lane with a bulging pocket. As I got in the car I caught my left testicle on the envelope. I doubled up with pain and banged my chin on the wheel. The horn blared. So much for security.

I put the tape into the stereo but did not turn it on. I started the car, hit the indicator and edged into the slow crocodile of evening traffic. I inched across the square and there were too many cars behind to see if the scarlet lady-bird followed. My testicle ached and I'd lost contact with my leg. Traffic gathered speed as we moved away from the business centre.

On the outskirts of town I hung a left into a filling station. While the attendant busied himself with the pump I opened the bonnet, pretended to check the oil. I watched the Porsche slow down and park about two hundred metres away, too far back to make out movement behind the tinted screen.

Out on the road again I accelerated to seventy and watched the Porsche swing in after me about a kilometre back. I turned on the stereo and pushed in the tape. It seemed to hiss for a long time before the dead man spoke.

*'Hiya, Johnny.*

*'First off I want to apologise for dropping this on you. Believe me I wouldn't do it if there was any other way. When I've explained it to you, when you know what's happened to me, I hope you'll appreciate how I've run out of options, that there isn't a satisfactory alternative to secure the future for Joan and the kids. Sorry for the emotional blackmail – but I'm stuck, no one else to turn to.*

*'If you're listening to this then I suppose I'm done for – Christ! That's an awful thought.*

*'If anything's happened to me, I mean like if I'm dead, stuff like that, then Walter Hartigan or a man called Bertram McRoarty will have arranged it.*

*'Jesus! Have I been stupid! Naive isn't the word for it. I could kill myself.*

*'Jesus Christ, maybe I have!'*

Tape hiss filled a long pause. At one point I thought I heard a sob – sadness or angry frustration, I couldn't be sure. In the main his voice was controlled – the public-man's prime-time-television voice that I'd grown used to these last few years. As the tape rolled hesitations and breaks crept into this his final tale and he grew hoarse as it went on. He sounded stressed-out, almost at the end of his tether.

*'Reason I can't go to anyone else is because what I'm going to ask of you is illegal, part of the great national sport of tax evasion.*

*'First you have to understand where I'm coming from and, more importantly, where I've been.*

*'Was a time when I used to think I was the smartest, coolest financial operator in Dublin. No one quicker or more able than P. Brett to organise your tax avoidance, vanish your excess profit – now you see it, now you don't.*

*'Let the rich sleep easy was my motto. One satisfied customer famously remarked in the bar of the Stephen's Green Club that I was better than Mogadon any day of the week. Was I devious! I invented more mousetraps than anyone else and they beat a path to my door, just like the man said they would.*

*'Then I came up with the ultimate mousetrap.*

*'I came upon it in Bonn five years ago during a seminar on taxation and monetary union. I met this Hungarian, Vilmos Lemptke, during a conference workshop and we got talking. He turned out to be Marketing and Development Director of North East Baltic Bank. What a machine that turned out to be! It makes the Space Shuttle look like a Model T Ford. Goes round exchange controls like a Lotus cornering.*

*'I stage-managed its launch in Dublin, steered it through the Central Bank. I was its first acting Chief Executive Officer in Ireland until it was well and truly up and running. I hand-picked the three non-executive directors, gave the board the gloss of super-respectability. I fed a*

load of business into it. I was The Man – I was Mr North
East Baltic.

'Then I head-hunted Bill Grattan as the permanent CEO.
To meet he's a nice guy – young, good-looking, sweet
talker, razor sharp, with a great track record in accountancy and a real fancy highfalutin law degree. A high-flyer
– best choice I could have made. Only thing you couldn't
find on his CV was his greed and the lengths he'd go to in
satisfying it. Financially speaking the guy has a sweet
tooth, but that didn't show until I introduced my ultimate in
mousetraps.

'Like all the best schemes it's essentially simple and
needs only the minimum of tweaking around the edges to
make it superficially legal. I targeted the middle-range
private operators. People assume that banks make their
money on big customers, never see that it's the hundreds of
smaller ones that are the real bonanza. I went after the
medium-sized shopkeepers, professional people – doctors,
dentists, lawyers – the guys and dolls looking for a home
for a spare twenty, thirty grand a year.

'Most of these people aren't interested in government-
backed investment schemes no matter how sweet the
incentives. They reckon if they put their heads above the
parapet to stick their dough in some Designated Area the
taxman is going to say, Hey! wait a second, where've you
guys been all these years you suddenly got that kind of
money to invest? And it is a good question even if it is
rarely asked.

'What the average punter really wants is to have his
money invested locally at reasonable interest and accessible
at all times. For that he's willing to pay, provided the end
result is sensibly less than the taxman's bite.

'Enter P. Brett and his Montego International Investment
Fund established in the Cayman Islands and operating into
Ireland out of North East Baltic Bank, Guernsey. Through
Dublin the punter invests in Montego International,
Guernsey, where his hot packet is cooled into a numbered,

*nameless account with instructions from the punter to invest in the products of North East Baltic Bank, Dublin. As an overseas investment account the profits are tax free in Ireland.*

*'The punter can go into the bank on Stephen's Green and draw out cash as required. Many don't want to do that, are afraid the Revenue Commissioners have guys in mackintoshes at every street corner. For those timid souls I can arrange for them to pick up their funds in London, Paris, Rome, wherever they want to go on holiday to enjoy their hard-earned thievery. Guy can walk in off the street and use an agreed name or number – it's that simple. The bank pays maybe three-quarters of a point less than the guy would get if he'd invested normally – maybe he has a few extra bank charges – but he does not pay tax.*

*'Basically that's it. I get a percentage, bank gets a percentage and the aggregate is less than what the punter would lose to tax – so everyone is happy. Everyone except the taxman, and what he doesn't know won't bother him.*

*'Way the system worked only two people handled Montego accounts – myself alone to begin with and later Bill Grattan as the numbers got bigger and it was necessary to have back-up in case anything happened to me. No one else handled those accounts and the computer files were encrypted. Within two years the investment was around a hundred and fifty million pounds and growing. The day-to-day management was in Bill Grattan's hands.*

*'Then a wheel came off.*

*'Joan asked me to help our neighbour, Kate Hartigan, Walter Hartigan's wife. You may have heard of him through his Knocklangan Hotel Group. Apart from hotels, he owns five pubs, seven betting offices, a string of newsagent shops, holiday homes, caravan parks and quite a number of other cash businesses. His daughter, Julie, is friendly with my son, Patrick, and Joan is often up in the house with Kate. Walter believed in beating his wife.*

*'Cut a long story short, I helped Kate secure a separation*

*and a barring order. Walter had made the mistake of having his wife as second director in a number of companies – Kate wasn't aware of it herself. He was such a bully she'd sign anything he put in front of her without question. I discovered it in a search in the Companies Office. I really screwed the guy and that was the start of my problem.*

'Two months ago I found a rat in my mousetrap.

'The big surprise came when I went into the bank and found Walter Hartigan in Bill Grattan's office. I'd only met the man a couple of times and, needless to say, we are not good friends. When he left I grilled Bill Grattan until he admitted Walter had a Montego International account. I combed the computer files but there was no trace of Walter Hartigan or any outfit resembling his group.

'I challenged Bill Grattan and we had a ferocious row. I threatened him with various things and he finally gave me the code that opened up another set of Montego International accounts.

'Talk about a parallel universe! There he was, good old Walter, with an investment of thirty million. I knew from the work I'd done for Kate Hartigan there was no way Walter had that kind of spare cash to hide. It had to belong to someone else, another group. But the really worrying thing was that Walter was not alone. There was another two hundred and sixty-four million in there from East European sources. I guessed then that Vilmos Lemptke wasn't just a marketing man.

'It took time but I finally got it out of Bill Grattan. He knew all about it. He was in it up to his neck. The harder I went after him the more he began to feel he held trump cards, that he had the hard men on his side. Like all desk-bound bandits the stupid prick thinks he can handle the men in the hills.

'Walter Hartigan is fronting for this creep, Bertram McRoarty, guy the underworld and the police call The Farmer. Basically what's happened is these guys, Grattan, Hartigan and this Farmer have turned my mousetrap into a *fucking washeteria for criminal profits. To top it all The Farmer has made an association with East European Mafia people to launder their money as well as his own. Vilmos Lemptke is up to his balls in it. Guy suckered me from the start.*

*'My big mistake is that my name is all over it. Mine is the signature with the Central Bank, the Companies Office, the Revenue Commissioners. Everywhere I turn in the legal entity that is North East Baltic Bank in Ireland I find myself looking back at me. Legally I'm the guy who set the whole thing up! Jesus Christ! I almost polished the brass plate.*

*'That little shit Grattan has even had the nerve to threaten me. He's really scared, even more scared than I am. He's done well out of all of this but not nearly as well as he expected. Guy finds he has a tiger by the tail and he can't let go. I don't know how true it is but when he wants to scare me he tells me that The Farmer has already killed two people over Montego International.*

*'Six months ago Tom McNamara and his wife were killed in a car crash. McNamara was assistant manager in the bank. Grattan claims McNamara found out about the accounts and threatened to go public unless he was compensated adequately. Grattan says he told Hartigan's Doberman – guy called Dutch Gaffney – and three days later McNamara and his wife were killed on their way home from the pictures. A container truck mashed her Ford Ka. I have no way of knowing if that's true, but it sure as hell could be.*

*'After I found out I did nothing for weeks except think how I was going to get myself out of this mess. I can't go to the police. I've got to extricate myself legally. What I've come up with isn't great, but it's the best I can do. I have documents drawn up and back dated to show I legally ceased being a director before Hartigan and the East Europeans began making investments. The papers should have been lodged with the Companies Office nearly two years ago, but I can claim the omission was the company*

70

*secretary's fault and, in any case, it's not unusual for papers to be lodged late.*

*'If North East Baltic is ever turned over by the Central Bank or the police or the Revenue Commissioners I'll be in trouble over Montego and the smaller investors. To a large extent I can shift the blame on to the punters as it is their responsibility to make a correct declaration of assets – they're the ones behaving illegally. My problem will be in promoting a product clearly designed for tax evasion. I might get rapped over the knuckles but I won't be involved in laundering criminal assets.*

*'I need signatures from Grattan and Lemptke – legally I don't need the other directors who know nothing anyway. Once I have their signatures I'll be on my way to a fresh start.*

*'I've made two copies of the accounts of Hartigan and the East Europeans. One copy is on diskette number one attached to this tape. After I made the copies I changed the access codes to Hartigan's and The Farmer's accounts – it's all on the diskette. While I was making the copies I noticed something that I don't think Grattan has picked up on for all his cleverness. I reckon Hartigan is skimming off the top of The Farmer's account. I couldn't swear to it, but he's moving small amounts consistently through Geneva. At present they come to a little short of a million and all go to a numbered account – NJ468S. Watch out for it on the diskette.*

*'Things are moving quickly now. The recent disclosures on banking charges have put inspectors into one bank already. Tribunals of Inquiry are getting close. I've got to move fast, get these papers signed. I've set it up with Grattan. Lemptke is flying in Sunday evening and I'll hand over my copy of the accounts if they sign the papers. The second copy attached to this tape is my insurance policy. I tell them if they try anything to harm me this copy goes straight to the Criminal Assets Bureau.*

*'That's the theory of it. If you're listening to this then for*

*some reason the plan hasn't worked. I cannot see why it will not work – I mean I'm not going to tell anyone about the Montego accounts. Johnny, if I'm dead I want you to send your copy of the diskette to the Criminal Assets Bureau straight away. Do it now. Get the bastards for me, Johnny.'*

There was a long pause full of a hiss of static that sounded eerie inside the car. It had grown dark and the Porsche's were the only lights in my mirror. It was maintaining its distance even though I slowed occasionally to see if it was paying attention. In a little while my old friend began to speak again. He sounded very tired.

*'Do you ever get to wishing you could do it all again, get it some way right second time around, not make the same bloody awful mistakes? But then maybe you haven't made the same mistakes or as many as I have. I've made a balls of it. I've screwed up my family and that's the worst thing you can do and the one thing that can't ever be undone. I know it's late in the day to be saying this, much too late and it sounds like whingeing to say it now, sounds as though I'm only making a sales pitch as usual, but I do regret cutting myself off from the family and from you. I've been thinking about you a lot these last few days. Back then we really meant something special to each other, you and me, the original blood brothers. We should have kept up. My fault I know. There was always something else, some stupid dinner to be attended, some sucker to be met, some goddamn deal to be done. But I should have made the time, should have never let the best part of my life and the best people I ever knew slip away from me. Christ, Johnny, I don't know – sometimes I think I've spent the last twenty years talking to the fucking man in the moon. I really miss you now, old pal. Like you used to say, no matter how far you travel you always have your arse behind you. I wish I had the old times back again. Getting hooked on money was my problem – worse than drugs.'*

Again he paused and I could hear the rasp of his breathing. He coughed drily and went on.

'That brings me to the second diskette attached to this tape. This gives details of what I think of as my pension fund. Twenty years now I've been building it and I have no intention of letting the taxman lay a finger on it – that is, if you'll help me.

'None of it represents profit from crime and, as such, it has no interest for the police. From the start, in my separate practice, I've preferred to take a slice of the action rather than fees. People used to complain that when they came to me for advice they left with a more valuable asset but owning less of it. The diskette gives all the details and how I'd like it distributed. It needs one code word to open it and that is your name as I knew you.

'You're going to need authorisations. I've left powers of attorney, letters of introduction, all that you'll need to deal with the funds. I've hidden them where Aunt Lil kept her post office savings book. It's the best I can think of right now.

'I can't ask any of the family to do this for me. I guess we've become what's called these days a dysfunctional unit. It's too late now to go into the reasons, much too late to start crying over it. I contributed greatly to the mess – I suppose I just got carried away doing what I do best. That and never going home or, times I did, never really being there.

'They couldn't handle stuff like this – that's why I need you desperately, Johnny. You're the only one I trust. Joan wouldn't be able for it – she's got a problem with the booze. Patricia is too wayward at the moment. She's going through a phase, really at war with me. Besides, the girl she shares the flat with used to be one of Hartigan's hostesses in that club of his. But Patricia will pull out of it – she'll straighten up. She's basically a good girl, just a bit fiery at the moment.

'Patrick won't listen to anything I say. He blames me for his mother's addiction – fucking Long Day's Journey Into Night all over again. Goes his own sweet way, does whatever he likes. I can't talk to him anymore. Besides, if he got *his hands on the money he'd start buying cars, living it up, taking that girl of his to all the night spots. Taxman would be on to him like a shot, have him for breakfast. I've worked too hard for it to see it slip away like that.*

'*I need you to teach them how to use the money without getting caught. They'll listen to you. I know we kind of lost touch and all that, but Joan still thinks you're the greatest and I know she'll make the kids listen to you. Besides, you'll have control and they'll have to do what you tell them.*

'*I've left my will with Oliver Pettit – he's my partner from way back. I've named you and Oliver as my executors – that way you have every reason to be dealing with my finances and it gives you the cover to handle the other funds not mentioned in the will. Oliver is the straightest guy I ever knew and you can trust him totally. I'd have asked him to handle the other funds only Oliver is as honest as the day is long and it would be against all he believes in to mess with truly hot money. Horses for courses, as they say, and that's why he was great as a partner.*

'*Don't think badly of me – try not to judge. I've done some dodgy things in my time but I've never been involved in anything downright criminal. I've taken a cut off the top when I've made big profits for guys who benefited from my mousetraps, but I've always seen that as the labourer being worthy of his hire.*

'*I don't want even to think what guys like The Farmer and his associates get up to. I've seen Hartigan's man Gaffney and I just know that man would sooner kill you than talk to you. Watch out for them – they really are dangerous. I think it's only a matter of time before someone catches on to what is happening at North East Baltic. I've told Grattan he's out of his tree to let them keep using it, but I guess they have too much of a hold on him now.*

'*Get rid of this tape. Burn it – don't leave it lying around.*

'*Again, Johnny, if you'd rather not do this, if you think it's too much to ask, burn this tape and the second diskette. Send diskette number one to the Criminal Assets Bureau.*

74

*I've made a fall-back arrangement that kicks in when Patricia is twenty-seven and that will tell her how to get to the pension fund. Trouble is though, they'll have no one to guide them in using it.*

*'I do need your help.*

*'God be with you, Johnny. Christ! I've never felt so lonely.'*

I ran the tape through one more time and let the ghostly voice of my old blood brother fill the cocoon of the car as I drove north in darkness, the lights of the Porsche behind a constant reminder that this was all happening in real time, that this was no movie and that my friend was really dead.

Listening the second time it seemed that as he talked Paddy Brett had begun to feel self-consciously embarrassed that he might be thought to be exaggerating the danger, had begun to think he was being melodramatic as he used up the tape. At the end, however, the danger had become real again for him. The despair in his final sentence hung trembling over the ominous hiss from the stereo.

The lights of Naas streamed past on my right and five minutes later the glow of Dublin was ahead. Traffic bunched as we slowed for Newlands Cross lights, but the Porsche hung back, let three or four cars overtake it. I headed for Ballsbridge and Jury's Hotel.

The hotel car park was stuffed. I loitered, waited for someone to shift. I put U2 into the stereo and Paddy's tape into the box *The Joshua Tree* came out of and stored it amongst other tapes in the armrest pocket. It was eight thirty. I saw the red roof of the Porsche across the parked cars and had almost reached a conclusion on the merits of confrontation when a car pulled out. I slotted into the space and headed for the hotel without a glance in the direction of the Porsche.

I hung about in the lobby and waited to see a tall, broad-shouldered man unfold from the Porsche. I strolled into The Dubliner.

Tuesday is a quiet night in town and the crowd in the bar had to be less than a thousand. I elbowed and kneed my way through to the timber and ordered a pint shandy. A charmingly scented lady was forced into me and her shoulder bag connected with my still-aching testicle. The barman looked quizzically at me, wondered what I'd said.

I watched the foyer in the mirror and saw him come in. I stood as straight as the pain in my groin allowed so that he'd see me. It was one of those tinted, smoky mirrors and I could see he was in his forties and had the build of a handy light-heavyweight. He was good-looking in a rugged Connemara way and walked with easy athletic litheness. He spotted me and hesitated. I hoped that after three hours of driving he needed the Gents. I raised my pint so he could see I was likely to be busy for a little while. Nature won and he headed in the direction of the toilets.

I gave him thirty seconds then backed out of the ruck. Driving out the gate I turned away from town and drove slowly, watching for cars that might suddenly pull out and follow, but there was no one. I went as far as the Merrion Gates and turned back toward Irishtown and the Industrial Enterprise Centre.

It's not a big sign – it's not a big building – but I never fail to get a secret thrill from seeing my name in lights. CONSTANTINE – NDT INTERNATIONAL LTD, the white-on-green letters announce to the world – at least that portion of the world that happens to be out and about in that area after dark.

I let myself in, punched in the numbers and locked the doors behind me. It's a basic engineering production facility and, depending on orders, I can have up to twenty staff employed before the Health and Safety people start getting stroppy. I have a small office and workshop at the back which I like to think of as the Research and Development Department. It's where I go when I feel an idea coming on – which is about three times a year. Halfway into the building is Des Lynch's office. He's Production Manager

76

and shares the space with Helen Foley who looks after accounts.

I manufacture only eight products, all for use in the field of non-destructive testing of engineering materials. Most people think that has to be a limited market, that demand must be easily satisfied but, thanks to the relative delicacy of the equipment and the rough and tumble of life on site, there is a constant demand for replacement. I go about a lot on sites looking for gaps in the market, thinking about what hasn't yet been invented, trying to stay ahead of the game. That's what I'd been doing in the Middle East when Paddy Brett had been looking for me.

I like what I do and at least it's constructive – in my case, non-destructive. I'd hate to think my life's work was a Montego International Investment Fund – a passel of greedy guys pushing pieces of paper from one bank to another making money on the backs of little people. My mousetraps are designed to catch real mice.

I switched on a computer and slid in diskette No. 1.

It was outside my experience and was full of references that meant nothing to me. Acronyms abounded and banks across Europe seemed to pass amounts backwards and forwards. I guessed that KHG was the Knocklangan Hotel Group and that VL meant Vilmos Lemptke, but that was as far as I could figure. I did see references to account number NJ468S and G, which I assumed was Geneva. At last mention the account held £964,000.

Diskette No. 2 lit up the screen with the request – PLEASE ENTER PASSWORD. I didn't hesitate – I'd been thinking of it on the journey.

I typed in ATHOS and it opened. He had been Aramis. Each of us had wanted to be D'Artagnan so we'd compromised.

According to what now appeared on the screen before me my friend, he of the crumbling house and potholed drive, owned £14,674,896.38.

I sat back and whistled.

It was all over the place – I remembered what Joan had said, how Paddy liked to keep his eggs in a lot of baskets. There were accounts in the Cayman and Virgin Islands, in the Bahamas, in Abu Dhabi, Amsterdam, Hong Kong, and even one in Newry and that made me smile. Why he'd thought such a diversity necessary or useful I could not figure.

There was a copy of a standard letter which had been sent to all accounts stating that John Constantine had power of attorney and was authorised, on presentation of listed documents, to use the account as he saw fit.

There was a brief note to me setting out how the money was to be divided. I should take one million pounds as a fee for handling the administration and advising his family to ensure they did not lose most of it to the Revenue Commissioners.

As the money was scattered far and wide and travelling expenses would be incurred he had deposited £220,000 in cash in a safety deposit box held in our joint names, fully accessible to either signature, with Hibernian Safety Deposit Company, Stephen's Green. He instructed that £20,000 of this should be given to Heather Skeehan, secretary to Bill Grattan, without the latter's knowledge.

A further sum of £100,000 was to go to Betty Halpin, his secretary in Paddy Brett & Associates, Investment Consultants, with advice on how she should handle it to avoid attracting attention. Attached to this bequest was the enigmatic request – 'Be nice to her, Johnny, she's been through a lot.'

The balance of the safety deposit money was to be used by myself as required for travelling and expenses.

He asked that I see to all the needs of his Aunt Lil and to this end I should set aside £200,000. He had a standing arrangement of a monthly payment to her and I should ensure it continued for her lifetime.

The balance of his pension fund was to be divided equally between Joan, Patricia and Patrick.

I sat thinking about all of this for some time before shutting down the computer. I put the two diskettes at the back of a file of nearly a hundred diskettes of obsolete designs and out-of-date sales accounts from the Middle East. I set the alarm and locked up.

Mine was the only car on Pearse Street as I headed home. The basement car park was silent as the grave and my footsteps echoed eerily. No one mugged me in the lift and I made it through my own security without being hit over the head. I put *The Joshua Tree* box in my tape collection – there are four shelves of it.

I used the lavatory and felt a lot better. I dialled my answering service.

A Betty Halpin asked me to contact her but left no telephone number.

Patricia Brett would like me to call at her apartment if I could – anytime after three tomorrow afternoon, she said. There was authority in her voice – none of the hesitation most people experience when talking to a machine.

Her brother had telephoned about an hour later and asked me to ring him in the morning. He was offhand, hesitant.

Oliver Pettit of Paddy Brett & Co. would like me to contact him as a matter of urgency. I keyed the number he gave into the memory of my mobile phone.

I poured three fingers of whiskey and eased it down while I watched the news on television. The latest Tribunal of Inquiry into corruption in high places was getting underway at Dublin Castle. Not since the French Revolution had there been anything like the number of tribunals we were experiencing. Ought to be a run on tumbrils and knitting needles, I thought sourly.

I hadn't pulled the curtains and my reflection stared back. I knew there was a flaw in what my old friend had said. It took a while before I figured it.

He had intended handing over his copy of the Montego accounts once they'd signed the papers. But he would have had to threaten them with the existence of the second copy to stop them having any ideas of harming him once they had the accounts. He would have had to say that if anything happened to him another copy would go to the police. Therefore Grattan and Lemptke had to know there was another copy – and if they knew so did Hartigan, The Farmer and the Russian Mafia.

'Fuck you, Aramis,' I said to the window.

I was angry.

I had managed to live my life in a reasonably honest, fairly uncomplicated way and made my own fortune. I didn't need Paddy Brett's troubles even if there was a million attached to them. God damn it! I hadn't spoken to the man in four years or so. Last time I'd met him we barely had time to exchange greetings as we headed in different directions at Dublin Airport. What had been between us in our teens was a long way behind us.

As far as I was concerned he could keep his clever mousetraps. I could live happily without knowing what went on at North East Baltic Bank. I didn't need hard men in red Porsches in my life. Even less did I need a ready-made dysfunctional family for whom I was expected to act responsibly and illegally, although I would still do it out of regard for our long lost youth and respect for the Joan I had once known.

Most of all I didn't need an old friend popping up in my life after quarter of a century to make me a present of a solid gold poisoned chalice.

I rose, switched off the television and paused as I realised there was a question outstanding. If Paddy Brett had told them there was another copy of the diskette, why had they killed him before they'd found it? Apart from it being incriminating evidence, the disk gave the new codes that opened the accounts. Whoever had it could (in theory) get at the money.

Come to think of it, why were they already following me? How did they know about me? Had they forced my name out of him before they killed him? Why hadn't he told them about Aunt Lil and left me out of it altogether?

Then I understood the scale of my problem.

What Paddy had overlooked in his calculations, had not allowed as a possibility, was that the killers might know of me. Clearly he had left the stash with Aunt Lil on the assumption that none of these people would be aware of our childhood relationship. My essential value as a repository of his ace-in-the-hole was my anonymity. But somehow they knew who I was, had even been waiting for me. If I sent the disk to the Criminal Assets Bureau they would know who had caused their downfall. I was not the anonymous agent Paddy had banked on. Somehow they knew he had left me something and rightly assumed it was the other copy of the diskette. But who was following me? And who had the first copy of the diskette, the one Paddy had intended trading for their signatures? I reckoned I was safer holding on to my copy than sending it anywhere. At least I would have something to barter with if the worst came to the worst.

Come what may I was in the game now and had to play the hand I'd been dealt.

Why hadn't I stayed on the beach at El Cotillo for another few weeks?

In the bathroom I told the mirror this was Dublin not Little Italy. Businessmen, top tax consultants, were not being gunned down in the streets as yet.

No one was killing inventors.

I went to bed and dreamed of ancient afternoons, of returning down Tinmen's Lane with Paddy Brett, school-bags dragging at our backs, and Aunt Lil at my mother's door, the aproned women waving to us as we slouched toward tea and currant cake.

# Chapter Five

I woke late on Wednesday morning. At seven o'clock the day was clear and sunny. It made me glad I owned a view all the way to the Dublin mountains. Even the river looked silver-clean. Tinmen's Lane flashed across memory's screen and I saw my parents and felt sad.

I thought about jogging, reminded myself of broken resolutions, but decided it was too close to peak carbon-monoxide time. Besides, I was no longer sure what lay in wait outside my door. Instead, I treated myself to a high-cholesterol breakfast of bacon and eggs – I've always tended to eat when I'm anxious or scared.

I collected my *Irish Times* and sipped coffee. There was a paragraph on page four that reported the nothing new in the Brett affair.

I showered, dressed disinterestedly, listened to the radio. My mind kept circling warily around the mess Paddy Brett had left me. It was what the Americans call a real and present danger. I could not come to terms with the gall of my one-time buddy to drop shit like that on me.

At eight thirty I phoned Windward – I felt sure Joan Callaghan would still be in Smirnoff land. I had no wish to speak to her, soured as I was by her husband's unwelcome legacy, but I had to find out what new disaster Patrick had in mind for me.

He answered on the third ring.

'Hi, Patrick,' I said, in the trendiest, youngest voice I could muster.

'Hiya, Johnny, thanks for ringing back,' he said, and his politeness made me even more chary of what I was about to hear.

'You rang,' I said, superfluously. Then I remembered my manners. 'How's your mother bearing up?'

'Fine, considering,' he said. 'Still asleep – I think she had a good night. Like to meet you this morning for a chat if I might.'

'Sure thing,' I said easily, watching my grimace in the mirror behind the phone. 'Like to come here?'

'Could we make it The Café of Eva Gonzalez?'

'The where?'

'The Café of Eva Gonzalez – it's in Sceptre Lane, near the College of Art and Design.' He laughed as he said it. 'Do you good to see where the young hang out, see how your taxes are spent.'

'Sounds all-round educational,' I said. 'When do you suggest?'

'How would ten suit you?'

'Ten sounds fine,' I said. 'See you there.'

I decided to partially make up for abandoned jogging by walking the kilometre to my appointment. I paused outside Magdalen's door wondering if I ought to say hello, check she was all right. It was bad enough having an old pal drop bastards like Dutch Gaffney and Hocks Mackey on my head without having them land on my friend's head also.

I decided against it, reckoned it would be wrong of me to interrupt any profitable work of mercy she might be engaged in. I skipped down the stairs and stepped out briskly into a great morning.

On the middle of Talbot Bridge I stopped to look down into muddy Anna Livia and squint about, see if there were any red Porsches or rugged light-heavyweights sneaking up on me. I seemed to be in the clear. I continued along the quay and up through Temple Bar.

The dressed limestone of Christchurch Cathedral was splendidly silver in the sun and I stopped to admire it and look for Porsches. I thought of the centuries of poor people who'd done their bit to leave middens for us to poke around in. They don't make 'em like that anymore.

I walked along messy Thomas Street. Most of the buildings look about ready to fall on to the traders. I squeezed between fruit and vegetable stalls and found the mouth of Sceptre Lane. It looks pretty much as it must have done to Dean Swift on evenings when he'd take a turn there mulling over the direction *Gulliver's Travels* was taking. Halfway down the lane the sun bounced blindingly off the new kid on the block.

The Café of Eva Gonzalez had so much glass out front you wondered why it didn't collapse when you opened the door. It was so trendy inside I doubted the sanity of an owner who would spend that kind of money in such an unfashionable area. Maybe it really was owned by Eva Gonzalez and perhaps she'd only recently made the descent of the Orinoco loaded with Inca gold. She was into bullfighting in a big way if the posters were anything to go by – either that or they were about to claim that Joyce brought Hemingway there for tripe.

Spanish guitars thrummed menacingly in the background – gave the impression a large bull might come charging through from the kitchen at any moment. Four people sat in separate islands of silence.

Behind the counter, smocked in duck-egg blue, a Dublin Jacqueline exaggerated her concern for hygiene as she arranged mouth-watering pastries with a too-small spatula.

'Morning, Eva,' I said, and her tired smile told me she'd heard that one too often.

'Whatcha like, pet?' Eighteen-year-old brown eyes took my measure.

'White coffee, please.'

'Bring it over t'ya.'

His hand on my shoulder was the first I knew of his arrival.

84

'Morning, Johnny,' Patrick Brett said, and sat opposite as Brown Eyes set the coffee in front of me.

'Morning, Patrick,' I said. 'Have something?'

'Usual, Liz,' Patrick said.

She returned his wink and made me feel old, out of it.

'Thanks for meeting me,' Patrick said.

I began to wonder where all this politeness might lead. From my brief experience of him, being pleasant twice in one morning was over the top as far as Patrick Brett was concerned.

'Nice place,' I said. 'I've never heard of it until this morning.'

'It's beginning to catch on. Pretty soon it will be too expensive for students and we'll have to find someplace else.'

'Are there any funeral arrangements yet?'

'Not yet,' Patrick said, stretching his legs, leaning back in his chair, making it creak. He yawned, shook his head like a diver surfacing. 'Pathologist is doing tests or something – man is up to his tonsils it seems. Cops say they'll get back to us soon as they can. You know a detective called Crotty? He seems to know you.'

'Yeah. Detective Sergeant Tom Crotty. Good guy, decent sort, bloody good hurler in his day.'

'Seems thick as a plank.' Patrick was watching me carefully.

'That's what he wants you to think,' I said. 'That's him dumbing down. Reckon he watches too much *Colombo*. When did you meet him?'

'He called to the house yesterday. Wanted to know when we'd last seen Dad.' He barked a laugh. 'That's rich – when did we last see Dad!'

The waitress came with coffee and an appetising croissant. Patrick neglected to thank her so I did it for him, but it was he who got her smile. I felt even older.

'Do you know,' he said, through a flaky mouthful of croissant and jam, 'every fortnight I had to go to Dad's office in Glasbury Street to collect the housekeeping money. Most times I wouldn't see him. Oh, he might be there all right, hiding out in his private office, but he wouldn't come out. He'd leave it to Betty Halpin to pass out the envelope of cash, dole out the drachma. Poor Betty used to be so embarrassed.'

Head down, he became preoccupied with the remains of his croissant. He looked so like his father I began to wonder how on earth the Paddy Brett I'd known could have become the megalomaniac control freak I kept hearing about. Hadn't anyone liked him? Man with that sort of money salted away – what was the point of treating his children in that fashion?

Patrick looked up.

'Wasn't it mad! Think about it! There he was on television telling the country how to run its affairs, telling us how we must accept monetary union, being interviewed by plummy bastards on *The Business Programme*, and all the while his family had to slope down to his skanky office for enough to keep going.' He shook his head. 'Fucking mad is what it was!'

'What's your explanation for it?' I was genuinely interested.

'Wish to Christ I knew,' Patrick said, earnest and sad. 'I really do. I'd love to know what it was we did to him that turned his face against us, made him cut off the money supply. I mean you could understand him falling out with one or two of us, but to fall out with the three of us all at once can't be explained. Maybe we didn't show sufficient gratitude, thank him on our knees often enough. Who knows, maybe he needed constant acclaim. We can't figure it. I sometimes think he went a bit mad when he started making pots of money, when he got that bank of his going and started buying and selling property.'

'And when *did* you last see your father?'

His eyes narrowed and he was suddenly wary.

'Must be the best part of four weeks now. It was over in

Fortress Glasbury. I was on collect-the-brown-envelope duty – Patricia and I took turns at being humiliated. Betty Halpin was paying me off when he made the mistake of coming out of his office too soon and he was forced to look at his son – one of the lesser inconveniences in the life of a Celtic tycoon.'

His bitterness was saddening. I changed the subject.

'What else did Crotty want?'

'He was trying to plot Dad's last movements. Mom told him we hadn't seen him in a bit. Mom always reckoned that one day Dad would shake off whatever madness had changed him, so she gave a fairly rosy picture of Brett family life to poor old Detective Crotty. Don't think he believed her. Mom told him how you were helping her wind up his affairs. That's when Crotty said he knew you – way he put it he seemed to know you well. Hope it doesn't cause you any bother, Mom telling him I mean.'

'No problem,' I said. 'I've played hurling against him on a few occasions years ago – that's how we know each other. That and a recent burglary at my plant that he investigated.'

I let a silence gather as I waited for him to tell me why we were meeting. He licked a finger and began mopping up croissant flakes – it made him seem younger, more vulnerable. When the plate was clean he looked up and I could see that he was embarrassed, blushing slightly.

'I rang Betty Halpin yesterday. It was brown-envelope day and we're broke. Betty is nice, but she couldn't do anything for us. She said I'd have to talk to Dad's partner in the other practice, Oliver Pettit. I rang him and he was polite and asked would I mind very much waiting until he'd spoken to you. He said you were joint executor of Dad's will. That true?'

'First I've heard of it,' I said. I was on thin ice and I took it easy. 'There was a message on my answering service from an Oliver Pettit last night – asked me to ring him as a matter of urgency. Must have been after you rang him that he rang me.'

87

'Did you ring him?' Patrick asked, leaning forward.

They must really be in dire straits, I thought.

I took out my mobile and pressed buttons.

'Mr Oliver Pettit, please,' I said. 'John Constantine here – he's been looking for me.'

'Oh, yes, Mr Constantine, yes he has.' She had a pleasant voice. 'Fact I just rang you again a few minutes ago. One moment please.'

Patrick watched me, drummed the table with his fingers.

'Oliver Pettit,' he said, his voice clinically dry.

'Morning, Mr Pettit. You were looking for me.'

'Thank you for ringing back, Mr Constantine. It's about my late partner, Paddy Brett, an old friend of yours I understand. You will have heard the tragic news. His son tells me that Joan has asked you to look after her affairs for the time being. I'm glad she has. Paddy named you and me as joint executors of his will. I believe his family are experiencing some pressing financial difficulties and I would like to attend to that as soon as possible, but I would prefer to clear the air with you before doing so. Would it be possible for you to drop by this office today, this afternoon at two fifteen perhaps?'

'I'll be there, Mr Pettit,' I said.

I put the phone away.

Patrick smiled nervously.

'Well?' he asked. 'Will we be able to get some cash?'

'Pettit wants to fix that straight away. I'm seeing him this afternoon.'

'But will we get money *today*,' Patrick asked, his eyes wide with anxiety. I was astonished that his need was so pressing.

I dug into my back pocket. I had three hundred and forty pounds on me. I peeled off two hundred and handed them to him.

'That do until this evening?' I asked. I didn't want him to think he needed to beg for charity. 'There should be plenty in your father's practice.'

88

He exhaled loudly.

'Thank you very much, Johnny,' he said, counting it. 'I owe you two hundred.'

The money relaxed him and he was smiling now, nodding his head to the beat of the flamenco that lightly filled the background.

'We had another visitor yesterday,' Patrick said. 'Man called Bill Grattan. He's the boss of North East Baltic Bank – the bank Dad was involved with. I'd never seen him before but Mom knew him. I listened.' He grinned and I smiled remembering the way he'd popped out of nowhere at the end of my visit to Windward.

'He was so full of shit – how he thought the world of Dad, went on and on about how fucking sorry he was. Sorry my arse! He wanted to know if Dad left any files with us, said that some information belonging to the bank had been mislaid. Seemed to me the guy had a problem. Mom was great. Drew herself up and told him Dad never needed to bring work home, had always said that the working day was long enough for anyone and a man needed time to be with his family. Jesus, she almost had me believing it!'

'Whatever they're missing it must be important,' I said.

Patrick shrugged.

'Grattan said if we found anything, any files, to give him a ring. I showed him out and he was full of patronising chat about what I was doing at college. Wanted to know if I was computer literate, went on about what a big fucking deal computers were. I told him I hated computers, anything to do with accountancy. Told him accountancy rots your mind – don't think he liked that.'

Patrick laughed and looked past me, his eyes widening with pleasure.

Candy Delamere trailed a perfumed hand across my shoulder, swung around me laughing – such a lovely sound, full of youth and sweetness. Way she was dressed my mother wouldn't have let her out of the house. She seemed to be wearing cast-offs someone had used polishing floors, but she still managed to look as though she'd stepped off the cover of Vogue. Her whin bush of red hair was restrained by an emerald-green scrunchie.

'Morning, Johnny,' she said, 'and how are you this lovely morning?'

'Much better now that I've seen you, Candy,' I said. You could only be in love with Candy.

She turned to a companion who slouched after her, but continued speaking to me.

'Meet our friend, Julie Hartigan, Johnny,' she said, then smiled at the girl. 'Told you he was a hunk.'

I stood and shook the small cold hand of a demurely attractive girl of Candy's age. Her fawn top had a golden elephant inset over her left breast and her ragged jeans emphasised her slimly rounded boyish figure. Her overly long face had a gauntly awkward strength that would become attractive with the years, but would be the bane of her existence until that good time. Her dark brown hair was pulled back too severely for that shape face.

'Hi,' she said, in the loquacious way the young have perfected.

She sat and smiled at Patrick who selected a wink from his quiver of greetings. Candy screeched a chair across the floor before leaning down to peck Patrick on the mouth proprietorially. She dropped down as Liz zipped from behind her counter to turn on a blinding smile beside me.

'All sleep well?' she asked, and giggled as though some great joke had just gone past. 'What will our young lovers have this morning?'

Candy raised an inquiring eyebrow at me. I spread my hands in open invitation. Miz Delamere interpreted that as *carte blanche* and began ordering right left and centre for herself and Julie Hartigan, who had the grace to look startled and ask, 'You sure?'

When all of it had arrived Candy pushed a plate of luscious cake in front of Patrick. Why hadn't I got a Candy to fend for me, I asked myself.

Candy picked up a fork, wiggled her slim hips.

'I shouldn't,' she said, 'but this is divine. Here goes.'

'You live close to Windward,' I said to Julie Hartigan.

She nodded, munched, waited to swallow before answering.

'Just up the road on the way into town. Big green gates – Knocklangan Lodge.'

'Same as the Hotel Group?' I asked innocently.

Julie frowned. 'Yes.'

'Which came first,' I asked, mainly to keep conversation going, 'the name of the house or the Hotel Group?'

'The house,' Julie said. 'Walter Hartigan called the Hotel Group after the house.'

Not many eighteen-year-olds refer to their fathers so coolly. I got the impression we'd hit her favourite distasteful topic. I passed, dropped it. I addressed Patrick.

'I'm going to see Betty Halpin now,' I said. 'Has she been with your father long?'

'Seven, maybe eight years I think.' He laughed. 'Mom used to reckon Dad was having it off with Betty. Poor woman's a brick short of a load – lift doesn't go to the top. But she's very nice. I like her – she's always been decent to me. There's some story about how Dad destroyed her father's company and the man killed himself – blew his head off with a shotgun. Way I heard it Dad is supposed to have felt bad about it – if you can believe that – and gave the daughter a job.'

'She's too old for him anyway,' Julie Hartigan said. Patrick and Candy looked sharply at her and she busied herself with her cake. I wondered what lay behind that odd comment.

'I'd better be going,' I said, rising. 'Might see you later this evening, Patrick. Nice meeting you, ladies.'

'Thanks for the assist,' Patrick said, and stood up – an outrageous courtesy for him.

I went to the counter and paid. Liz was thrilled with my tip, gave me one of her special winks.

91

'See yez,' I said to the beautiful threesome as I passed their table and they chorused farewells before settling down to serious conversation.

I walked down Thomas Street and stopped to look at reflections in a window. No one seemed to be interested in me. I walked on and wondered what Grattan's visit to Windward the day before really meant.

He had to be looking for the diskette – that was obvious. So Paddy hadn't given it to him on Sunday night. Had Paddy met Grattan or Lemptke on Sunday?

Had he been robbed of the diskette and killed on the way to the meeting? Hartigan was the most likely candidate for that scenario if Paddy was right in thinking Hartigan had been skimming off the The Farmer's investments. Maybe Lemptke and his East Europeans had other irons in the fire and had reasons of their own to try for the diskette.

I stopped thinking about it.

It was coming up on eleven thirty when I turned into Great Georges Street and headed toward St Stephen's Green.

Glasbury Street is decrepit, totally uninteresting and consequently is picked out on all maps as a feature of Historic Dublin. I'm sure Tourist Board guys have combed *Ulysses* for a mention of it – even an anagram in Serbo-Croat would make them happy, anything that would get it into the Literary Walks section of their brochures.

Like an outraged governess fastidiously drawing in her skirts, the narrow frontage of O'Connor's bookshop tries to pretend it's alone, not squeezed between the stale-smelling doorways of two pubs – The Ball and Pocket to the right, The Whetstone to the left. Unlike its competitor – modernised about twenty years ago and now on its way out – The Whetstone has had hardly anything done to it since Robert Emmet cruised it of an evening and as a consequence is on its way back.

Between it and the bookshop was the door that led to the first floor of O'Connor's. It carried a burnished brass plate that announced to the world and his wife should they glance that way that Paddy Brett & Associates, Investment Consultants, were constantly available – step right up, folks.

I pressed the button.

'Who is it?' Her voice was high pitched, frightened.

'My name is Constantine. I'd like to speak to Miz Halpin.'

'Johnny Constantine?' The voice was brighter now.

'That's right.'

'Come in, come in.' The buzzer sounded.

The staircase was a steep tunnel with a whiff of mould in the air. Difficult now to imagine a family had bided there once, that children had shouted gaily on their way to school, clattering down those steps in the proud morning of vanished empire.

She came to the top of the stairs and I slowed my ascent to let her get used to me – sudden movements are always bad, as upsetting to the naturally timid as they are provocative to the congenitally aggressive. Cautiously she stared down and I guessed the hand behind her back held some weapon, some notional means of defence.

'You *are* Johnny Constantine, Paddy Brett's friend?'

Her voice was tight, hysteria not far away. I realised I was still a threatening silhouette against the grime-strained glow from the intricate fanlight behind me. I had a sudden flashback to a childhood hideout in the People's Park and the complicated series of passwords Paddy Brett and I had worked out for every day of the week. And it *was* a good question. Was I still Paddy Brett's friend? I pushed that to the back of my mind.

'The same,' I said, and paused, leaned against the wall, my head waist high on her as I waited for her to go on.

'Oh, I'm so glad to see you, Mr Constantine, so glad you've come. Paddy often spoke of you, about when you were boys together. Please do come up and excuse me standing here like a peeler.'

Slowly, so that she would not feel I was crowding her, I followed her into an office that was beautifully decorated, warmly intimate, wallpapered with secrets. Thick pile silenced our footsteps and not the smallest sound came to us from the busy street.

Guiltily, her smile shy and self-effacing, she brought from behind her back an old-fashioned book-keeper's ebony ruler and laid it neatly on a splendid mahogany desk that had to be worth twenty grand – it gleamed like a freshly unhusked chestnut.

'Please sit down,' she said, indicating I should take the high-winged chair behind the desk as she prepared to sit in front of it in an understandable if sad attempt to restore a familiar order, recreate the life and times that had meant so much to her.

I swivelled the chair and sat down, resting my elbows on the warm mahogany, and examined Betty Halpin in the light from the window behind me. Slim and of medium height, I guessed she was a few years younger than myself – probably hovering on the wrong side of forty. Her face was younger, curiously bland – a well-formed bone structure that was neither beautiful nor plain. Her expression was childlike in its innocence, her skin unlined and of a paleness that was in stark contrast to impossibly black, swept-back hair streaming to a chignon pierced by a tortoiseshell comb. Lively emerald eyes pleaded for fairness in an unjust world. Her mouth was truly remarkable, arresting in its uniqueness, as though all her allocation of beauty had been concentrated in its proffered gentleness and wide symmetry – like a cat's tail, it had a life of its own and it quivered tremulously every so often.

Something about her warned of nascent discord, an aura of instability framed her. I had the distinct feeling that trifling with this woman could be calamitous.

'I've been trying for weeks to contact you, Mr Constantine,' she said. 'I've been ringing your home and your office almost every day. Paddy would check in with me on his mobile every morning to know if I'd managed to get you – he was so anxious to talk to you. Your phone kept ringing out. I've never known Paddy to be so agitated about reaching anyone. Yesterday was the first time your answering service cut in, Mr Constantine.' She looked at me accusingly, as though unable to understand how a phone would not reply automatically.

'Call me Johnny, Betty,' I said. 'When I go away I turn everything off.'

'It's been so difficult,' she said. 'All the clicking, those noises on our phone – I kept thinking we had a fault on the line but Telecom said no. Of course you can't believe them, they're half asleep most of the time. Have you any idea what's happened, Mr Constantine – Johnny?'

Her fingers riffled imagined piano keys on the desk's edge and she swayed as she played.

'I know very little, Betty,' I said.

Something odd began to happen in her eyes and at the corners of that mobile mouth.

'I'm trying to piece together an outline of his movements,' I said. 'What do you know about last Friday, say?'

'I've no idea where he's been for most of the last fortnight,' she said. 'He kept in contact by phone. I think he suddenly got very busy at the bank. He rang from there several times, but mostly he was ringing on his mobile. He came in last Wednesday, this day week. He signed a few cheques and went again almost immediately. He hadn't shaved and that's so unlike him. After that he could have been anywhere – out and about, hither and yon, here and there.'

She yawned, seemed to become bored by our conversation, looked down at the desk for some time. I said nothing.

'Haven't been able to sleep again,' she said, looking up quickly. 'Always difficult to figure where he is, you know – Scarlet Pimpernel. They seek him here, they seek him there – know what I mean? He could be at a board meeting, or in some pub, or some bed.'

She smiled dreamily and it was a sobering experience. Something wild came into her face, a sliver of chaos, as though she'd decided now was as good a time as any to have that nervous breakdown she'd been promising herself. Distractedly she patted her chignon, an old-fashioned gesture, and smiled secretively, lopsidedly and returned with a weird coyness to piano playing on the edge of the desk.

'We're to be married, you know,' she said, glancing up shyly from her playing. 'Not right away, but soon. The quotations for invitations and hotels are on my desk. Just as soon as we can find the time we're headed for Mexico and divorce – the Irish thing takes much too long, far too expensive.'

She smiled again, if what she did with that sensual mouth could be called a smile.

'Course we didn't wait. We've already had our honeymoon here.' She caressed the mahogany of the desk. 'This will always be our special place.'

I said nothing, but got ready for any eventuality. I even began to wonder if she had an ulterior motive in sitting me in Paddy's chair, if she'd arranged it to get between me and the door. Betty Halpin was only starting – she'd been without an audience too long.

'Course he can be a bit of a bastard when he wants,' she said – a grin, a dismissively forgiving wave. 'Handsome is as handsome does! You men – you get away with so much. I've never gone along with those trollops he brings up here. Always forgive him though, provided he puts the oriental on our desk. I've never minded those flibbertigibbets – it's girls like that Heather Skeehan I object to, years too young for him. They're only out for what they can gouge out of him and he can never see that.'

It was unreal. I was dumbfounded by her performance, by her present tense, but I managed to ask my question casually.

'And who is Heather Skeehan?'

'An avaricious bitch,' she spat back. 'Joined North East Baltic when it opened – I think Paddy knew her father, or he'd had his eye on her. She was only a slip of a girl then. What am I talking about? She's still only a slip. She had him all to herself for two years. Poor fool, he even gave her the apartment in Donnybrook – course that was before the price of apartments went through the roof. Probably worth two hundred thousand now. Seven years ago he bought it for sixty. Man is made of clay and woman has made a mug of him! She sure did. She's sleeping with Bill Grattan now. Just can't keep her legs together.'

She tinkled imaginary ivories some more, swayed wildly as she played. I began to wonder if she was having some sort of attack, asked myself if I should ring for a doctor. Suddenly, she was still, bolt upright.

'Bitch was here yesterday. Cheek of her!' she said, her lovely mouth a narrow line. 'Said Bill Grattan sent her. Wanted to know if there were any bank files here, any computer records. I know what she was after. Sniffing around to see what she could pick up. I think he's gone back to her and he doesn't want me to know. That's why he's staying away.'

Without warning she seemed to shift down a few gears, became the timid mouse of our initial meeting.

'Tea? Would you like some tea?'

'Tea would be very nice,' I said, smiling.

'Won't be a moment,' she said, and left.

I heard her rattle cups, fill a kettle somewhere down the hall. She began to sing 'Raglan Road' in a Dietrich voice – she was quite good.

I gently opened the drawers of Paddy's desk. Then I tried the three filing cabinets against the wall. Every drawer was empty.

Behind me her laugh was low, a chillingly guttural chuckle.

'Shredded,' she said, standing in the doorway, waggling her finger at me as though I'd been naughty. 'Confettied –

97

just like I promised myself I'd do if he ever went off with that bitch again. That's it, isn't it? He's no more dead than you or me. Probably over in Connemara with her as we speak – like he used to be three years ago. Over in that cottage in Maam Cross. All she ever had to do was waggle those hips of hers – and her with hardly an arse at all on her. God! He's such a fool! Men! No use him sending that pair of eejits around here pretending they're gardai to cod me into believing he's dead. Paddy trying to pretend yer man across the street has the place under observation. I know who he is, I'm on to him.'

I swivelled the chair and looked out into the street. He was window shopping, but it was definitely odd – he didn't look the type that would be into frilly underwear, lace nighties, crotchless panties. From where I sat I could see he was getting thin on top and his sporty zip-up contributed little to his massive shoulders. Come to think of it, he might look cute in black lace.

'You know him?' I asked Betty.

She came around the desk and peered out quickly, drew back.

'Yes,' she said. 'Paddy called him Hocks Mackey. There's another one he called Dutch Gaffney. They've been taking turns at hanging around there these last three weeks. Are you trying to tell me they're for real?'

I spoke casually as I looked out the window.

'I really don't know, Betty. Where did you shred the files?'

Her eyes narrowed. 'Whistled up a mobile outfit. Wait until he gets the bill!'

'When did you last see Paddy?'

'Friday morning. Put his head round the door – asked if I'd managed to contact you. I spoke to him again twice during the day – I remember because the line was so bad. He must have been in the car. He said he'd see me Monday.'

Her eyes fell and she moved toward the door, paused, and turned back to look straight at me.

'It's a bluff, Johnny, isn't it? He's off someplace with her, isn't he? Just doesn't want to hurt my feelings, that's it, isn't it? I mean he's really all right, not dead, nothing bad like that?'

Her eyes pleaded with me, begged me to say yes.

'No, Betty,' I said. 'I've seen him in the hospital. I'm very sorry.'

She was nodding, her lips moving, and she looked about her as though she would run somewhere, hide from my words. A kettle began whistling and she ran toward it. I turned back to look out the window. In the street the big man continued to be fascinated by the lingerie.

Footsteps and the sound of rattling china brought me swivelling about as she returned to the room. Betty Halpin carried a tray of tea things and, apart from high heels, a small white scarf at her throat, a gold cross and chain, she was entirely naked and utterly unconcerned. She set down the tray and resumed her seat opposite me. She stirred the pot before pouring.

'I hope it's not too strong,' she said, then laughed lightly. 'Paddy always says you should be able to trot a mouse on it.'

I was fascinated by her heavy nipples and their purple-brown areolae. Her wide bush of pubic hair was thick and curly, as improbably black as the hair on her head. I took the cup she passed to me and she added sugar and milk in silence. She nibbled a biscuit between sips, crossed her legs without a care in the world. I tried to keep looking her in the eye.

'Joan and the children are anxious about their situation,' I said.

She nodded thoughtfully before brushing crumbs from a surprisingly resilient nipple.

'I never understood why he put them through such hoops – especially young Patrick,' she said. 'Did you know the kids took it in turn to come here every fortnight for the housekeeping money? That was shameful and, besides, there was no call for it. We had tucks of money here. Way things stand, right now there's about two hundred thousand on call and more again in fees in work-in-progress. Paddy just won't agree to letting his wife have what she should have.'

Betty looked over her shoulder, then leaned forward confidentially, her fine breasts swinging out.

'Paddy claims no matter how much he gives her she drinks most of it. Poor woman! It's an awful affliction.'

'So there will be no problem in letting the family have cash for the funeral and other expenses?'

'Funeral? What funeral? Paddy won't agree to them getting a shilling. I bet you any money he'll stick to his old routine as soon as he gets back from the West.'

I looked at her and in a little while she looked away, folded her arms stubbornly, as though she had said all she was going to say. Her nipples squinted at me over her forearms.

'He's not coming back, Betty,' I said. 'He's dead.'

She began humming and bouncing her crossed leg, looking everywhere except at me. I remained silent and in a little while the humming stopped.

'He was Betty's friend,' she said, without warning. 'Betty's only friend.'

Tears came soundlessly, big globules that rolled down to drip on to her breasts, her eyes glazed and that startling mouth hung open.

I sat without moving – there was nothing I could do.

Later, when her tears had ceased and the strange, mesmeric humming had begun again – was she aware she was doing it? – I rose and came round the desk.

'I'll have to be going, Betty,' I said. 'Will you be all right?'

It was weird to be addressing a naked, goose-pimpled woman in an office.

'No,' she said. 'I won't be all right. Betty will never be all right again. The files are all with the Ballsbridge practice. I didn't shred anything. I wouldn't do that to him.

100

He transferred them last week. I don't know why. Maybe he didn't trust Betty any longer. Oliver Pettit has the files now – and the accounts. You're going to have to talk to him about money for Joan. Why didn't he trust me, Johnny? Was it because of that Mr Carmody? Was he afraid for me, was he trying to protect me? I wouldn't have cared – I would have died for him.'

'What Mr Carmody?' I asked.

'Man who came here threatening Paddy. I heard them shouting. Paddy never used to shout. Oh, I know Paddy said after he'd gone that it was only business, but I could see he was really frightened. I heard Carmody give Paddy ten days to do whatever he was supposed to do.'

'Is there anything I can do for you?'

She seemed to be totally unaware that she was naked.

'No. I asked you here because I wanted to be sure. To be certain I wasn't hearing the voices again. I knew you would tell me the truth – Paddy always said you were the best.'

'Betty, I'd like to send a friend along to fix your phones for you, cut out all those noises.'

'That's very kind of you – hardly seems worthwhile though.'

'You never know,' I said, lamely. 'I'll send him anyway.'

She looked up at me and nodded absently.

'Now we never will make love,' she said. 'Goodbye, Johnny Constantine. Thank you for coming.'

The humming began again as I was leaving the room. I felt a sense of total helplessness at being unable to utter a word of comfort to help her in a grief made more poignantly intense by her strange behaviour. But at last I'd found someone who truly grieved for Paddy Brett.

At the foot of the stairs I hesitated, took three deep breaths and let myself out. I paid no attention to the knicker enthusiast on the other side of the street.

I crossed to Dream Bathrooms at the corner of Glasbury Street and paused in front of a display of gross mirrors to

101

watch a multiple image of Hocks Mackey saunter after me. Nonchalance was not his forte. He was big and looked as though his boxing career had been a pretty savage and short-lived affair.

I walked on past the Central Bank and into Temple Bar. I saw Detective Sergeant Tom Crotty go into The Duckless Drake, Angel McDonagh's Historic Pub – that's what it says over the door. Angel opened it for the first time all of three years ago.

The Duckless has to be the noisiest pub in Dublin – Angel even gets accused of playing pub-noise tapes to force up the decibels. He does the business though – you have to give him that.

It was early, but even so the pub was three-quarters full and Angel's famous shouting waiters were building atmosphere. Plates of meat were coming across the counter faster than clay-pigeon pulls. There was the usual demand for the bottled water of mythical bogholes. Overall, the mating calls of cellular phones gave the lounge the frenzied charm of a picnic in hell.

Crotty was at the bar in full chat-up mode, already *en rapport* with a tall pleasant-looking young woman who seemed a trifle taken aback at the speed of the proposition she was listening to, possibly wondering where this handsome brute had come from in the middle of a perfectly ordinary mid-week toasted-ham-and-coffee. Like Angel, Crotty does the business. I squeezed through and stood beside him.

'Johnny, how's it hangin'?' he said, through a mouthful of something. 'This is my friend ... God, love, what's your name again? Head like a sieve.'

'Anna,' she said, tilting her head back, 'Anna Rellehan.'

She smiled a nice smile and I hoped she wouldn't be too disappointed when she found out about Crotty's little hedonistic ways.

She'd just taken a sip of coffee when I said to Crotty, 'I see you favour the rotary method of mastication.'

Anna Rellehan sprayed the counter and Crotty patted her back and smiled at me.

I turned to pick up my glass of Guinness and in the mirror saw Mackey standing just inside the door watching me and Crotty. Suddenly he turned and bulled his way out through three young women coming into the pub.

'Always nice to meet a gentleman,' one of them called after him.

'How's the Brett thing going?' I asked. 'Like I said, I have a personal interest – even more so now. His wife has asked me to help wind up his affairs.'

'So I believe,' Crotty said, 'so she was telling me.'

'You've been to see her?'

'Up there yesterday. Now there's a great bit of property. Jaysus, way things are going, rundown an' all as it is, she should get three-quarters of a million for it. One of them pop stars'd snap it up, turn it into a shrine, help the tourist trade. Christ, I've been offered a hundred and twenty thou for my inner-city gaff. I paid thirty-seven for it five years ago. Hey, Angel, give us drink here before the whole town becomes a fucking theme park. Where d'you live, Anna?'

Anna Rellehan hesitated only a couple of seconds.

'I share an apartment with two girls – down by the river.' That was as much as she was telling for the moment. 'Your office around here?'

'Harcourt Street,' Crotty said. 'Garda Headquarters.'

'Oh,' Anna Rellehan said.

'KGB,' Crotty said, leering. 'You have to do as I say or it's the Bog of Allen Gulag for you. Right!'

'Right,' she said, smiling, feeling much more secure.

'But how's it going?' I asked, dragging him back.

'Not great, to be honest,' he said, 'but don't go telling that to the papers. Forensics aren't finished yet. Jaysus, there are so many bodies around these days and there's so few staff to deal with them. There've been two murders since Brett was found, but thank Christ they're not high profile like him. I reckon we should ask for some of the

103

Lottery money – maybe that way we might start to get somewhere. Anyway we do know time of death to be somewhere between eight and eleven Sunday night – nothing like pinpoint fucking accuracy. Killed somewhere and brought to Bullock Harbour. Not a thing in his pockets except loose change – nothing at all, not even a wallet. Imagine that – an accountant without a wallet! Could be a contract job – all the rage now. You know anything about it?'

He was smiling but I knew he was serious and it didn't pay to get the wrong side of Crotty.

'No more than I've read in *The Irish Times*,' I said.

He stared soberly at me as I drank.

'He had a penthouse just around the corner,' he said. 'I've just come from there. One of those apartments people queued for overnight when they went on the market – mainly rich guys, dentists and the like. He must have bought it as an investment. Arm and a leg, I'd say. Funny thing though, there's so little in it. I mean the guy's rich and he lives in this swell gaff and the place looks as though he was just camping there. I mean there's hardly any furniture and he's been living there two years. Neighbours see him come and go regularly. Think about it, there are only two chairs in the whole apartment. Television set on a stand in the corner and that's the living room furnished. Guy can't have been expecting many visitors. Neighbours can't remember ever seeing any. Found a pair of women's black tights – only sign of anyone else having been there. Weird. Was he like that when you knew him?'

'No,' I said.

He looked hard at me, then reassembled his good-humour face and turned back to Anna.

I had one of Angel's Historic Ham Sandwiches and another Guinness – I would have to get back to serious jogging. I answered Crotty's politely thrown words which became fewer as his interest in Anna Rellehan sharpened. I learned between the lines that the body was unlikely to be released for burial before Monday, more likely Tuesday.

In a while Crotty ignored me completely and I reckoned crime and punishment had dropped off his agenda for that afternoon at least. Anna went to ring her office, tell them something she'd eaten hadn't agreed with her and Crotty and I chatted amiably. Anna returned fresh-faced and eager to be at it. She and Crotty left. Anna blushed a little, looked quite bridal and sweet in an old-fashioned way as she nodded, shook my hand, said it had been nice meeting me.

I finished my Guinness slowly and thought of Paddy Brett sitting in his empty apartment on one of his two chairs watching television. Unlikely that the second diskette was hidden there – but he didn't have it on him when he was found. If someone hadn't killed him to take it off him, the most likely hiding place was the safety deposit box. I would need the key and that meant going back to Aunt Lil.

In the mirror I saw Hocks Mackey shoulder through the crowd to stand at the end of the bar. I waited until the barman started pouring the pint he ordered. I finished my drink and walked out.

# Chapter Six

Mackey kept a shambling hundred metres between us all the way along Nassau Street. On Kildare Street I was tempted to try losing him by slipping in and out of the Shelbourne Hotel, but then decided there wasn't much point. I continued out Baggot Street and down into Pembroke Road. Halfway along, a white stone plaque marked the offices of Paddy Brett & Co.

The building had been beautifully restored, all its original features preserved. An attractive middle-aged woman presided over an incongruous space-age arrangement of consoles and VDUs in a glass lobby. She looked up from a word processor and smiled.

'Mr Oliver Pettit,' I said. 'Name's Constantine – he's expecting me.'

'Oh, Mr Constantine, yes of course.'

She pushed buttons, announced me.

If they want to do him justice Oliver Pettit's epitaph should include the words, 'He was the Neatest Man.' Most of a foot shorter than me – which made him around five-four – he held himself ramrod straight. His suit looked as though it had been pressed with him in it. Gently courteous and without a trace of obsequiousness, he led me away to his inner sanctum which was – well, neat. His desk was so uncluttered I wondered what it was he did all day.

He smiled a lot, showed the neatest teeth. For a decorous

time he was conventionally doleful about the late principal of the firm, but then shot his cuffs in a life-must-go-on gesture and got down to business.

The original of Paddy Brett's will was with his solicitors, but Pettit handed me a letter from the solicitors and a certified copy of the will. The substance of the letter was that Oliver Pettit and I were executors. With the exception of a couple of small bequests, the bulk of the estate was to be divided between Joan and the children. The will included the deceased's property and his interest in the two practices. All very straightforward, Oliver said.

He then gave a succinct account of how he and the other two remaining directors of the company proposed buying out Joan's interest in Paddy Brett & Co. It was clear that a plan had been developed since Paddy's death.

The buy-out would be spread over five years to ease the company's cash flow and minimise the beneficiaries' tax liabilities. All the figures, books, etc., would be made available to independent auditors if so desired, but he suggested – with a neat smile – that it might be advantageous for all concerned if the whole transaction remained between the two of us and out of the domain of the Revenue Commissioners. He would handle all funeral expenses and would make thirty thousand pounds immediately available to Joan and the children.

I told him I'd go along with him for now and pocketed the cheque he gave me for Joan.

'I understand you have all the files for the other company, Paddy Brett & Associates,' I said.

'Betty Halpin's been on the phone to me this morning, told me you'd been with her,' he said. 'She's very upset, poor soul. That company is completely independent of us here in Ballsbridge.' I noticed a definite shade of emphasis on that 'completely'. 'I haven't had time to sort through everything, but it does seem that the family can expect to do very nicely out of it. Betty reckons there's the bones of seven hundred thousand there and she's hardly ever wrong about things like that.' His smile seemed to indicate that he was aware of other things in which she might not be quite so accurate. 'Of course,' he went on, 'we shall have to look at it in the overall context to see that we minimise their exposure to tax.'

'That it then?' I asked.

His eyes widened slightly and his chair moved back.

'Well there are a few bits and pieces – directorships here and there and he was chairman of a few companies – those will take a little while to tidy up, but there's not a lot involved. I'm not sure about North East Baltic Bank. He was very prominent in that, was the first acting CEO when it was set up as a matter of fact. It was something he kept very much to himself – and that's saying something for a hands-on operator like Paddy. I've been picking up the oddest vibes about the bank, rumours of rumours so to speak.'

I had the feeling Mr Neat was buckling on his parachute.

'What kind of vibes?' I asked blandly, giving him my innocent stare.

His chair moved another couple of inches back from his desk.

'Well, I've been hearing stories about offshore activities, particularly a product called the Montego International Investment Fund that Paddy was instrumental in setting up. Word has it there's a lot of money involved.' He massaged the bridge of his nose before continuing. 'Could be it's what got Paddy killed. I certainly can't think of any other reason why anyone would want to murder him.'

At last I'd found someone interested in why Paddy Brett had died.

'You reckon there was something illegal in this Montego Investment thing?'

Oliver Pettit looked at me for ten seconds before deciding I had to be having him on.

'Of course it's illegal,' he said calmly. 'They wouldn't be rushing hell for leather to invest in it it wasn't. I know quite a few people who are heavily into it and happy the way it works. I wouldn't recommend it myself – I don't believe in that kind of exposure. But it's no more illegal than a lot of other things and money knows no morality.' He smiled bleakly.

'Why would anyone kill because of Montego?'

'I've been tossing that around,' he said. 'One answer could be money laundering. Me, I don't like what I hear about this man Vilmos Lemptke – he's chairman of the bank. Friend of mine investigated him on the international scene, made inquiries in Bonn and Berlin. He didn't like the way people looked at him and clammed up when they heard the name. Montego is wide open to abuse. Could be there was some kind of falling out at the bank. Besides, Bill Grattan, the CEO, has been on to me asking if Paddy left anything belonging to the bank here. They seem to be missing some files, something like that. Doesn't sound good from the bank's point of view. Also, Grattan has the name of being something of a sharp operator.'

'Have you spoken to anyone about this?'

'You're joking, of course,' he said drily. 'It's none of this company's business. I'm telling you about it only because I know you have the family's interests at heart and you need to be on your guard in case anyone drops it on you.'

'Do you know any clients of Paddy's that might be tough enough to kill him?'

'Paddy Brett made a practice of never allowing his right hand to know what his left hand was doing.' He said it without rancour, merely stating a fact of life. 'I only know the clients of this company. Some of them can do pretty wild things at times, but none in a truly criminal way, if you get my drift. Sure, they cheat and lie to the taxman, but they're not going to go out and kill someone. My money is on Montego International – there's millions of reason there, enough to kill for.'

We left it at that and set a date three weeks ahead when I agreed we'd look at the details of the buy-out offer to Joan and the kids. He walked me to the front door and we shook hands. I felt he was a guy I could do business with.

It was three o'clock when I strolled through the Wolfe Tone memorial into St Stephen's Green. I sat on a bench in the afternoon sunshine. I was tired of walking but felt it was doing me good, felt that by the time I'd completed my appointments I would have had as much exercise as if I'd gone jogging earlier.

From the corner of my eye I saw Hocks Mackey hesitate then step behind some bushes. I took out my phone and punched in Gerry O'Connell's number. Gerry is one of those wizards that knows everything about electronics and communications – he's the guy the politicians use when they don't want the police to know. He often contributes to my inventions, even shares one of the patents with me.

'Johnny,' he said, 'how can I help?'

I told him about Betty Halpin's noisy phone, gave him the address, told him it was urgent.

'What do I do if there is a bug?'

'Leave it,' I said. 'Don't tell Betty what you've found. Give her a story.'

'You got it,' he said, and rang off.

It was the only way they could have known about me so quickly.

I'd arrived back in town late on Sunday and gone to bed almost immediately. I'd driven to see Aunt Lil on Tuesday and they'd been on my tail that morning. Betty Halpin had been ringing me for weeks. Whenever Paddy rang in she'd have told him she'd failed to make contact. Whoever killed Paddy knew he wanted to get in touch with me badly. Two and two would have made four as far as they were concerned. It didn't take genius to put me high on the list of possible recipients of that diskette.

With old friends like Paddy I didn't need new enemies!

*

110

Fifteen brisk-walking minutes brought me to the five apartment buildings that make up Joyce Court. Staggering originality has named the utilitarian six-storey blocks after characters in *Ulysses*. Dedalus House turns a drab façade toward the Liffey and I leaned against the river wall and studied its brickwork's patchy efflorescence for some time. The Joyce thing has been taken to extremes. Why not Kinch's Keep or Conmee Towers or Molly's Mansion? For sure the property market's still not ready for Biddy-the-Clap Flats.

It was a big squawk box with over twenty brass name plates, most of which were empty. Number eighteen announced Brett and Coady in neat typescript. I assumed Coady was the flatmate. I pressed the button and stooped to listen.

'Who are you looking for?' she asked.

'Miz Patricia Brett,' I shouted into the speaker, and she laughed behind me.

I turned and faced a young woman of not more than five and twenty. I smiled then, both because I realised how silly I must look and because she had that frank openness that makes you happy to look into the clear face of youth.

'Miz Coady, I presume,' I said, bowing.

She was tall, wore an elegant coat that added to her natural poise and gave her an air of having just left a fashion show. Shoulder-length dark hair framed a tanned squarish face relatively free of make-up and her eyes were the translucent green of toppling waves.

'Mr Stanley, no doubt,' she said, mockingly. 'What can I do for you?'

'Name's Constantine, Johnny Constantine, friend of the Brett family. Patricia rang me, left a message for me to call this afternoon. Her mother has asked me to help sort out her father's affairs.'

'That ought to hold your interest,' she said, 'there were enough of them, that's for sure.' She was laughing again, searching her pockets, but the key turned out to be in her shoulder bag.

'Patricia's late. You'd better come up,' she said, and led the way in.

The lobby was tiny – parties of more than five would have to split up to enter the building. We were silent as we waited for the lift. The lift doors juddered as they closed. She pressed five and I spoke, mainly to restore momentum to the lapsed conversation.

'That's the trouble with these new apartments, not enough room to swing a cat.'

'Oh, plenty of cats get swung around here,' she said, and grinned wickedly.

In the small space, millimetres between us, her warmth was intimate, her perfume light and sensual.

The girls shared a standard Dublin hutch built in the name of centre-city renewal, first step on the property ladder, student accommodation, tax avoidance, slum for the twenty-first century – take your pick. All things considered it wasn't a bad apartment even if it was a bit tight around the shoulders. Someone was house-proud to a fault – the place was excessively tidy as though a prospective purchaser might be due any moment.

Coady pirouetted out of her coat and went through to the only bedroom. Beyond her I had a view of a large double bed with ornate modern brass ends and a bemused looking giant panda propped against fluffy mustard-yellow pillows. Muted pastel shades washed into each other and the sitting-dining room had a seductive ambience that was very feminine. I felt clumsy in the small space. The double bed nagged in the back of my mind.

'Drink?' she asked, rattling bottles on a silver tray, opening a cute fridge concealed in a veneered cabinet beneath it. Twisting cubes from an ice tray into a silver bucket she looked at me over her shoulder. 'Before you say anything I better warn you I'm out of tonic.'

'Whiskey would be nice, if that's OK,' I said, and dropped into an easy chair that was easier than it looked.

'Ice?'

'No thanks.' I knew if I stayed too long in that chair I'd never walk upright again.

Coady's movements were elegantly assured – nothing fussy, everything handled neatly and efficiently, effortlessly raising mundane gestures through three or four gears. In profile there was a stubbiness to her features, the blunt roundedness of a river-worn cobble that contrasted oddly with her slim, firm body, her long supple hands.

Full on she had a youthful sternness of purpose. Her chin and mouth bespoke a personality that would brook little disagreement, that seemed to proclaim opinions came fully formed in this model and batteries were most definitely included.

Before folding gracefully into the chair opposite she managed to convey with the tiniest of befuddled gestures that I had taken her customary seat. Crossing her long slender legs she looked coolly at me and began probing.

'Cheers,' she said, raising a gin and white Martini. 'Old friend of Casanova you say – how old?'

'G'luck,' I said, and downed a lash of ten-year-old. 'Forty-five this year,' I said, and was pleased that my pretence of misunderstanding made her laugh. 'Why do you call him Casanova, Miz Coady?'

'Della, Johnny, call me Della,' she said, and sipped some drink. 'You ought to know if you really are an old friend of the family.'

She bounced a slim ankle and her smile did things to her face that dropped three or four critical years from it, took away the sophisticated disdain I had begun to find unpleasant.

'I was a boyhood friend of Paddy Brett and the more I ask around the more I realise how much he must have changed since I knew him. Last twenty-five years or more we weren't close, didn't fraternise.'

'Well you could say he was something of a ladies' man – more accurately, a pole vaulter, if you're familiar with the term.' She was smiling over the rim of her glass, but I

113

sensed a tenseness in her, an unease. 'Do it at a bus stop in a blizzard in fact. A cocksman as they say in your men's magazine. Surely he must have been like that when you knew him?'

Her face clouded, her mouth thinned out. 'Funny thing though, he was such an adolescent when it came to women, a real dickhead. Then you hear he was such a financial whiz – hard to equate the two.'

'We had a restricted upbringing,' I said, leaping to the defence of my generation.

I finished my whiskey. With a slither of tights she unfolded like a carpenter's rule and was on her way back to the drinks tray with my empty glass while I was still absorbing the wave of musky perfume her body-rush had poured over me.

'Those days people weren't as liberal minded as they seem to be now,' I said, addressing tightly dimpled buttocks. 'Word on the street was a lot more religious back then and sex was in its infancy. Paddy married our child-hood sweetheart, you see. After that we kinda lost track of each other.'

'You mean he wasn't into cradle-snatching in those days.'

'Not that I'm aware of,' I said, slightly mystified at her direction.

'He sure as hell made up for early abstinence these last few years. Patricia's had cause to be embarrassed by him on a number of occasions – never knew when her dad was going to end up bedding one of her schoolfriends. Messy! What do you do when you're not assisting the widows of old friends, Johnny?'

I was conscious of a coldness in her voice.

'I'm a civil engineer, but I'm kinda retired – work when I have to and that's not often. You?'

'I work in a night club,' she said. 'Must be nice to be retired at forty-five.'

'Way to go.'

'You married?'

'No.'

'Divorced?'

'Never been married.'

'Gay?'

'Not so's you'd notice.'

'What exactly are you trying to do for Joan Brett?'

Somewhere in the last few questions – which I thought had overstepped the mark – the mood had changed, even the room temperature seemed to have dropped.

'I'm trying to rationalise Paddy's assets.'

'You haven't by any chance been deputised to evict me from here in the course of your rationalisation?'

Delia Coady dealt it softly, skimmed it at me like a Mississippi gambler and I knew then this was a kitten with claws.

'No,' I said. 'No one has suggested I try any such thing. What's more I wouldn't go along with it if they had. Why do you ask?'

'C'mon, Johnny, you're not dumb. Joan doesn't like the arrangements here. Reckons I've led her daughter into unnatural practices. She has no idea of the depth of our relationship – at least has only one idea of our relationship.'

She tossed her hair defiantly, felt much better now that she'd nailed her knickers to the mast. I shook my head slowly.

'No one's mentioned anything like that to me. I'm here because Patricia rang and asked me to call – I have no other agenda. I don't know why Patricia's asked me, but I'm hoping she can throw some light on her father's business or any connections he had.'

I was trying to be polite, make conversation, but I'd picked the wrong word.

'What do you mean by connections? Who've you been talking to?'

Delia Coady was sitting up straight now, hackles raised. I wished I knew what this was about, what she thought I was implying. Then I said to myself, you don't need this.

115

'I think maybe I should call back another time,' I said.

'Don't give me that crap,' she suddenly spat at me. 'I don't give a damn who did for that chauvinist prick Brett. He had it coming for all the screwing around he did, for the fifteen-year-olds, for the way he messed up people's minds, his mental extortion. I've only just got through unravelling what he did to Pat and I'm not standing idly by while her crazy alcoholic mother or daddy's old pal screw her up again. You got that?'

Della Coady was one woman who didn't look beautiful when she was angry. I wondered what she meant as I watched the rise and fall of her shapely bosom. In the confines of that small apartment even the walls seemed to be heaving.

'Yeah,' I said, putting down my unfinished whiskey, preparing to lever myself from the chair, get the hell out of there. 'I think I got that.'

A key went into the lock and I swung to face the front door. Della Coady was on her feet and moving in the instant.

Last time I'd seen Paddy Brett's daughter she'd been crying, but now, standing in the doorway, hesitating at the sight of a visitor, I had a chance to see her properly. As tall as Della Coady, she held herself regally in a model's end-of-catwalk pose, her body in subtle equilibrium, a woman in the full bloom of physical allure, a magnificent presence in total command of that small room.

Della Coady went to her, reached out and took the coat from Patricia's shoulders, encircling her with such delicacy I could have sworn they kissed as Patricia caressed the hand that removed the coat and swayed into the room, smiling, speaking as she came.

'Mr Constantine, Johnny, I'm sorry to be late – I got stuck in traffic. I've just been talking about you.'

With her eyes Della Coady dared me leave as she carried Patricia's coat into the bedroom. I picked up my drink.

'Hi, Patricia,' I said. 'Who was talking about me?'

Della returned, began rummaging amongst the bottles.

116

'Usual?' she asked Patricia.

'Well, OK,' Patricia said. 'But only a teeny one, keep you company – it's too early for me.' She turned back to face me. 'Patrick rang. He said you had coffee with him this morning and that you were arranging some money for Mom and us.'

Della mixed a barely pink Campari and soda, added ice and slid an orange slice on to the side of the glass – very professional. Patricia sipped, smiled up at her approvingly. Della orgasmed.

'Yeah,' I said, over my glass. 'I have a cheque here for your mother from Oliver Pettit – something to be going on with.'

'I hope it's decent, we are kinda short right now.'

'It should keep things ticking over until we get things fully sorted out.'

That was the worst answer I could have given. Patricia's face went cold.

'Johnny, I know you mean well and I know you were a friend of my parents when you were kids together, all that stuff. You probably feel it's your duty to do things by the book, but let me explain a couple of things to you. I didn't get along with my father. He had this view that his daughter should behave like the Virgin Mary. One of the ways he had of seeing to it that I had the least opportunity to do anything else was his control of the money.

'All my life – and the same goes for Mom and Patrick – I had to beg for money, wheedle it out of him. Now that he's dead whatever money he has is rightfully ours. I don't intend begging anyone else for it. You can talk in front of Della – she and I have no secrets between us. So how much did Oliver Pettit give you and what's the deal on the balance?'

I told her exactly what Pettit and I had discussed, told her the value of the cheque I carried for her mother and what had happened in Glasbury Street. I was tired of the whole thing, fed up to the teeth of being followed, of having potential murderers dogging my footsteps. I felt like telling Patricia and Patrick they were old enough to look after themselves, that it wasn't my war. But something told me I couldn't get out of it that easily. When I finished she was smiling.

'Thank you very much, Johnny. You're very kind to help us like this. Please don't think what I said means that I'm ungrateful – it's just that Dad was such a difficult human being. I don't know how to explain him – he was an extraordinary man. One moment he was kindness itself and the next he was the world's number one fascist, had to have everything his way and we had to jump through the hoops he held out.'

She was silent for a moment. Della Coady reached out a hand to my glass, but I covered it and shook my head. Patricia suddenly grinned.

'Did Betty Halpin take her clothes off?'

'How do you mean?' I asked, but failed to hide my embarrassment.

'You're a gentleman, Johnny,' she said, laughing. 'I believe she does it often. Dad told me he sometimes came in to find her at her desk, not a stitch on, totally unaware she was doing it. Her father was ruined when Dad closed down a whole series of companies. As I heard it, one night her father walked naked into her bedroom, said goodbye, put a shotgun under his chin and blew his head off right in front of her. Ever since, when she gets upset, she takes her clothes off. She sort of lost it that night, went a bit queer in the head – wouldn't blame her. Dad felt responsible – that's why he took her on as secretary. He could be very kind at times.'

Patricia threw a reproving look at Della Coady, as though daring her to contradict. She became serious again.

'But there's more money than that, Johnny, isn't there?'

This time I had no problem looking surprised.

'How do you mean? More money where? Do you know of other businesses?'

Patricia's face clouded.

'I don't know,' she said. 'I heard it in the club last night.'

'What club?'

'Place where Della and I work, Doxy Moran's. It's owned by a neighbour of ours at home – Walter Hartigan. Used to be a neighbour that is until Mom and Dad helped Kate Hartigan get a separation. I think Kate was a director of a lot of Walter's companies and Dad got working on it. Dad was brilliant at things like that. Anyway, when I packed in university Walter offered me a job. He did it to annoy Dad.' She grinned. 'I took it for the same reason. It's where I met Della.' She smiled at her flatmate. 'Dad really stitched up Walter for Kate.'

'Or to get close to Julie,' Della said.

'Leave it,' Patricia said, her voice low.

'Who told you there was money somewhere else?' I asked.

'Well no one actually said there was money. Walter Hartigan asked me what I knew about you and what your relationship was with Dad. Wanted to know if you were some kind of sleeping partner of Dad's. He said that North East Baltic Bank was looking for some files Dad had that seem to be worth an awful lot. Dad was a director of the bank. He asked me if Dad met you on a regular basis, wondered if he might have given the files to you. Did he, Johnny?'

'I haven't met your Dad in four years,' I said, and hoped she'd missed the evasion.

'That's what I thought,' Patricia said. 'But after Walter had spoken to me about it, I saw him at a table with Spike Carmody and they both kept looking over at me. Made me feel uncomfortable.'

'Who's Spike Carmody?' I asked.

'He's The Farmer's man,' Della Coady said. 'Just like Dutch Gaffney's Hartigan's man. Carmody's the only man I ever saw make Gaffney sit up and take notice. And Dutch Gaffney is what you might call a really hard man.'

'God's sake,' I said, 'who's The Farmer when he's at home?'

'Bertram McRoarty's his real name,' Della Coady said.

'He lives out beyond Rush – has a big farm out there – I think that's why he's called The Farmer. He's big time, into everything. Carmody comes to the club now and then, usually with these Russians or Hungarians – real heavy guys.'

'What goes on in Doxy Moran's?' I asked.

The women glanced at each other quickly.

'Whatever you want,' Patricia said.

'What's that supposed to mean?' I asked.

'It's a night club, that's what I mean,' Patricia said. 'Just like you'd find in London or anywhere else.'

'Did Hartigan tell you any more about this file that's supposed to contain the treasure map?'

'I'm not joking, Johnny. Hartigan thinks it's worth an awful lot of money.'

'I'll watch out for it,' I said. 'Funny thing though, Betty Halpin told me some girl called Heather Skeehan came round to see her. She was looking for some file the bank thought Paddy might have taken with him by mistake. You know this girl? She seemed to annoy the hell out of Betty Halpin.'

Patricia froze, then looked at Della Coady. She turned back to me.

'Dad shacked up with Heather Skeehan in an apartment in Donnybrook. She joined the bank when it first opened. Maybe he knew her before that and got her the job. She's the same age as me.'

'I heard he started sleeping with her when she was fourteen,' Della Coady said.

'Della!' Patricia said, and the word crackled in the air like a ringmaster's whiplash. It surprised me. I had thought Della the dominant one. Patricia looked steadily at me.

'If Heather Skeehan is asking after a file then what Hartigan said is true. Bill Grattan, the boss at the bank, is keeping her. Dad used to think a lot of him, but last time we met he had nothing good to say about him.'

'When did you last see your Dad?'

'We met by accident in the Dun Laoghaire Shopping Centre couple of weeks ago. We chatted about this and that and then had the usual flaming row. What annoyed me was he only stopped to talk because he was avoiding someone from his old home town. He was very uptight – I'd never seen him so nervy and jumpy. Wanted me to pack in the job at the club, didn't want me near Walter Hartigan he said. Wanted me to go back to university. Said he was sorry he'd ever put this apartment in my name. Jesus, he was really into his control thing. I walked away and left him – no point arguing when he was in that mood.'

'Chauvin was his middle name,' Della Coady began, but stopped when she saw Patricia's brow crease.

'You didn't see him last weekend, did you?'

'No,' Patricia said. 'But I do know he was close to home 'cause he was in the local pub on Sunday. So the barman of The Sandcastle said – I called in there last night on my way to see Mom.'

Patricia rose, moved gracefully to the drinks tray, set down her glass with the finality good hostesses use to signal the end of the gig.

'I'm jacked,' she said. 'Got to have some sleep before I go to work.'

I finished my drink, levered myself from the chair and was surprised I got out without a sucking sound as I broke free.

I took my leave of them, told Patricia I'd see her at the removal whenever the body was released. She saw me to the lift, asked me to tell her mother she'd try to get to see her the following afternoon. She thanked me again for what I'd done and said she hoped I wasn't angry for her sharp words initially. The lift stuttered open and I got in.

'Take care, Johnny,' she said. 'Hartigan's people are dangerous. I don't like this business of the missing file.'

'I'll keep an eye out for it,' I said, as the lift doors scraped shut.

On the way down I wondered if she was telling me all she knew. Why hadn't she speculated on who could have killed her father?'

*

The usual load of junk mail waited for me at my apartment with a couple of bills thrown in for good measure. Helen Foley at the plant had sent a fax. A young engineer had phoned asking if I'd be interested in an idea he had for quality control of driven pre-cast concrete piles. He was flying home from Bahrain on holidays and had given a contact address in Tipperary. I scribbled a reply to Helen on the back of her fax – told her to set up an appointment.

I checked my answering service. I'd had one caller – Gerry O'Connell. I dialled the number he'd left.

'You were right, Johnny. Both phones have bugs. Whoever owns them is about ten years behind the times – if not more. It's no one in Ireland – I'd bet money on it. It's East German equipment and very old stuff at that. Make sense to you? It's not the boys in blue, that's for sure.'

'Yeah, Gerry,' I said, 'it kinda makes sense. Betty Halpin know what you were at?'

'No idea. I told her it was a Telecom problem and wouldn't be fixed for at least a month. I don't think it's top of her worry list right now.'

'Thanks for the quick reaction, Gerry.'

'My pleasure.' He hung up.

Six thirty and the evening scramble for home in progress, I decided to give the traffic another hour, let the roads clear. I walked round to Jockey Redden's pub behind my apartment block and took a seat at the counter. Willy Redden, the son and heir, Jockey Two as he's known, laid an evening paper next to me.

'Usual, Johnny? The monkfish is good if you're eating.'

'Yes, please,' I said. 'I'll try the monkfish. Caught it yourself?'

'Off the fuckin' bridge,' he said, pouring a glass of Bud.

Paddy Brett hadn't made the evening news. There was a lot of front page coverage of investigations into bank over-charging.

'Great to see the fuckin' bank managers gettin' it up the

arse for a change,' Willy said, putting the Bud in front of me, leaning on the counter. 'Near fuckin' time. Like I keep saying, our monthly statement reads like something from the Valley of the fuckin' Kings – no one could fuckin' understand it. Charges for this, interest on that, interest on the fuckin' interest.'

Willy had taken a package tour to Luxor two years before and couldn't stop talking about it. Claimed he was studying hieroglyphics in his spare time.

'We need a Tribunal of Inquiry into overcharging in the pub trade,' a voice said from somewhere along the bar.

'Yez are never fuckin' satisfied,' Willy said, and moved down to argue with the offending voice.

Willy was right – the monkfish was good and so was the baked potato. I had a coffee after to drift up to seven thirty.

I lowered the windows when I hit the Merrion Road to take advantage of the sea breeze. It was a clear blue evening as I drove through Dalkey around eight. I parked on the Vico Road to enjoy the view and force Hocks Mackey to drive past and park further on.

They were sticking to me like glue.

I tried to rationalise the situation.

The primary question was, which diskette was Grattan looking for? Was he after the diskette Paddy Brett failed to hand over in exchange for signatures on Sunday night or the second diskette copy Paddy Brett told them he was holding to ensure his own continued safety, the disk that now lay in my files in Irishtown?

If Paddy was killed on the way to the meeting then someone other than Grattan or Lemptke had the diskette – plus the papers Paddy wanted signed. The likely candidate was The Farmer.

But he was the driving force behind Hartigan and was at least an associate of Lemptke. If The Farmer had organised Grattan and Heather Skeehan to ask after missing files and instructed Hartigan to have his man follow me, then it meant he was searching for the second diskette if he really had killed Paddy Brett and already had the first one.

But that did not make sense if one presumed The Farmer to be intelligent. Why kill Paddy until he knew where the second diskette was?

If The Farmer hadn't killed for the first diskette then the likely candidate was Hartigan and his reason had to be the need to cover up his whittling away of The Farmer's investments.

That they were inquiring of Oliver Pettit and Betty Halpin about files and also following me seemed to suggest they were unsure who had a diskette and were merely covering all the angles.

There was a further possibility that there was some independent operator – perhaps one of the East Europeans – who had killed Paddy for the diskette and had yet to try blackmailing The Farmer through Hartigan or Grattan.

If that was the case maybe Paddy Brett had not told anyone about leaving a tape and they were on my tail simply because of the tapped phone calls.

One thing was sure – someone was serious enough about something to commit murder and that was scary.

I looked out toward Bray Head and asked myself for the hundredth time why I bothered living centre-city when I could have the finest view in Europe. I hit the key and drove on. I didn't look at Mackey as I went past his white Opel. In the mirror I saw him indicate and move out after me.

I drove sedately all the way to Windward and slowed to a walking pace after I'd passed between the piers to observe Mackey drift by at ten miles an hour. I parked in the forecourt and noticed that the ponding of my previous visit had dried up.

'Evening, Johnny, nice to see you,' Patrick said, opening the front door before I reached it.

'Lovely evening, Patrick,' I said, and breezed past him, turned in the hall, waited for him to close the door and lead me into their living room.

I hope I never forget that first sight of her, that tingle of surprise.

It was a feeling I remembered from a time when a boat I stepped into moved out from shore and I realised too late there were no oars – a small sense of panic, a momentary loss of balance.

And yet she was quite ordinary. There was nothing exotic in the way she was dressed. I don't recall what she wore other than that it was the sort of sensible, stylish, end-of-summer woollen stuff thirty-something women wear of an evening when they're not expecting anyone other than old friends.

It was her aura of calmness that struck me, the sense of someone totally at home in her own skin, of someone waiting to be recognised. That and her face, those eyes.

Joan Callaghan was holding court, enjoying being the centre of attention, the inevitable glass in her hand.

'Johnny, it's good to see you,' she gushed, a trifle loosely but, I felt, at this point in the evening still in control. 'Meet an old and great friend of mine, Kate Hartigan.'

'How do you do,' I said, and shook the hand she smilingly held up to me.

'A pleasure,' she said, her voice low, throaty. 'Joan's been telling me all about you.'

I looked around as though for a seat, but really to take my eyes off her in case she noticed how much she affected me. I found her enormously attractive, had a sudden inexplicable desire to take that long face in my hands and kiss that lovely mouth.

'You mustn't believe most of it,' I said, as the springs of my chosen armchair closed on me like an iron maiden. 'I'm afraid Joan only remembers the good times.'

'What else is worth remembering?' Kate Hartigan asked, and sipped from her glass.

She had good legs, what I could see of them below the long skirt of her knitted suit.

'I take it you still prefer whiskey,' Patrick said, handing me a glass, proffering a small jug of water.

125

'Thanks,' I said, and drowned the whiskey – it was a long drive home.

'What's the news, Johnny?' Joan asked. She turned to Kate Hartigan. 'As I told you, Johnny is trying to find out how we stand financially. I hope it's good news, Johnny.'

Remembering Patrica Brett's annoyance at my reluctance to tell all, I passed her the envelope Oliver Pettit had given me. Patrick was on his feet instantly and moved behind her chair to read over her shoulder.

'That's to be going on with,' I said.

'Thirty grand,' Patrick said, beaming, reading the cheque his mother held up.

Kate Hartigan smiled. 'Now that's what I call loot,' she said.

'How does it look apart from that?' Patrick asked.

'Very good,' I said. 'According to initial estimates there should be over a million there. Of course you're going to have to get at it slowly to avoid losing a lot to tax. Oliver Pettit is putting a package together to buy out your interest in the accountancy practice over five years and he's doing an audit on the other consultancy. He says he'd like to get together with me in about three weeks' time. He's offered to take care of the funeral expenses directly if you wish.'

'That's great news,' Joan said, smiling. 'I think you could freshen our drinks on the strength of that, Patrick.'

'Mine's fine,' Kate Hartigan said, holding her hand over her drink.

Patrick poured one for his mother, his back toward her, shielding the drink from her.

'You think we're wise to allow Oliver Pettit to put a package together for us?' Patrick asked the question as he handed the drink to his mother.

'Pettit struck me as being an honest man,' I said. 'Unless you have any reason to think otherwise I'd be inclined to let him handle it. You have to remember that bringing in outsiders opens the door to the taxman.'

'Oliver Pettit did some of the work on my settlement

when Paddy took on Walter and I found him honest as the day is long,' Kate Hartigan said.

'Paddy always claimed Oliver was dead straight,' Joan said.

'If you wish you can join me in the discussions with him,' I offered Patrick.

'I'd like that,' Patrick said. 'It's not that I don't trust you – please don't think that. It's just that I'd love the experience of seeing how these things are done.'

'It's not as exciting as you might think,' Kate Hartigan said to him. 'It's all very boring in a way – least that's what I found.'

'I had a phone call from Aunt Lil,' Joan said, over her glass.

I wondered if Aunt Lil had said anything about my visit.

'I was thinking about her this afternoon,' I said. 'How is she?'

'Better than I would have expected,' Joan said. 'She's one tough old lady.'

Joan sipped her drink, spoke to Kate Hartigan.

'Aunt Lil and Paddy adored each other. We all lived in this terrace called Tinmen's Lane – tiny houses. Some years ago Paddy bought the house either side of Aunt Lil's and he knocked the three of them together – hired an architect to do it. It's really quite a lovely place now. Have you ever seen it, Johnny?'

'No,' I lied smoothly. 'Aunt Lil deserves the best – she was always great to me. She was wonderful when my parents died.'

'Johnny's parents were killed in a car crash,' Joan explained for Kate's benefit. 'It was so sad, the car was a present from Johnny. Isn't that so, Johnny?'

'Yeah,' I said, annoyed with her.

Kate Hartigan glanced sharply at me but said nothing.

'What'll we do with all the money, Ma?' Patrick asked.

'Well, first off we're going to do a job on this place,' Joan said. 'Any chance of a loan of Eddie, Kate?'

'He's very busy,' Kate said. 'Half of Killiney are looking for him. I'll ask him.'

'Who's Eddie?' I asked.

'Steady Eddie Delaney,' Patrick said, and laughed. 'The demon gardener of Killiney and the last of the Bolsheviks.'

'Don't mind him,' Kate said. 'Eddie Delaney is from County Clare, same as myself. We're neighbours' children. He's been doing my garden ever since I came to Dublin – a great worker.'

'Dynamite with a shovel,' Patrick said, laughing again. 'Don't ever get into a political argument with him. Talk about Trotsky – only trotting after Eddie.'

A doorbell sounded and Patrick leaped to his feet. When he returned from the hall he was followed by Candy Delamere and Julie Hartigan.

'Hi, everybody,' Candy said, and Julie muttered something.

Patrick was putting on a jacket.

'Where are you all off to?' Joan asked.

'The Sandcastle,' Patrick said. 'Now that we're in funds we may as well celebrate.'

'That's not a nice thing to say, Patrick, and your father not even buried,' Joan said, looking po-faced.

'He's being cremated, Ma, as you well know, but let's not go into that now. You can do the mourning bit. I'm taking these babes down for a jar.'

'Did you put on the alarm?' Kate Hartigan asked her daughter.

'I thought you were upstairs,' Julie said, her face sullen.

'Did you remember to close the door behind you?' Kate asked, in wry exasperation.

'Oh, I'm out of here,' Julie said, and tried for a Delamere flounce as she left the room. It was no go – Candy owned the patent.

The First Lady of Flounce gave us a mere matinée

performance and her usual 'Byeee' before exiting. Patrick followed her out with a silent wave.

The front door lashed shut. The windows rattled.

'One of these days he's going to take the door off the hinges,' Joan said.

'It's dreadful the way they do that,' Kate said. 'Julie's becoming impossible. I bet she's left the back door unlocked.'

'Patricia said to tell you she'll try to get out to see you tomorrow,' I told Joan.

'When were you talking to her?'

'This afternoon,' I said. 'She asked me to call and see her. She was worried about you, wondered if you were going to be all right for money. I told her what Oliver Pettit had said.'

'Did you see Betty Halpin?' Joan asked casually, and I knew it was a loaded question.

'Yes,' I said. 'She's very upset. Found it hard to accept that Paddy is dead.'

'Hah!' Joan said. 'Bloody sure she did. Woman is mad. Be glad to see the back of her.' She looked into the empty fireplace.

I stole a quick glance at Kate Hartigan and found her pulling a glum face at me.

'I must be off,' Kate Hartigan said, standing, brushing her clothes.

I knew I couldn't let her get away and I was on my feet instantly.

'I'll run you home,' I said. 'It's dark.'

'Not at all,' Kate said. 'I'm only up the road – there's no one going to run away with me. You and Joan have loads to talk about.'

'I've got to go anyway,' I said. It was only a white lie – I had no stomach for a couple of hours of Joan's maudlin talk.

'Why can't the two of you stay?' Joan said, in what was suspiciously close to a whine.

'I'll be uneasy until I've checked the house,' Kate said.

'I'm sure Julie's left it open – it wouldn't be the first time.'

'I've got to run, Joan,' I said. 'There's a guy calling to see me.'

'Knowing you, Johnny Constantine, there's probably some woman calling,' Joan said coyly, attempting a joke, and I was suddenly very annoyed with her, cross that she should give a totally wrong impression of me to Kate Hartigan when she knew so little of how I lived.

On the way to the car Kate Hartigan stumbled in the dark and grabbed my arm. I had a fleeting sensation of her firm body before she righted herself. Her perfume filled the air around me. I felt very happy and I laughed involuntarily as I handed her into the car.

'What's funny?' she asked, as I got in beside her.

'I was just thinking of finding your house wide open,' I said, covering up, feeling foolish.

'Well it won't be funny if it happens once too often as I'm sure it will,' she said.

Her house was indeed only up the road – just past the white Opel with the bulk of Hocks Mackey trying to make himself invisible.

'Wonder who that can be?' Kate Hartigan said, turning, looking back. 'Maybe I should ring the police. We have a Neighbourhood Watch scheme and we're always being asked to use it.'

Why, I do not know, but I decided on the spur of the moment to involve her.

'That,' I said, 'is Mr Hocks Mackey, a gentleman employed by your husband. He likes to follow me around.'

'Left here,' she said, suddenly.

I braked hard and turned tightly between the granite piers that bore the legend Knocklangan Lodge.

Railings gleamed whitely in the headlights as I drove along a tree-lined black carpet that unrolled slickly and without blemish. About the time I began to feel we should be seeing the lights of Belfast the house came into view.

It was a big house – at least eight bedrooms I reckoned –

and the creeper that clung to the entire facade was going flat out for *The Guinness Book of Records*. Light showed in two downstairs windows and a hall light outlined the delicate tracery of a semi-ellipse of fanlight. I swept around on the raked gravel and parked next to a three-year-old Toyota Camry.

Kate Hartigan had not spoken since her peremptory direction. Now she threw open the car door and slammed it shut almost before I heard her say 'C'mon in.' As I stepped out of the car she had the front door open and was marching into the hall. I followed slowly and saw her pick up the telephone and dial briefly. I knew she was ringing the police.

'Yes,' she was saying, as I closed the door behind me, 'Kate Hartigan of Knocklangan Lodge. Yes, a white car. Very suspicious. You can ... good! It's a comfort to know you'll do that. Thank you very much. Yes, I will. Good night to you and thanks again.' She rang off.

The hall was large and airy, the colour of ivory, the floor a black and white mosaic that could have been an early Bridget Riley. A set of excellent hunting prints mixed in with framed photographs hung on the walls. Beyond an archway and lit by uplighters a graceful curve of stair rose like an organic growth in search of the upper level. I surprised myself in an oval of bevelled mirror and thought I looked nicely tanned but oddly scared.

'There's a fire in here,' she said, and entered a reception room to our right.

I followed slowly, admired her tight flanks as she crouched to start the gas fire. She rose and crossed a meadow of fawn pile to a glass-and-stainless-steel trolley with drinks. She began rattling bottles.

'Will you stick to whiskey?' she asked, looking at me over her shoulder.

'Whiskey's fine,' I said.

Someone in the house was into uplighters – either that or she had a relation in the electrical trade. The ornate plaster ceiling floated a trifle eerily on a frieze of sporting

131

amoretti, gambolling putti, atop blood-red walls against which a small fortune in antique furniture demurely awaited the admiration of the connoisseur or the covetous eyes of vagabond gypsies.

'Do you really take that much water in your whiskey?' she asked, swaying hippily toward me, offering a glass and a jug.

I was childishly pleased that she'd noticed.

'Not really,' I said, adding only a small amount this time. 'I thought I might get caught, have to stay a long while with Joan. She tends to overdo the hospitality.'

'Don't I know,' she said. 'Do sit down.'

I looked around and opted for the primly stuffed chesterfield as the least likely to damage my spine. Back at the drinks trolley she took her time fixing something exotically complicated involving slow pouring from three bottles. It started out amber but in the end turned carmine – that could have been something to do with reflections from the walls.

The clinging knitted suit moulded itself to her neat figure. Long athletic legs suggested tennis-filled summers, winters on Austrian slopes. Frizzling copper hair in tight individual coils was massed and mounded like some exploded electrical appliance (an uplighter gone berserk?).

The face was too rectangular, too freckled, too dominated by puckish green eyes to be in any classic mould – but up close and within that orbit of radiated charm all critical faculties were suspended, paralysed.

As she turned, I sipped a molten mouthful of fourteen-year-old.

'This is terrific stuff,' I said, holding the glass up to the light. 'Where've you been all my life!'

'Oh, I've been around,' she said, swaying to a chair opposite. 'You just haven't been looking.'

She smiled, raised her glass in salute, drank some.

'How long has Mackey been following you?' She watched me carefully.

'Since I got back from Spain on Sunday, I think.'

132

'Howja know who he was?'

'Betty Halpin told me. Paddy Brett told her. This man Mackey has been watching Paddy's office in Glasbury Street for some weeks.'

'Why was he doing that?'

'I have no idea. Do you know him?'

'Yes,' she lowered her drink to her lap. 'He's a thug. My husband, Hermann the Hun, employs people like that. Mackey is usually accompanied by his boss, man called Gaffney. He really is a thug, scum.' Her lip curled as she spoke.

'Have you told the police about this?' She looked hard at me. 'I would.'

'No.' I said. 'I'm wondering why he's following me.'

'It has to be connected with Paddy's death,' she said. 'You say he was following Paddy?'

'According to Betty Halpin he was.'

'I wonder if he was following Paddy on Sunday night – he might have seen what happened.'

'He might have done it for all I know,' I said.

'Were you and Paddy really the big friends Joan says?'

'We were once, I suppose. We went everywhere together up until we were seventeen, eighteen maybe. Then he went to college in Dublin and I went to Cork. We kinda grew out of one another round about then. Mostly I saw him on television after that.'

'He was a very odd guy,' Kate Hartigan said. 'Don't get me wrong. I owe him my life and when I say that I'm dead serious. I'd still be on my knees to the bastard I married if it hadn't been for Paddy Brett. But for all that he was an odd man out. I couldn't really figure him and, you know, I don't think he wanted to be figured. He lived up there in his head and that was one wild attic, I reckon.'

'When did you last see him?' I asked.

She thought about it. 'You know I'm not at all sure when it was. Must be several months. He finalised my settlement over two years ago. Up to then we met on a regular basis to

133

sign papers, compare notes, answer queries from Walter's solicitor, that sort of thing. What I found most strange about him was the way he treated Joan. I'd always had the opinion from listening to Joan that he was a distant, cold, calculating financier – accountant type. But when he came to help me he was totally different. I found him warm and amusing. Oh, he was distant in some regards – like I say, he lived in his head – but he could turn on the charm, be very pleasant. Why he was so set against Joan I'll never understand. But then, I'm no one to talk about happy families.'

'Tell you something that amazes me,' I said, pleased to have someone with whom I could compare notes. 'When we were young we were an inseparable threesome. You don't usually get two fellows and one girl as constant companions – I mean it was a pretty intense friendship. After we qualified at university, when Paddy suddenly told me he and Joan were getting married, I reckoned it was a marriage that would have to succeed, last forever. I mean we'd really meant an awful lot to each other. I must admit I was jealous at the time.'

'Maybe they used it all up when they were young, maybe they should never have taken it further. It happens you know.'

'Sure, OK, that can happen. But why take it out on the kids? I mean, Joan's a mess, but then she may be that way because of Paddy's behaviour. But the children were not to blame, they never asked to be involved. Paddy Brett was an intelligent man – I can't understand why he would force his children to come begging to him for housekeeping money on the one hand and give Patricia an apartment on the other. It doesn't make sense.'

'It never does with intelligent men,' Kate Hartigan said. 'I lived with one for fifteen years and I'm still trying to figure it out. Maybe Paddy was trying to excuse his behaviour, salve his conscience, when he gave Patricia the apartment.'

'Maybe he bought it for another reason and changed his

mind,' I said. 'The stories I'm hearing about Paddy Brett and his women make him sound like some sort of desert sheikh. I find them astonishing, totally out of character with the man I knew. Especially stories about girls of fourteen and fifteen.'

Kate Hartigan's face froze over and her body language told me I'd stepped on a mine.

'What stories are you referring to?' Her voice was curiously flat as she spoke.

'Well, there was no particular girl mentioned,' I lied, 'it was just general comments. I understand one long-term girlfriend – if you consider a couple of years long term – Heather Skeehan, she seems to have been only sixteen when he shacked up with her. After all, Paddy would have been about forty at that time. That's a bit old for sixteen in my book.'

'I've heard Joan speak of her,' Kate Hartigan said. 'I never realised she was only sixteen. That's criminal as far as I'm concerned.' Her face had turned to stone. 'But then, that's just a woman's view.'

'Please!' I said, 'Don't go all feminist on me – I think it's outrageous as well. That is precisely why I don't understand what happened to the guy I knew.'

'It still doesn't explain why my husband is having you followed,' she said, relaxing slightly. 'Were you an associate of Paddy Brett, did you do business with him?'

'No, I hadn't spoken to Paddy in several years and we've never done a day's business together. The Paddy Brett I'm hearing about now is a total stranger to me.'

'Then why is my husband having you followed? It is my husband who's behind it you know – unless Gaffney and Mackey have stopped working for him, and I don't believe that for one minute. Walter likes to have thugs around. He's one himself behind that slick veneer.'

'Talking to Patricia Brett today she said your husband has been asking her if Paddy left any files belonging to North East Baltic Bank in her keeping. Maybe that's why they're following me. She said there was a guy called Carmody came into the club where she works – your husband's place, Doxy Moran's – and he was also looking for files. This Carmody, he works for some weirdo called The Farmer. Betty Halpin said that Heather Skeehan called to see her and was asking for files. Oliver Pettit says that Bill Grattan, manager of the bank, was in touch with him about missing files. Everyone is looking for files.' I smiled at her. 'Hope you're not looking for any.'

Kate Hartigan had gone pale and she stared at me for a long while before suddenly rousing herself.

'I'm sorry. Would you like another drink?'

'No thanks,' I said.

'Those are very serious people,' she said. 'Carmody is every bit as dangerous as Gaffney, if not more so. I've met him and his boss, The Farmer – where do they get these names? His real name's Bert McRoarty. They came to a hotel we were staying in years ago in Galway. Walter spent a whole evening with them. They scared me. I don't know how Walter knows them. He said at the time McRoarty was thinking of building a hotel and was asking him to act as a consultant.'

She sipped her drink and I was content to look at her, absorb her. Then she surprised me.

'Joan says that Paddy had money hidden away – hot money – and that she's asked you to find it.'

That was all I needed. Maybe Joan might consider an advertisement in the Lost and Found section of *The Irish Times*.

'Far as I'm concerned,' I said easily, 'the only money I know about is the value of the two practices Paddy was involved in. If he had any other money I know nothing about it.'

Kate Hartigan looked me in the eye.

'I want you to know where I'm coming from, Johnny,' she said, evenly. 'I'd like to see Joan fixed up. Now I know you've found out that Paddy died worth over a million and that's great news. But I figure from what I knew of Paddy Brett there has to be an awful lot more – and so does Joan. He had to be loaded – he was iceberg man, eight-ninths or whatever beneath the surface. He was the kind that takes the prayer rug out from under the bed each night and faces Wall Street or maybe Threadneedle Street and recites five decades of the Dow Jones, the Footsie and the Nikkei. Wherever he put it, in whatever bolt hole he secreted it, I will bet all I own – for which I will never stop thanking him – that there's a hell of a lot of it, enough for a small revolution as they say down in my part of the country. Plus the fact that my husband and his truffle-hunting thugs rooting around looking for a rip-off means there really is money there.'

I stayed looking at her long after she'd finished her speech.

'Anyone got any suggestions where I should start looking for this mother lode?' I asked, not without a tinge of sarcasm.

'I'm sorry,' she said. 'I have no idea where it might be. I've said what I think mainly to warn you. My husband and his friends are dangerous people. I would hate to see you get hurt – that's my only reason for saying what I've said. I feel I owe Paddy Brett something for all the good he did me, for giving me back my life.'

Kate Hartigan put her glass on the table and looked apologetically at me.

'I'm sorry about this,' she said, 'but I have to go. Wednesday nights there's a meeting I must attend. I'm a part-time counsellor – battered wives, families in trouble. Experienced people, women like me who've been down that road, are in demand. Maybe some other night you're calling on Joan you can drop in on your way home. I'm nearly always here and there's a stock of that whiskey.' She smiled, laughed lightly. 'Money wasn't all Paddy screwed out of Walter for me.'

I set down my empty tumbler and stood up.

'I'd like to do that,' I said.

I began following her out into her ivory hall and suddenly I knew I had to see her again – I couldn't leave it at that. We were almost at the door when I halted and she turned to see why I'd paused.

'Would you have dinner with me tomorrow night?' I asked, almost blurted. 'Or whenever . . .? I mean sometime when you're free, not doing anything special.'

Kate Hartigan seemed flustered, didn't seem to know what to say.

'It's ages since . . . I mean it's been some . . .' She swallowed hard, held up a finger, smiled. 'I'll start again. I would love to go to dinner tomorrow night.'

'Great,' I said. 'Good. That's settled then. Is there anywhere special you'd like to go?'

'Surprise me,' she said. 'I should warn you – the last time I was in a restaurant I was with Julie and it was a McDonald's.'

'Julie and Patrick and Candy introduced me to The Café of Eva Gonzalez this morning.'

'My goodness! What a hectic life you lead.'

'Your daughter's a charming girl,' I said.

'Now that really is a man's perspective.'

Kate Hartigan opened the door.

'I'll call for you at seven thirty – OK?' I stood there smiling at her.

'I can't wait,' she said, then laughed. 'I actually mean that.'

'Night,' I said.

She let go the door, folded her arms, hugged herself in the sudden cold but remained smiling broadly at me.

'Night, yourself,' she said.

I walked to my car and she didn't close the door until she'd waved as I drove away.

It had been a long day but I felt great.

# Chapter Seven

Thursday morning I was dressed for the road at six fifteen.
I'd slept well, felt I could face another day of assorted
hoodlums.

On reaching home after leaving Kate Hartigan I found
my answering service had only one message. I'd listened to
it several times before going to bed.

They had decided it was time to come out of the wood-
work.

Even on a recording Bill Grattan had an anchor man's
boom to his voice, asked me to ring him at North East
Baltic Bank at my convenience on Thursday – but not
between one and two.

I made toast, ground coffee. I sat at my window and
watched dawn unfurl its multi-hued banner over the molten
silver of the river.

It was time to visit Aunt Lil again.

At six fifty I eased up the ramp from the basement car
park and crossed the bridge.

No white Opels.

No red Porsches.

No light-heavyweights.

No Hocks Mackey.

I drove west on the quays into Phoenix Park. I left the
park by the Chapelizod Gate and went to Palmerston before
turning on to the Western Parkway to meet the south-bound

N7. I turned for Naas and put the hammer down. Nothing followed me – I was certain of that.

I let the car take me through the sweet morning and planned my evening with Kate Hartigan.

Somewhere in the middle thirties, I thought. Must have married in her teens to have a daughter Julie's age. No wonder she looked so cross when I spoke about sixteen-year-old Heather Skeehan shacking up with Paddy Brett.

Didn't seem to be the clubby, lady-who-lunches type. Did she have a regular man? Did she have a man regularly? I didn't think so. I felt she wouldn't be the type to accept an invitation from a relative stranger if she had a regular guy. I mean she wouldn't, would she?'

Kate was such a reliable name, such a steady name; a solid Agas-and-soda-bread country ring to it. No-nonsense Kate. Kate of the d'Urbervilles. I'll take you home again, Kate. Have my Kate and eat her. Kiss me, Kate.

Where had Kate ate? What kind of restaurant did she like?

Surprise me she'd said – what did that mean?'

Solid country cooking I bet – none of your nouvelle cuisine, Impressionists' plates, come-away-hungry jobs. Probably ate like a horse – slim women like her always did.

Swanson's – that would fit the bill. Best of both worlds. Snobby, full of Ritzy nonsense but the food was good. Only trouble – your parents had to reserve a table for you at birth, certainly before the christening. Not too far to drive afterwards – breathalyser.

Not counting the small escapade in Fuertaventura – that was an old-friends-and-lovers thing – I hadn't been involved with a woman since Disaster in the Dolomites three months earlier. Might have made a go of that if I'd been twenty years younger or she'd been ten years older. It had been the kind of affair a man of forty-five can delude himself into thinking he's enjoying until he runs out of puff. Good while the going was good though, right up to the point where she reckoned I was too set in my ways – headed straight for what she called selfish bachelordom.

She could be right. Nice lady though – one of those square-shouldered young career women – dry toast, decaff, jog three times weekly. Kind you see early mornings in pin-stripe, razor-sharp trouser suits with shiny Samsonites, determinedly high-heeling the cobbles toward the Financial Centre or the Law Library as though they had a date at the OK Corral.

She was pretty up-front in her views, told it how it was – I give her that, even if it was a bit hard to take at the time. Wasn't that I didn't suit her, she said – matter of fact I wasn't what she'd call demanding. I was fairly OK in the feathers – no earth mover, she reckoned, but what the hell – an orgasm was an orgasm when you came down to it or went down on it. I had the dosh, the pad and, not being a nine-to-fiver, I could rear the child she proposed having at the optimum point in her life cycle and leave her free to pursue a rewarding legal career complete with all those dinners law folks seem to attend every second Tuesday.

But, and it was a big but, she reckoned I was inherently selfish. Wanted the freedom to go places whenever I felt like it. A man couldn't be relied on to put his shoulder to the wheel, his nose to the carborundum if all he could think of was heading off to the Great Barrier Reef for three months at a time. Certainly couldn't expect his wife to drop everything and go gallivanting around the world with him at a moment's notice.

She left me – abandoned me – north of Bassano del Grappa. Claimed she was running out of precious mate-search time and couldn't afford to waste holidays on lotus eaters, lost causes. Last seen Padua-bound with matching luggage and the matching-minded, up-and-coming (definitely the latter) property developer I'd been foolish enough to introduce to her.

I concentrated on my driving.

Over quarter of a century has past and still I get a lift when I reach the house with the green gable that means I'm almost home. In all these years of using it as my landmark I've never inquired who owns it. Perhaps subconsciously I don't want to know. Maybe if I did find out it would no longer be mine, my own special landfall that marks the beginning of childhood's territory, the limit of my earliest run.

Suddenly, I remembered something and braked hard by a random rubble wall. I left the car and walked along by the wall searching in the concrete coping until I found the spot where three children had written their initials in the wet concrete thirty-two years before.

There we were – JC PB JC. The first JC was hers and I felt a piercing sadness for the loss of what she'd been. But she was young yet, a whole new life ahead of her, and as my mother always said, God is good. I got back in the car.

From the green gable on into town what features there are in the landscape have immediate association for me. On that municipal dump Paddy and I went ratting. Joan never went with us. She was afraid of rats – the only thing I ever remember her being afraid of. Over there, between those two horse chestnut trees, the three of us routed the Waldren gang and Paddy and I got into trouble over Joan's black eye. There, in that meadow, from that tree branch, we dropped naked into the summer river. But surely it used to be bigger, as wide as the Mississippi, as deep as the Amazon, not a small bog rivulet overgrown with bulrushes!

The car plunged into narrow streets between small houses, past the occasional derelict mill of massive Valerian-infiltrated masonry to reach the modern, alien, town square. How many hovels were levelled to accommodate its glass and neon shopping mall where well-dressed stranger's children laugh from glittering escalators?

It was not yet ten o'clock – too early to bother Aunt Lil. I loitered and sauntered, wandered aimlessly for over half an hour, constantly doubling back and watching for watchers. Satisfied that I was not being followed – feeling ashamed of my paranoia – I slipped into Tinmen's Lane, a salmon slithering into its native delta, that once happy alley now waiting resignedly for the inevitable demolition ball and release from mouldering loneliness.

142

Aunt Lil was cautious. I'd never known her to call 'Who is it?' from behind a locked door. I told myself it was because she wasn't expecting me, but her relief when I shouted a reply and she'd thrown wide the door was enormous – and not solely because it was me.

'I've been so worried since you were here,' she said, when we were sitting in her kitchen, the kettle on and cups on the plain deal table between us. 'Mrs Morgan said there was a man asking where you were reared. Came down the lane yesterday. She told him she'd only just moved into the street and didn't know anyone.' Aunt Lil laughed. 'Imagine May Morgan saying a thing like that and her and all belong to her born in that house.'

'What did this man look like, do you know?' I asked.

'I didn't see him of course, but May said he looked like trouble – for all the world like a fella that'd be collecting rents. Frightener's eyes, she said, fish on a slab. Not from around here either. Had a Dublin accent. May watched him after she'd closed the door, saw him try a few other houses. But most of the houses are empty now during the day – young couples out working their hearts out to pay off mortgages when they should be rearing children. Too busy to see they're giving their youth away.'

'What did he look like?' I persisted gently.

'May said he was sort of average with sandy hair. She said he had a beautiful pair of shoes – why, I don't know. Desperate mean-looking man she said.'

'You should be careful,' I said. 'There's a lot of petty crime about.'

'Don't I know,' she said, 'and a lot of it is far from petty, I can tell you. I think I'm the only house in the lane that's not been burgled and that's only because they think I have nothing, living here on my own as I do.'

'I must put in an alarm system for you.'

'I don't want one of those, thank you very much. Paddy said the same thing. My heart wouldn't stand it if it went off in the middle of the night. That would be worse than being robbed. Dr Collins has me on a pill a day for my heart as it is. Mrs Nolan three doors down put one in – blows the neighbourhood out of it every second day taking in the milk.'

Over tea the conversation turned to Paddy Brett and his funeral. I told her the earliest the remains would be released for burial was Tuesday and that the funeral would be Wednesday most likely. I invited her to stay with me, to come to Dublin on Monday, but that threw her into mild panic. She didn't want to leave the house unguarded, she said, but it was really because she hadn't spent a night away in over forty years, not since she'd carried off her newly-conceived son to await his birth – her very own Flight into Egypt. Besides, she told me, Joan had invited her to stay and she looked forward to seeing Patrick and Patricia. I was a little annoyed until I remembered she was talking about her grandchildren.

I was glad that in the excitement of seeing me Aunt Lil never asked why I'd called. My problem was I needed to be alone in the house. I didn't want to admit I was there to collect what Paddy had hidden. I didn't want her to know it existed – that way it could never get her into trouble.

In the end she solved my dilemma for me. She needed to go to the shop on the corner but had been worried about leaving the house unguarded ever since she'd heard about the stranger. After she'd gone I moved quickly.

Paddy's alterations to the house did not extend to Aunt Lil's bedroom which was more or less exactly as I remembered it the day Paddy brought me there to show how clever Aunt Lil was at hiding things. I recognised the wardrobe and the dresser. The old brass bedstead was as shiny as I remembered it, the knobs splitting, worn through by Aunt Lil's polishing.

On a shelf covered with a white cloth bordered in Limerick lace a two-foot high statue of the Virgin Mary raised her plaster face to heaven. A rosary dangled from the hands that were locked forever in what Paddy Brett called the regulation praying grip with overlapping thumbs. I took it down and turned it over. A cloth was stuffed in the opening at the bottom of the hollow statue. I pulled it clear and the envelope with my name on it tumbled out. I slipped the envelope in my pocket and shook the statue, but that was all there was. I wondered if the statue had become too heavy for Aunt Lil and she'd stopped hiding things there.

When it was time to go – after I'd eaten the compulsory rashers, sausages and eggs – I said goodbye to Aunt Lil, held her frail bird's body to me, kissed her cheek.

I left Tinmen's Lane the way the locals do on Sundays, by a narrow passage that looks as though it's the back way into a house but actually leads into the graveyard of St Patrick's Church – the path we took to Mass on Sundays and in the early morning of fasting Lent when a Catholic God hung like a thundercap over Tinmen's Lane and no one had ever heard of priests or bishops having children.

I loitered in the front of the church like a jilted bridegroom and paid careful attention to everything in the street. Satisfied that I was free of company I hurried to where I'd parked my car.

Ten miles after Kilkenny, the road behind clear of traffic for as far as I could see, I rounded a bend in a small wood and saw a picnic sign. I turned in, wheeled about in the gravelled space surrounded by fixed rustic furniture and parked with a deer's eye view of the road through sundappled foliage. All was still and silent beneath the green canopy. Two minutes passed before an immaculate Morris 1000 rounded the bend after me, a silver-haired dowager holding its steering wheel at arm's length. Several more minutes and a Donegal registered BMW lashed past. I got a good look at the driver and knew he had no interest in me.

I took out the Blessed Virgin's envelope and slit it. Like the diskette had predicted, I was looking at the authority to collect almost fifteen million pounds.

There was something else. I turned the envelope and a key fell out.

*

145

Between Kilcullen and Naas I pulled into the hard shoulder and got out my phone. Directory inquiries gave me the number of Swanson's Restaurant and, after I'd abased myself sufficiently, a phoney French accent took a booking for that evening. Thursday had to be a slow night. I rang 'message waiting' and got Helen Foley at the plant.

'Guy called Grattan at the North East Baltic Bank keeps trying to get you. His secretary – Heather Skeehan – wants you to ring soonest.'

Helen gave me the number and I eventually got through.

'Mr Constantine, thank you for returning our call.' Heather Skeehan had a soothing, sing-song voice with an unflappable tone. 'Our manager, Mr Bill Grattan, is anxious to talk to you about Mr Paddy Brett. Would you be able to meet him today?'

The dash clock had two fifteen.

'Would fourish be OK?' I asked.

'That would be fine, Mr Constantine. I'll tell him you'll be here around then. Looking forward to seeing you.'

I wondered if anyone else had been looking for me and punched in my own number. It rang twice and was picked up and that surprised me.

No one spoke. I heard a couple of clicks.

'Hello,' I said. 'That you Maggs?'

Breath was exhaled. Magdalen is the only other person with a key to my apartment. She looks after things when I'm away and I pay her a retainer to straighten things out on a regular basis.

'Johnny, that you Johnny?' Maggs said, her voice shaky.

There was a buzzing.

'It's me. I'll be home in an hour,' I said, and cut the connection.

Those clicks worried me, I drove one-handed and called up Gerry O'Connell's phone number from the memory.

'Sorry to bother you again, Gerry. I need another phone checked – my own. Could you do it soon, I mean in about an hour. I'm just passing Naas – I'll be home in forty minutes.'

'Sure thing, Johnny.'

'I need a sweep of the apartment as well.'

'What are you into now? Must be one hell of an invention.'

'I'm going nuclear,' I said. 'Don't go up to the apartment. Meet me in the basement car park.'

In the event I made it to the apartment in a remarkable thirty minutes. I slammed into the car park and found Gerry leaning against his Mondeo. He had his bag of tricks beside him.

I briefed him in the lift.

'Johnny ...' That was as far as Magdalen got before I kissed her and that surprised both of us. I clamped my hand over her mouth.

'Sweetheart,' I said, into her wide eyes before whispering in her ear. 'Play up to me. I think the place is bugged.'

Magdalen's eyes went even wider. I took my hand away slowly. She was a born actress.

'I'm so glad you're home, Johnny,' she said. 'Sean had an accident at the cooker.'

Gerry quietly assembled his gear and began examining the phone as Magdalen and I rabbited on about a bad scald from boiling water. She kept shaking her head to indicate it never happened. She was so good she had me worried – Sean and I are mates.

Gerry looked at me, pointed to the phone, nodded sagely. He began moving around the apartment.

Magdalen looked horrified but kept talking as she took up the notepad I keep by the phone. I gave her my pen.

'Yesterday I let in Telecom man to fix phone,' she wrote.

I went into the bathroom and closed the door. In a while I flushed the lavatory and immediately opened the four tiles that hide the wall safe. I put the Virgin Mary's envelope in the safe and spun the combination.

Gerry did all four bedrooms, the lounge, dining area, kitchen and bathroom. He even went into the broom cupboard. Magdalen and I kept up a stream of nothing conversation. Gerry beckoned to me and we both retired to the bathroom and closed the door. Gerry turned the shower on full. I was beginning to feel like James Bond.

'I'm beginning to feel like fucking James Bond,' I whispered in his ear.

'I'd prefer Magdalen if it's all the same to you,' he whispered back, and cracked up silently at his own joke.

'You really are popular,' Gerry said, finally getting control. 'Same stuff as Glasbury Street. East German I'd say. Load of rubbish but effective in a noisy way. Phone's bugged. So are three of the lamps – lounge, dining and master bedroom. What do you want me to do?'

'Take them out,' I said, and went back to Magdalen.

'That's it,' Gerry said. 'That's the last one.'

We were in the kitchen. Magdalen had made coffee.

'You're a brick, Gerry,' I said. 'Send the bill to Helen.'

'No sweat,' he said, collecting his gear. 'Get it out of you on the next great invention.'

It was four thirty. I rang North East Baltic Bank and spoke to Heather Skeehan. I told her I was delayed but that I'd be along within the hour. She said that was fine, but to ring the bell as the bank would be closed.

'This Telecom man,' I asked Magdalen. 'What did he look like?'

'Like a Telecom man,' she said. 'Mind you he had an accent. I thought he must be from down the country. I was using the vacuum when he called. I left him here when I had to go collect Sean from playschool. He said he'd lock up. Sorry, Johnny.'

'Great,' I said. 'Marvellous. Rasputin could come in and you'd take him for Skibbereen Sam.'

'That's not fair, Johnny,' Magdalen said, hurt.

'I'm sorry,' I said. 'Didn't mean it. I must go. I've got to get to the bank.'

'I need to talk to you, Johnny,' Magdalen said.

I was on my way to the door.

'Back in an hour,' I said. 'I'm already late. Can it hold until then?'

'OK. See you in an hour.' She grinned. 'You're a nice kisser.'

I left the car in the basement and walked to St Stephen's Green as there's no place to park. The North East Baltic Bank building was once a small hotel. Funny thing, years ago I spent a night there with an American girl I met in the bar of the Shelbourne Hotel. A marble and glass front had been added since then and the bank's name was in foot-high gold letters. I rang the bell and wondered how life had gone for my American lady.

A white-haired man prised apart the slats of the venetian blind behind the glass door. He looked at me for about five seconds then opened up.

'Miz Skeehan is expecting you,' he said.

He locked the door behind us and led me across the empty banking hall and around the counter to where a young woman sat at a desk. There was no one else about so I presumed the bank staff went at five. The porter walked away and left us.

I must have had a subconscious notion of what the sixteen-year-old mistress of a forty-year-old accountant would look like because the young woman was a definite letdown. She was the epitome of the bank clerk, the proto-typical mouse. Her desk was clear apart from a telephone, a VDU and keyboard, two printed sheets of paper and one she was writing on. Her eyes were a pale grey. The brown uniform was a mistake.

'Mr Constantine, it's so nice to meet you,' she said, leaning back in her chair, very assured for such a young person in the Irish banking system. 'I've heard so much about you I feel I know you. Paddy Brett used to talk about you quite a lot.'

Good old Paddy!

'In that case call me Johnny,' I said. 'I've heard a bit about you too. Maybe we should get together after banking hours some evening and talk about old friends.'

This was the woman to whom Paddy Brett had left twenty thousand pounds.

She opened a drawer and took out a business card. She wrote on the back and pushed it across to me.

'Mr Grattan's expecting you,' she said.

I picked up the card and put it in my top pocket. She looked at me and silently mouthed what I took to be the words ring me.

She picked up the phone and punched buttons.

'Johnny Constantine is here.'

She listened, hung up. Suddenly she winked at me and it felt as though the Mona Lisa had flashed a tooth.

A door to my right burst open and Bill Grattan came out fast.

'Johnnnyyy Constantiiine,' he boomed, his hand reaching out to me.

The few inches he was shorter than me had been added to his shoulders. Built on the lines of the renowned brick privy, the false smile and overly suave greeting suggested the content could also be similar. A career in motion pictures was an option for this guy.

'Come on in,' he said, sweeping his arm towards his open door. 'You needn't hang around, Heather. George and I will lock up.'

She didn't move from her desk, just sat there looking at us. Then she seemed to decide something and tapped the sheets of paper, put them neatly on the corner of her desk.

'OK,' she said, still without rising. 'Good night, Johnny.'

'Night,' I said, and went into his office.

He was hearty. God, was he hearty! He was a one-man Lansdowne Roar.

Hear him tell it Paddy Brett was the spiritual descendant of John Maynard Keynes. The Celtic Tiger owed a lot to Paddy's breadth of vision and economic perspicacity together with his unrivalled political astuteness and ability to see the broader picture. The Department of Finance,

Uncle Tom Cobbly an' all, were indebted to him in most areas of taxation. His contribution to every damn thing had been nothing short of enormous. This guy had index-linked superlatives.

Eventually I could hardly see him for the clichés piled high between us. Then, for a while, I thought we were on either side of an open grave instead of his quarter acre of desk. I grew tired of his eulogising.

'So, now that he's gone,' I said, looking him in the eye over his steepled fingers, 'you reckon the country's banjaxed?'

I could see he wasn't sure how to take that, but he finally decided I had to be joking.

He laughed tightly. 'Paddy always said you had a sense of humour,' he said.

There it was again. I refused to believe Paddy Brett had ever found reason to discuss me with this asshole.

'I'm sorry to have been late for our appointment,' I said, 'but it was kind of outside my control. I hope you'll forgive me if I say my schedule has been compressed and I've got to be getting along shortly.'

'Of course, of course,' he said, and leaned forward on the desk. 'Joan Brett told me you're looking after her interests and I wanted to tell you how things stand here at the bank.'

He took his time, elaborated on the sterling work that Paddy Brett had done in establishing North East Baltic in Ireland, how he'd built up healthy offshoots in London. Liverpool and Manchester. I heard how the boy wonder helped the farming community with European grants, cut EU Gordian knots to the bank's advantage. All of it boring and all done to give him time to size me up, get a handle on my general reaction to financial dealing, my appreciation of the world of money. I went dumb, made it difficult for him.

'Paddy was a director of the bank,' he continued, 'and as such is due monies – we are looking into that at the moment

151

and should have the figures worked out in a few days' time. His shareholding alone is worth around two hundred thousand at today's value and we can discuss that with Oliver Pettit if you agree – last thing Paddy Brett would want is the taxman getting his sticky fingers on his hard-earned money.' He laughed, sat back in his chair.

I continued my silence – something I learned from the Arabs.

He came forward again, leaned his elbows on the desk.

'Thing we often talked about here after board meetings, Paddy and I, was what we got to calling the number-eight-bus scenario. In other words what we had arranged for our companies and our dependants in the event of being run over by a bus. Paddy used to say his family was going to be OK because in his corner he had the most honest man he'd ever known – and that was you, Johnny. He talked about you so often I knew he must have left you clear instructions on how he wanted things handled.'

He nodded sagely, returned his fingers to his favourite steeple. 'With a friend like that a man's rich. Yes indeed – a man is rich with friendship like that.'

I looked at him and said nothing, blinked only when I had to. He began shifting his feet beneath the desk.

'We've got a delicate problem here at the bank, Johnny,' he said, putting his hands flat on the desk. 'I trust that what I am about to say will be treated in the strictest confidence.'

His eyebrows shot up questioningly.

I made no move.

'I can rely on your confidence, Johnny, can't I?' His voice was a trifle harsh, exasperation was peeping through.

'Bill, let's get this straight,' I said. 'I don't want to know any of the bank's confidential matters. Got nothing to do with me. For one thing, I don't even have an account here. What I don't know I can't tell, so don't tell me anything you don't want told, OK?'

That gave him pause. True to form he decided to laugh.

'You're right, of course, Johnny. Our problem is that

there are some files gone missing, sensitive material. Paddy was last to have them and we feel he must have taken them off the premises. I was wondering if perhaps they were in the papers he left for you.'

'What papers are you referring to?'

'I always understood from our conversations that he was leaving you instructions in the event of his death,' Grattan said.

'I'm not aware of any,' I said. 'Joan Brett asked me to help sort things out and that's the only reason I'm getting involved. You should ask Oliver Pettit or Betty Halpin – they may know something. I certainly don't.'

'But he always said you'd be the one to talk to.' He sounded desperate now.

'I'm sorry, Bill,' I said, getting to my feet. 'Last time Paddy Brett and I talked must have been three, four years ago. He didn't say anything about looking after his affairs then. Matter of fact I can't tell you what we talked about because I don't remember. I gotta go – I have an important appointment. I'll be meeting Oliver Pettit in three weeks' time and I'd be grateful if you could have sent him on the details you talked about by then.'

He saw me to the door, made one last effort as he crushed my hand.

'If you should receive any papers left for you by Paddy please keep an eye out for bank files.'

I told him I would.


Twenty after six I got to my apartment and knew I was going to be late for my date. In the rush to get in I dropped the keys twice before I swung the door open and found myself looking down the barrel of a gun.

'Sweet Jesus Christ! Where the fuck did you get that?' I exploded in genuine terror, raising my hands in front of me, throwing myself back against the door.

Magdalen's hand wobbled and she lowered the gun.

'Christ, you gave me a fright,' she said, shakily. 'When I

heard messing with keys I thought it was Gaffney or Carmody.'

I noticed then that the television was on and heard the unmistakable dialogue of *Star Trek*®. I saw Sean's eyes peering over the back of the chair.

'Hiya, Sean,' I said, and waved. He kept staring.

I walked past Magdalen into the bedroom and threw my jacket on the bed. I was stripping off my shirt as Magdalen followed me in.

'I am sorry, Johnny,' she said, 'but I really am scared.'

'Where did you get that gun?' I asked, facing her, dressed only in my underwear.

Her jaw stuck out. 'I'm minding it for a friend,' she said, defiantly, holding it in front of her.

'Would you point the fucking thing somewhere else,' I said, and went into the bathroom.

Magdalen followed me, sat on the lid of the lavatory while I lathered my face. She pointed the gun at the floor. She looked contrite and miserable.

'Why?' I asked, and started shaving.

'I was trying to tell you before you went out. Spike Carmody was here this morning. Jesus, Johnny, tell me you have nothing to do with those people. I mean Carmody's The Farmer's man. He's deadly. He kills people. Why is he here?'

I looked at her. 'How do you mean he was here? Was he in the apartment?'

'I got scared downstairs. I came up here with Sean – your locks are better. Hope you don't mind, but ever since Gaffney and Mackey were here I've been frightened. Ring at the bell and I peeped through the spy hole and saw Carmody. Christ, Johnny, he's worse than Gaffney.'

'If that had been Gaffney or Carmody at the door just now, would you have shot them if they got in?'

'Fucking right I would,' she said, and opened up a whole new personality.

I finished shaving.

'May I take a shower?' I asked.

154

'Sorry,' Magdalen said, and left, closing the bathroom door.

I turned on the shower and let it run. I opened the safe and sat on the lavatory lid warm from Magdalen and went through the documents Paddy Brett had left me. They told me how to go about retrieving the material he'd stored in the Hibernian Safety Deposit Company in both our names. Told me what I would need by way of identification. As an afterthought he wished me luck and once again I thought grimly of how much I would have preferred he had found someone else to look after his family. He said nothing about bequeathing me Gaffney and Carmody!

'Would you mind turning the other way while I dress?' I asked Magdalen, and she went and sat at the other side of my bed.

'Afraid I'll find out your little secret?' she asked, giggling.

I got out clean underwear and a cotton shirt and began dressing. I paused to ring Kate Hartigan. She answered on the third ring.

'I'm sorry, Kate,' I said, 'I'm not going to make seven thirty. Around quarter to eight I'd say. Things got a bit piled up.'

'No problem,' she said, laughing. 'I'm running late myself. See you.'

Magdalen was watching me.

'Kate, is it? Haha!'

'What are you haha-ing about?'

'Should see your face when you said Kate. Nice is she?'

'No,' I said. 'I only date Medusas.'

'They good in bed?'

'So so.'

'Straight up, Johnny, what the hell is going on? Why're Gaffney and Carmody calling here? What have they got to do with you?'

Magdalen was pleading with her eyes and she seemed genuinely scared.

'It's my friend, Maggs, the one who died, Paddy Brett – somehow he seems to have got tied in with those people.'

'That accountant guy found dead out in Bullock Harbour? He was your friend? One who was married to your Vico widow?' Magdalen's eyes were wide with surprise.

'Yeah,' I said.

'So that's it! So that's what it's all about. Jesus!'

'What do you mean?'

'Way I heard it, there's an awful lot going down over that guy. Joe – you know, man who calls to me in the evenings – he plays golf with this guy who's boss of the Baltic Bank of something. This guy says there's all sorts of tax shit could hit the fan – says there could be loads of guys running for cover in the next few months. Reckons it could make the Ansbacher Accounts scam look like piggy bank stuff. Some of Joe's clients are in trouble over it. Joe says it could lead to the mother of all tribunals.'

'What do you know about The Farmer?'

'You remember The General? This guy is The General in spades. He's far-out heavy shit – take my word for it. Spike Carmody and a man called Paco Ryan do his cleaner dirty work. The dirty dirty work he does himself. The man is an animal – stay well away from him. Tell me again you have nothing to do with them.'

'For what it's worth I have nothing whatsoever to do with them.'

'You mind if Sean and I stay the night? We'll be very quiet – we'll take the small bedroom.'

'Course you can. Move in until all this is over if it makes you feel safer. Use the big room – there's a television there. But for Christ's sake don't shoot anyone.'

I rang her doorbell at twenty minutes to eight. I must have broken the speed limit ten times on the way. It's no cure for butterflies to know that it's quite ridiculous at forty-five to feel nervous calling for your date. I felt myself in a reprise

156

of the night thirty years before when I'd walked on stage and fluffed my three lines in the school play.

When she opened the door I was glad I'd worn my best suit, hadn't turned up casual.

'Hi!'

Such was the utter inadequacy of my greeting – I didn't trust myself to say more until I'd grown used to the full impact of her.

Kate Hartigan wore a black suit with large black cloth-covered buttons. High heels brought her up to chin level and her electric copper-red hair was spectacularly bunched into a mass of tight curls. A double string of cultured pearls adorned her neck still tanned from summer.

'At last, a man of his word,' she said, smiling, waving me in. 'Quarter to eight means seven forty-five – you sure you're Irish?'

I turned to face her in the ivory hall as she closed the door. I think I knew then that this was something very serious. I hadn't felt so attracted to a woman since I'd lost Margaret Hourican to God. It made me even more nervous, made me feel more ridiculous.

'Would you like a drink before we go?' she asked, smiling that reckless smile.

'It's a nice evening,' I said, my voice hoarse, 'let's move on while there's light in it. I've booked a table at Swanson's – I hope you like it there.'

'I've never been, but I know I'll adore it. I'll get my coat.'

She returned with a long black coat draped around her shoulders.

'I don't think it's cold out,' she said.

'No,' I said, inanely, 'it's not a bit cold out.'

We stood in the hall looking at each other without speaking.

'I think we'd better go,' she said, in a little while.

'Yes,' I said. 'It's time.' I had no idea why I said it.

I held the car door for her and she left a banner of

157

perfume in the air as she slid across me. I got behind the wheel and she began to laugh.

'What's so funny?' I asked.

'That's the second time someone's done that,' she said. 'Held a car door for me, I mean. You did it last night as well. I could get to like that.'

'I'll work on it,' I said.

Swanson's is one of those restaurants people will eulogise when it finally closes – they'll say what a marvellous ambience it had when they're sure there isn't a chance of exaggerated claims being verified. It's been through all the culinary fads and styles. Over the years interior designers have gone mad there. Yet it remains a constant in the capital's night life, rightly celebrated amongst the Beautiful People as the place to be ripped off amongst presumed peers. Normally I wouldn't be seen dead in the place.

It was a magic night – one of those evenings when everything goes right, when the restaurant staff are friendly, the food up to expectations, the wine smooth as silk. There was just the right size of crowd – a number of tables remained empty, reserved for theatre folk who still hadn't arrived by the time we were leaving – yet there was always enough to create a pleasant buzz without detracting from the level of service.

I couldn't take my eyes off her. That strong face held me enthralled – wildly mobile one moment, hesitant and unsure the next. Now and then she became shy, diffident and, once, asked why I was staring and left me flustered, embarrassed. Forty-five and behaving like that!

We talked about everything and anything and I have no idea what that means, what it includes. I remember slivers of conversation, words that jumped out at me, phrases that connected with events of the past days, that opened vistas into her earlier life.

She said that getting married at seventeen and having a child at eighteen tended to make a woman old before her time, especially when her husband was a man like Walter Hartigan.

158

'We hardly ever went anywhere together,' she said. 'Only holiday I ever had was when he took me to Paris once. I had to stay in the hotel while he attended to business. For all of three days I hardly left the hotel lobby. He was violently jealous, hated me to talk to strangers.'

Like the oyster, she covered her irritant in nacre, referred to her husband as Hermann, Attila, had a variety of soubriquets for him, made jokes about him – sarcastic, ironic – hid the deep wounds he had inflicted.

Paddy Brett had been her saviour and she told me a little of what he had done to gain her the independence she now had – but I wondered what it was she knew about her husband's affairs that had enabled her to force him into letting her keep the house, to have an income. It was not a typical Irish story of separation from a difficult spouse, there had to be more to it. Somewhere along the line she'd got something on Walter, something serious and Paddy had helped exploit the advantage. But it was none of my business and I let it pass.

'Why are you single?' she asked at one point.

Any other time I'd have laughed it off, said no woman had asked me to marry her, the usual guff of the long-distance bachelor. But that night I had no answer, no real answer to give those candid, inquiring eyes. I knew that all the silly answers I'd ever given were covering something. I think I realised that night it was time to stop pretending, inventing impossible scenarios involving Margaret Hourican, stop using her as an excuse. She had gone her own way, chosen her God before me, and I should have moved on, made my own life.

'I don't really know why,' I said, and for once it was the truth. 'Selfishness I suppose,' I added, thinking of Bassano del Grappa and another woman who'd had enough and walked away.

Kate Hartigan shook her head slowly. 'No,' she said. 'I can't wear that – you don't seem the type. It's something else, but it's none of my business.' The conversation moved on.

We left in starlight before eleven, a romantic moon riding high to the south. I held the car door again and loved her laughter. All the way back to Knocklangan Lodge she leaned against me, filled the car with her scent, smiled in the darkness.

'There's a great brandy waiting to be opened – the last of Attila the Hun's stock,' she said, as I held the door for her.

'You're a toff, Constantine,' she said, dancing out of the car, taking my hand, drawing me after her.

We settled in her sitting room – I once more on the chesterfield, she opposite – twirling our brandy glasses and wondering in our separate ways what to do next as we made the only stilted conversation of the evening. In a while silence descended on us and we sat staring at each other, becalmed.

Her smile faded slowly and, simultaneously, an awareness came to us that something unusual was happening in that room, something chemical building in the atmosphere, as though an osmosis or ion exchange was taking place or a new force field was growing between us.

We opened our mouths to speak, to break the tension that had become unbearable, but were pre-empted by the sound of clear young laughter and footsteps in the hall. The door burst open and the two girls were upon us.

Candy Delamere looked fabulous in a black leather jacket that stopped midway down her shapely thighs. Apart from shoes it seemed to be all she was wearing – that and a gossamer wisp of emerald chiffon round her beautiful neck. Her head was thrown back as she entered the room and her laughter faded to a sly cat-smile when she saw me. Eyes full of green devilment swung to Kate Hartigan as though in that maturely sensual face she might find confirmation of some illicit act she half suspected.

I wondered what it was Julie Hartigan had done to herself and it was some moments before I realised she'd fluffed out her hair and added make-up. In The Café of Eva Gonzalez she'd been the quintessential first-year undergraduate,

160

uptight, nervous about everything. Now she was assured, at ease, a shade sardonic – a tabby on the prowl.

'Why, Johnny Constantine! How nice to see you again,' Candy said, in her best Southern Belle accent, as though she'd just put down *Gone with the Wind*. She strutted her stuff across to the fireplace and pivoted, smiling a queenly smile.

'Candy and I are going to The Sandcastle to meet Patrick and some of the guys,' Julie said, offhandedly, nodding hello in my general direction. 'We're all going to a party in Trinity. I won't be home – I'll stay over with Candy, OK?'

'It's only Thursday,' Kate said, rebuke in her voice.

'It'll be a great party,' Candy said, supportively.

'College is barely open,' Julie said. 'Don't worry, Mom, there will be plenty of time to study later on.'

'Where have I heard that before?' Kate said resignedly. 'Well I'm sure there's no stopping you so have a good time and mind yourself.'

'See you in the morning,' Julie said. 'So long, Johnny.'

'Do try to behave,' Candy said, and threw a wink at us adults before making for the door, doing her thing. At the door she paused, turned her sly smile on me.

'Cute suit, Johnny,' she said, and was gone.

We heard the front door close behind them.

'I'm not too sure I approve of Candy,' Kate said. 'She's very grown-up for her age. But then I suppose I'd have behaved the same if we'd been as free of inhibitions in my day. Probably did anyway when you boil it down.'

'I like Candy,' I said. 'I like the way she stuck up for Patrick when she thought I suspected him of having had a hand in his father's death.'

'You cherish loyalty in your women, do you?' Her head was tilted back, her smile slightly mocking. 'What else do you expect of them?'

I said nothing, sipped my brandy, looked at her and waited. I was as unsure of how to move this thing forward as I was certain that there was something to be moved. I felt clumsy, felt it best to do nothing in case I knocked something over.

161

A long fingernail tapped a small tattoo on the empty glass cupped in her hand. She looked about her, slightly agitated now.

'Johnny,' she said, then paused for a few moments. 'I'm very nervous,' she said. 'It's been a long time since ...' She looked at the ceiling.

I said nothing.

'I'm afraid I'll disappoint ...' She stopped again.

'There's all the time in the world,' I said. 'There will be other nights.'

She smiled then and it turned into a slightly wicked grin.

'I'm chickening out, aren't I? That won't do. I've been chickening out too long.'

'Maybe we both have,' I said, and suddenly knew what I meant.

'Would you like another brandy,' she said, then thought about it. 'Putting it off again – I'm impossible!'

'I've still got some,' I said.

She looked at me for almost a minute then stood up. She put her glass on the trolley and moved toward the door.

'As Julie's not coming home you can put the chain on the door,' she said. 'We can switch the burglar alarm on from the bedroom.'

She walked out into the hall and I heard her go upstairs.

I finished my brandy and after a while put off the lights before going into the hall to do what she'd asked.

Hours later we finally did it.

Kate began laughing then. Said it was like riding a bicycle – something you never forgot.

We had another brandy and I promised that one day I'd count all her freckles.

It was Kate who started it the second time.

'You know,' she sighed. 'I really don't care.'

'Bout what?'

'Why you're not married,' she said, and got on her bike.

# Chapter Eight

In the morning, spatula in hand, I stood at the cooker in yesterday's shirt sleeves and dared the eggs to spit. It was a beautiful day in the outer world – the corn as high as an elephant's eye or something. Larks sang in the clear air. I felt an ode coming on – a sexy haiku at the very least. Every fibre tingled with Kate vibrations.

I wondered who else in Dublin that Friday morning was standing at a cooker having such profound thoughts – then told myself to get real. Get a life, I said aloud to the man reflected in the window.

I'd just stopped lecturing myself, had checked the toast and poured the hot milk into a jug before it could do the usual, when Julie arrived home from her night on the tiles with Candy and Patrick.

The outer porch door slammed and the kitchen door burst open. She stood stock still when she saw me.

'I do not believe this,' she declared theatrically.

Without make-up she looked even younger, child pale and vulnerable. I felt guilty, felt I'd been caught with my finger in the honey pot. I had an urge to explain something, but I wasn't sure what. We stared at each other for several loaded seconds before an egg spat and hot oil landed on my wrist. I jumped.

'Fancy bacon and eggs?' I asked, waving the spatula at the cooker. I smiled a crooked smile, knew I looked none too bright.

'Fucking hell,' she said. 'Bloody woman's gone nympho now – any dick will do it seems.'

It was a tribute to the carpenter who'd made the kitchen door that it remained a door after she'd lashed it shut with all the strength of her young years. On her stormy passage through she tested the internal door for good measure and pounded up the stairs like a Hitler Youth.

Moments later her mother came into the kitchen.

'Julie's home,' she announced brightly. 'Found everything you needed?'

'Oh, yes,' I said, but I was more or less transfixed, spitted by a surge of left-over lust that shot through me as I looked at her. The turquoise blouse was nipple tight – my palms itched with memory of them – and the pleated beige skirt swirled and floated as she walked, danced really, across the kitchen to slap a toothpaste-fresh kiss on my ravening mouth.

She leaned back in my embrace, gulped air and grinned, shook her head in joyful laughter.

'There's just nothing like it, is there?' she said. 'You just can't whack it.'

We were on the second pot of coffee and trying to behave when Julie returned in sweater and denim cut-offs. She bustled about the kitchen, noisily not talking to us, putting together a breakfast full of rattling crockery, slammed drawers, loud toast. Kate winked at me and said nothing until things quietened down again.

'How'd your evening go?' she asked, when next her daughter went hustling past the table, nose in the air.

That got Julie's attention, really pushed the plunger, added that back-breaking straw. Meryl Streep couldn't have done it better. Oscars have been awarded for less than that akimboed, foot-tapping, offended innocence in the morning sunlight of the kitchen.

'Christ, Mother! Have you no shame!' Her eyes began to leak and her lower lip trembled rather prettily. 'Jesus, he only arrived last night and you're screwing him already.'

'It's actually Johnny's second visit,' Kate said, precisely, and I wondered if she had some moral probationary span for such eventualities. As though sorry she'd given what might be considered an excuse when no excuse was needed, or had read my mind, she hastily added 'Not that I'm aware of any maturing period and, in any case, adults don't have to explain their actions – as I'm constantly being told by someone.'

'Christ! At your age!'

Julie, bowl in hand, back against the draining board, began stuffing cereal into her mouth, snuffling as she ate.

'You'll discover age has nothing to do with it,' Kate snapped, and went on the offensive. 'For God's sake, do you have to make that racket while you're eating!'

That did it. Slivers of breaking bowl flew around the kitchen and the girl raced for the door with her mother's 'Get out of my sight' ringing in our ears. We heard a door slam upstairs. Kate rose and closed the connecting door in the sudden silence.

'Sorry about that,' Kate said, resuming her seat, trying to smile. 'Julie's becoming more difficult to handle as time goes by. Blames me for our semi-dysfunctional family – that is, she plays both sides to suit herself. Sometimes she even accuses me of having driven Hermann away – Christ! I had to get the police a couple of times the bastard was going to beat the two of us to blue rags. No reason for her to be rude to you all the same.'

'I'm not worried,' I said. 'In a way I can't blame her – kids expect grown-ups to behave like adults and are always surprised when they do.'

'I know what you mean,' Kate said, and began putting our dishes in the machine.

I handed the remaining ones to her.

'I've got to go,' I said. 'Got to see about sorting some stuff at the plant.'

She turned from the dishwasher, put up her arms and kissed me. We were really into it, getting back to where we'd left off, when I opened my eyes and saw the man watching us.

He was standing in a drill of the herb garden, the shelf of his gaunt chin resting on hands that cupped the handle of a hoe. He wore clay-stained black clothes and a soft broad-brimmed oddly sinister hat. The ends of his shapeless baggy trousers were tied with hairy green gardening cord. An unlit briar pipe was clamped in his teeth, the capped bowl pointing down, as he watched us impassively. Feeling my attention shift, Kate looked up at me, then followed my gaze.

Suddenly embarrassed, she stepped clear of me, automatically drew her hand across her lips and waved to the man. She mouthed OK, gave him a thumbs up. He nodded gravely, conspiratorially, and turned back to his work as though he'd been waiting for her signal, her all-clear. His powerful broad shoulders swayed rhythmically as he worked.

'That's my Eddie,' she said. 'Steady Eddie Delaney, best gardener in Ireland. Sometimes I think I can hear plants purr when he's around. I'd better go talk to him – he worries about me when there are strangers here. Will I see you tonight?'

'Will you want to?' I asked. 'I really mean that. I don't want to push my luck.'

'You know,' Kate said, nodding slowly, 'I believe you do. I'll make a stew and I'll expect you when I see you.'

She took a fast peek into the garden, saw that Steady Eddie had his back to us, and kissed me sweetly before going out to join him.

Her slim figure swayed daintily as she side-stepped across onion drills and I waved to her smile when she glanced back. Then I went about my business.

It was touching ten when I reached my apartment. I rang the bell in case Magdalen was in shooting mode and then put my key in the lock. There was no one at home.

I was naked, putting away my worn clothes, when I heard the door being opened. I wrapped a towel around me before Magdalen called out 'That you, Johnny?'

'No,' I shouted. 'It's Butch Cassidy.'

She came into my bedroom. The woman lacks all modesty.

'Where's Sean?' I asked.

'Playschool,' Maggs said. 'Had a nice evening did we?'

'Pleasant.' I said. I walked into the bathroom and Magdalen followed me and sat on what was becoming her favourite seat.

'Hope I'm not bothering you,' I said.

'No problem,' she said, then realised I was being sarcastic. 'Ooh!' she said. 'Touchee this morning, aren't we. I see we were wild-oating last night.'

'Whatja mean?'

'Nice one in the small of your back. Love to see what the front is like.'

'If you don't mind I'd like to take a shower.'

'Go right ahead.'

I got into the bath, drew the curtain, put the towel on the end of the bath and turned on the shower. I was resolved not to be intimidated in my own bathroom.

'Like to tell me about her,' Magdalen called out. 'Want the woman's slant on it?'

'No,' I shouted. 'Had enough slant for one night.'

'Like me to get in there with you and improve your slant?'

'You are kindness itself, but no thank you.'

'A day may come when you'll wish you hadn't said that,' Magdalen intoned philosophically. 'I take it she took the longing off you last night?'

'Don't want to talk about it,' I said, turning off the shower, wrapping the towel around me, getting out of the tub.

Magdalen began rubbing my back with another towel.

'This is jolly,' she said, rubbing briskly, goosing me playfully.

167

'God's name, where did you pick up a word like jolly?'

'Old English bloke used to live in Baggot Street. Really decent type, retired stockbroker, very generous. Used to say it all the time. Every time he managed it he'd say "That was really jolly, Polly." Kind of a catch phrase.'

'You should write your memoirs,' I said, moving away as she began to get too playful.

Suddenly she pulled down my towel and began laughing as I grabbed it from her.

'I knew it,' she said. 'Knew she'd do it. Right on your arse.'

Maggs sat back, grinned up at me as I wiped condensation off the mirror, checked the stubble left by Kate's tiny razor, debated with myself whether or not to shave properly.

'You're no Bruce Willis,' Magdalen said, reading my mind.

I began to lather.

'When you're ready, check your phone,' Magdalen said. 'It rang several times last night.'

'Why didn't you answer it?'

'Didn't want to give you a bad name,' she said, but I knew that wasn't it at all.

I padded out as I was and picked up the phone. There were three messages. The agency that handles the rental of some of my properties had queries. A solicitor I'd never heard of had a client interested in developing a site next to some old sheds I'd picked up for buttons years before – wondered if I'd like to talk sale or joint venture. The third was an oddly accented voice, ould Dublin trying to be classy.

'This is Mr Carmody,' he said. 'I'd like to speak to you as soon as possible.' That was it. He left a number before breaking the connection.

I got out my mobile and put his number in the memory.

I went back to the bathroom and Magdalen.

In the condensation of the mirror she'd written – JC xxx Kate. I wiped it clean.

'Very funny. That was your friend – the one and only Spike Carmody. Wants me to ring him as soon as possible. What do you think of that?'

'You have any sense you won't.'

'I'll have to sooner or later,' I said.

'Don't meet him in a dark place,' Maggs said, and left the bathroom.

In a while I heard the front door slam.

They must have chosen him for his air of solid security. He was very big, and handsome with it – a young Samson. You had to wonder if standing inside the lobby of the Hibernian Safety Deposit Company was the best he could do with all he had going for him.

He smiled easily, was the personification of politeness when I presented myself in the glass and chrome reception area that Friday morning. I gave him the letter and identification Paddy Brett had left me together with my passport.

He catalogued it all in a book, made a packet of it and put it in a blue plastic folder. I saw his lips move but he spoke so softly into a phone that not a sound leaked out around the mouthpiece – it was a feat in itself. He placed the blue folder on a stainless steel plate, pressed a button and the folder was sucked through his desk with a slurping sound.

'Cute,' I said.

He nodded. Someone must have told him his forte was being the strong silent type. I stood looking out at the street and waited.

At the sound of a soft buzzing I turned in time to see a section of what I had assumed to be stainless steel cladding swish gently aside. A young woman emerged and stood behind the glass screen separating her from the lobby. She nodded to the gentle giant. He pressed a button and locks on the street door behind me snapped shut. He pressed another button and the door in the glass screen swung open. The Queen of the Vaults emerged and spoke softly.

169

'This way please, Mr Constantine.'

I followed her swivelling derrière down a short carpeted staircase and heard the stainless steel panel close behind me.

'I hope you know your way back,' I said.

She turned her neat head. 'Trust me,' she said, and gave me the standard Hibernian Safety Deposit Company smile. I wondered if she and Samson ever made love in the vaults before opening time.

I'd never been in one of those places before but it was like the movies so I knew what to do. I showed her my key. I signed her docket, absolved her from all blame. She gave me the box and led me to a booth that contained a table and two chairs.

'When you're ready to leave press the button,' she said, smiled and closed the door softly behind her.

I looked about in the small room but could see no obvious sign of a lens. The odds were I was entirely alone.

I opened the box.

It was neat and tidy. It contained a series of envelopes. I started at the back of the box.

There were three sealed envelopes – one each for Joan, Patricia and Patrick. They were quite slim – not more than two sheets of paper in each I thought.

Next was a bulky, open envelope addressed to grey-eyed Heather Skeehan. It contained two hundred one-hundred-pound notes. A single sheet of paper was wrapped about them. 'For the good times, love, Paddy,' he'd written on it.

Four bulky open envelopes followed, all addressed to Betty Halpin. Each one contained two hundred and fifty one-hundred-pound notes.

The balance was a group of envelopes addressed to me. They contained further hard copies of the letters of introduction, powers of attorney, referrals, etc. and instructions on how he wished the money distributed – all as I had already seen on the diskettes he had left me. Like Betty Halpin, I also received one hundred thousand pounds.

170

I went through all the envelopes again carefully. I took them out of the box singly and laid on the table.

For absolute certain the second copy of the diskette showing the Montego deposits was not there.

Paddy's killer had to have it.

I put the three family envelopes in my inside jacket pockets. I put the letter addressed to Heather Skeehan in my back pocket. I thought about taking Betty Halpin her money but decided it was safer where it was for the time being. I folded five thousand of it and stuck it in my pants pocket. She might need something to be going on with. I shut the box and pressed the button for Vault Woman.

I watched her slide the box back into its burrow and returned her smile. Following her upstairs was even sexier than going down.

'Have a nice day,' she said, seconds before the stainless steel mouth of her cave closed on her.

I nodded my thanks to Samson as he handed back my passport and papers. The front door locks snapped open. I felt like Steve McQueen bustin' out.

It was turning into a sunny day as I walked the short distance to Stephen's Green. I'd barely rounded the corner when I saw the pair of them bearing down on me.

Hocks Mackey wore the zip-up I'd seen him in before and looked like a man flexing himself for a troublesome encounter. His companion had to be Dutch Gaffney. Of slighter build, wearing sports jacket and cords, he had an air of menace and a purposeful stride – he looked cool and dangerous. They were both tightly focused on me and I halted, stopped dead in my tracks.

They can't do anything here, I thought, not in broad daylight, not on St Stephen's Green of a Friday morning. They kept on coming.

'Johnny,' the voice said behind me.

Never again will Garda Detective Sergeant Thomas Crotty look so beautiful.

'Morning, Tom,' I said, smiling, and from the side of

171

my eye I saw Gaffney and Mackey veer away and cross the road and pass into the Green.

'I've just been over to your pal Brett's bank.' He jerked a thumb at North East Baltic. 'Been talking to the manager. Fancy a coffee or something?'

We were outside Bendini & Shaw's so I followed him in. Had Tom Crotty suggested I board his space probe I'd have joined him. I knew there had to be a reason – Crotty just isn't the coffee type.

'It's a funny thing,' Crotty said, 'but every time I come out of somewhere on this Brett business I seem to run into you. You wouldn't be following me around, Johnny?'

He laughed, bit into an apple slice.

'This is only the second time.' I said.

He shook his head. 'You were in Bullock Harbour as well.'

'I can assure you I am not following you around.' I smiled my politest smile.

'You been hearing anything about your pal's bank?'

'Nothing in particular,' I said. 'I don't bank there if that's what you mean.'

'Don't mean that,' he said, munching. 'Word on the street is it could be in trouble for offshore activities. Mind you, quite a few of the banks seem to be into that right now, when they're not overcharging customers. You hear anything like that?'

'No,' I said.

'Seems to me it's one of the few things that could explain your pal getting killed. Everyone I talk to has only the good word for him. But someone did kill him. I was in with Brett's partner in the accountancy practice – he says the two of you are joint executors. You come across anything odd in your friend's estate?'

'No,' I said. 'I'm waiting for Oliver Pettit to tell me what the score is. He says it will take maybe three weeks to come up with the figures.'

'Nice-looking woman, the widow. Heavy on the sauce

I'd say. She have any ideas? She might tell you before she'd tell me.'

'Not that I'd be able to tell you anything I heard in confidence,' I said. 'As it happens his family are as much at sea as I am as to who could have killed him.'

'She's going to be a wealthy woman by all accounts.'

'Jesus, you're not suggesting she had anything to do with it?'

'Wouldn't be the first woman to knock off her husband. But, as it happens, I don't think she did it.'

'Do you have any leads at present?'

For a few moments he watched the video of number three in the charts – the music was too loud but the young woman's gyrations were hypnotic and sexy. He tore his eyes away, looked sheepishly at me.

'Not a bad song,' he said. 'Nah! We've no real idea who killed Brett or why it was done. That plastic bag over the head is unusual. If it was a drive-by or a belt of a hammer it might be different. The bag is kinda freaky. We've been trying to trace his movements Saturday and Sunday, but no luck. Secretary – that mad woman in Glasbury Street – she says he'd been acting odd for a couple of weeks. But she's so fucking odd you wouldn't know whether to believe her or not. Why do you suppose he employed a March hare like her?'

'Oliver Pettit seems to think highly of her ability as a secretary,' I said. 'Way I hear it her father committed suicide in front of her and it kind of upset her balance permanently.'

'Heard that too,' he said, 'and the funny thing is that it was Brett who drove her father to it I'm told. Brett was the one who bankrupted her father's companies, drove him into the ground. You think she's mad enough to have killed him? The bag over the head might fit with her.'

'You can't be serious,' I said.

'Don't suppose I am,' he said. 'Anyway, you can let the family know they can have the body Monday. They should get a phone call sometime today about it.'

'I'll tell them,' I said, and slid off the stool to join him.

We walked outside. There was no sign of Mackey or Gaffney.

'Give you a lift?' I asked. 'I'm just across the street.'

'Going anywhere near Donnybrook?' he asked.

'Right by it,' I lied.

We crossed the road and got into my car. I saw the pair of them through some bushes inside the railings. I drove out listening to Crotty talk about hurling.

Across the street from the Garda Station in Donnybrook he looked in at me before closing the door.

'Thanks for the lift. You hear anything while you're looking after the widow be sure to let me know.'

'For sure,' I said, and moved off as he slammed the door.

I drove to Irishtown and the Enterprise Centre and parked outside my plant in the slot marked JC. I hadn't been in the office in working hours for three months but it was comforting to see that no one had parked in my space. There was a new girl in Reception. She was very young.

'Where's Jenny?' I asked.

'Jenny left,' she said. 'Gone to the States – had one of those Morrison Visas. What can I do for you?'

'Oh, I don't rightly know,' I said. 'Work hard, be conscientious, try to represent the company cheerfully at all times, that sort of thing.'

I walked past her desk and pushed open the door to Parts Assembly as she began to protest and tell me I couldn't go in there.

Des Lynch was inside.

'Well hello there, Marco Polo,' he said.

'He just walked past me, Mr Lynch,' the young woman called from the door.

'It's OK, Bernie,' Des shouted. 'I'll explain it to you later.'

For an hour Des told me how things stood. Helen Foley joined us and we had the closest thing to a board meeting

174

we are ever likely to have in Constantine NDT International
Ltd. Helen has a great sense of humour and it comes in
handy because Des takes life very seriously. They are both
shareholders.

Two of our earliest models were sinking into obsoles-
cence and Des and Helen felt that maybe they ought to be
discontinued, made a strong case for retirement on the
grounds of age.

'You wouldn't be hinting that they're not the only things
that should be retired?' I asked, jokingly. Some of their
remarks seemed to be getting kind of personal and
pointed.

Des got upset, thought he'd insulted me, rushed to deny
any such implications. Helen just laughed.

'You should get married,' she said, 'you're getting
touchy.' Then her eyes widened as she read something in
my face, saw she'd scored a hit.

'Hey, hey, Des,' she said. 'Things are happening. The
boss is in love – how about that! She really must be some
woman to lasso this man.'

I was embarrassed. 'You're getting ahead of yourself,
Helen,' I said.

I changed tack and went into Des's reasons for dropping
the products from our range. Turned out there was a new
American version of one and a German variant of the other
that had taken over the market.

'They have wider fields of application and better recording chips,' Des said. 'OK, our price is better, but
contractors aren't too worried about initial cost when the
product is broad spectrum and more or less stupid-proof for
unskilled operatives.'

'Maybe it's time The Brain went into deep space once
more and invented a newer and better mousetrap,' Helen
said, and the echo of Paddy Brett's expression brought me
back to the business in hand.

We ended with a quick review of the financial position –
good – and the number of employees – eighteen, two less

than critical mass as far as the Health and Safety people were concerned.

When they left me I took out Heather Skeehan's card. She was an assistant manager it said. On the back she'd written the address and phone number of her apartment in Donnybrook. Beneath that a mobile-phone number had been pencilled in plus a small note – 'best'.

It was twelve forty – chances were she was out to lunch. I dialled her mobile. She answered on the third ring.

'Can you talk?' I asked.

'I'm sitting on a park bench in Stephen's Green,' she said. 'The sky is blue. The pigeons are closing in on my lunch. Been wondering when you'd ring.'

She sounded very assured, in control.

'You know who this is?'

Her chuckle rolled down the line to me. 'You're unmistakable.'

'I have something for you,' I said.

'Hoped you might,' she said, and did her chuckle thing again. 'How would you like a light lunch in my place tomorrow around one? Probably best we shouldn't be seen together.'

'Sounds fine,' I said. 'I take it you'll be alone?'

'He goes home to momma at weekends,' she said. 'You like sweet or dry wine?'

'Leave it to yourself,' I said.

'Wise,' she said. 'See you.' She broke the connection.

Cool, I thought, definitely cool. My phone rang.

'This is Bernie, your receptionist, Mr Constantine,' she said. 'Sorry about this morning.'

'You have nothing to be ashamed of, Bernie,' I intoned, the way Redemptorist priests used to say things when I was a kid. Bernie was obviously puzzled by that – it was a few seconds before she spoke.

'There's a Mr Gaffney here to see you.'

'I'll be five minutes,' I said. 'I'll ring you back.'

I took out the papers Paddy Brett had left me, the letters

to his family, Betty Halpin's money, Heather Skeehan's envelope and the key to the safety deposit box and put them in a bubble pack. I rolled back the carpet, opened the floor safe and stowed the packet.

I went into the production area and collared Des Lynch.

'There's a guy coming in to see me now called Dutch Gaffney. I want you to interrupt us after five minutes.'

Des looked oddly at me but nodded and I went back to my office.

'Show Mr Gaffney in please, Bernie.'

My door opened and Bernie stepped in.

'Mr Gaffney,' she said.

He came in slowly, like a cat suspecting a trap. He was around five-eleven, slim, with thinning sandy hair. Then I noticed his shoes. They were unusually patterned, highly polished, and I knew I was looking at the man May Morgan had spoken to in Tinmen's Lane. He had a mean face – May Morgan had been right about that too. The shadow of an old scar ran down his right cheek and I reckoned the chances of it being from a forceps delivery were slim. His eyes were pale green – like May said, fish on a slab. I thought of a shack in the mountains and felt very cold.

'Morning, Mr Gaffney,' I said, without rising. 'Thank you Bernie.'

He took one of the chairs the other side of my desk as Bernie closed the door softly.

'Mr Hartigan wants to see you,' he said.

He sounded as though someone had hit him in the larynx at some stage.

'And who is Mr Hartigan?' I asked, and thought I was being pretty cool.

'Husband of the woman you fucked last night.'

He looked calmly at me and the room went very quiet.

'Get out of my office,' I said.

He sneered then. 'You're going to have to talk to him unless you want something to happen to the bitch.'

'Are you threatening me?' I leaned forward on the desk. He didn't even blink.

'No,' he said. 'You deaf? I'm threatening her. Now are you coming or not? It's all the same to me – I'd just as soon cut her.'

I stared at him, looked into those empty eyes. He was a terrifying man.

I knew he didn't care – knew he really would slice into Kate without a thought, knew that Magdalen's story about her sister was true.

Des Lynch walked into my office through the door to the production area. Gaffney hardly glanced in his direction.

'Sorry, Johnny,' Des said, 'didn't know you had company.'

'I'm leaving now with Mr Gaffney,' I said to Des. 'We are going to visit Mr Walter Hartigan of the Knocklangan Hotel Group. I am going in my own car.' I turned back to Gaffney. 'Where are we meeting him?'

Gaffney showed no reaction.

'Cairngorm, his house in Foxrock,' he said, and smiled a vicious smile, 'if that's OK with you, Mr Constantine.'

'I should be back here by four o'clock,' I said, looking at Des. 'Please wait here for me.'

Des realised then that something was wrong. He looked mystified but nodded.

'I'll wait here until you get back,' he said.


My car clicked rhythmically over the joints in the concrete pavement of Strand Road as I hung behind Gaffney's Volvo. Hocks Mackey drove, held it at a steady thirty. The tide was way out and there was a nasty smell of rotting seaweed – at least I hoped it was only seaweed. Small stick-like figures with tiny clockwork dogs walked by the edge of the sea. Closer in, a couple of silhouettes were digging for lugworms. Faded graffiti said 'SAVE OUR STRAND'.

I swore softly, cursed Paddy Brett for his presumption in thinking he could just drop his problems, his leftover

178

villains on the old pal he hadn't bothered with for twenty-five years. And now it was worse – I'd dragged Kate Hartigan into the manure business.

We turned at Booterstown Avenue, again at Leopardstown Road and plunged into leafy Foxrock where the houses, set well back from the prying eyes of passing peasants, play hide-and-seek in acre plots. Autumn was entering the first weeks of a long run and here and there a rope of smoke rose lazily to fill the windless air with the smell of burning leaves.

Mackey turned down a lane almost too narrow for his car. I followed quickly and came close to piling into the Volvo's rear in the small turning circle at the end of a cul-de-sac. In front of it automatic wrought-iron gates were opening slowly. On either side of the gates tall, closely spaced conifers cut off the view. Beyond the gate the tree-lined drive curved sharply obscuring the property within. I looked up and caught the glint of a lens in the trees. Mackey drove between the piers that bore the name Cairngorm. I let out the handbrake and followed.

I took my time, let him get well ahead of me. As soon as we cleared the bend we were in open parkland and that surprised me. There had to be about four acres of it – worth at least a million an acre. It was hard to believe so much open ground still existed in that expensive suburb. Walter Hartigan was doing well if he owned this – or did it belong to The Farmer?

A golden mare trotted the other side of the white fence as I dawdled along and rolled her eyes at me when I called out to her. Her foal pronked behind, drunk on the magic of existence.

I drew in next to Gaffney's Volvo on the gravel of Hartigan's forecourt. On the other side of him was a sleek grey Jaguar XJ6.

It was a beautifully proportioned house of two symmetrical storeys clad in whispering ivy. White paint glistened and the house faced south to sparkle in the sun. It looked as if someone polished the windows and the ivy leaves on a regular basis, maybe every day. A large roof overhang, the soffit and dentils painted white, neatly capped the facade. At each corner CCT cameras arced lazily in slow-sweep inter-lock pattern.

Modern stained-glass panels surrounded the wider-than-normal front door. A fixed CCT eye looked down coldly. Gaffney rang the bell. I stood behind him. Hocks Mackey remained leaning against the car. No one said anything. I felt menaced, not nearly as nonchalant and cool as I hoped I looked.

''Tis you,' the cantankerous-looking woman in the apron said when she opened the door. She turned on her heel and left it to Gaffney to push the door in fully.

It was a Sunday-Supplement interior. Film directors need look no further for the set of their next costume drama. A Roderic O'Connor, all wild reds and whorls of colour, hung above a sensational hall table. Doing sentry duty next to it, an antique grandfather clock hit the quarter chime as we entered. On a low table an exquisite small Wejchert sculpture waited patiently to be noticed.

It got better the further in we went as Gaffney led me down a side hall to the door at its end. A split second before he turned the door handle he hit the door with the flat of his hand – a mere token politeness.

Walter Hartigan was at a desk in a book-lined study. It was a corner room and windows on two sides flooded the interior with light. The room deserved an Einstein or a Yeats. No common or garden skulduggery should be plotted there.

He had on a great shirt – Italian, I reckoned. It was buttoned at the neck and he wore no tie. Older than me, he looked like a film star of the thirties, right down to the small tooth-brush moustache. Tanned like myself, he had the look of a man that exercised, pumped iron a couple of times a week. His strong black hair was combed straight back and the eyebrows met in one continuous bar. His hairy hands rested on the desk as he leaned back in his seat. A fawn corduroy jacket hung over the back of his chair. Magenta suited him.

'Mr Constantine,' he said, 'good of you to come. Do please sit down.'

Like a friendly bank manager with bad news on the overdraft, he waved toward a chair in front of his desk. I sat and looked over my shoulder. Gaffney was leaning against the wall next to the door as though I might make a break for it. I moved my chair sideways so that I could keep him in my peripheral vision.

'It's about your friend Paddy Brett, Mr Constantine,' he said, smiling tightly.

'No it's not, Mr Hartigan,' I said. 'It's about your wife.'

His smile slipped away slowly and he leaned forward on his desk.

'What do you mean, Constantine?'

I flicked my thumb at Gaffney. 'That animal over there threatened to cut your wife if I didn't accompany him. If he hadn't – I wouldn't be here. I'm not at anybody's beck and call. Now for her sake I don't want to go to the police. But if you don't do something about that son of a bitch behind me I will. Am I making myself clear to you? My friend Detective Sergeant Crotty is very interested in your Mr Gaffney.' I hoped I lied effectively.

'That true?' Hartigan said, looking seriously at Gaffney.

Gaffney shrugged. 'He knows Crotty – me and Hocks seen them talking.'

'Not what I meant,' Hartigan said. 'You threaten to cut the woman?'

'Yeah,' Gaffney said, lazily, without much interest. 'Got his attention.'

'Wait outside,' Hartigan said.

Gaffney sneered at me, levered himself away from the wall, turned slowly, slid out of the room closing the door softly.

'I'm sorry about that, Mr Constantine,' Hartigan said, leaning back again.

I rose, walked to the window, got my thoughts together. I had to decide quite a few things fairly quickly. I walked back and stood in front of his desk.

'I want you to do something for me, Hartigan. I want you to understand that I am interested in the woman you call your wife. She does not think of you as her husband for reasons best known to the two of you, reasons I have absolutely no interest in. I am going to continue seeing her for a very long time I hope. So I would ask you to do the decent thing and stay out of her life. If I see that Doberman of yours anywhere near her, in the neighbourhood even, I'll have the police on both of you. Good day to you.'

I headed for the door.

'I'll make a deal with you,' he said.

I turned. 'How do you mean you'll make a deal?'

'You give me what Paddy Brett left you and you can have her. I won't bother you further.

He was standing now. He was about an even six feet.

I frowned. 'How do you mean?'

'You know damn well what I mean.'

I looked as puzzled as I could. 'I've been asked by Brett's widow to help tidy up his estate. I'm an executor of his will. Far as I know he hasn't left me anything – I wouldn't have expected him to leave me anything and I don't need anything from him. Is that why you sent that cur after me, allowed him to threaten Kate? As to you letting me have Kate – the lady is not yours to give to anyone. And furthermore, you don't bother me one bit.'

He winced slightly at her name. I had the feeling he was unsure of his ground, that he had been working a bluff, hoping I would admit to something.

'Brett left you papers, records,' he said. 'That's what I was told.'

'Whoever told you that is getting it up for you,' I said. 'Now remember – you put that Gaffney on a choke chain.'

I slammed the door behind me. Gaffney was lounging against the wall, one leg crossed, hands in pockets. He had his head back and laughed softly as I went past.

'Good ride, is she?' he asked, and sniggered.

Gaffney never expected it, never reckoned a middle-aged guy would have it in him. To be honest, I even surprised myself.

I once shared site camp in South Yemen with a Turkish engineer, Vedat Ozberki, who'd been pipped for a boxing bronze in the Olympics of his youth. To pass the time in those long-ago starry nights he showed me how to hit someone if you really meant it. Dutch Gaffney was the first ever full-scale test of how much I'd learned.

It worked exactly as Vedat said it would, but I have to admit luck and surprise were on my side. I came around so fast he hadn't time to react and the momentum of the turn added to the haymaker I landed to Vedat's exact specification. His head against the wall did the rest – man was surely caught between a rock and a hard place. Gaffney collapsed and in dropping knocked a Waterford glass vase that showered a thousand crystals on the fallen thug.

Hartigan wrenched open his door, stared at Gaffney, then at me. I pointed to the man on the floor and tried for my best Bogart.

'Like I said – a choke chain, otherwise I'll have to do something about him.'

I felt terrific but it was good to be in the open air again. Mackey was at the white picket fence stroking the neck of the mare. I hoped he couldn't see I was trembling.

I sat into my car and sprayed gravel as I turned. I drove out quickly and found the gates closed when I reached them. I waited, but kept the engine revved. They didn't open.

'Fuck it,' I said, and hit the accelerator.

Looking back I could see one side off its hinge. I hoped Gaffney's head hurt at least as badly as my hand. With a small shock I realised how much Kate Hartigan meant to me that I could react so violently and out of character to Gaffney's insult. And that felt good too.

*

183

All the way back to Irishtown I kept thinking of Gaffney and his threat to Kate. Hartigan looked as though he could control Gaffney, prevent him from harming her. But should I tell Kate of the threat?

It would only worry her unnecessarily, I thought, probably start her thinking of possible danger to Julie. I couldn't see Hartigan harming his own daughter.

Hartigan didn't have the diskette – that seemed pretty certain. So who had killed Paddy?

If it was The Farmer, why was Carmody trying to contact me?

That left only Lemptke and his East German friends. If the bugs in my apartment were anything to go by, then Lemptke seemed the most likely candidate. But why would he operate independently?

And whose side was Grattan on? Could he have decided to strike out on his own? Was Heather Skeehan in it with him? The derisory way she'd said 'He goes home to momma at the weekends' did not say much for her supposed intimate relationship with Grattan.

'Who's yer man Gaffney?' Des Lynch asked, when I got back to the plant. 'I wouldn't like to meet him in a dark alley of an evening.'

I made an excuse, told some lies, but asked him to keep an eye out in case Gaffney came snooping around. Des nodded but I knew he didn't believe me.

It was coming up on three o'clock and I decided it was time to deliver Paddy Brett's letters to his family. I opened the safe and took out the three letters.

I found parking immediately opposite Joyce Court.

Patricia answered on the second ring.

'Who is it?' the box squawked.

'Johnny Constantine.'

'C'mon up.'

The door buzzed and I pushed into the lobby.

The lift doors opened on an overly made-up young woman carrying a small bag. Scarlet-tipped prehensile fingers taloned the arm of a furtive-looking elderly guy with the air of a man desperately needing the world to understand that it wasn't what it seemed, that she was really his daughter. But even he knew that daughters didn't dress like that going for weekends with their fathers. The love bite under his ear did nothing for his identity problem. He avoided my eyes, but she winked as she stepped out of the car.

In the lift the smell of sweet perfume was stifling, made breathing almost painful, and I reckoned he'd be lucky if he lasted the first night with her.

The Visigoths had been since I was last in the lift, had even recorded their passing. We now knew that TJ was having an intensely physical relationship with AN. The gender of the pairing remained a mystery.

In the hall on Patricia's floor the noise from her neighbour's apartment was incredible – the Spice Girls had to be in simultaneous orgasm in there.

I pressed her bell.

She wore something black, brief and tubular – what came out each end was fabulous. Turquoise costume jewellery highlighted ears, neck and arms – big clanking crusty baubles that only a woman of her height and youth could carry off with casual elegance.

'Afternoon, Johnny,' she said, then looked at her watch. 'You caught me as I was just about to leave.'

I wished I had that effortless knack of telling people how much of me they can have.

'I was in the neighbourhood and thought I'd drop by,' I said, and showed her my village idiot's grin. 'Wanted to ask you a few things.'

The door to the bedroom was slightly open but the room was in darkness. I wondered if Amazon Coady was in there making out with the other member of that *menage à trois*, the giant panda.

'Care for a drink?' she asked. Never had enthusiasm known such bounds.

'Not really,' I said. 'Won't delay you.'

185

I avoided the easy chair that had come close to sucking me under on my first visit and sat on a simple kitchen affair that seemed solid enough.

'Your father left this for you,' I said, fishing out the envelope, making sure I was giving her the correct one.

She looked closely at it, turned it over, smelled it. She made no move to open it, just stood there tapping it against her thumbnail.

'Where did you get this?'

'If you don't mind I'd rather not tell you right now as it might get someone into trouble.'

Ice formed in her eyes. She sat opposite and leaned forward.

'Actually, Johnny, I do mind. I mind very much.' She was serious, angry but composed. 'I told you before. One of the things Dad did that drove me wild was the way he treated us as imbeciles – patronised us, made out we didn't know our arse from our elbow. Would tell us nothing of the real situation. We were always either on our way to the poor house or off to sunny Spain. Like I told you, Walter Hartigan seems to think Dad left lots of money – something to do with North East Baltic Bank. Seems to believe he left it with you.

'Now I don't mind Walter and his friends leaning on me – I can cope with that. But Dad is dead and I won't have you taking his place and not telling me what's going on. I won't accept you playing his smug little games like some self-appointed Galahad. Now please tell me where you got the letter.'

I shook my head. 'I believe your father was killed because of something he knew – something special about someone's business. I don't know what that was but I'd never forgive myself if somehow I caused another death. If I do find this money that Hartigan thinks was left to my safekeeping I can assure you I'll turn it over to your mother, Patrick and yourself. For the moment I must ask that you put up with my arrogant assumption that I know best. I thought you would want to have that letter as it is addressed to you.'

'Do you know what's in it?'

I shook my head. 'That's exactly as it was when it came into my possession.'

'Was there one for Mom and Patrick as well?'

'Yes.'

'Have you given them theirs?'

'No, not yet.'

'What are these few things you wanted to ask me?'

I was surprised she didn't open the letter.

'Your father was to meet Bill Grattan and a director of North East Baltic last Sunday night . . . '

'How do you know? Who told you that?'

'Take my word for it. Do you remember if Walter Hartigan was in the club on Sunday night last?'

She thought for a moment.

'Yeah,' she said. 'He was there. So were Gaffney and Mackey. Mackey was a bit pissed as usual. Gaffney was his nasty self. Don't tell me you suspect them?'

'Not if they were there all night – up to around one in the morning.'

'They were there until later than that,' she said. Suddenly her eyes narrowed. 'Come to think of it, there was a call for Walter around midnight – it was Bill Grattan. That have anything to do with it?'

'Don't know,' I said. 'It could mean that Grattan was ringing to say your father hadn't arrived – or that he'd killed him and needed help.'

'You must know a lot more than you're telling, Johnny. Have you really found Dad's fortune?'

'When your father's two practices are sorted out and his Bank shares and other bits and pieces totted there's going to be around one and a half million pounds. That's not bad for a boy from Tinmen's Lane.'

'You even sound like him,' she said, exasperation in her voice. 'You know, I reckon you have found the money

187

Walter Hartigan asked me about. Suppose someone kills you the way they killed him – what happens to us?'

'I won't be in a position to worry about it.' I was annoyed by her self-centredness. 'Have you thought about who might have killed him?'

Her eyes almost closed and I felt I had been mentally accusing her in the wrong. She had given a lot of thought to her father's death.

'I have no idea,' she said. 'I don't think it was Walter Hartigan. He wouldn't have killed him until he'd got his hands on whatever it is he thinks Dad had that was valuable. Walter's brutal but smart, and killing Dad before he had what he wanted wouldn't be his style. I don't think killing people is his style anyway. He's not straight but he's not a gangster. I think it's much more likely to have been The Farmer or someone like him.'

'Walter could have killed him in anger.'

'When Walter's really angry he gets icy cold – I've seen it and it's not nice. Ask Kate – I believe you get on well with her.'

'Got to let you go,' I said. I'd be damned if I'd rise to that bait. She must have heard from Patrick who'd have the story from Julie Hartigan.

I nodded to the unopened letter.

'I'd prefer you kept that secret for the time being. Anything in it to shed light on your father's death you might let me know.'

Patricia was still in her chair staring at the envelope as I let myself out. She didn't look up as I closed the door behind me.

# Chapter Nine

There were no messages on my answering service back in the apartment. I looked in the second bedroom but there was no sign of Sean or Magdalen apart from his pyjamas and her nightdress.

I stood under the shower for some time. I felt nervous, felt somehow compromised, as though I'd lost some essential freedom now that I had Hartigan and Carmody breathing down my neck. I thought of Paddy Brett and swore softly at the way he'd decided he could buy his way into my life, foist his sleazy associates on to me.

I skimmed the razor over my face, slapped on some of the lotion Bassano Woman said suited me. I put on a dressing gown and lay on the bed.

This should not be happening in Dublin, I told myself. This is the kind of thing that happens in Chicago or New York. I thought about the snippets I'd read in the papers – the odd murder surfacing here and there that seemed to belong in the lives of some drug-crazed souls, some forgotten underclass. But nothing organised, no Capones, no Mobs, and all the farmers I knew were interested mainly in the Common Agricultural Policy.

It was hard to believe a man could walk into your office and threaten to disfigure the woman whose bed you'd just left. Even harder to think you truly believed him capable of it, accepted the likelihood that he would do it.

It certainly looked as though someone had killed Paddy Brett because he knew things about how their money was laundered. It did not explain why they were following me. Paddy had changed the computer codes when he copied the accounts – without one of the diskettes they had no easy way of getting at their money. Whoever was following me did not kill Paddy Brett – if he had then he would already have the copy that was not found on the body. Crotty said Brett hadn't even carried a wallet. That meant Hartigan didn't have it; neither did Carmody and his boss, The Farmer. Lemptke and his East Germans seemed the most likely people, the only suspects left. But they were supposed to be associates of The Farmer.

Then there were all those Irish investors that stood to lose if Montego came into the public domain. Maybe there was one amongst them pissed off enough to do for Paddy Brett. There was something horribly casual about Paddy Brett's death – a blow, a plastic bag. Somehow it would have been more understandable if he'd been shot. There was a nastiness in the use of that plastic bag, something weird – just like Crotty had said.

Suddenly a picture of Kate Hartigan came to me – maybe I dozed off, had a dream. Her face had been sliced open like a melon. I sat up, my heart beating wildly – it had been very real.

I fumbled with the bedside phone and dialled her number. She answered on the fourth ring.

'Kate?'

'Johnny?'

'Are you OK?'

'Course I'm OK. Why wouldn't I be OK? Are you OK?'

'Yes, yes,' I said. 'I had this dream.'

'You inventors always go to bed this time of day? Why didn't you tell me? We could have done it together.' She laughed.

'That stew,' I said.

'The stew? You were dreaming of stew? So much for us girls.'

'Have you made it?'

'Johnny Constantine, what in God's name are you on about? Are you a stew fetishist or something? It's a skirts and kidney stew and it's been on these last twenty minutes.'

'Would it hold until tomorrow?'

'You can't make it tonight?' She sounded disappointed.

'I want to take you out,' I said. 'I want to look at you by candlelight.'

'I've got candles,' she said. 'But you can take me out. Oh, can you take me out! Don't think I can't keep my stew and my candles for another night. When will I see you?'

'Seven thirty.'

'This is the life,' she said. 'You'll get your reward in heaven or someplace.'

I lay back and thought about her.


Magdalen woke me with a cup of coffee.

'Great for some,' she said.

I sat up, pulled my dressing gown modestly about me.

'Thanks,' I said. 'How's Sean?'

'Outside,' she said, nodding towards my living room. 'Left on the *Enterprise* ten minutes ago.'

Just then *Star Trek*® music burst on us as Sean came through the door.

'Can I have a Coke?'

'Hi Sean,' I said. 'Coke's in the fridge.'

'Say thanks to the nice man,' Maggs said.

'Thanks, nice man,' Sean said, already halfway out the door.

'I met Dutch Gaffney today,' I said.

Magdalen became very still, grew pale.

'Where? Here?'

'No. He came to my office. He threatened me.'

'Johnny, listen to me,' Maggs said, sitting on the bed. She was serious, intense. 'You said you knew hard guys.

191

Get them now. Get them fast. Pay them to break the bastard's arms and legs in forty places. Gaffney means whatever he said. He'll kill you, Johnny.'

'He didn't threaten me,' I said. I was impressed by her intensity, felt the fear emanating from her.

'Who did he threaten? Did he threaten Sean? Did he threaten me?'

'No. He threatened this woman I know.'

'The widow? This Kate of yours?'

'Kate,' I said, watching her eyes.

'He'll do it, Johnny, whatever he said he'd do to her, he'll do it. Get those guys now, today, don't wait.'

'Jesus, Maggs, this is Dublin, it's not New York!'

'Oh, Christ! How can I explain this man to you? He's an animal, a mindless animal, Johnny. Christ, if you knew the half of what that bastard's done you'd be terrified like me. Get those guys, Johnny, and make sure they're tough.'

I got off the bed and went to the bathroom.

I felt distinctly uneasy.


I dressed carefully but casually – Donegal tweeds, no tie.

I rang Dunlinny House and booked a table for two by the french windows. It's just beyond Bray. A fine old country house from colonial times – trust the Brits to build in the right places. Good solid country cooking too – plus a short breathalyser-free journey back to Kate's. It was a bit late in the year for the gardens but the lawns were always charmingly peaceful – hence the table by the window.

The Friday evening traffic almost put me in a bad mood. I still managed to reach the Vico road before six thirty and stop for my usual daydream of where my life might be if I got myself organised.

I rolled between the tilting piers of Windward at six fifty.

I had not phoned ahead. I did not want Joan organising a Smirnoff soirée.

Patrick answered my knock.

'Johnny,' he said, surprised. 'Come on in.'

This time we walked past their living room and down a shabby hall into a large kitchen at the rear. I understood then what Joan had meant when she said they'd spent the last ten years camping in the house. This section looked as though the builders were expected shortly. I marvelled at the mind of my old friend – how he could have assets of around sixteen million and have his family living like this. How to punish your spouse! Mad, totally mad!

'How nice to see you, Johnny,' Joan said, half rising from the table.

'I've interrupted your meal, I'm sorry,' I said.

They were having what we used to call tea back home when I was a kid.

'We're just having a snack,' Joan said. 'Will you have a cup of tea?'

'No thanks. I'm in a hurry this evening. I was talking to Sergeant Crotty today and he tells me they've finished their forensic work.'

'Yeah,' Patrick said. 'We got a phone call this afternoon. We've only just got back from Mulligan's, the undertakers. They'll organise everything. Removal to the church on Monday night arriving five thirty, cremation after ten o'clock Mass on Tuesday. Bill to go to Oliver Pettit.'

He looked quickly at his mother. Joan was close to tears.

'I want to arrange a lunch on Tuesday, Johnny, invite the people. I'm sure there will be a lot of Paddy's business acquaintances there. I know Paddy would have wanted that. But Patricia and Patrick are totally against it. What do you think?'

'Doesn't matter what Johnny thinks, Ma,' Patrick said. 'We're not going – Patricia and I. You can arrange a lunch if you want one.'

'See what I mean,' Joan said, appealing to me.

'Not fair to drag Johnny into it, Ma,' Patrick said.

I stayed quiet, hoped they would leave me out of it. I took out the two envelopes.

'Please don't ask how I came by these,' I said, 'at least

not for the moment, not just yet. Paddy left them for you. I don't know what's in them.'

I handed the envelopes to them. They were staring at me and it was a moment or two before Joan reached out and took hers. Patrick laid his on the table in front of him and looked at his mother. She began to cry silently, holding the letter pressed to her breast. I felt utterly uncomfortable, totally inadequate.

'I'd better be off,' I said, speaking to Patrick. Joan was in a world of her own, her eyes fixed on the table. 'If there's anything in those that might help ... That might indicate who ... That might tell us ... You could give me a ring, Patrick.'

He nodded and turned back to his mother. I think he was close to tears himself then. I left the kitchen, my footsteps sounding hollow in the echoing hall.

I was glad to sit into my car and drive out.


My mind was still full of the two of them as I turned into the drive of Knocklangan Lodge more sharply than I intended and almost hit him. He had to throw himself sideways and the effort tripped him – or maybe it was the spade on his shoulder that threw him off balance. He sprawled in a heap at the side of the drive. I stood on the brake and peeped out, rushed back to him.

He was very fast for a man of his size. I was still five paces from him when he was on his feet and turning to face me, the blade of the spade flashing like some ancient weapon as he whirled about. Planting his feet firmly – I was reminded of samurai in Japanese films – he looked at me coldly, silently, as though I was the footpad from hell.

'Are you all right?' I said. 'I'm very sorry – I must have taken the entrance too quickly.'

For some reason – as though wanting to show this dangerous-looking man I was unarmed – I held my arms out from my sides, palms open towards him. Thirty seconds of silently standing there and I began to feel foolish – Cool

McFinn, the Irish Ninja. I let my hands fall. He lowered the spade slowly, cupped his hands on the handle and I realised it was Steady Eddie Delaney, Kate Hartigan's gardening angel. I wondered where his hat was.

'You're Eddie Delaney,' I said. 'My name's Constantine, Johnny Constantine.'

I took a pace toward him, held out my hand.

'You should watch where you're going,' he said. He made no move toward my hand so I took it away. "People with fine cars should have more fucking manners.'

'I said I'm sorry – it was just one of those things.' I felt bad about it but there's only so much you can do.

'It's always the same with you upper-class shits – it's always just one of those things. Bollocks to the lot of you. In future mind where you're fucking going.'

He did the gardener's shoulder-arms and strode out the gate like a Wexford pikeman in search of Vinegar Hill.

I sat in the car gathering my composure and thought of that gaunt face, the hotly glaring eyes, his off-the-wall comments, and wondered what the world had done to him to store that amount of bitterness. I gave up and drove on to the house.

Kate Hartigan opened the door in a knitted dress of palest blue. I did the only thing possible under the circumstances – I reached out, took her in my arms and kissed her. If it had been possible, I would have inhaled her.

She stepped back, shook her hair, started laughing.

'Why do I feel like I'm sixteen again?' she said, and literally hurled herself back into my arms.

'Johnny Constantine,' she said, in a while, 'take me out or take me to bed. If we don't do one or the other soon we'll be in trouble here on the doorstep.'

'Get your coat,' I said.'

'Where are we going?' she asked, laughing, as I handed her into the car.

'It's a surprise,' I said, or sang, I can't remember. I felt younger than her sixteen, felt the way I'd felt when forever still had real meaning.

'I nearly hit your beloved Eddie Delaney,' I said, rolling over the spot, braking for the exit.

'Where?'

'Right here,' I said. 'I swept in a bit fast – he had to make a dive for it. I think it was mostly my fault, I'm ashamed to say. I wasn't thinking properly, not concentrating. He could have been nicer about it though – I mean there was no harm done and I apologised.'

She started laughing. 'Did he call you a middle-class shit – that's his favourite at the moment. It used to be bourgeois shit. He nailed up a picture of Che Guevara in the toolshed a few weeks ago. Eddie is your old-fashioned Bolshevik right enough – Karl Marx would have adored him. Poor man's not the full shilling, you know, not all there. Like that since birth – I've known him since childhood. We're both from the same mile of road in County Clare. He's been in love with me since then – kinda heartbreaking really.'

She mused, looked out her window, and I revelled in the scent of her.

'He very nearly had his chips tonight,' I said.

'When I got married,' she said, then frowned. 'No, when I made the Great Mistake' – she made some inverted commas – 'allowed Walter the Halter to lead me into slavery in Dublin, Eddie followed me like a dog. That's why I employ him, he's part of my life. I'll tell you a secret – sometimes I think of him as the only dowry I ever had. Isn't that a mad way to think of someone?' She laughed. 'You wouldn't mind but he has a wife and four kids.'

With the sun on my right and my darling on my left I drove into the Dublin mountains and there was not a happier man in the whole of Ireland that evening.

Dinner was wonderful. The first two courses went by while we watched two beautiful children squeal, scream and cheat each other through their own version of croquet on Dunlinny's lawns until the chill of dusk brought mother and tantrums.

Looking at her lovely oblong face as daylight lost out to

candlelight I knew I would fight a hundred Gaffneys for her – give it my best shot at any rate. Hartigan had to be a fool to have driven her away.

I told her the arrangements for Paddy Brett's funeral and she said she'd like to go with me. I told her I was thinking of going down the country Sunday to fetch Aunt Lil, bring her up to Joan for the funeral. Only then did I realise I hadn't spoken to Joan about Aunt Lil, hadn't made any arrangements. I decided it was not important – in any case, Aunt Lil could stay with me. I wondered if anyone knew how to contact Paddy's brother and sister – there were only two left of the family that had scattered to the four winds. Last I'd heard they were in Australia and Canada. They were considerably older than Paddy.

'Julie's gone to Galway with Trevor,' Kate said, smiling. 'Won't be back until Saturday night or Sunday morning. We have a free house, as she says herself.'

'Who's Trevor?'

'Boyfriend. Mind you, he's more of a manfriend. He's a geneticist at Trinity. Nice fellow, but old for her. I haven't said anything. She's just waiting for me to object. Keeps telling me what a mature person he is, regularly mentions he turned thirty this year. If I say a word she's going to demand I let her move out of the house and I'm not doing that for at least another couple of years.'

'She's got to go sometime,' I said.

'Don't you start,' she said, but smiled. "She really is becoming extremely difficult. I know all those hormones are supposed to be wildly active round about now, but Christ, they shouldn't obliterate good manners, common decency. I hope you won't mind if she gives you the odd tongue lashing – excuse it for my sake, please.'

She looked beseechingly at me. 'I'm so afraid she'll mess things up between you and me. I don't want anything bad to happen to us. Like I said, I haven't been this happy since I was sixteen and I don't want it to stop.'

Kate reached across the table, squeezed my hand.

197

'I promise not to let a cross word pass between me and Julie – no matter what the traffic is like the other way.' I took her hand in both of mine and kissed it. Kate looked about quickly, embarrassed by the gesture.

'You'll need loads of patience,' she said. 'She's so inconsistent – for weeks she's been going on about how she hates Walter. Yesterday she found an old hairbrush of his at the back of my wardrobe and she's hidden it away as though it was the Turin Shroud. I can't make her out. Still, she's in Galway – think of all that freedom we have until Sunday morning.' She grinned wickedly and her foot came up along my leg beneath the table.

By three o'clock I had to admit I was flagging.

'You need brandy,' she said.

'Races the heart,' I said.

'So does the other,' she said.

We sipped and talked. In a while she leaned toward me, looked at me earnestly as I caressed a tumid nipple.

'Do you think I'm a right trollop?'

'You serious?'

'Yeah.'

'No.'

'Most Irish men your age think a woman shouldn't like sex.'

'Howja know? I mean how many Irishmen my age have you had sex with?'

'There you are. That's what I mean.'

'How do you mean that's what you mean?'

'First thing you want to know is how many others there've been.'

'I never said that. It's you said that.'

'No. It was you said that.'

'Well yes, but it was you who brought up sleeping with other guys. Said guys my age think women shouldn't have sex – hell! Why are we talking like this? How did we get started on this?'

'Men,' she said, leaning back, looking ahead, sipping brandy.

'Women,' I said.

'It's been five years,' she said, after a while, and looked at me.

I said nothing, leaned over and kissed her chastely.

'Thanks,' she said.

'Don't mention it,' I said.


One o'clock Saturday found me searching Donnybrook for Onion Lane. Kate and I had slept late, then done what all young lovers do on Saturday mornings.

My first port of call had been to the plant to pick up the stuffed envelope Paddy Brett left Heather Skeehan. Then I drove around for a while. I went to Phoenix Park and dawdled to see if anyone followed. I drove out the Castlenock Gate and back in by the Cabra Gate, then all the way across the park and out the Knockmaroon Gate. I went through Ballyfermot, Bluebell, Drimnagh. As far as I could see no one stayed with me.

Appropriately enough it was the greengrocer who put me right for Onion Lane and I drove slowly along the row of recent, four storey, tree-named apartment blocks until I found Ash House. Heather Skeehan had an apartment on the fourth floor.

She was seal-sleek in skin-tight pants and almost-see-through blouse. Her hair hung to her shoulders and the glasses were gone – probably replaced by contact lenses. She had a really sexy figure and I could see now why Paddy Brett had given her the apartment and still felt guilty enough to leave her twenty thousand pounds. Her smile could mean anything.

'Come on in, Johnny,' she said, stepping back, cocking a provocative hip. 'Did you have trouble finding me?'

'Not really,' I said, 'the greengrocer knew his onions.' From her look I knew straight away I wasn't the first with that and I quickly added, 'In a manner of speaking.'

It was a reasonable size of apartment. I reckoned it a two

bedroom job, about nine hundred square feet. Worth around a hundred and eighty, maybe more. Not a bad parting present I hoped the 'good times' had been worth it.

A table was laid in the window overlooking the Dodder. She was house proud and had a flair for minimalist decoration. On a sideboard I noticed a photograph of herself and Bill Grattan on their stomachs on a beach somewhere in the sun. They were both tanned and naked.

'We went to Lanzarote last year,' she said, seeing the direction of my glance. 'Wish I could live there always.'

Heather took a bottle from a silver ice-bucket and poured two glasses of wine.

'Cheers,' I said. It was good wine and I smiled appreciatively. 'You have splendid taste, if you don't mind me saying so.'

'Don't mind in the least. Fact I'm rather proud of my knowledge of wine – but I try not to be a bore about it. I can thank your old friend Paddy Brett for that. I was sixteen when he first took me in hand, in a manner of speaking, and taught me – among other things – how to appreciate wine and how to make love to him. But it was an Arab in Tangier that taught me how to really make love.'

She grinned broadly, raised her glass in a silent toast and drank.

I wondered what that gem of information was meant to convey but held my peace.

'You know, Johnny, I feel I know you,' she said, moving back, going to the window. 'Paddy talked about his young days quite a lot and you were a big part of his life. Do sit down.'

She gestured and I took a seat at the table. Heather went to the fridge and came back with two plates of smoked salmon. She took a salad bowl from the fridge and put it between us.

'Do you like French dressing?'

'Never leave home without it,' I said.

All through lunch she talked about Paddy Brett, was

dismayingly frank about his sexual preferences. She told me, laughing all the while, how he liked her to dress in gymslips, schoolgirl clothes. There was an over-ripeness to her conversation that I found disturbing. She was at pains to tell me she still had the clothes somewhere, as though she imagined I might share his fantasies having grown up with him. I let her talk on, pretended to a sophistication I didn't feel, and did not ask any questions. It seemed she wanted me to think of her as the totally liberated woman for whom the little controllable whimsies of men were her passport to securing a place at the top of the pile.

'This is quite a nice apartment,' I said at one point, eager to change the subject. 'When did you buy it?'

'Didn't buy it,' she said, laughing. 'It was Paddy's. He put it in my name when he got tired of me – at least when I started to look older and couldn't carry off the little-girl stuff the way he liked. Do I shock you?'

'Well, yes,' I said, 'to be honest, I suppose you do. I'd rather not know about it if it's all the same to you.'

She seemed to think that deliciously naive, commented to that effect, said she could get to like me.

She made coffee and poured two glasses of Grand Marnier.

'You said you had something for me,' she said.

'Yes,' I said. 'I got it in the post with other stuff.'

I took out her envelope.

'It was open in the packet I received,' I said.

She took out the note and read it. Her face clouded over with anger. She tipped the money on to the table. French dressing spread over some of the notes.

'That it?' she asked. 'That all you have for me?'

'Yeah,' I said, 'that's it.'

She left the table and began pacing, made it obvious she wanted me to know she was praying for control, trying to be calm, to be reasonable with me. She halted on her side of the table, put her hands on the back of her chair, looked down at me.

'In case you think I don't know what this is all about, Johnny, in case you think I'm just on a fishing expedition, let me tell you what I think – what I know – you have, what Paddy Brett left you. And he left it to you because you were his one true friend.'

She said it mockingly, derisively, and I knew I could get to actively dislike Heather. She began at the beginning, spared me none of the salacious details of her sensual education under the tutelage of Paddy Brett, sketched the development of the North East Baltic Bank as she knew it from the bed and desk of its first acting Chief Executive Officer. No one could accuse Heather of being a slow learner and she must have developed a proprietorial feel for the bank early on – sometimes she called it by name, other times referred to it as 'our' bank, once or twice even called it 'my' bank. Heather knew all about Montego International – to hear her tell it she seemed to think it was her brain child, her special project. It rankled sorely with her that Paddy had denied her access to the Montego files, had not given her the codes.

Heather claimed to have handpicked Grattan, said she'd been the first to draw him to Paddy Brett's attention as a possible CEO. She told me how she'd had Grattan in her bed even before Paddy had grown tired of her – securing her base, she called it. She knew about Hartigan and The Farmer, had a fair idea that something heavy was happening through Vilmos Lemptke. Most of all she knew Paddy had made copies of certain files.

'Let me explain something, Johnny. I'm the one who told Paddy Brett what was going on down at North East Baltic. He'd stopped coming in regularly, thought he could leave it to Bill Grattan. I told him what was happening with Montego. Grattan is a child. He's greedy, wants everything he sees. Thinks he's a wheeler-dealer. He has no savvy when you come right down to it. Far as I'm concerned he's just a boy with a bag of balls. At least Paddy was smart – no matter how much he wanted to get up little girls' skirts

202

he always kept an eye to business. Once Grattan's in bed with me I can get anything out of him. That's how I found out about Hartigan, how they're helping themselves to The Farmer's money.

'Grattan and Paddy were the only ones with the codes to the Montego accounts. I couldn't get at them. When I found out what Grattan and Hartigan were up to I told Paddy – he promised to give me the codes so that I could keep tabs on what was happening. Instead of that he changed the codes on Hartigan's and The Farmer's accounts – all that Grattan can get to are the Irish investors, the small beer. Paddy must have left you the codes, the way into the accounts.

'Paddy came here last Sunday at five o'clock in the morning. I had to put on a show for him.' She laughed – harsh and cruel I thought. 'Had to let him have his favourite honeypot one more time. He was like a little boy, had even become a little pathetic, greedy for it. He said he wanted to talk to his son that day – that he hadn't seen him for four weeks. He told me he was meeting Grattan and Lemptke that night. He wanted out of being a director of the Bank.

'Can you believe it – at the end of the day he didn't have the balls for it. Well I have. I wanted those codes, but he said they were in a safe place, that he would give them to me once he was out and I could do whatever the hell I liked with them. Well he's out now – not the way he reckoned it, but I want my share, what I'm entitled to. You may as well give me the information, Johnny. It's no use to you – no way you can get at the Montego accounts, but I can. I'll make us both rich, Johnny, I mean really, really rich. You on for that, Johnny, do you have the balls for it?'

'That's not the right question,' I said. 'The question is do I have these codes you're looking for and the answer is I don't. I'm sorry you've told me what you have. I am really not interested in what is going on in your bank. The whole thing sounds very dubious if not highly illegal and I sure as hell want nothing to do with it.'

'Johnny, Johnny, this is Heather you're talking to. I'm

203

the girl who listened to three years of pillow talk about how you and Paddy Brett and Joan Callaghan were the Three Musketeers. I know that in the end he only had you to turn to because the other musketeer had become an alcoholic. I figure – I know – he had to give the stuff to you to mind for the kids – there just wasn't anybody else he felt he could trust. You'll notice I haven't said a word about Paddy's own stash. That's because I'm not interested in that. I'll be happy to settle for the Montego accounts – the Irish investors and The Farmer's dough.

'You can hold on to the stuff Paddy's been squirrelling away for years – there must be quite a bit by now. I only ever knew a little about that and none of it passed through our bank so I have no way of dealing with it. You can keep that if you like, Johnny. That could be part of your share – I mean who's going to know? He did leave it to you, didn't he?'

'You are way beyond me now,' I lied steadily. 'I don't know anything about this Montego thing you talk about and I'm certainly not aware of anything outside his two prac-tices and his directorship entitlements from the bank. Maybe you should talk to Oliver Pettit.'

'Johnny baby,' she said, almost cooed. 'You are out of your league, out of your little tree. You haven't thought this thing through. I know what to do, Johnny. And I'm entitled to my share. I've spent six years taking it every which way from those guys – it's my turn to dish it out. If you won't play ball with me then I'll just have to put a joint venture together. I could go talk to Hartigan, tell him what you have. Or maybe I'd do better talking to The Farmer. Then again maybe I ought to try good old Vilmos Lemptke. I've been to bed with him, you know. He's quite a guy, really kinky, really gets it on. Him and those guys he brings to town now and then would have you singing in no time, really break your balls. Why go that route when you could let Heather make you rich? Just lie back, enjoy the ride, let Heather do all the work? Now don't keep telling me you don't know what I'm talking about.'

I knew I'd made a big mistake. I should never have assumed she'd just be pleased to get the money. I should have anticipated another agenda. By giving her the money I'd confirmed I'd received a message from Paddy Brett. It was too late now. I felt a noose tighten a few notches. I got to my feet, determined to face her down.

'That was a very pleasant lunch,' I said. 'Excellent food, lively company. What more could I ask for? I'm sorry you refuse to believe me. I'll have to be off I'm afraid.'

Heather Skeehan leaned against the wall – as svelte a package of malice as I've seen.

'Door's there, Johnny,' she said, flicking her head. 'You walk out that and you've made a bad enemy, turned down a good friend. You're not a bad-looking guy, Johnny, we could have fun together – all we need is money. I have the motor, you've got the key. Let's make a go of it together.'

I shook my head, walked past her, opened the door.

'I mean it, Johnny,' she said. 'I'm not going to hang about. I'll make an alliance if you force me.'

'Woman's got to do what a woman's got to do,' I said, and left.

I closed the door gently and let out my breath before starting down the stairs. On the top step I paused as I heard her throw something, heard it break.

I went down the stairs slowly with a horrible feeling that my back was exposed.

'Why have giraffes long necks?' Sean asked, as soon as I let myself into my apartment. 'Ma said to ask you. She said you know everything. She said you're a silver engineerling. What's a silver engineerling?'

'Someone who knows everything,' I said.

In the second bedroom Magdalen said 'Hah!' I heard her beating pillows. In a few moments she joined us. She was beautifully dressed, looked very well, very young.

'You look wonderful,' I said, and meant it.

Maggs smiled, did a curtsy. 'Thank you, kind sir. We

205

went to the zoo today – saw the elephant and the kanga-roooooo.'

'No we didn't,' Sean said. 'They didn't have a kangaroo. Why're giraffes' necks long, Johnny?'

'To reach the leaves on the trees,' I said.

'Oh!' Sean said, and looked disappointed. He went to the television and fiddled until he got Tom and Jerry. I watched it with him for a while. They had Deputy Dog to follow. I'm a sucker for Deputy Dog.

'I'm going to crash for a while,' I said, when DD was over, and went into the bedroom.

I kicked off my shoes, lay on the bed. Magdalen followed me in.

'Did you do anything about getting guys to deal with Gaffney?' she asked, sitting on the bed.

'No. I don't think that's going to be necessary.'

'Why? You think the bastard is going to commit suicide?'

'No,' I said. 'I think we're just getting a bit carried away here. God damn it, this is not Miami, Maggs. This is Dublin. Things haven't got that bad yet.'

'Oh, no! This is Dublin, right! This is the town where guys on a motorbike can pull up to a car at a traffic light and shoot a woman journalist in broad daylight. Wake up and smell the coffee, Johnny. Gaffney and Mackey don't give a shit. They just do things. The Farmer – he's gone Common Market, can bring in guys from wherever for a contract job – no one ever hears from them again. That's why they can't tie him in with anything. Only way to deal with the Gaffneys of this world is to meet fire with fire.'

'I've got a date, Maggs,' I said. 'I want to have a snooze before I go.'

She looked at me for a while, her lower lip clamped between her teeth. Clearly she would argue further if I gave her space. In time she relented, grinned sadly.

'How's the romance going? This Kate being nice to you?'

'Yeah,' I said. 'She's being nice to me.'

'Good,' Maggs said. 'She ought to – you're a great catch.'

She stood up, seemed about to leave, then turned back.

'Going to ruin those slacks,' she said.

Before I could stop her she'd opened my belt and was at the end of the bed tugging my trousers off.

'Hey!' I said.

But she was folding my pants, putting them on a hanger. She threw a rug over me.

'Sleep tight,' she said and left me, closing the door behind her.

I didn't dream.

Ten seconds after I hit the doorbell Kate Hartigan filled my arms with the pure electricity of life and I knew that everything in my day since I'd left her that morning was unimportant.

'I'm scandalously ready for you,' she gasped, after we'd untangled our tongues, brought our hyperventilating down to something close to panting. 'Christ! I've been waiting all day. This is crazy!'

'Welcomes don't get any better,' I said. I did my James Cagney voice. 'This ain't a gun I have in my pocket, sweetheart.'

'We have a visitor,' she said, furious, her brow creasing. 'Of all the bloody nights she has to pick this one. Jesus! I don't know how I'm going to get through this. Joan Brett's inside – just dropped in out of the blue. I had to ask her to stay to dinner – poor woman is having a bad time of it. We'd better go in quick before she puts the vodka bottle on her head.'

I followed in a daze. Kate wore a silk blouse – fine lines of burnt sienna on a silver background – and a tight cream skirt moulded to plane of hip, curve of haunch, maddeningly sensual as she moved. I could think of nothing but possessing her there and then, that very minute, anywhere, do it over and over, again and again.

'Hello, Johnny,' Joan Callaghan said, her tone husky – the martyr waiting for the lions to enter. Her shocking complexion could have done with make-up. All in all she was a mess. Given time any decent industrial chemist could have identified the main course of her last four meals from the stains on the black tracksuit that ballooned formlessly about her and reduced her to sad sloppiness. She looked like someone who'd spent the afternoon drinking.

'Hi, Joan,' I said, as enthusiastically as I could. I took a chair opposite her at a kitchen table laid for four. There were fresh flowers on the centrepiece and I could see that Joan was getting between me and a memorably intimate dinner. I wondered who the fourth place was set for.

Kate grimaced behind Joan, shrugged her shoulders before turning to twist ice-trays into a bucket. Glasses clinked and whiskey was put in front of me without my asking. Kate's fingers trailed lightly across mine and exchanging ions crackled. Joan was very fast – noticed I hadn't been asked to name my poison.

'Didn't know you two were drinking buddies,' she said, trilling a brittle-icicle laugh, nervously primping her hair, holding out her empty glass for a refill. Kate tried to deflect her.

'We're going to eat after this one. Would you prefer a glass of wine?'

Joan knew her proofs. 'I'll have a Smirnoff just to be sociable,' she said, nodding in a ladylike way, her eyes awash with Russian magic.

'I'm half expecting Julie,' Kate said to me, nodding at the fourth place. 'She rang from Galway to say they might be home early. I don't know if Trevor is coming.'

'You don't like Trevor, Kate,' Joan said, narrowing her right eye to focus on her hostess. 'You don't like the idea of his being a genetics man – all that sex stuff. I hope you've told Julie about the dangers of sex.'

'It's all right,' Kate said. 'I trust her – besides, I put the pill in her tea.'

'You don't,' Joan Callaghan was astonished. She tried to turn her chair sideways to follow Kate's wanderings around the kitchen, but began to slip from it and clung to the table.

'Only kidding,' Kate said. 'Julie put herself on it six months ago. It made me sad but I suppose there's no point in trying to keep out the tide.'

Kate sat at the table to sip a sherry. She looked at Joan sympathetically and she ran the sole of her stockinged foot up the inside of my thigh. When she encountered resistance she looked dreamily at me and smiled. I took a drag of my whiskey and let it trickle down slowly.

'I can't stand it the way young people today shack up together,' Joan slurred, hanging over her vodka. 'There's no morality now, no respect for the laws of God or man. It was different in our day. We valued purity, knew that we should keep ourselves for marriage.'

Joan was addressing a point some four miles distant between me and Kate. There was not a trace of irony in her face as she switched her eyes to me over the rim of her glass. Kate Hartigan snorted, was having none of it.

'I won't have you behaving like one of those born again virgins, Joan Brett. Kids today are doing what we'd have done a lot more of if we hadn't been full of all that hell and damnation put out by black-skirted wankers tossing off in presbyteries all over the country. Good luck to the young people – let them have at it while they're fit and able and let them thank God for the rubber tree.'

'Thass an appalling thing to say,' Joan said, from the Smirnoff pulpit. 'I brought Patricia up to do the right thing at all times.'

Kate couldn't let it go. 'I hear she does,' she said drily, looking at me to see if I appreciated her comment. 'Herself and Della Coady are into novenas in a big way.'

'You're behind the times,' Joan said, coldly, drawing herself up. 'Patrick tells me Patricia has finally managed to get that baggage Coady out of her flat. I understand she's sharing with a much nicer class of girl now, one that won't interfere with her studies with all night shenanigans like that strap Coady used to do.'

Joan threw back the remains of her vodka and put

down her glass loudly, none too politely signalling refill time.

'I'm taking up the stew,' Kate said, rising.

Immediately, as though on cue, the front door banged and we heard people laughing in the hall.

'Holy Christ!' Kate said, and looked at me in exasperation. 'This place is getting like Heuston Station. Who's coming now!'

The kitchen door burst open and in poured the Irish entry for the Rio carnival.

Candy Delamere was spectacular in the simplest of dresses – what you saw was what you'd get if you should get that lucky. She had on her thousand-watt face. Patrick Brett had his hands on her supple hips and he either pushed her ahead of him or was drawn along in her wake. He looked happy until he saw me and then his mother. Julie Hartigan was subdued, seemed over the pique of the previous morning – even so, the look she threw me was far from welcoming. An athletic young man of about thirty followed Julie and I presumed him to be the boyfriend Kate disapproved of.

'Where did you lot spring from?' Kate asked, her back to the cooker as though prepared to defend her stew to the last dumpling.

'I think I'll try another, Kate,' Joan said, pushing her empty glass forward. Kate ignored her.

'Got back early from Galway and we met in town,' Julie said. 'Didn't know you were having a party.'

'I'm not,' her mother said. 'There's not enough stew to go round but I could knock up some Spanish omelettes if you don't mind waiting.'

'No hassle, Kate,' Patrick said. 'We're on the junk-food trail.'

'Mrs Hartigan to you, Patrick,' Joan chided her son.

'Oh don't start that again, Joan,' Kate said, waving her hand to the tall young man. 'Trevor, I'd like you to meet Johnny Constantine. This is Trevor Wallace, Johnny.'

'How'r'ya,' he said, grinning, and I liked both him and his solid handshake.

'And have you had a nice day, Johnny?' There was a chuckle in Candy Delamere's voice as she put the question, as though there was some fabulously funny joke I wasn't yet aware of – either that or my fly was open.

'Even better now that you're here,' I said, smiling at her lovely mischievous face.

'Oooh! Isn't he the sweetest man?' Candy said to Julie. 'Why don't our men say things like that to us?'

For some reason I got the distinct impression that Julie had been discussing me with Candy earlier in the day. There was a discreet emphasis on the word our, and I saw Candy's eyes flicker sideways to observe Kate.

'Come on, you two, move ass,' Patrick said. 'Let's get to junk-food land – I'm starving.'

'I've just got to run upstairs,' Julie said.

'We'll wait in the car,' Patrick said.

'Whose car?' Joan asked.

'My father's,' Trevor said.

There one moment, they were gone the next – like a dust devil in the desert. Suddenly it seemed as though real life had gone out the door.

'Wish I had their energy,' Joan said, moving her empty glass in a circle. Kate refused to see it.

'Let's have dinner,' Kate said. 'You must be starving, Johnny.'

She took a tea-towel and began removing plates from the oven.

The first whiff of skirts and kidney stew brings me back to childhood with the speed of light. Kate Hartigan would have got on well with my mother. Wine buffs would probably think it sacrilegious, but we didn't care, threw caution to the winds, and polished off two bottles of fine Burgundy with the stew – whiskey wasn't all that Walter Hartigan had laid down. In fairness to Kate and me, it must be said that Joan Callaghan had most of a bottle despite Kate's best efforts to limit her intake with some degree of courtesy.

Mostly the conversation revolved around Joan's maundering reminiscences of our golden youth – memories that grew ever more gilded as time and wine slipped by. It was pretty much a solo performance that needed only an occasional interjection to keep alive. I listened with half an ear, spent most of the time enjoying the wondrous face of my love. Kate smiled with embarrassment, now and then indulged in a little surreptitious footsie beneath the table. Neither of us was prepared or expecting it when Joan asked her question.

'Was Paddy here on Sunday night?'

Out of the blue it came. One moment it was all maudlin talk – Joan and Paddy and Johnny being the fab three – and the next there was a stunned silence. It even seemed possible to me that Joan had been pretending to indulge memory to create a false ease, to lull us into an unpreparedness and catch us off balance.

'What do you mean?' Kate almost stammered in surprise.

'Just what I asked,' Joan said, and I noticed her gaze was no longer focused on infinity. 'Did Paddy come here Sunday night? That's a pretty straightforward question as questions go.' Her words wobbled but held together. Suddenly Joan Callaghan didn't seem so drunk anymore and no longer held her glass as though her life itself depended on it.

'No,' Kate said, recovering, very positive. 'He was not here Sunday night.'

For the life of me I couldn't say why I didn't believe her, but I knew then she wasn't telling the truth.

'Why do you ask?' Kate said, defensive now, not looking at me, not including me in the conversation.

'Patrick told me Paddy called at our house around seven or eight. I was asleep and Patrick wouldn't wake me. Patrick had no idea why he called, but said Paddy was sober and they didn't fight as they usually did. For some reason Patrick got the impression he was calling here.'

'Well he didn't,' Kate said, believable now as she turned

212

a bright look on me. 'Cheese? Who'd like some cheese? I'm afraid that's all there is by way of afters.'

'Love some,' I said, and smiled to reassure her.

'Funny,' Joan said, not letting go the bone. 'Patrick was sure his father came here.'

Kate Hartigan put a plate of Irish cheese and crackers in front of me and I made myself busy.

'Why would he come here? I mean all my financial and legal stuff's been sorted out for nearly two years. It's ages since Paddy's been here.'

'Patrick didn't seem to think he was coming to see you,' Joan said, a trifle doggedly now, her head down. 'He got the impression that Paddy wanted to meet Julie.'

Kate became very still, concentrated on Joan. The two women seemed to have forgotten my presence, discounted my existence.

'Why would he come to see Julie?' Kate said quietly, casually, but I felt that the pin of an obscure grenade had been pulled.

For seconds Joan stared at her friend's benignly defiant face that seemed to dare her to accuse, to demand that she substantiate some unspoken allegation. The moment passed, Joan blinked, backed down, took refuge in Smirnoff speak.

'Would there be another drop of that lovely wine going?' Joan's mouth had gone lopsided again and her focus floated free to infinity.

'What about a liqueur?' Kate asked decisively, collecting plates, rattling cutlery, setting out fresh glasses, and I knew that some crisis had passed. 'I'll put on coffee.'

By eleven thirty that evening Kate and I were demented, would gladly have put Joan Callaghan out of her misery if we thought there was the slightest chance of getting away with it, when literally, we were saved by the bell. Joan and I waited in silence as Kate went to see who was calling at that hour.

It was Patrick Brett.

'Came back to give you a lift home, Ma,' he said.

'You needn't have,' Joan said. 'Johnny will give me a lift when he's going.'

My heart sank, but Patrick grinned crookedly at me and persisted.

'The others are down in The Sandcastle. We're going to a party in Howth. I wanted to see you safely home before we went.'

Joan beamed, was suddenly the proud parent. She finished her drink and got shakily to her feet.

'I don't think you should be going to parties right now,' she said.

'Let's not go into that again, Mom,' he said. 'Did you have a coat?'

'She didn't,' Kate said.

Joan kissed my cheek, said she'd be in touch. Patrick said goodnight as he led his mother away, Kate on their heels.

I slumped back at the table and heard Kate shout something, then a pause before a car started. The front door banged and Kate came back in. She marched across the kitchen and took my hand, pulled me to my feet. I followed her and we barely made it to the bed.

Later I came down and collected our clothes off the stairs in case Julie was earlier than we reckoned. I brought up the Benedictine and a couple of glasses.

'You're getting to be a habit with me,' Kate said, dreamily. 'Who wrote that?'

'Dunno,' I said. 'Definitely Nobel material. We could write to the Booker people about it – deserves a wider public.'

'Say something nice to me – it's your turn.'

'I can't go a day without you. You are my sunshine. Without you my copy of Herodotus is, well, just another copy of Herodotus. Without you Abu Dhabi is just another city in the desert. How am I doing?'

'Great, she cried, throwing her leg over and mounting him,' Kate said, laughing.

She was a woman of her word.

214

# Chapter Ten

I woke at five thirty that Sunday, her belly warm against my buttocks, her body spooned into me, her long fingers doing delicate, exciting things.

'Thought you'd never wake, lazy lump,' she said, and bit my shoulder. She continued her rummaging. 'Aha!' she said, 'and the dead awoke and spoke to many.'

I will remember that morning always, not only for the awfulness that daylight brought, but equally for the sheer delight of Kate Hartigan, for her sweetness, the intensity of pleasure and sustained excitement I drew from her supple body and how our coupling seemed to go on and on, moving in and out of waking and sleeping until we lay spent in each others arms, welded together.

'Someone's going to have to throw a bucket of water over us,' she said in a while, and the convulsion of her laughter popped me out like a pippin and I rolled on to my back. We must have slept for a while – next time I looked at my watch it was six thirty.

'You awake?' she whispered.

'No.'

'I'm worried about Julie. She stayed out again last night. I think she's getting serious about Trevor. Oh, I suppose I don't really mind her sleeping with him – she's got to get on with that at some stage and I think he's reasonably responsible and can be relied on to take precautions even if she

215

doesn't. Christ! I shouldn't say that. She's a good girl, knows what she's at. It's just he's that bit older – I hope she won't be hurt. She's so full of anger these days. Do you know what she did last night? I spotted it as they were going out.'

'What?'

'Remember me telling you about that hairbrush she found, the one belonging to Walter? Well, last night, when she went upstairs that time – I thought she was changing her pants or something – she collected it. I saw her stuff it into her bag. Why do you think she'd do something like that?'

'No idea,' I said. 'Probably something quite simple – not much point in worrying about it.

'Seems like only the other day she and Candy were kids – all that was bothering them was how to winkle out the price of the latest CD. Now they're young women – loaded guns. What is it someone said about putting seventeen-year-olds in charge of Maseratis?'

I remembered then what Candy Delamere had said the first time I met her. How Patrick couldn't have had anything to do with his father's death as he'd been in bed with her and if I wanted proof I could ask Julie Hartigan as she'd been with them. Julie Hartigan might not be the innocent her mother thought. But then, who ever was? I reckoned there was no point in explaining that to Kate.

'What would madam like for breakfast?' I asked.

'Ooh! Do I get it in bed?'

'Madam gets everything in bed.'

'Bacon, egg, toast, coffee – and orange juice, lots and lots of orange juice. I need fluid replacement, Hodgkins, I've had an exhausting morning.'

In underwear and trousers – in case Julie came home – I hied myself to Kate's kitchen and made breakfast, a thing I like doing. I brought two trays and the kitchen transistor to the bedroom. Kate had missed the National Lottery result and wanted to get it after the eight o'clock news. In cool nakedness Kate reclined in mounded pillows and I sat on the edge of the bed.

216

I felt very happy – I remember that.

I remember how we laughed, how Kate put marmalade on her nipples and had me lick it off while she became hysterical with laughter. I remember how the news began on Radio 1 and we listened with half an ear waiting for the Lotto numbers.

It is crystal clear in my memory how the announcer said some new initiative would be tried in Northern Ireland and then, suddenly and with the shock of earthquake, I heard her say 'body of a woman' and then 'Tinmen's Lane' and how 'foul play had not been ruled out'. It was over so quickly I was stunned.

'What is it? Are you all right? Are you feeling sick?' Kate was bolt upright in bed.

By then I was on my way, rushing for the phone.

Radio Eireann were obtuse – more likely it was me, too inarticulate to ask my questions.

I dialled 999 and the operator abused me for blocking the emergency number when I could ring the local Garda Station. I told him to stuff himself and fumed as I waited for directory inquiries to answer.

In a pale-grey dressing gown Kate Hartigan descended the stairs at a run and asked what was happening at the precise moment Julie came in the front door and set off the alarm.

'Oh, Christ!' Kate snapped, and ran to the control panel under the stairs.

'Shit! Bloody woman is humping again!' Julie said, and ran past me up the stairs as her mother called crossly after her and the operator put me through to the Garda Station.

'And why would you be inquiring might I ask?' The accent was broad Kerry, the words delivered like a sack of coal.

'Look, I didn't hear all the news. Just that the body of a woman had been found in Tinmen's Lane.'

'That is correct, sir. What is your interest, please? Who am I speaking to?'

'I have a great friend, Miss Elizabeth Meagher, she lives in Tinmen's Lane. Has anything happened to her? She lives in number seven.'

'Are you a relative, sir?'

I knew then Aunt Lil was dead and I stared in horror at Kate Hartigan. I'd led them to her – without me they would never have found her. It was the story of my parents all over again – I'd done the same to Aunt Lil. If only I'd stayed away, arranged for her to send the stuff by post. If Paddy Brett had kept his nose clean . . .

'Fuck you Paddy,' I shouted passionately.

'I beg your pardon,' the voice said.

'What is it? For Christ's sake, Johnny, what is it?' Kate said, her hand on my arm, pulling, demanding.

'Aunt Lil,' I said. 'Sweet Christ, Aunt Lil is dead.'

'Is the lady your aunt, sir?' The policeman's voice had not altered in tone.

'Not my real aunt,' I said to no one.

'Who am I speaking to, please?' The policeman was regretting he'd told me as much as he had.

'I'm on my way,' I said, and heard him say something as I hung up.


I took the Wexford road and once on the dual carriage-way I put the hammer down. Racing along the Bray bypass I thought of Tom Crotty and how I could get help from him by letting him know early of the connection – he would find out sooner rather than later, if he hadn't already.

Driving one-handed I had the operator put me through to Harcourt Street Station. He was off duty so I told a few stories about him and the officer-in-charge finally accepted I had to be a friend and gave me his home number. A woman answered.

'For you,' I heard her say.

'Crotty,' he said. 'This had better be good.'

'Tom, Johnny Constantine,' I said.

'Johnny, what are you doing up at this hour of a Sunday?'

'It's the Brett thing, Tom. It was on the news. His aunt was murdered down home – at least the radio has it that your colleagues down there say foul play is suspected. It has to be connected. I'm on my way there now.'

'Shit,' Crotty said. 'Give me your number and I'll ring you back.'

I was entering Gorey when the phone rang.

'Yeah, Johnny,' Crotty said. 'There's no doubt she didn't die a natural death. They suspect it was in the course of a robbery. Place was torn apart. Could have been after the woman's savings. Christ! There are some right bastards out there. I've told the lads that a friend of mine is on the way. I presume you were their mystery caller who knew the woman but didn't give his name?'

'Sorry about that,' I said. 'I was kinda confused. She was very dear to me. I used to call her my aunt although we're not related.'

'You should have given your name. Ask for Sergeant Goldsmith. He's a good guy but don't give him any bullshit. Do you know of any connection between her death and Brett's? It would be one hell of a coincidence. Maybe she was looking after something for him. You any ideas?'

'No,' I said. 'But if I think of something I'll let you know.'

'Do that,' Crotty said.

I drew into a parking slot outside River Street Garda Station as the liquid green numbers on the dash flashed to ten thirty. Five doors down was the old building where Paddy Brett and I started school at age four. I remember it yet for the marvellous man who told fairy stories to us children as we huddled about an old stove. Refurbished now – almost beyond recognition – a snazzy shingle announced it to be the home of a group practice of solicitors. At the turn of the century it was the barracks of the Royal Irish Constabulary.

Freshly painted blue and white outside, the Garda Station

219

within was a mess of government fawn and green. The air was stifling. Somewhere to the rear I heard the echoing screech of furniture being dragged about – at least I hoped that's what it was. A big man with a long, exhausted face stood at a counter and wrote in a ledger with an incredibly short stub of pencil that only a chain smoker could hold properly.

'Yes,' he said, and looked briefly at me from beneath ragged eyebrows before going on with his writing.

'My name is John Constantine,' I said. 'I rang earlier this morning to inquire if the woman in Tinmen's Lane was Elizabeth Meagher. Maybe it was yourself I spoke to.'

'Deed it wasn't,' he said, raising his head, fixing me with genuinely baby-blue eyes, remarkable in that sad face. 'Sergeant Hopkins you spoke to and he's gone to Mass and a well-earned breakfast this last hour. He told me of your call and how you refused to give your name.'

He spoke ponderously, as though imparting something arcane and wise.

'Sorry about that,' I said.

'What's done is done,' he said, pontifical in his forgiving, snapping shut the ledger for emphasis and made me wonder if I hadn't fallen foul of Flann O'Brien's mysterious policeman. 'My old friend, Tom Crotty, rang and told us you'd be coming. I'm Sergeant Shortall.'

'How do you do,' I said and held out my hand. He scrutinised it as though it was an exhibit in court before taking it and working my arm slowly, like a bilge pump.

'Might I ask what happened?' I said, when he gave my hand back.

'Not me you should be talking to,' he said. 'Detective Sergeant Oliver Goldsmith is expecting you and I warn you 'tis many's the joke he's heard on that name and unless yours is fierce original altogether I'd keep it to myself if I were you.'

He raised the counter flap and beckoned me in. I followed him down a corridor that smelled of antiseptic to a room at the rear of the station. A heavy set man with prematurely greying hair and a chest problem wheezed and burbled at a rickety desk that creaked and swayed beneath his writing hand. He looked up as we came in and his eyes were red and watery. For all that he was a handsome man.

'Tom Crotty's friend, John Constantine, the one who wouldn't give his name on the phone,' Shortall intoned and closed the door, like a head prefect delivering a culprit for chastisement.

'How is Crotty?' he asked, standing, shaking my hand, indicating the chair at his desk. 'He still playing?'

'Far as I know,' I said. 'Looks fit enough anyway.'

'Mad whore,' he said, and failed to get his handkerchief in time to stifle the first of three massive sneezes. 'Christ! I should be in bed. Wasn't for this business in Tinmen's Lane I would be. What's your connection with the deceased?'

'I was reared in Tinmen's Lane and had many a meal in her house with my friend, her nephew, Paddy Brett.'

'Yeah,' he said. 'Crotty told us that – so did the neighbours. When did you last see her?'

'Thursday last,' I said, and he went into a paroxysm of coughing and snorting.

'Sorry about that,' he said. 'Can you tell me about your visit?'

'We talked about Paddy Brett and the arrangements for the funeral. She was going to stay with Brett's widow – I was going to bring her to Dublin.'

I told him about the funeral arrangements for Paddy Brett but nothing about men with mean eyes and fancy shoes inquiring of my rearing. He made occasional notes, snuffled a lot.

'Sad,' he said. 'The poor woman! Do you have any reason to think the deaths are connected?'

'Well, as Crotty says, the wonder would be if they're not. How did it happen?'

'The neighbour, Mrs Campion in number ten, called to her at seven, asked was she going to the pictures with herself and Mr Campion. She said she was tired, was going to make an early night of it. On their way home after the pictures, about eleven, the Campions saw her door open and went in when they couldn't get an answer. They're not in the better yet of what they found.'

Goldsmith wheezed as he stooped to the bottom drawer for a packet of photographs. He tilted them out on the desk in front of me. He sat back and watched me as he dabbed at his nose with the handkerchief.

I thought my heart would break. After the first four photographs I had to walk to the window to compose myself before going on. They had robbed her of all dignity, reduced her to a rag doll. She lay in an unnatural pose in the centre of her ransacked living room. It was appalling to think what had gone on in that room.

Goldsmith said nothing. He watched me silently – even his wheezing seemed to have ceased.

They had turned the house topsy-turvy. Everything was smashed. Each room was littered with the debris of her treasured possessions, but I kept returning to the photographs of herself and the most treasured possession of all that they had taken – her life. Even death had not robbed her sweet face of its kindliness – that remained beneath the stray wisps of grey and leaped out at me from the grainy black-and-white close-ups.

'How did she die?'

Goldsmith sighed. 'Preliminary examination suggests a massive heart attack brought on by the savagery of the assault.'

'What else?' I asked. Like Aunt Lil herself, I wanted the truth, wanted to be told.

'If you mean was she sexually assaulted, the answer is no. We will know more when the pathologist arrives tomorrow.'

'Did no one hear anything? Surely she must have screamed, shouted for help.'

'Those old houses,' Goldsmith shrugged, 'the walls are thick. Besides, everyone was watching television. My guess is she probably had the heart attack early on when the beating started.'

'They beat her then?'

'Yeah,' he said, not looking at me. 'Punched her a lot in the body.'

'Surely someone must have seen them arrive or leave?'

'Why do you think there was more than one?'

'The state of the place, the way it was ransacked.'

I had a vision of two thugs – one slight and sandy-haired in fancy shoes, the other heavy and burly in his zip-up. Then I imagined a third, suaver man, in his fancy house waiting at his desk for a phone call that would tell him they'd found the stuff the old lady had hidden for the man who'd never known she was his mother.

'I think I'll go for a walk,' I said. 'I need some air.'

'There's no point going down Tinmen's Lane,' Goldsmith said. 'House is boarded up pending the arrival of the forensic lads from Dublin – they don't work Sundays because of the overtime ban.'

'Do you want me to stick around?'

'Not a lot you can do. Who'll be making the funeral arrangements?'

'I suppose I will,' I said. 'The Bretts, what's left of them, are scattered all over the world – maybe dead. I don't think anyone knows how to contact them anymore. I'd say Joan Brett – Paddy's widow – is the closest relative available. I'm looking after her affairs so it's probably down to me. I'll be more than happy to see it's done right.'

I gave him my card, told him how best to keep in touch. He stood and shook hands, said he'd let me know when the remains were ready.

Sergeant Shortall nodded, eyed me sombrely as I passed him.

I left the car where it was and walked the quiet Sunday streets of my home town that now no longer held anyone

223

dear to me. A lone child under the eye of a sad young woman kicked his ball to me in the park and I tapped it back. His smile faded when I didn't return it the second time and his young minder spoke sharply to him. I felt like telling her to be nice to him, that you only get one chance and then it's gone forever.

I was crying as I went down Tinmen's Lane and I stopped outside my parents' house and for the thousandth time silently begged their pardon. I stood outside the hastily barred door of Aunt Lil's house and could not cease weeping. After a while I realised I had company.

'Hello, Johnny, I'm very sorry for your trouble,' May Morgan said, and I took her outstretched hands in both of mine.

'May, how are you? It's good to see you. Aunt Lil was talking about you only the other day. Isn't it awful?'

'A fright to God! Sarah Campion said 'twas terrible what they must have done to her. And the way the place was destroyed – and poor Lil loved that house and the grand way Paddy did it up for her. He was real good to her, and he's dead now as well. God but 'tis a cruel world. She's as well off to be shut of it. Can I offer you a cup of tea?'

I thanked her, but went on my way. I needed to be alone.

I sat in the park for a longish time, not thinking of anything but really thinking of everything – of all the days and people of my life that would never come again. For some reason I became sad that Aunt Lil would never now meet Kate. I knew they would have hit it off – two women who had known trouble in their time. I realised then that I'd wanted to show Kate off to her, that I was proud Kate was interested in me, proud that we made love together. Aunt Lil would never have a day out on me now.

I thought of Paddy Brett and how I'd cursed him for a lifestyle that had taken Aunt Lil's only life. I realised then, sitting within a stone's throw of my parents' house, that he had done no worse than I had myself. Neither of us had intended what we had caused.

224

I walked up by the gasworks to where Cronins had their undertaking business, but a boy hopping a ball against a wall had no memory of there ever having been such a place in his street. He knew where Cronin's Funeral Parlour was and told me how to get there.

Sean Cronin recognised me despite all the years, saw me coming down the street and came to meet me with outstretched hand and his decent, not-entirely professional, sympathy. He surprised me – told me I needn't bother myself about details. Aunt Lil had been to see him three years before and given him her list of how she wanted it done, who was to be told, where Masses were to be said – St Patrick's Church and the foreign missions – the choice of coffin and the acknowledgement and remembrance cards.

I gave him Goldsmith's name and asked him to let me know the arrangements when he could and to send the bill to me. He said there wouldn't be a bill unless something unexpected came up. Aunt Lil had thought of everything. she would leave the world owing no one a penny.

I asked him to arrange a lunch in a local hotel afterwards and that would definitely be on me.

I returned to the car and took the Dublin road. I no longer cared if anyone was following me.

I hauled into a Statoil station after Kilkenny and rang my apartment. There were three messages – each one from Betty Halpin. She sounded husky, lisped a little, and I thought she was being her dramatic self. I should have caught the hysterical note, but I didn't.

Each time the message was the same – to ring her as soon as possible. The first message was stored at eight fifteen on Saturday, the second some two hours later. The last message was rung in at noon Sunday. I decided to wait until I got to Dublin before calling her.

Continuing to think of Aunt Lil, I reckoned it wasn't fair not to make the effort to contact her relatives. I wondered if

Joan had done anything about Paddy's surviving brother and sister.

I took the M50 at the Clondalkin roundabout and cut across to Killiney. At four thirty I rolled between the piers of Windward.

It had been raining in Dublin. Fat drops fell from the trees to splatter against the windscreen. Windward looked even gloomier as I wheeled about on the waterlogged forecourt and left deep tyre tracks in the bare clay. I parked next to a Rover.

Joan Callaghan Brett opened the door to me and I knew instantly she was on her Russian magic carpet – Smirnoff had left her more than breathless.

'Johnny, I'm so glad you're here,' she cooed, focusing on something about a mile behind me. 'We were just talking about you.'

Considering her condition she did a passably graceful pirouette, let the door slip from her fingers, left it for me to close, and floated ahead into the room they lived in. Her visitor was a balding elderly priest, all dandruff and glasses, who clutched a whiskey to his chest and gave me a lens-glittering, Deo-gratias nod from the depths of the best chair (the one with the cigarette burn under the rug) as his flat lips parted unattractively over yellow, celibate teeth.

Joan was quite the lady – a Killiney Madame Bovary – and waved airily at me as she introduced me to him.

'Meet our oldest friend, Johnny Constantine,' she said. 'This is Father Mulhall, Johnny. Father has been a great comfort to me over the years and has been our spiritual mentor since we came to live at Windward.'

As she spoke, Mulhall kept nodding his overly large head abstractedly. Like a pile hammer, it seemed to drive his slight frame deeper into the chair. He didn't get up. Instead, he extended a slightly shaky, liver-spotted talon as though he expected me to kiss it, all the while clutching the whiskey to his breast the way he'd been taught to hold a ciborium. He said nothing but nodded with a degree of understanding that was encouraging – at least he wasn't deaf.

Things were different in the Brett household that day – the drinks were openly on display. The sideboard held several bottles and there was an array of mismatched Waterford glass. Presumably Joan was holding some class of long-distance wake.

'Whiskey, Johnny?' Joan asked, drifting toward the sideboard. She wore an olive-green dress that was a little tight for her, would probably have fitted a few years before. Her make-up had been done with care and she no longer looked a caricature of her former self. She looked what she was – a forty-four-year-old stressed-out widow with a drink problem. That day I could feel genuine sympathy for her.

'Whiskey's fine,' I said.

'It's not as good a whiskey as your friend, Kate, stocks,' she said, almost gaily, but with a little too much emphasis on the word friend, and handed me a fair lash of whiskey. I added about the same of water and noticed how steady her hand was as I gave her back the jug.

'I called with bad news, I'm afraid, Joan,' I said.

'I don't think things could get any worse, Johnny,' she sighed, settling back in her chair.

Mulhall continued to nod, pile-driving away.

'Aunt Lil is dead,' I said.

'Oh no!' Joan said, and rose up in her seat.

Mulhall stopped nodding.

'What happened? Her heart?'

'Well yes,' I said. 'Her house was broken into. She was badly beaten, but seems to have died of a heart attack in the course of the robbery. I heard it on the radio this morning.'

I told her of my trip, my visit to the police, the undertaker's story and how we would know the final arrangements on the following day.

Joan was speechless. She finished her drink and returned to the trading post, collecting Father Mulhall's empty glass on the way. He resumed his pile-driving.

227

Joan handed him a full glass and settled opposite me once more.

'I wondered if you'd contacted Paddy's brother and sister,' I said.

'No,' she said. 'We have no idea where they live. Bonny is married and living in Canada. I think Jimmy moved from Australia to Borneo or somewhere like that. Paddy was so much younger than any of them. Paddy used to always say he was the last shake in the bag.'

Joan blushed then, surprised me.

'Excuse me, Father, that's not a nice thing to say,' she said.

Mulhall parted his lips briefly and his glasses glinted. He waved his free hand in absolution.

'I'd like to go to Aunt Lil's funeral,' Joan said, 'I'd like to go to the removal as well. Will you be going, Johnny?'

'Yes,' I said. 'I wouldn't miss it.'

'I'll have to see what Patricia and Patrick are doing – they didn't know Aunt Lil all that well. Could I travel with you, Johnny, if they get awkward and refuse to go?'

I hoped they would be able to attend, but told her she could come with me if they felt it was not their concern.

'Father will be saying the Mass for Paddy on Tuesday,' Joan said, more to bring Mulhall into the conversation than from any real need to increase my store of knowledge.

Mulhall came alive, spoke for the first time and astonished me.

'A sad occasion. A wonderful, wonderful man,' he said.

He had the most marvellous voice – soft and carrying, mellifluous, the sort advertisers would kill for. Suddenly he was a different person, a real presence in the room, a mouse that sang.

'I was just saying before you came in,' he went on, 'how we know not the day nor the hour.'

'True, true,' I said warily, and my worst fears were confirmed when Father Mulhall took off on flights of

228

fancy. He was one of those people who find it hard to begin a conversation but who never stop once they do.

Twenty minutes went by during which Mulhall awarded Paddy so many accolades – the Palme d'Or for parenthood, the Oscar for husband of the century, Knight of Columbanus for devotion to his Maker, the Nobel for services to humanity – that I felt he clearly could never have known the man. Joan took it all quietly, took up pile-driving where Mulhall left off.

It got to me in the end and I finished my drink and waved Joan away when she tried her usual trick.

'I have to go,' I said, adding vaguely, 'I must make arrangements.'

'I wonder if I could impose on you?' Mulhall said.

'If I can be of help,' I replied cautiously, and dreaded what was coming.

'It's my car,' he said. 'It's been giving trouble. I wonder if you wouldn't mind waiting to see if it will start. If it won't, might I cadge a lift into Blackrock?'

'Oh, you're not going too, Father,' Joan said, dismayed.

'I must, dear lady,' he said in his mellowest tones, and I could see how so insignificant a man could charm the socks off women.

The Rover's engine turned asthmatically, refused to catch, and I was stuck with the man with the golden voice. We said goodbye on the doorstep to a slightly unsteady Joan. I waited until Father Mulhall sat into my car before putting the question to her.

'The letter,' I said. 'The letter Paddy left for you. Does it throw any light on what happened to him?'

Joan Callaghan began to cry. It was weird and very sad. She just stood there and tears streamed down her face. She didn't sob or sigh – her eyes just overflowed. She wept as I have never seen anyone weep – it was almost unemotional. In a while she pulled a handkerchief from a pocket and lightly dabbed her eyes.

'Candy will be annoyed with me,' she said. 'She helped

me with my make-up. No, there was nothing about who killed him. He said he might have to go away for a while. He said if anything should happen to him that Oliver Pettit would help me. He said that he was leaving instructions with you. That I was to be guided by you. Is that true, Johnny? Did he leave instructions with you?'

'Yes,' I said. 'But please don't tell anyone.'

'Oh, he said that too. He said I wasn't to tell anyone. Twenty-four years and all he can write is that I'm not to tell anyone that he couldn't trust me. Maybe he thought I should throw myself on his funeral pyre and be done with it the way eastern women are supposed to do. What kind of a mind had he, Johnny? What sort of man does that to someone who only ever wanted to love him? Can you tell me, Johnny? Did he leave you instructions like that? What to tell the old cow at home?'

'I'm sorry, Joan,' I said, feeling that this conversation could end in hysteria. 'I'm not happy with what he's left me. What he left me could get me killed the same way it may have got him killed. That's the only reason I'm asking you not to tell anyone for a while. He left you a great deal of money and he laid the onus on me to transfer it to you and the kids. Now please stay quiet about it until I tell you the danger's past. I'm asking for your silence out of self-preservation – I really do not want to die just yet. It might also get you killed if we are not careful.'

She looked hard at me, then decided I was serious.

'We'll talk about it when the funeral's over us,' she said. 'I won't tell anyone, I promise.'

Mulhall smelled of drink and incense and resumed talking about Paddy Brett as I turned the car and drove slowly out the drive. I had intended calling in on Kate before contacting Betty Halpin, but I decided against it – she would not thank me for landing Mulhall on her.

He talked on and I turned on to the road for Blackrock. As we approached the gates of Knocklangan Lodge Father Mulhall dropped his bombshell.

'Strange – that's the last time I saw poor Paddy,' he said, pointing to the entrance. 'This day a week ago. I passed him as he was turning in that very gate.'

I felt a tightening in my chest.

'Sunday night?'

'Yes.'

'Around what time would you say, Father?'

'Nine o'clock or thereabouts. I was down with poor Mrs Kavanagh in St Columba's Nursing Home. She's not at all well, you know. In fact I must call in on her again tonight.'

I do not know what Father Mulhall said on the remainder of the journey into the presbytery in Blackrock. Even as he stood in the road thanking me profusely and offering himself and my door as perfect targets, an accident waiting to happen, telling me over and over how decent I was, part of my mind was remembering the question Joan had asked at dinner the night before and the way Kate had denied that Paddy had been in her house on that fateful Sunday night.

I pulled into a lay-by on the Merrion Road and rang my apartment. Betty Halpin had telephoned again while I'd been at Windward. I noted her address.

I rang Kate Hartigan. She answered on the fourth ring.

'Was it bad?' she asked.

I told her how my day had been, what I had seen and who I had spoken to. I did not tell her about Father Mulhall.

'Are you ringing from Joan's?'

'I'm on my way into town. I have to meet my associates at the plant.'

Immediately I wondered why I'd lied. What part of my mind had felt it necessary to conceal a visit to Betty Halpin?

'Will I see you later?'

'No. I don't expect to finish until very late.'

There was a long pause.

'Is anything wrong?'

'No. There's nothing wrong.'

'You're sure? I have this bad feeling suddenly. Tell me I shouldn't have a bad feeling.'

'There's nothing wrong and you shouldn't feel bad.'

'It's just that this means an awful lot to me, Johnny, more than maybe I'm ready to say right now.'

'Me too,' I said. 'Pucker your lips – something's coming down the line to you.'

Before I cut the connection I promised to ring her in the morning.

In Ranelagh I stopped for a sandwich and coffee and realised how hungry I was.

Rain misted down as I drove into Rathmines. It was not the easiest street to find and I had to ask four times before I found an authentic local who actually knew where he was and recognised the address.

It was one of those short streets tucked away from the main thoroughfares – opposing rows of two-storey, semi-detached, five-bedroomed, early thirties houses in rich red brick with quoin stones in Wicklow granite. The housing boom has set the going rate for such a house at around four hundred thousand pounds. If Betty Halpin owned hers she had a nest egg worth talking about.

I parked and walked the tree-lined pavement until I found number twenty-two. The front garden was well kept and the gate had felt the caress of a paint brush in the not-too-distant past. Flakes peeled from the front door and the area around the escutcheon was worn bare of paint. There were no lights within but it was only a little after seven and there was still plenty of daylight. I thumbed the brass nipple with the word 'press' outlined in white and heard a bell ring deep within.

After a minute full of silence I rang again. Looking up, I walked backwards from the door and saw the curtain of an upstairs window draw aside and an excited Betty Halpin wave before she disappeared. Lights came on downstairs and the door opened. She ran toward me with outstretched arms. It would have been funny if she hadn't been so hysterical and hadn't a face that looked as though she'd gone three rounds with Mike Tyson.

Everything within whispered of the owner's genteelly straitened circumstances. Betty Halpin clung to me one-handed as she secured the door behind us and led me to her lair at the back of the house.

You don't often see a fully operational nineteenth-century kitchen in end-of-the-millennium Dublin. Betty could put herself on the tourist route and make a few shillings out of it.

She was crying, kept saying my name over and over and I knew it was best to let her cry herself out before trying to make sense of her condition. Something very bad had happened to harmless Betty Halpin.

In places her face was tinged with purple, her left eye was almost closed, her wrists were bruised, the fingers of her right hand in swollen sausages. There were faint outlines on her throat that could have been made by fingers. Beneath my encircling arm she quivered, whimpered like some terrified animal, and her words didn't make sense as she tried to tell it all at once while she snuffled and choked. I talked in a low voice, soothingly slow, and gradually she calmed, began to listen and, finally, to make intelligible conversation.

'They wanted to know what files Paddy left with me.'

'Who wanted to know?'

'That man Mackey, the big fellow, and Gaffney, the weaselly man. The two that stand outside the office.'

'When were they here?'

'Friday night.'

'What happened?' I asked.

Betty seemed to drift away then. Her gaze slid past me, out and away to focus on infinity. At that moment I felt she wasn't aware of who I was.

'Gaffney is really sadistic,' she whispered. 'Just like my father. Did I tell you about my father? He started fucking me when I was seven – kept at me for years until he died. Want to know how he died, my fucking Daddy? Paddy took everything he owned off him, ran him into the ground, and I could have cheered – I did in my heart.

'The last night – I was twenty-eight then but I was still scared of him, terrified, he was such a brute of a man – he came to my bedroom. At that stage I was all he owned, all he controlled. He hadn't done it to me in years and I discovered that drunk as he was I was too strong for him. I threw him out and he went for his shotgun and came back upstairs roaring, swearing he'd kill me. He was saying it was all my fault, that I was the one that had robbed him.

'I beat him to it, wrestled with him, pushed the muzzle under his chin and blew his brains out with his own finger on the trigger. It was all over the ceiling, down my nightie – blood, shit, brains. Christ! What a mess, some of it in my mouth even. Agh!'

For a while then she was out of control and I held her to me as she trembled and bucked like a trapped wild thing. Slowly that changed to the weird humming I remembered from our first meeting, the sound of some internal motor being brought under control. After a bit she had it together again, even drew away a little, but held on to my hand, pressing it tightly, uncomfortably.

'What happened on Friday night?' I prompted.

'They pushed their way in when I answered the door. You don't expect that – you never think callers are just going to knock you down in your own hallway. Mackey held me for him – he has hands like steel bands.' Betty rubbed her wrist, looked at her swollen hand as though it belonged to someone else. 'Gaffney lashed me across the face over and over and then started choking me. He'd hold on until I thought I was going to die, then he'd let me breathe again. He hooked his fingers into me down there and I was sure he was going to pull my insides out. I fainted several times and woke up to find him slapping me across the face like the nuns used to do only a lot harder.'

234

'What did he want? Don't try if it hurts to remember.'

'Oh, I want to remember. I want to hold them clear in my head. That's where I went wrong with Daddy – what he was doing I pushed to the back of my head, refused to think about it for years until it was packed so hard that my head hurt nearly all the time. I should have kept it up front, looked at it every day until I was mad enough to take the carving knife to him. I'd recognise that blond bastard Gaffney in the dark of hell.

'I think it must have gone on for maybe an hour. They kept asking about the computer records. Seemed to believe Paddy had given me something or told me passwords. I had no idea what they were talking about. Eventually I must have fainted and when I woke I was under this table. Most of my clothes were torn off, but I don't think they did it to me. I'm so sore down there but I'm sure it's from his fingers.'

Betty seemed to have stepped out of herself, to be talking about someone else, as she recounted what had happened, but now something snapped and she was back inside herself again. 'Nothing new in it of course, I've been having that since I was seven, ever since the night he took me on his knee.' Her eyes suddenly opened wide and she looked into some terrifying corner of her mind and it came out of her in one long cry, 'Daddyyyyyy!'

Her scream was all the more shocking for being low, continuous, an almost impossible feat of breath control. I realised then I was hearing the scream a seven-year-old child had learned, the only one allowed, one that would not alert the neighbours to what was happening in this house of horrors. I held her tightly as she heaved and sobbed, held her until she dried up and became very still, almost cata-tonic.

'Are you all right? Can you cope?' I asked, feeling help-less and inadequate.

'I let him down, Johnny, I betrayed him. First I told them I'd shredded the files but then I told them Paddy and I

235

sent them to Oliver Pettit. I couldn't stop myself, Johnny, I had to do it, they were hurting me so much. I let Paddy down – after he'd looked after me, gave me a job, fixed it so that everyone believed Daddy committed suicide, stood by me during the whole lousy business, helped me when those rotten relations tried to have me certified and put away so that they could get their hands on this house. In the end I let him down.'

I shook my head. 'No,' I said, 'you never let him down, Betty – you're the one that stuck by him, his best pal.'

'Do you really think so, really think so?' Full of tears, her eyes pleaded for approval and I nodded encouragement.

'Have you told the police?'

'No. You see I'm the mad woman of the neighbourhood, the suicide's daughter. Those bastard cousins of mine would jump at something like this. They'd love to see me sent off, get their hands on the house – it's worth a lot now, you know, might make half a million at auction, way house prices are. If I went to the police now my relations would start saying I'm not able to look after myself properly, that I should be some place where I'd be safe. After Daddy died they gathered round like vultures, said I should be in a home. I told them I had a home. They talked in front of me as though I didn't speak English, as though I was some kind of dummy. Asylum is what they meant, the bastards. Get the stupid bitch out of the way is what they really meant.'

'Have you eaten today?'

'Not hungry.'

'I think you should go to bed. You're cold and you need sleep.'

'Will you stay for a bit, Johnny?'

'Only if you promise to go to bed.'

She laughed softly and it was a nice sound.

'You're just after the one thing.'

'Right,' I said, standing. 'Now it's up to bed at once you go and no naughty temper show.'

That surprised her. It surprised me – I couldn't remember when I'd last heard that old nursery jingle my mother always used when it was time to hit the pillow.

'Please don't pay any attention to the state of the house, Johnny. I haven't been able to do a lot with it these last few years.'

It was a tight squeeze but I continued to hold her close as we mounted the stairs. At the top the house ran out of decent carpet and we were into make-do threadbare land. Her room was at the back of the house and I suspected it was the smallest bedroom and the one she'd grown up in.

'You get into bed,' I said, staying outside, drawing the door almost closed after her. 'Call me when you're ready.'

I waited and heard her open and close drawers. I wondered if she was going to do her Lady Godiva bit again and was apprehensive when she called and said I could come in.

She wore a simple white nightdress with small pink bows. She was propped against the pillows. She had beautiful creamy shoulders that made her bruises seem even more shocking. Her hands rested palm up on the counterpane.

'You look beautiful, Betty,' I said, from the doorway.

Betty Halpin smiled at me seconds before her face crumpled and she hid behind her hands and wept. I didn't know what best to do. I thought I might frighten her if I held her naked shoulders. I drew a hand away and held it. In a while she stopped crying.

'Do me a favour, Johnny, lie down with me until I fall asleep.'

I took off my shoes, lay on the bed and put my arm around her as she snuggled beneath the clothes.

We were silent for a long while. I wanted to kiss that beautiful mouth but I knew I could not keep the promise it would imply.

'Don't know what I'm going to do for a job now,' she said. 'Don't suppose you need someone to be loyal to you.'

I was embarrassed and didn't say anything.

237

'I might have to sell the house after all.'

I thought then I might as well tell her.

'Paddy left you something, Betty,' I said.

The effect on her was electric. She shot up in bed and turned to me.

'What, Johnny, what did he leave me?'

'He left you a hundred thousand pounds.'

'Where is it, Johnny? Do you have it with you? Can I see the letter?'

I was dumbfounded. 'No,' I said, 'I don't have it with me. I left it where it would be safe, but it's yours. I brought five thousand of it with me in case you needed it. I've left it on the bedside table.'

'But the letter, Johnny, you have the letter?'

'There was no letter, Betty,' I said.

Her face fell and she thought for a while. Then she brightened.

'It was in a box, wasn't it, Johnny, the money was in a box. You just missed the note he left me, that's it, isn't it?'

I shook my head. 'No, Betty, there was no letter.'

She fell back on the pillow and tears welled in her eyes once more.

She had no interest in the money.


I think I slept a little on Betty Halpin's bed. When I woke she was snoring lightly and I extricated myself from her and left as quietly as I could. I double locked her front door and dropped the key in the letterbox.

I felt drained as I slid into my slot in the basement car park.

I sat there going over my day and the memory of Aunt Lil and Betty Halpin. I think it was then I realised I was going to do something about it, that this whole business had gone too far, had cost too much. People should not be able to do that kind of thing and get away with it.

I took the lift to my floor. I closed the door behind me and hit the lights.

Magdalen stood outside the second bedroom in her nightie, the automatic held two-handed and pointed straight at me just like she'd learned from television.

She put down the gun when she was satisfied it was really me.

'You know I could get very tired of finding a gun pointing at me every time I come home,' I said.

'I'm sorry Johnny, but I wasn't expecting you. I mean when you didn't come home last night I assumed you were with Kate. Then when it got to half eleven I reckoned you and she were at it again.'

I went into my bedroom and began peeling off my clothes. Magdalen followed me in and sat next to me on the bed.

'I'm really tired, Maggs,' I said.

'Had a rough day?' she asked, patting my naked knee sympathetically.

'You might say that,' I said.

'Like a cup of tea and a rasher sandwich?'

'Terrific,' I said.

Maggs beamed happily and left.

I never did get that sandwich.

I was asleep in two minutes.

# Chapter Eleven

Monday morning was clear and sunny. I slept right through to nine fifteen. I opened my bedroom door and called out but no one answered and I realised that Maggs would have taken Sean to playschool.

I made coffee and toast and went back to bed. I rang Kate.

'And how are you this fine morning?' I said, all breezy.

'Something's wrong, Johnny,' Kate said. 'I haven't slept a wink thinking about it. What is it?'

'Sweetness, light of my life, there is nothing wrong,' I said, more heartily than I truly felt. 'You're imagining things.'

'Oh, Christ!' she said. 'Are you sure? I have this appalling foreboding and I can't shake it off. I sense a change in you.'

'Forget it, Kate. It's nothing. I'm just a bit low after the death of Aunt Lil and you've picked up on it. Nothing to do with you or us – OK?'

There was a long pause.

'OK, Johnny, OK. As long as you're sure. When will I see you?'

'Are you going to the removal tonight?'

'Joan has asked me to ride with her to the church. Will I see you there?'

'I'll be there.'

*

I was dressing when the phone rang.

'Johnny? Tom Crotty.'

'Morning, Tom.'

'You figure out any connections yesterday when you were down home?'

'No, nothing really.'

'Goldsmith tells me he reckons your aunt's house was turned over professionally and then the place broken up to make it look like a regular amateur burglary. That's his theory for what it's worth. What would you make of that?'

'Sounds like someone looking for something specific.'

'That's what he thinks too. Now suppose, just suppose, your pal Brett left something with his aunt, to mind for him like, what would you think it could be?'

'Haven't a clue,' I said. 'Why ask me?'

'Because I can't help feeling that you're involved in all of this. I just keep running into you, Johnny – this stage it's gone beyond a joke. Goldsmith tells me you were down with the old lady last week. What was that all about?'

'I went to see her because I knew she'd be very upset and I wanted to make arrangements about bringing her up to Dublin for Brett's funeral.'

He was silent for a while.

I waited.

'You wouldn't have been picking up something, would you, Johnny?'

'No,' I said. 'I was there to sympathise and make arrangements.'

He paused for a longer while.

'You still there?' I asked.

'Yeah,' Crotty said, exhaling loudly. 'You think of anything interesting be sure to give me a ring, Johnny.'

I pulled the bed together, tidied my bedroom, had a run at smartening up the bathroom, cleared the kitchen of all traces of toast and coffee and decided enough was enough on the household chores for one day.

Magdalen had collected the paper and left it on the

kitchen table. There was a headline about bank overcharging and calls for a tribunal to look into reported irregularities. There were statements from the main banks claiming such mismanagement was impossible with the kind of internal checks they had in place. However, they assured the public, their self-regulatory machinery was in full swing to demonstrate all was as it should be.

As usual the Central Bank was prevented by its constitution from letting the world know what it was doing with the public's money. A spokesperson for them said it was perfectly normal in all European countries for Central Banks to keep that kind of thing to themselves so why should the Irish feel miffed if they were told to leave financial matters to their betters.

It was a small item, at the foot of the Business and Finance page. The Overseas Development Director of North East Baltic Bank, the influential Vilmos Lemptke, was in Dublin to represent the bank at the funeral of Paddy Brett. In an interview in his suite at the Hyperion Hotel, Mr Lemptke said all the right things about his departed colleague and confirmed he had no knowledge of any rumours circulating in financial circles about problems relating to illegal offshore accounts. North East Baltic was the cleanest whistle in town.

I dug out my directory of hotels in Ireland and Great Britain. The Hyperion Hotel was a member of the Knocklangan Hotel Group. They were keeping it in the family.

The doorbell bonged and I walked lightly to the door and peered out. Even through the distorting lens of the fisheye Candy Delamere looked gorgeous. Patrick Brett looked intense.

'Well, well,' I said, 'good morning to the pair of you. What a lovely surprise, Candy.'

'Morning, Johnny,' Patrick said, and gallantly handed in the fair one ahead of him.

Candy Delamere wore sweater and jeans as they were meant to be worn.

242

'What a fabulous place you have, Johnny,' Candy said, walking towards the window. 'Wow!' she said, exaggeratedly. 'Now that is what I call a view.'

'Sorry to burst in on you, Johnny,' Patrick said. 'I owe you this.'

He handed me a roll of notes and I put it in my pocket.

'Thanks, Patrick,' I said.

'No, thank you. It was very necessary.'

'Is all this yours?' Candy asked, wandering about, touching things. 'These are nice,' she said, and stood in front of a pair of Connemara watercolours by James Le Jeune.

'Yeah, it's all mine,' I said.

'We'll see you at St Lawrence's Church tonight?' Patrick asked.

'Yes, I'll be there.'

'That letter you gave me, the one from Dad,' Patrick said, wandering about, not looking at me. 'It didn't say anything that might tell who killed him.'

'Don't suppose he expected to die,' I said.

Patrick looked out at the river for a few moments before turning to me.

'He wrote that you would tell me, tell us, where there was a lot of money. At least that's how I interpret what he wrote. That true?'

I looked him in the eye. 'Yes,' I said. 'But I'm not going to talk about that just yet. Would you like some coffee?'

'No thanks,' he said, looking quarrelsome. 'Why can't you talk about it?'

'Because it could get you killed. It may have got your father killed.'

I wasn't expecting it and was surprised when he glanced quickly at Candy and she turned and walked back to the window and the view.

'That sounds a bit dramatic,' he said, smiling, and I had a feeling he wasn't taking me seriously because he knew something I didn't.

I tried a shot in the dark.

'Maybe if you told me what you and your father discussed before he died that Sunday night it might change my mind.'

Patrick grew pale. 'Who told you?'

'Your mother told me. She said you told her your father called while she was asleep. She was under the impression that after that he went up to Knocklangan Lodge for some reason. What did you and he talk about? Was there a specific reason for his visit?'

Candy turned from the view and dropped into a chair. She crossed her legs, folded her arms and looked straight at Patrick. I had never seen her so serious. She seemed to be waiting for him to discuss something she was tired of arguing about.

'Christ! You can't tell Mom anything anymore. Yes I spoke to him that Sunday night. He suddenly deigned to give us the benefit of his company, started one of his let's-be-pals-together bonding speeches. He did that when he was sober, you know. I preferred him pissed and insulting. At least then you knew where you stood with him. The other way you never knew what he was working round to – a load of patronising bullshit.'

'What did he talk about?'

'The usual – how he'd done his best to understand me, tried to be a good father. Then a load of cobblers about his own youth, how he'd had to work hard for things, climb the ladder of success with ten tons on his back – the usual shit I've heard a hundred times. He could go on all night with that kind of rubbish – often did. He said he had an important meeting that night. Said he might be going away for a while – which was a laugh considering that was the first time I'd seen him in four weeks.'

'Did he go up to Hartigan's?'

'Far as I know.'

'Did you see him later when you went up there?'

'Who said I was up there later? Christ! Who's telling you all these things?'

I turned to Candy. 'I understood from what you said that Julie had been with you that night. I assumed you went there.'

She could have murdered me. 'I never said we were up in Hartigan's.'

'You told him!' he snarled at her. 'Christ! What else did you tell him?'

She was furious but was not one to be subdued.

'OK, so I told him that you couldn't have had anything to do with your father's death, that the three of us – you and me and Julie – were making out. So what! It's a free country – no law against what we were doing.'

'Were you there when your father left?' I asked him.

'No,' he said. As he spoke he looked directly at Candy as though daring her to contradict him and I knew there was more.

'That what happened, Candy?' I asked.

'Yes,' she said, automatically, looking at him, ignoring me.

'And was your father alive and well when you left?'

I don't know what prompted me to ask the question, or to phrase it in that fashion, but from the way they both turned to stare I knew it was crucial.

Patrick spoke. 'Yes. My father was alive when we left.'

It seemed to me then he had been waiting for days for someone to ask that question, that he had been tormented by the need to give the right answer. Candy just stared and said nothing.

'That it? That all?' I asked, not knowing how to progress the inquiry.

'Yes,' he said. 'That's all I know.'

A key turned in the lock and Magdalen burst in and stood stock still when she saw my visitors. She looked fabulous in a white leather trouser suit and new hair-do.

'Hi,' she said, into the surprised silence, then closed the door.

Candy glanced at me and one eyebrow shot up as she grinned wickedly.

245

I made the introductions and Magdalen improved my celibate image no end by asking them if they'd like coffee and scones while casually tossing her handbag on the settee and slinging her jacket after it.

'We were just going,' Patrick said. He looked hard at me. 'See you this evening, Johnny.'

I saw them to the door.

Candy smiled at me. 'Have a nice day, Johnny,' she said, and winked.

'I know I have a black tie somewhere,' I shouted at Magdalen that evening, over the noise of Tom and Jerry. Sean believes in all-round sound when he watches cartoons. I was tearing drawers apart, throwing stuff in the air. 'It's all your fault,' I shouted, 'you and your mania for tidying.'

'I never saw a black tie,' Maggs said. 'Anyway, no one wears a black tie anymore except maybe immediate family – thing of the past. You have a nice grey tie in the wardrobe that will do fine. You going to be staying out all night again?'

'None of your damn business,' I said, but regretted my tone immediately. 'I probably won't get home.'

'You staying with your famous one-nighter again?'

'What's a one-nighter?' Sean asked – kid never misses the important bits.

'Now that is definitely none of your business,' I said to Magdalen.

'Something to take to bed when you're feeling scared,' I said to Sean.

'No need to get huffy,' Magdalen said. 'Just asking so's I'll know not to let anyone in.'

'I'll knock three long and two short,' I said.

'I know anything about men,' Maggs said, 'you'll knock once and be out like a light.'

Too early by ten minutes I stood at the back of St Lawrence's and to pass the time tried counting the congregation. The Irish adore funerals it always seems to me. That evening there was a fair scattering of elderly local people who, I felt, couldn't possibly have known Paddy Brett. Maybe they were practising or, at this late stage in their lives, hoping that if they went to enough funerals their own, in turn, might amount to something memorable.

Sizeable as their number was they were still lost in the vaulted space of the parish church. To someone of my generation it is incredible and heartwarming how the Catholic Church has lost its hold on the minds of the Irish people. One or the other has come of age – and for my money it is not the men in black. The clergy are on the run in more ways than one – and it's the women who've seen them off.

The attendance increased as it got closer to six. Serious suits began arriving. I recognised faces from television – captains of industry, members of the Dail, a well-known surgeon (Montego material), members of the Irish Management Institute, several famous rugby players (why, I couldn't figure).

Bill Grattan strode in, glancing about, but not seeing me. He was accompanied by a tall foreign-looking gent who cut a considerable dash in a long black overcoat. A swarthy handsome man, his strong hair was dyed the colour of his coat. He had the air of a man who wished others to take him as seriously as he took himself and I presumed him to be the one and only Vilmos Lemptke. Behind them came Heather Skeehan who did not miss me – she gave me so fleeting a smile I looked the other side of me to see if it had been meant for someone else.

Oliver Pettit came neatly in, walking with the precisely balanced steps of a fencer. He was accompanied by the receptionist I'd met at his office. Betty Halpin, looking neither left nor right, genuflected and knelt in the second last pew. I remained with my back to the wall.

The coffin was wheeled in and behind it came the Brett

family – Joan, pale but very erect and carrying herself with an old pride, flanked by her progeny, both of whom looked very handsome. Candy Delamere came behind them and proved it was possible for a Stradivarius to play second fiddle. Bringing up the rear behind the chief mourners were Kate Hartigan and Julie.

Kate searched about with her eyes and found me. She smiled eagerly, incongruously, and I grinned back with all the warmth I could muster.

A bell tinkled and an altar girl preceded good old Whiskey Mulhall to the rail to welcome the remains of Patrick Brett to Mother Church. Mulhall really had a voice that did not need amplification. In fairness to the man, he stole the show, ran away with it, and for once Paddy Brett had to be content with second billing.

As the sonorous voice rolled out to me over the heads of the congregation I became absorbed in a contemplation of Paddy Brett's last hours. Somehow that slid into thoughts of Kate Hartigan and, most inappropriately, a sensual reverie of her naked beauty. So wrapt was I that I never felt her approach and my first inkling of her presence next to me was her whisper.

'You never change – always the back of the church.'

I turned and there was Margaret Hourican, Sister Camilla, smiling her fabulous smile. She wore a navy suit that on her was sensational, showed how truly magnificent a forty-something woman can look.

Why couldn't she have grown old like the rest of us, developed lines on that lovely face, become less gut-tearingly desirable? It wasn't fair. There should be some compensation of nature dictating that a woman who dumps a guy for God must develop bad breath or something, anything at all that would be a slight consolation. She should not become calmer, more radiantly lovely, offer a man blinding flashes of the youth and beauty they had shared. I spoke without thinking, straight from my centre.

'You're as desirable as the day I met you, Margo. If you

were to say now, this very minute, come with me, I'd follow wherever you led.'

I meant every word of it without any attempt at flattery, or of being in any way provocative. It surprised me almost as much as it took her aback.

Her lips parted on a sharp inhalation and a shadow washed across her face. Her eyes grew large and I was aware of an emotional intensity in her that brought her hands up as though warding off some threat. But then strength flowed back into that beautiful face and she breathed deeply, smiled gently.

'In God's house, Johnny,' she said, lightly reproving.

'He never loved you like I do.'

It was out before I could stop it.

She turned away, went and knelt behind Betty Halpin. Suddenly my emotional world was topsy-turvy and I walked out to wait in the open air.

Later, outside the church, while the Brett family were still in the front pew receiving the condolences of the congregation, I found myself with three women. I introduced them to each other, found it strange to be the connecting link.

'It was a nice service,' Betty Halpin said, and I was glad for her sake that the light wasn't good and what remained of her bruising beneath her heavy make-up was hardly noticeable.

'I'd never have thought Paddy would want to be cremated,' Kate said. She turned to Margo Hourican. 'I thought cremation wasn't allowed by the Church.'

'There isn't an objection as far as I know. I think there used to be but, like a lot of things, it's gone now. They burned enough women as witches in their time, that's for sure,' Margo said, and surprised both women listeners.

'Cremation's awful,' Betty Halpin said, and shivered. 'There's no place to visit.'

'How did you get here?' I asked the three of them.

Kate had travelled with Joan and Patrick, Betty had come

by taxi, and Margo had been taken by a visitor to the hospital who lived near the church.

They piled into my car, Margo refusing Kate's proffering of the front seat in favour of sitting behind with Betty. On the way Kate continued to probe Margo, fascinated by her casual rejection of all the stereotypical ideas on religion Kate felt Margo should have. I saw Betty to her door.

'So that's the famous Kate Hartigan,' she said on her doorstep. 'You sleeping with her, Johnny?' I never expected Betty Halpin to ask so blunt a question.

'Yes,' I said.

Betty nodded. 'I hope you're happy,' she said. 'Hope it keeps fine for you. Watch out for that bastard of a husband, Johnny, he'll try to kill you.'

The door clicked shut and I could feel the awful loneliness of her half-million pound house close around her.

At St Malachy's Hospital I walked Margaret Hourican to the door.

'I like your Kate,' she said. 'She likes you. I hope it works out.'

'I don't take back a word,' I said, and wished that kissing nuns goodnight was accepted practice after removals.

'I'll see you tomorrow, Johnny.'

'Like me to call for you? Wouldn't be any bother.'

'No thanks. I'll manage,' she said, and slipped away from me into the antiseptic isolation of the hospital.

I drove in silence until we were almost in Dalkey.

'Why did you break up?' Kate asked, shattering my train of thought, confusing me.

'How do you mean?'

'How do you think I mean? Jesus, the pair of you standing outside the hospital! I mean, Johnny, even a hardened creature like me recognises it when she sees it. Must have been a very hot number while it lasted – or is it still on the boil?'

'It was over twenty years ago. We were only kids.'

'Will you look at the man's face!' Kate said, scornfully.

'We were only kids,' she mimicked. 'It's all over your face, Constantine, but I must admit I like that. You must have been crazy about her so it was she who packed it in.'

'It was a long time ago,' I said.

'I can see I'm going to have to keep an eye on you,' Kate said, drawing closer. 'Do to you what that nun should have done.'

Later, in bed, making it for the second time, Kate drew back from me, swayed her breasts across my chest, worked her hips against me.

'That nun ever kicks the habit I'll kill her,' she panted.

I could not be sure which woman I made love to that night.


I left Kate Hartigan's warm bed the following morning in dawn's pale light. The house was very quiet. I let myself out with a minimum of noise. At six forty I rang my own doorbell – anything was better than getting shot.

Magdalen was in hip-length night attire and very fetching.

'Don't you have anything more revealing than that?' I asked sarcastically.

'Next is skin,' she said, walking ahead of me, hiking up her nightie to prove it.

'Any calls?' I asked, heading for the bedroom.

'Undertaker, guy called Cronin. Said to tell you the funeral of your aunt is all set for tomorrow after ten o'clock Mass in St Patrick's. Removal there tonight arriving six thirty. End of message, sir.' Maggs saluted, the raising of her arm uncovering her attractive bush.

'For God's sake, Maggs,' I said, 'put something on.'

I shaved and showered. Maggs stuck her head around the door while I was dressing to let me know she was popping downstairs to see to her accountant – breathe life into him before he got too tied up in his *Financial Times*.

I decided to have another couple of hours' sleep and went back to bed.

The smell of bacon grilling, coffee perking, woke me and I joined Magdalen and Sean in the kitchen. Sean was working his way through a bowl of mixed cereal – he was collecting the toys from two different types. He broke off long enough to throw 'Hello, Johnny' in my direction. I nodded, man-to-man stuff – it's what he likes.

'How's the love life going?' Maggs asked, setting down my breakfast.

'You're incurably romantic for a lady who leads a confused existence.'

'What's a confused existence?' Sean asked.

'It's what your mother leads,' I said.

'Your future I'm interested in,' Magdalen said. 'Like to see you settled before I die. Nice removal last night, was it? At least you don't look as though you were drinking.'

'Very quiet,' I said. 'I drove a nun home before going to bed.'

'That must have been a new experience for you.'

'Not as new as you'd think.'


I wore my charcoal pinstripe just to let people know I could be as bourgeois as the next guy. I was stuck with the same grey tie.

The church was full and that made me wonder until I heard someone say it was a holy day of obligation. That explained why every pensioner within a radius of two miles seemed to be there.

Whisky Mulhall was in his element playing to a full house. He even chanted and I wondered why U2 hadn't snapped him up long ago. I was a bit suspicious of the Offertory, wondered what his charming acolyte slipped him. His voice really soared after the Communion.

Bill Grattan said a few words; Paddy Brett was born in a log cabin and was cut down in his prime before he could reach the White House – something along those lines. He actually made a half-assed comparison with JFK – something which got people looking askance.

252

Everyone I expected to be there was there – even a few old faces from Tinmen's Lane which I thought was nice and damned decent of them to travel all that way for a man who'd left the old neighbourhood so long ago.

Margaret Hourican did not look in my direction.

Kate came with the Bretts and gave me a smile on the way in as she followed them to the top of the church.

Betty Halpin looked my way and smiled her wan smile.

I wondered where I'd seen the big handsome man before when he pushed through the side door and leaned against the brick wall the other side of the aisle to me. It was the absence of a spade that threw me, that and the coarse suit that looked as though it had been pressed under a mattress. The kind of suit inmates of mental hospitals were forced to wear before they were evicted from their institutions and thrown into the community.

Steady Eddie Delaney was a good-looking man when he was all cleaned up and the four-button suit made him look broader, leaner, hard as a board. There was something of the old black-and-white cinema gunslinger-come-to-town about him. He looked coldly at me and made no effort to acknowledge my nod. I felt like stepping out and slapping leather just to see if he had a sense of humour.

Whiskey Mulhall gave me a pious smirk as he preceded the coffin out to the hearse. Tight-lipped and dry-eyed, Paddy Brett's family brought up the rear. As usual Candy Delamere was stunningly erotic in the purest way and smiled angelically at me as she brushed past trailing a scent as fresh as new-mown hay.

In the crowd outside I came up behind Margaret Hourican.

'Morning, Margo,' I said, smiling.

She turned slowly and smiled, her gaze level, her face calm.

'Morning, Johnny. At least Paddy got a good day for it.'

'He was always lucky,' I said, for something to say, knowing then that whatever had happened between us the night before would not be repeated – Sister Camilla was firmly in charge. I was polite for form's sake.

'Can I give you a lift to Glasnevin?'

'No thanks, I've got to get back to the hospital. One of the nurses drove me here and she's waiting for me.'

'Aunt Lil is going to the church tonight down home.'

'I saw it in the paper,' she said. 'I'd love to go but I can't. I'll pray for her.'

'Do,' I said, 'she'd like that. Last time I was with her she asked all about you.'

'I hope you gave a good report of me.'

It was a small chink, the barest trace of light.

'Oh, I did. I told her you hadn't changed, that you were as beautiful as ever.'

She held out her hand. 'Goodbye, Johnny. Look after Kate, she seems very nice.'

And that was it. Sister Camilla left me to join the line that was waiting to kiss Joan Callaghan.

I looked around the crowd in front of the church. The famous were talking to each other with wary heartiness. I caught Bill Grattan watching me and acknowledged his embarrassed smile. Vilmos Lemptke was keeping a beady eye on me from the other side of the hearse and immediately focused his attention and conversation on some dignitary when I caught him at it.

I saw Della Coady, head held high, force her way close to the hearse to speak to Patricia. She kissed her before turning to shake Patrick's hand. Her point made, she stepped back with a defiant toss of her head.

'You're a hard man to catch up with, Mr Constantine,' he said at my shoulder.

I turned to look at the handsome light-heavyweight who had followed me in the Porsche on my first visit to Aunt Lil.

'You have the advantage of me,' I said, smiling as easily as I could.

'Oh, I have that right enough,' he said, and I detected a

Northern accent. 'But you know me by now all the same. Name's Carmody and I've been ringing you. My boss, Mr McRoarty, would love to have a wee word with you. At your convenience, of course – we'd hate to put you out now, upset you unnecessarily like.' He had a horrible smile.

To my left I saw Kate Hartigan watching me, her face drawn and pale. Beyond her, leaning against the railings, in a pool of space as though no one wanted to be near him, Dutch Gaffney stared at me with that flat, baleful look of his. I had the feeling of being surrounded and it was far from pleasant.

'I'm afraid I'm fairly occupied at present, Mr Carmody. Immediately after this I have to go to my home town to another funeral. A dear friend, Miss Elizabeth Meagher, aunt of the man in the coffin over there. You might know of her. She was murdered last Saturday night.' I said it coldly, turning to him fully. The crowd kept us closer than would be normal for two strangers and I could feel his breath on my face.

'Say again,' he said, his eyes narrowing.

'I think you heard me the first time,' I said. 'Maybe you might ask Mr Gaffney over there about it – he should have all the details if you're interested.'

He looked about quickly, found Gaffney and stared at him. Gaffney levered himself away from the railings, took his hands from his pockets and glowered at us.

Carmody looked at me. 'When will you be back in town?'

'Thursday, probably,' I said. 'But I'm pretty busy even then.'

'It wouldn't take long,' he said. 'Just a few points to be cleared up – a few key issues, as I'm sure you know.'

'Ring me,' I said, as nonchalantly as I could.

'Oh, I will, I will,' Carmody said. 'But matters are coming to a head, Mr Constantine, and they won't wait. I'll ring you Thursday.'

He moved away and later I saw him squared off and talking to Dutch Gaffney – they did not look as though they were planning a holiday together.

'Are you OK?' Kate said, slipping in next to me. 'There are an awful lot of not very nice people around here. I'm not going to the crematorium. I won't see you now until tomorrow night, right?'

'The lunch after the funeral tomorrow is organised for twelve thirty. I should be back by six at the latest.'

'Will you ring me tonight?'

'Yes.'

'I saw you talking to your nun. You sure you're a free man?'

I looked her in the eye, answered honestly. 'I think so.'

She pressed against me in the crush of people and squeezed me gently before moving away. She didn't look back.


'I thought there would be a great belch of flames when the little doors opened for the coffin to roll through,' Candy Delamere said, as we drove through Drumcondra.

In the blue Opel in front Patricia drove her mother and Patrick. Candy had opted to keep me company, but I think it had more to do with a temporary coolness between herself and Patrick. She stuck out her tongue at him every time he looked back. Whatever it was, it was not a serious rift.

Few stayed with the funeral to the bitter end. At the crematorium they were politely efficient but, like everyone else, they had to keep to schedule and there could be no hanging around. The actual cremation could not be carried out for another four days due to pressure of business.

After such a disconcerting start to the day I found Candy's company exhilarating, like being twenty-one again. Her perfume filled the car.

'You're thinking of hell,' I said.

'No such place,' she said, then added as an afterthought,

'except for some people. Why does a man with your kind of money drive a Xedos?'

'It's as much car as I need.'

'If it was me I'd have . . . '

'A Porsche,' I finished for her.

'A Volvo big enough to put a wardrobe in,' she said, laughing at me.

'Was Paddy Brett really OK when you left Knocklangan Lodge that Sunday night?'

Candy spun sideways, faced me from the corner of her seat.

'You're real mean,' she said, 'always asking sneaky questions. Why can't you leave it alone?'

'Because there are all sorts of pressures building up and there's a danger for people if we can't discover what really happened. Besides, Paddy Brett was once my great friend.'

'We didn't think he was all that great,' Candy said, after a while of staring out the window her side.

'Who's we?'

'Us girls,' Candy said. She paused for a bit before continuing, rushing into it as though she had been waiting a long time for the right audience. 'He was a dirty old man if you really want to know. He had a thing about girls of four-teen, fifteen – it was awful, nasty. Then when Patrick and I started our thing he thought I was easy meat. I haven't told Patrick a tenth of the times his father tried it on with me.' She was getting angrier. 'Seven weeks ago he was at it again. From what he said I knew he must have been spying on us – me and Patrick and Julie. I was glad when I saw the bastard stretched out that night.'

She knew immediately that temper had made her say too much and she rushed to cover it, draw away from it.

'Your great pal was not a nice man, Johnny, I'm sorry to tell you. Not nice like you. Mind you, that's relative.' She grinned wickedly. 'Julie is pissed off with you since you started sleeping with Kate. But I've told her you're not like Patrick's dad and she needn't worry about you coming after her like he did. He really went after her, you know, it was terribly embarrassing. Used to wait in his car down the road from the school. Everyone had it copped. Patrick gave out shit to him over it, had a huge row with him. Your old buddy could be very nasty, Johnny.'

Candy paused for breath, waited to see if she'd succeeded in distracting me. I decided not to press home on her 'stretched out' comment – there was no point in antagonising her.

'You amaze me,' I said.

'The letter he left Patrick was sad. Anyone would think he was the poor misunderstood father instead of the sharp accountant with a drink problem and a tendency toward paedophilia.' Candy spoke scornfully, rapidly, like someone who'd been practising her speech for a long while. 'Course Patrick only saw the drink problem, refused to get his mind around the deeper one. Yuk!'

'Did Patricia know about this fondness for young girls?'

'Let's get one thing straight, Johnny, there was no fondness in the way he went after girls. Sure Patricia knew, had to know – she never confided in me, she's much too old – but her father must have gone after her girlfriends, he'd have to, it was his nature. Patrick tells me he was always rowing with her. Wouldn't surprise me if he tried his own daughter. When she took the job in Julie's father's club, Patrick said his father told him his sister had become a prostitute.'

Candy laughed. 'Fair play to Patricia! Patrick told me she used to tell her father she could make two hundred pounds a night on her back and didn't need his money. She could really wind him up. Mind you, in the end of the day, I think she really loved him more than Patrick did.'

'Would you be upset if I asked you to leave us when we get back to the house? I want to talk to the family.'

Her eyes saucered and she grinned excitedly. 'You're going to do the reading of the will bit? I'd love to be a fly on the wall for that. I'll go home – matter of fact you can drop me on the way. Is Patrick going to be rich?' She giggled, clapped her hands. 'I might get my Volvo.'

'I'm sure he'll tell you all about it. I feel duty bound to talk to them privately – I hope you don't mind, I'd hate to upset you.'

'You know I believe you would,' she said, 'and that's what makes you such a nice guy.'

Outside her gate she leaned across and kissed my cheek. It felt wonderful.

'Have a lovely last-will-and-testament morning. Give Patrick bricks of money. By the way, I think you and Kate were made for each other.'

She jumped from the car, winked, waved and was gone.

'Let's all have a drink,' Patrick Brett said, and went off to get them after I'd relayed Candy's apologies and explained that she would be along later.

Joan tossed her coat on to the table and sank with a sigh into her favourite chair. Patricia picked up the coat absently and wandered out with it.

'Well, that's that, Johnny,' Joan said, despairingly, close to tears. 'I never expected they wouldn't do the cremation for days. I can't stop thinking of him lying in the coffin up there.'

She paused, wiped her eyes. 'Quarter of a century! Seems it's only yesterday we were swimming in the Ownaglas. Remember, Johnny? Maybe I'll throw his ashes in there when I get them.'

'You could do worse,' I said.

Memories jostled each other in that room and I was uncomfortably aware of all the young years I'd shared with this woman.

I was uneasy. Perhaps my emotions had been unhinged by the meeting with Sister Camilla the previous night – the reappraisal of how deeply she had impinged on my life that had come when I was suddenly confronted with her mature beauty.

Joan rambled on, staring ahead into the past.

'We really came a long way, didn't we? Funny the way life speeds up – everything seems to get faster as you grow older. You looked well talking to Margaret Hourican last night. Pity you two never made a go of it. You should never have driven her into that convent.'

'Pardon?' I was astonished by her remark.

'You should have married her – it would have been good for both of you.'

Amazing the way people jump to conclusions. As Magdalen says, presumption is the mother of all fuck-ups.

Joan sighed, looked at me. 'I hope your news is as good as you indicated, Johnny.' She looked about. 'I really would like to do something with this place.'

Patrick came back with a tray of drinks and for once did not grudgingly hand one to his mother, even managed to smile with some tenderness as he gave it to her. He set Patricia's on a coaster at the head of the table. He had a whiskey for me and a beer for himself. I hoped he was taking it easy, especially now that he was about to become rich.

Patricia returned, the epitome of the ice maiden, her face composed, ready to repulse boarders.

'You going to tell us where we stand, Johnny, or maybe you don't think we're old enough yet to know what our father left us?' She looked scornfully at me over the rim of her glass.

'Please, Patricia,' Joan said, 'Johnny is only trying to be helpful.'

'Oh, I think you're old enough,' I said, 'your father certainly did. Each of you is a millionaire several times over.'

What is it about that magic figure one million? Thanks to the National Lottery it has become the unit of currency in the world of prizes. No one wants to win less.

It got them. Patricia and Patrick shot up straight in their chairs, mouths open. Joan looked confused.

'Bloody hell!' Patrick said. 'You sure, you absolutely certain?'

'You know where this is and how to get it?' Patricia asked, doing her best to appear calm, as though a guy dropped by every other afternoon with millions.

'I know exactly where it is and I have all the authorisations I need to get it. There are strings attached – you can't just take it and start spending. It's in offshore accounts and you'd be wide open to the taxman – and maybe other interested parties – if you were to bring it back suddenly, be seen to have loads of dosh. You're going to have to operate carefully and not draw attention to yourselves. There may be another tax amnesty sometime in the future and you might consider at that stage that it's worth losing some to tax to get it back into the country to use openly – but that would depend on how you got around explaining where it came from to begin with.

'There are powerful people involved who may have killed Paddy and who may feel they have some rights to this money. We are going to have to be careful for a while yet. In the meantime, I have some suggestions for you.'

# Chapter Twelve

Around three in the afternoon I hit the road for my home town. Patricia helped her mother pack a few overnight things when Joan insisted on coming with me. It was the last thing I wanted, but could not refuse to take her to Aunt Lil's funeral.

The weather held and the sky to the south was clear. While I'd been explaining the ramifications of the Irish tax system and how it applied to Dublin's newest million-aires, Joan had worked her way through three vodkas and, as a result, was cruising as smoothly as my Mazda. I don't think she was aware how wealthy she was, it hadn't got through to her yet. She was just happy that she could stop worrying about how she was going to get by. Besides, it wasn't just Dublin she was leaving behind her as we drove south.

'I'm really looking forward to doing something with the house,' she said, easing back in her seat. 'God, how tired I was of trying to get Paddy to do something. He could get so nasty about it.'

'Well, that's all in the past now,' I said, too quickly.

'I won't go on about it, Johnny. You must be tired of listening to me.'

'Not at all,' I lied, and launched into an extended version of my tax advice. That achieved the desired result and soon she was asleep. Patricia had told me Joan had taken anti-depressants that morning which made for a pretty heavy mix when vodka was added.

While I rambled on about taxation I kept an eye on my mirror and noted that a blue Mondeo was staying with me but too far back to make out the driver. I accelerated and slowed in a random pattern just to make sure I wasn't imagining his intentions. He held on to his end of the elastic.

Joan woke on the outskirts of Carlow, her biological clock telling her she needed a Russian interlude. I pulled into the first hostelry we came to and watched the Mondeo cruise past with Hocks Mackey at the wheel.

'You know,' Joan said, moving in the direction of the Ladies, 'I think I'll change my mind and have a vodka and tonic instead of tea.'

Twenty Smirnoff minutes later we were on our way and the Mondeo fell in behind as we cleared Carlow. It stayed with me all the way to the hotel I'd booked us into. We signed in, dropped off our things and went straight to the church after Joan had overdone it with her make-up.

It was a Tinmen's Lane affair. They were all there and very few young people amongst the mourners – which was a pity, because Lil Meagher loved young people, always had great time for them. Outside the church, after the brief evening service, Joan and I were the centre of interest to all the neighbours we hadn't seen in twenty years. I enjoyed it and I was happy to be there.

Dinner with Joan was miserable, on top of which the food was overcooked and poorly served. Joan drank too much and became maudlin. Odd looks were cast in my direction when I escorted her to her room. She seemed capable of looking after herself so I accepted a sloppy peck on the cheek that slid around to my mouth. I was glad to cross the hall to my own room.

'I'm in bed,' I said, when she picked up the phone. 'What are you doing?'

'I've got this big – seriously big – black dude in bed with me,' Kate said. 'New service they have here in the capital.

Deal is, he cleans the house from top to bottom, every nook and cranny, does the lot and stays until you're totally satisfied. Firm called Surrogates – quite reasonable too. Bed and board while he's here and a fiver for himself when he comes.'

'What are you eating?'

'You don't want to know. Joan behaving herself? Not there next to you I hope! How'd the removal go?'

'Willy Cronin does a good job. All the neighbours were there. Even the detective on the case turned up. Lot of people attended out of a sense of outrage at the way she died. Loads of flowers – more than Paddy Brett got. I was astounded at the number of people who came up to me to sympathise. I was pleased at the way they took me for a relative. It was really nice and I was glad for Aunt Lil's sake. Is it true what they say about black men?'

'Every word,' Kate said. 'A yard if it's an inch.'

'Have fun,' I said. 'See you tomorrow night.'

'If I'm not too exhausted.'

We buried Lil Meagher on the side of a hill in driving rain. At the graveside a small altar boy had to be restrained when the umbrella he seemed to be trying to blind the old priest with threatened to tumble him into the hole. Heavy and impermeable, the dark brown clay turned to sleech in the downpour. The coffin made an ugly sucking sound as they finished lowering it. A quavering decade of the rosary was torn away on the wind and shredded in a hedge of hawthorn. In the end most were glad to slither and slide down to the cars.

I'd invited everyone back to the hotel for a last meal in honour of Lil Meagher. I was pleased when most of Tinmen's Lane showed up, wandering in shyly, not wishing to be thought forward or grasping, but not ready yet to part forever with the ghost of Lil. It was a lovely, sad affair and I was glad I'd done it. We all had our stories and tales of her goodness and two old men got a bit carried away and, for the first time in their lives, made halting speeches, spoke from the heart of the many neighbourly kindnesses of the woman who'd left us.

Joan was quiet for most of it and worked her way steadily through the best part of a bottle of wine. I didn't try to stop her – it suited me for her to sleep all the way to Dublin.

Hocks Mackey was in the bar when I went in search of the manager to settle the account.

He leaned on the counter, an empty shot glass and a half-full pint of Guinness in front of him. A brown, tide line of stout marked his upper lip. It was nearly two in the afternoon and we had the bar to ourselves.

'Nice funeral?' he sneered. 'She was a game old bird for her age.'

He drank from his glass, looking smugly over it.

I turned and left the bar. I heard him laugh softly behind me.

I found the manager and paid.

I was trembling and I realised that for the first time in my life I actually wanted, deeply desired to take the life of another human being. But not Mackey, I thought. No, not Mackey. He was thick as two planks – he went where he was led, did what he was told. Dutch Gaffney was the one. Even Hartigan didn't want anyone killed – he had objectives he wanted achieved and would always prefer the easy way. But Gaffney liked his work, enjoyed it.

I collected Joan from her room and we left town. As we went through the level crossing at the marshalling yards I saw the Mondeo move up, shorten the distance between us. We cleared the town traffic and Mackey closed down even further. I had the feeling that something different was happening. He was no longer in tailing mode. There was something edgy and aggressive in his driving, the way he was crowding me, as though he had a purpose.

Traffic was light and we were still some distance from

265

the dual carriageway, but the road was broadening and we were heading into a stretch of straight wide road.

Joan had fallen asleep shortly after we'd cleared town and I looked to check her safety belt. She seemed secure enough.

Mackey closed up further until I could see the grin on his face. Then he was using a mobile phone and I knew something was happening. The road was clear and straight for nearly a mile ahead and I pushed the car to eighty. Mackey stayed with me, the phone to his ear.

If the driver of the container truck had not been wearing a white shirt I might have missed the relevance of his approach, not made the connection. It came round the bend far ahead and I saw from his white sleeve that he also had his hand to his ear and suddenly I knew for certain it was no coincidence as Mackey began to reel me in. The memory of what Paddy Brett had said about the assistant manager of North East Baltic Bank having been killed with his wife on the way home from the pictures came back to me and I sat up.

The truck came on and I could see the driver's grimace as he prepared himself. I was absolutely certain then of what they planned to do.

Mackey began his move, accelerated. He swung into the hard shoulder and it was clear he intended getting between me and the wall that was coming up, force me out into the path of the container truck that had begun an appreciable drift out of its lane.

I did not intend what happened. What I did I did out of self-preservation and mainly reflexively. I moved in towards the wall to block Mackey and simultaneously took my foot off the accelerator. His choices were to hit the wall, rear-end my car, or try to get out and around me in the space between me and the truck. He was much too close to brake.

He opted for passing outside me. I saw the pothole at the last moment and swerved out to avoid it and that sealed

266

Mackey's fate. He must have thought I was going to take him in the side and he moved out further. He seemed to lose control then, perhaps he panicked, and half his car met the truck head on. I heard the impact as I sailed through between the truck and the wall.

I accelerated. Ahead of me the road was clear. Behind me I could see smoke, heavy and black. The container truck was broadside to the road by then and I could not see if there was any traffic behind it. As I swept around the bend a car went by on the other side of the road. I drove on to Dublin, my hands trembling on the wheel. We were at the M50 before Joan Callaghan awoke.

'Oh, we're almost home,' she said, and flipped the visor to check herself in the mirror.

Rain had not yet reached Dublin as we drove into Windward. Dark clouds hung over Bray and it looked as though the evening could be wet. It was barely after five.

Joan was out of the car as soon as I stopped and was working her key in the door before I'd begun opening the boot for her luggage. It was very still within the circle of trees that surrounded the forecourt. So still I heard the small creaking the rope made. I turned in the direction of the sound and saw her. I strolled across to her.

Who had climbed so high into the tree to fix the children's swing? I felt a surge of pity and hoped it had been Paddy – he'd always loved to climb, was always the most adventurous. He was the one who would go out until the branch broke and dropped him laughing into the Ownaglas.

It was an old horse chestnut and memory flooded me with remembered smells, the sticky feel of spiky burs as they split to disgorge mahogany pearls, and I could hear Paddy roar as he shook the branches to shower us with conkers.

She watched me through sullen, lowered lashes, twirling slightly, one foot on the ground, thin arms raised to the frayed ropes. Slim as she was, Julie Hartigan was almost jammed into the grained wood of the weathered seat.

'Not a great day for a swing,' I said. 'Like a push?'

'No thanks,' she said, not looking at me, continuing her semi-swirl.

We were silent for a minute or two and it got to her. She inclined her head and looked at me in a combative way.

'Am I that bad?' I had to ask.

'All adults are bad,' she said.

'That why you can't wait to be one?'

'I hope I don't turn out the way the ones I know have.'

I passed on that. I strolled in a tight circle, mainly to check if we were unobserved from the house and was glad to see we were well hidden by the shrubbery.

'You saw him too, didn't you?'

Her head came up fast and she twirled to face me.

'Who? Saw who?'

'Paddy Brett.'

'Mr Peeping Tom? Mr Whispers? Mr Pishwishwishwish? Paddy the perv?' Her face grew angry. 'Oh, yeah! I saw too much of the bastard – him and his roving hands and his hot breath.'

'No,' I said, not letting her distract me. 'I mean you saw him the night he died.'

'Who says I did?'

'Everybody knows.'

'Who the fuck is everybody?' She was really angry now.

'You know I think fuck is losing its impact – if your generation keeps on using it as you do it will be dead in no time.'

'Then we'll think of some other fucking word, won't we! Who's been talking to you?'

She stared belligerently at me, dared me to speak. I didn't betray anyone's confidence, didn't mention Candy Delamere's reference to seeing Paddy stretched out. All I did was raise a who-do-you-think eyebrow and let presumption kick in. But she jumped to a conclusion I was not expecting.

'I don't believe this,' she said, very still, no longer swivelling. 'My own mother! Christ, what that woman will do for a fuck! She told you! Jesus Christ, she told you. Well it wasn't Patrick. It happened before he arrived – we didn't even tell him. Me and Candy took Patrick away and he didn't know until the following morning.'

'Where did you go?'

'We came here and partied until all hours. Mrs Brett was out like a light – she'd miscounted her tablets again.'

'Why are you protecting Patrick?'

'Because he didn't do it. I was there. His father was dead before Patrick arrived. He never even saw him. Candy and I kept him at the front of the house. Patrick is brilliant, sensitive. He's going to do something great with his life. He can't take shocks like that.'

'You're sweet on him, aren't you?'

'No, I'm not sweet on him. Jesus, where did you learn to say things like that? We fuck, we talk, we have a serious relationship. Is there something wrong with that?'

'Not a thing,' I said. 'Just makes me wonder. How does Candy fit into this serious relationship?'

'Typical bourgeois reaction,' she snorted, disgustedly. 'She's his numero uno, but she knows about us. We're open about these things. We do it together. So fucking what!'

'Like you say, so fucking what. Who else was there that night?'

'She was.'

'Your mother?'

'Yeah, her.'

'Who else?'

'No one else. But he was killed in the garden. He did it – or he fucking arranged it.'

'Who?'

. 'Her husband – Hartigan.'

'Your father!'

'He's not my father – he's just her husband.' She began a semi-rotation, switching back and forth in a semicircle. 'You going to tell the police?'

'Don't really know. I don't think so – what the hell, it's hardly my business, don't see the point in causing trouble.'

That surprised her, merited her looking me straight in the eye.

'Just as a matter of interest,' I said, then added sarcastically, 'and please be brutally honest if you think it's none of my business. Where does your young man Trevor fit in all of these serious relationships?'

She grinned, enjoyed that.

'Trevor has his uses. At thirty he can hardly believe his luck that he's making it with an eighteen-year-old. He's in permanent shock.' She laughed harshly. 'Poor guy, I can lead him around by the dick.'

I considered her judgement. Were we like that at her age? I couldn't remember. We certainly wouldn't have said it like that, but we probably thought it.

'Got to go,' I said, moving away. 'Might see you later.'

'She's making dinner for you. Trev and I are invited as well. Should make for an interesting evening.'

She smiled smugly then and I knew she had something up her sleeve. I had the feeling it wasn't going to be nice.

I had taken three steps when there was the sudden roar of a motor, a mechanical snarl close at hand. I whirled to my left and saw Steady Eddie Delaney, arms above his head, apply a chain saw to the branch of a tree. I hadn't seen him or heard him move during my conversation with Julie Hartigan.

He did not look in my direction. I watched him until the branch sagged away from the trunk and came down slowly, tearing a way through the overgrown shrubbery. The crown of his hat was full of sawdust. He turned slowly to look at me. I nodded but he only stared. I waved my hand in a forget-it gesture – I was tired of theatricals.

I collected Joan's overnight bag from the car and Patrick answered the door.

'Didn't know the last of the Mohicans worked here as well as at Hartigan's,' I said, by way of greeting.

'Who . . . ? Oh, you mean Eddie. He used to work here regularly until Dad decided it was costing too much.' He waved me in, but I shook my head, handed him the bag. 'That was before Dad lost interest in everything to do with us and the place,' he went on. 'Dad was actually trying to get at me when he stopped employing Eddie. He reckoned I should be the gardener, should earn my keep. He couldn't understand it when I told him I never asked to have a garden in the first place. Will you not come in?'

'Got to be going,' I said. 'I'll talk to you again in a few days. If you have any problems, ring me. Remember what I said about not telling people the true state of play.'

'Sure, Johnny,' he said. 'I'll keep in touch.'


'Now that was worth waiting for,' I said, easing her away so that I could look at her.

'You miss me?' Kate asked.

'Utterly. Your pal from Surrogates gone?'

'Packed it in at three o'clock this morning. Couldn't stand the pace. Told him my regular man was good for five rounds and he couldn't hack it.'

'What's cooking?' I asked, disengaging. 'Smells wonderful.'

'Typical man,' she said, taking the lid off the dish. 'Didn't know when to expect you so I made braised steak. If you don't start keeping regular hours you're going to think all I can cook is stew. I've invited Julie and Trevor. I should say Julie has invited Trevor. I had hoped to have fed them before you arrived, have you all to myself. What matter!'

'I know,' I said. 'I met Julie at Windward.'

I sat at the kitchen table set for four and sipped the Jameson Kate put in front of me. I rose and turned on the television.

'You mind if we watch *News at Six*?' I asked.

'No. What's a woman to do if her man won't talk to her?'

271

Once again the news showed tireless barristers girding up their loins for the latest Tribunal of Inquiry – shot after shot of briefcase-carrying suits in search of that yellow brick road, the fabled money trail. They all looked tanned from the Cayman Islands. I concealed the shock of recognition when I saw power-suited Bassano Woman purposefully crossing the cobbled courtyard of Dublin Castle loaded down like a prospector's burro.

For the umpteenth time the inquiry had been halted as the legal fraternity agreed to split hairs, play semantic tennis, in an all-out effort to extend the search and the fee income by delaying the proceedings. Someone threatened to take the whole shebang to Brussels.

'That is brilliance,' I told Kate. 'Can't you just see it? Insist on making the case in the first official language! That way you need English-, French- and Irish-speaking barristers. At a stroke you can treble the fees.'

An intrepid reporter braved the wrath of the Incorporated Law Society to expose the shoddy treatment meted out to its members. He barely concealed his glee as he pointed up how they were forced to work for two thousand pounds a day and have their practices ruined by becoming typecast as specialists of the extended quest, being dragged screaming into becoming millionaires before their time.

'You know,' I told Kate, 'the Law has to be the best gig in Ireland, *Riverdance* notwithstanding.'

It was a small item. An accident on the road south of Carlow that had caused a massive tailback of traffic. Diversions were in operation and motorists were advised to take alternate routes. There were pictures of the container truck slewed across the road, the barely recognisable Mondeo.

The driver of the car was dead. The truck driver was in hospital in Kilkenny and was stated to be comfortable. Names were not being released until next of kin had been informed. Kate was in time to see the pictures of the vehicles.

'Oh, my God!' she said, and sat down slowly. 'No wonder the driver is dead.'

'Yeah,' I said, and left it at that as I heard the front door bang and the sound of footsteps in the hall.

Trevor seemed anxious at dinner. I put it down to his being closer in age to Kate than to Julie. The atmosphere was strained to say the least, but was helped to an extent by the decent bottle of wine he'd brought.

From the start it was plain that a row was brewing between mother and daughter – war clouds hung over a fine dinner. I thought Kate handled it well. She ignored all of Julie's obvious tiger traps, deflected most of her shafts and patiently refrained from reacting when one struck home. Nevertheless, it became tiresome and I hoped it would pass quickly.

It began in earnest over coffee. I had an inkling something was coming when the young people grew quiet, tense. Julie's cheeks were on fire and her hands trembled slightly.

Kate sensed it and rushed to fill a longish silence with talk of a Harvey Keitel film she wanted to see. I remember she was laughing when Julie cut across her.

'Who's my biological father?'

Kate set down her cup, looked carefully at her daughter.

'What on earth are you talking about?'

'You know, you know.' Julie was positively quivering.

'Course I do. Same as you do. What are you on about?'

'Tell her,' Julie hissed, turning to Trevor. 'Tell her what you've found out.'

Trevor looked like a man who wished he'd learned the Indian rope trick before coming to dinner. He glanced quickly at me and then at Julie.

'Don't mind him,' Julie said dismissively, nodding in my direction. 'Looks like he's going to be hanging around for some time so he may as well know.'

Kate was staring at Trevor.

'What is it that Johnny may as well know, Trevor?

What's Julie talking about? What have you found out? I wasn't aware that there was an investigation going on. Don't tell me tribunal fever is catching on in the private sector.'

It wasn't a bad attempt at a joke under the circumstances but it fell flat.

'Look, Mrs Hartigan . . .' Trevor began, but Kate cut across him.

'I don't know what this is about but whatever it is I'm sure there's no need to stop calling me Kate.'

'Kate, this is embarrassing . . .'

This time Julie cut across him. 'Tell her, tell her, for Christ's sake tell her.'

Trevor spoke in a rush, needing to get it said and out of the way.

'Julie asked me to carry out some comparative DNAs. One sample was Julie's, one was hair from a hairbrush and one was yours, Kate.'

Trevor became absorbed in his coffee, held it in front of his face with both hands, hid behind it. Kate was very pale.

'What's going on here?' she said finally. 'What do you mean comparative DNAs? Samples? How do you mean one was mine? I wasn't asked for any samples. What is this, Trevor?'

'Julie brought me some hair from your comb,' Trevor said. 'She told me the hairbrush belonged to her father.'

'He's not my father,' Julie said, livid, passionate. 'You said he couldn't be my father.'

'That's not exactly what I said, Julie.' Trevor said to her, in a rather schoolmasterly way. He turned to Kate and me. 'I want everyone to understand what I did,' he said.

He looked very uncomfortable, like a man who could think of a number of places he'd rather be. When he spoke he took refuge in the manner he probably used lecturing.

'The hairs from the brush were coarse and for the most part broken hairs. Only seven hairs had roots attached. I got a decent amount of DNA from them, but they were old.

274

I had plenty of your roots, Kate, and I had a cheek swab from Julie. I did a standard DNA fingerprint. The DNA fingerprint from the hairbrush does not match either of your profiles. I'd rather have a better sample – preferably blood – before stating categorically that your husband and Julie are not related.'

'So that's why you went on about the hairbrush,' Kate said, almost to herself. 'And all the time I thought it was for a different reason. Well, I can tell you now I don't know who was using it last, don't know if Walter even owned it.'

'You said it was his,' Julie shouted, on her feet now. 'I asked you and asked you – and every time you said it was his.'

'Julie, please!' Kate said, but her daughter was pacing the kitchen now, her fists held out.

'Don't try to fob me off this time,' she cried, still shouting, 'I want to know – I have a right to know. I'm not related to that scumbag you married. I refuse to be related to him. I don't accept it. You must tell me the truth. Who is my real father?'

'Your father is your father, Julie,' Kate said, and lost me as well as Julie. 'There isn't anything more to tell. There are no secrets, no skeletons in cupboards. I don't know whose hair was on that brush – and I'm genuinely not sure the brush was your father's. I said it was his because it seemed important to you that it should be. I thought you wanted it as a memento. I thought you were blaming me for the separation, regretted your father was no longer living with us. I'm sorry you feel so badly about it and I wish with all my heart it could be otherwise, but it's not and never will be. I can't change that. I'm afraid you're stuck with what you see.'

Kate looked at me then and I smiled supportively. Julie had begun to cry and Trevor looked as though he'd definitely decided to attend Indian-rope-trick classes.

'You're hiding it from me, treating me like a child,' Julie sobbed. 'I just know I'm not his daughter, I couldn't be.

Why won't you tell me? Can't you see I have a right to know?'

I felt sorry for Julie as she pleaded with her mother, sorry that she had such a lousy parent in murderous Walter Hartigan.

'I've told you all there is to tell,' Kate said, pale and trembling. 'I'm sorry, but you'll have to live with it same way I have to.'

Julie stared at her mother through leaking eyes for some time before turning to hapless Trevor.

'Let's go,' she said. 'I told you she wouldn't tell the truth.' She turned and left the kitchen.

Trevor rose, looked apologetic.

'That was a lovely dinner, Kate. Best food I've eaten all week. I'm sorry about this, but Julie insisted.'

'I don't know how things stand between you and Julie, Trevor, and I don't wish to interfere. Fact is it would probably be the worst thing I could do,' Kate said, her eyes cold and level. 'But I do take enormous exception to someone eating at my table while they're secretly studying my – for want of a better word – samples. That was rotten and I do not forgive you for it. Leave us now and say no more.'

Kate waved disgustedly in the general direction taken by Julie and Trevor left after a grimacing nod to me.

'That's what comes of having a geneticist for a boyfriend,' Kate said, wryly smiling. 'Christ! The sneaky little shit! When I think of it! And Julie – I never thought she felt that badly about Walter. I hope to Christ she didn't take up with Trevor just because she reckoned he could check out Walter.'

I stood up, began clearing dishes, and we heard the front door bang.

'Constantine,' Kate said, smiling wanly, 'one of these new men you are not. Sit down and talk to me. Drink your coffee, pour a couple of brandies. I really need one after that.'

I poured two brandies, served up the last of the coffee

276

and sat opposite. Kate smiled, reached across and pressed my hand.

'Kate,' I said, 'we need to talk.'

She groaned. 'Oh Christ! You're not going to say something awful, are you?'

I looked at her for some time, then went around the table and kissed her. I went back to my chair and took both her hands in mine.

'That discussion tonight,' I said. 'You have to tell me, it's very important. A matter of life and death – believe me. Had that anything to do with Paddy Brett being killed here that Sunday night?'

She opened her mouth to deny, but I reached up and gently put a hand over her lips.

'He died here. I know that, Kate. The police don't know it. Only a few people who were here know it. Now how did it happen? That's vital. That car crash you saw on the news tonight – I did that. The dead man is Hocks Mackey – he was trying to kill me. I think Walter sent him to kill me because he's panicking. He's terrified The Farmer, McRoarty, is going to find out what he's been up to. There's an awful lot more to this than you could know. Please tell me how it happened because if you don't I may not be so lucky the next time. And believe me there will be a next time unless I can stop it.'

Kate was staring at me.

'How did you find out?' she asked.

'Julie told him,' he said, behind me, and I felt the breeze from the open door to the garden porch.

I whirled about, rising as I turned.

He was freshly shaved and wore the yak-hair suit I'd seen him wear to church. Beneath it he wore an old fashioned collarless shirt with brass stud gleaming at the throat. He looked the vengeful preacherman from a hundred movies, Once again I was struck by his stature and calm good looks that were at odds with the wildness in his eyes. At that moment Steady Eddie Delaney looked anything but steady.

277

'You want to know what happened?' he asked me aggressively. 'I happened.'

'No, no, no, Eddie, don't do this,' Kate Hartigan sobbed, standing at the sink, holding on to it for dear life.

But Eddie was going to do it and I wished I knew what it was he was going to do. I took a step back as Eddie took one forward.

'Your kind,' he said, his voice a low growl. 'Money, that's all you are. Big fucking moneybags. Think the whole world was put there for you to wipe your feet in, stick your prick in. He was a bastard that Brett. Wanted the whole world. See him on television telling us all how to work for nothing so that the fucking economy would prosper. Celtic fucking Tiger! What he wanted was to fuck children. Wanted young Candy. Then wanted my daughter. That was the rock he perished on. I don't give a shit now. I'm finished but at least he'll never threaten another child. You can do your worst. Get the police, but keep away from my daughter.'

I knew then who Julie's father was and I looked at Kate.

'You can't do this, Eddie. Think of your own children, your wife,' Kate moaned.

'I don't care,' Eddie said again.

'That Sunday night, Eddie,' I said. 'You took Paddy Brett's wallet and some papers he had?'

Eddie Delaney frowned, looked hard at me, and Kate stopped sobbing.

'How did you know?'

'What did you do with the papers?'

'I buried them.'

'Could you please dig them up?'

'Why?'

'Do it, Eddie,' Kate said, facing him red-eyed.

He looked at her for several seconds then turned to me.

'Come on out and I'll show you where they are,' he said.

'No,' Kate cut across me harshly. 'Get them, Eddie.'

He swayed as though he would throw himself at me, but then he turned and left.

I poured another brandy, topped up Kate's.

I watched her sadly, waited for her to speak.

She lowered herself slowly on to her chair.

I waited.

When she spoke she addressed her drink.

'I told you Eddie's not the full shilling. He's always been a little gone in the head.' She looked at me then, her eyes full of despair. 'But when he was young he was so beautiful that you could tell yourself, you wanted to believe, that it was just youthful wildness – if you loved him, that is, and you were fifteen and you lived in a tiny place on the sea where the next parish to the west was in America.'

Kate shifted in her chair, looked at the cooker as though a jury sat there and it was beholden on her to explain herself. She sipped some brandy.

'My father was a hard man – unbelievably hard. He lived by the code of his generation. He had no time for women as far as I could ever make out. God alone knows why my mother married him. When I became pregnant I contemplated suicide. You see, there was no other way out in that place, in those days. Walter Hartigan saved me. He came on holiday and hired my father's boat to go fishing. They got drunk together, Walter and my father, and that was how he found out about me. Walter wanted me then, once he knew I was pregnant, and my father gave me away into slavery.'

Kate laughed harshly, looked at me.

'Dramatic, isn't it! But that was what it was although I didn't know it then. At the time. Walter was a God-send to me, a life saver. Of course I should have asked why he wanted to marry a girl carrying another man's child. I was young and terrified, persuaded myself it was my beauty he craved. Later I discovered the truth. Walter is impotent. Walter Hartigan cannot get it up. He will do anything to conceal that fact. Everything he is stems from that. That was the only reason he wanted a wife and child – to prove he once could get it up.

'I told you Eddie is my dowry. He followed me like a lost lamb, but we were never lovers again. He had nowhere to go in Dublin so I got money to him, helped him get on his feet. When Walter bought this place I got him the job here and from it he became known in the area. Walter doesn't know Eddie is Julie's father – that was one secret I kept from everyone until tonight. Eddie got married, had children. Even so he has this thing – always sees Julie as his only child, his special one.

'The price I paid for having Paddy Brett sort out my problems was his being close to Julie while he was helping me. Paddy Brett was the nearest thing to a paedophile I've ever come across, but I didn't know that until we were almost finished with Walter. When I found out I told him to keep away from her, but he only laughed, said I was mistaken, that I was being silly.

'I wasn't home that Sunday night when he came here. He went out back and found Julie. He spoke to her, must have propositioned her, but she ran away. Eddie was there and heard it. They had a row. Paddy turned on the power, treated him as an uppity servant and it was a red rag to a bull. Eddie hit him with the spade. Later he put a freezer bag over his head – it's the way he gets rid of unwanted pups after he's trussed them up. I told you Eddie isn't right in the head.'

'So that explains how Candy and Julie saw him stretched out,' I said.

'They panicked and took off with Patrick when he arrived,' Kate said. 'When I came on the scene Paddy was dead. Eddie was going to give himself up but I persuaded him that his family needs him. The kids are young and there's been too much pain for children already. Besides, he didn't really mean to kill him, not in the accepted sense, even though he did tie that bag over his head. We put him in the car and I drove to Bullock Harbour. Eddie can't drive. We walked home our separate ways.'

She was silent for a while. 'Will you report this?' Kate

280

looked at me, her eyes begging me. 'Nothing good can come of blaming Eddie. He reacted badly to a provocation. As I say, he's not the full shilling.'

We heard Eddie coming back.

'Let me handle him,' Kate said, 'he'll do what I tell him.'

Eddie Delaney carried a plastic supermarket bag that had obviously been buried in clay. He laid it on the chair Trevor had sat on and stepped back. Small lumps of clay fell to the floor as I opened the bag. Inside was a plastic wallet with papers, a leather wallet with cash, credit cards, the usual personal things. The last item in the bag was a computer diskette.

The papers related to Paddy Brett's resignation as a director of North East Baltic Bank and had pencil crosses indicating where they were to be signed. They were dated some two years back. He never did break free.

'Well, moneybags, what are you going to do now?' Eddie asked, scornfully.

I took the papers and walked to the sink, collecting a box of matches on the way. They were damp, slow to catch fire, and I had to use three matches. I held them over the sink and watched them burn until the heat made me drop the last fragment. Eddie Delaney stared, his forehead creased in a frown. Using the supermarket bag I handed him the wallet. 'Destroy that,' I said. 'Burn it, don't just bury it. Do it now, Eddie, and maybe you won't ever be caught.'

He stared at me. 'You're not going to report me to the police?'

'Let the police look after their own business,' I said. 'I no longer have an interest in who killed Paddy Brett. Burn it, Eddie, do it straight away. It's the only thing that connects you to it. No one else is going to talk.'

Eddie Delaney studied my face, wondered if he could trust me. I knew for sure if he decided he couldn't he would try to kill me.

'He means what he says, Eddie,' Kate said. 'Please burn

it. I'm going to lock up now, Eddie. Why don't you go home?'

He nodded slowly and left us.

Silence descended on the kitchen.

'And how do we stand, Johnny Constantine?' she asked. 'Is it over between us?'

I sat at the table again, picked up my brandy.

'That depends on you,' I said.

'Do you mean that?'

'Yes.'

She sat opposite me. 'When Eddie came in tonight I thought we were finished. My whole world came tumbling around me again. Just when you're getting it together, I thought, just when you're seeing the glimmer of a chance of maybe having a little of the happiness others take for granted. I felt total despair. You sure you really mean that? Can we forget what you heard tonight?'

'I won't forget it, but it no longer means anything to me. My friend didn't die here. My friend died somewhere along the road between seventeen and forty-five. The man who died here had nothing to do with me and I owe him nothing. As far as I'm concerned Eddie Delaney defended the one he loved and I don't blame him for that.'

'So he can go home to his wife and kids?' Kate said.

'Why not?'

'I'm so glad you see it like that. That way, if you see what I mean, the innocent don't get hurt.'

'Oh, you're wrong there. A lovely lady is dead because of all this and that cries out for vengeance. And don't think there isn't more violence to come as long as this diskette is lying around. But that's for tomorrow. It's time we were in bed.'

Kate Hartigan stood and leaned across the table.

'John Constantine, I could get to love you,' she said, smiling.

We went to bed.

*

282

A magpie machine-gunned the garden at dawn and woke me. I eased out gently from Kate Hartigan's bed, but even so I disturbed her.

'Johnny, where you going?'

'Got miles to go before I sleep,' I said.

I rolled across and kissed her longingly.

'You look beautiful,' I said.

'You can say that every morning if you want to,' she said. 'When will I see you?'

'I'll ring you.'

I slipped out of the house into the chill of a pearly grey dawn. I took my time and looked about carefully. If Walter Hartigan was sufficiently panicked to try killing me in a road accident there was every possibility he would grow desperate enough to try more direct methods. I was very conscious of the diskette in my pocket.

As soon as I cleared the gates I stood on the brake and the car screeched to a halt. I felt a little paranoid for having done so, for having had the mad notion that Gaffney might have fixed my car during the night.

I halted on the Vico Road and watched the sun rise.

I thought of Kate and of how we'd made love and of how beautiful she was. That morning I knew that Margaret Hourican, or the remembered vision of Margaret Hourican that I'd been carrying, was no longer with me. I was Kate Hartigan's man and that pleased me.

'The hell with you, Gaffney,' I said, aloud, to the risen sun. I let out the clutch and drove on.

I went to the Enterprise Centre and the plant. No one followed. The Merrion Road was empty all the way behind me as I crossed the tracks at the railway crossing. I was about to put the key in the lock when the guard from the security company called out and frightened the daylights out of me. I let myself in unsteadily and keyed in the alarm code. I went through to my Research and Development Department and stuck the diskette in the computer.

It was the second copy.

I stored it with the first copy and locked up.

No one followed me.

In the basement of my building I parked in my usual slot and froze as I saw the big guy get out of a car across the aisle behind me. He was six-two or three of very wide, flat man. He wore dark slacks, black shirt and the kind of leather jacket that used to be favoured by the Special Branch. He had the face of an unsuccessful sparring partner. He stood at the rear of his car, his hands held in front of him like a soccer player making a wall.

I debated with myself. Should I back out and run for it or should I brazen it out fearlessly? I decided to try being brave and stood out.

'Mr Constantine?' he said.

'Yeah,' I said, and clicked my clicker, locked the car.

'Mr McRoarty would like to see you,' he said. He made no move toward me.

'And your name is?' I asked.

'Ryan,' he said. 'Paco Ryan.'

'You a colleague of Mr Carmody's?'

He seemed to like that. He smiled, looked quite amused, rolled his shoulders.

'Yeah, you might say that,' he said, and decided on a replay. 'I'm a colleague of Spike's.'

'I need a shave and a shower and a change of clothes,' I said.

'Fine by me,' he said. 'I'll wait here for you.'

'OK,' I said. 'I'll be about three-quarters of an hour.'

'Suit yourself,' he said.

I walked past him heading for the lift and decided to try a funny, show I wasn't scared. I turned, made a gun of finger and thumb, pointed it at him. He was very relaxed as he stood calmly watching me.

'For a minute there I thought you were going to pull a gun,' I said, and grinned my you-don't-scare-me grin.

He smiled, shook his head.

'Not part of the tour this time around,' he said.

He'd won that one, I had to admit. I was glad when the lift doors closed.

'It's me,' I said, ringing my own doorbell.

This time Magdalen wore a housecoat.

'She can't be looking after you properly if you're out of bed at this time of the morning,' Maggs said, locking the door as I made for the bedroom.

'Do me a favour,' I said. 'Stick on the kettle and make some coffee.'

'What's happening?' Maggs shouted, ten minutes later.

I peered around the shower curtain and she was sitting on the lavatory.

'I have an appointment with Mr McRoarty. His colleague Mr Paco Ryan is waiting in the basement for me.'

For a moment I thought Magdalen was going to be sick. I stood back under the shower again, but Magdalen hauled the curtain aside. I did the best I could with my hands.

'Maggs!' I said, indignantly.

'Don't go, Johnny. Whatever you do, no matter what he says, don't go.'

I got out of the bath and turned my back to Maggs. I wrapped a towel about me.

'Magdalen, my sweet, please wait in the kitchen,' I said.

I decided on a cotton open-neck and Donegal tweeds. Reddish brogues with strong toecaps seemed right in case I had to kick someone in the groin.

Maggs had poached eggs on toast for me.

'You're out of rashers,' she said, slamming the plate in front of me angrily.

I ate in silence and held my tongue until I was sipping coffee. Maggs sat in front of me bouncing her crossed leg.

'I'm going out to see The Farmer,' I said. 'If I'm not in touch with you by twelve o'clock tonight please ring Harcourt Street Garda Station and ask for Sergeant Tom Crotty. Tell him where I went and tell him it's all to do with the Brett case. OK?'

Maggs looked at the ceiling, shaking her head.

285

'Christ's sake, Johnny, don't go. That's one man who doesn't care who he kills. He has the people. He's got these foreigners with thick accents who'd cut your throat as quick as look at you. Think about it! They might never even find you again. Lot of good this Crotty will do you if you're in some bog.'

'I've got to go, Maggs,' I said. 'I've got the fire behind me. I can't stay put. You won't forget now, sure you won't. Sergeant Tom Crotty – he's a detective. You'll like him, he's a decent guy.'

The kitchen door opened and Sean came in rubbing sleep from his eyes.

'Why're you here for breakfast, Johnny?' he asked, yawning, kissing his mother.

'Thought I'd drop in see how you were getting on,' I said.

He went to the cupboard and took out the cornflakes, found a bowl and came back to the table.

'I've got to go,' I said. 'Have a nice day, Sean.'

'Have a nice day,' he said, pouring milk.

Magdalen followed me to the door.

'Don't go, Johnny,' she said.

'No other way, Maggs,' I said. I felt scared.

As she held the door open I stooped and kissed her.

'Don't forget,' I said. 'Tom Crotty.'

'I won't forget,' she said.

# Chapter Thirteen

Outbound traffic was heavy until we hit the airport road. I put the hammer down to stay with Paco Ryan's Saab.

I'd said there wasn't much point me dragging him all the way back again when he'd offered to be my chauffeur. I'd watched his eyes to see if I could detect if a return trip was actually on the cards. I might as well have looked into a black hole.

A few miles beyond Swords we hung a left down a road I had never noticed before and after a couple of miles we turned into what was more a boreen than a driveway. There was nothing remarkable about the entrance – no big piers, nothing like that. Just an ordinary six-bar farm gate that could have done with a pot of paint.

Because the house was in a dip we had to cover nearly all of almost a mile of boreen before it came into view. It was a beautiful house, low and spread out in a south-facing crescent like I had never seen a house designed before. It had a warm red-tiled roof and the front was covered in a creeper that was turning to gold. The pebble of the gravelled forecourt was deep and we left tracks in it as we slid up to the door.

I don't know much about horses but the four roans – two blues, one red and one strawberry – looked pretty aristocratic behind the white picket fence of the adjoining paddock. Their heads came up on our arrival and they conferred briskly.

My shadow went ahead of me as I scrunched to the front door. It opened before Paco Ryan could ring.

He was about five-eight in mud-spattered riding boots. He wore britches and a green army-surplus sweater with shoulder patches. He was about fifty, I reckoned, with a ruby-red good-apple complexion. He was slim-hipped and that tended to emphasise the wedge of his trunk, the heavy powerful shoulders. I could see it wasn't for his possessions alone he was called The Farmer.

He was hearty and courteous.

'Mr Constantine, a pleasure to meet you at last. Good of you to come out. I'm Bert McRoarty. May I call you Johnny?'

'Don't see why not,' I said, and shook the dry, goal-keeper's hand he held out. It was like catching a piece of weathered oak.

'Come in, please,' he said, and stood aside to wave me into a gracious hall.

Had I been led there blindfold I could easily have imagined I'd ended in a drawing room in elegant Belgravia. We were barely seated when a young woman – clearly a maid in the film they had to be making in another part of the house – brought in a massive silver tray with coffee things. Silently, and without once looking at either of us, she poured and left us to our own devices.

The Farmer was not a man to act in haste. He discussed the present boom the country was enjoying, the sterling exchange rate and its implications for farming, inquired if my inventions were doing well on the foreign markets, made some intelligent remarks about doing business with Arabs.

I had declined a third coffee before he came to the point.

'I suppose you are wondering why I've asked you here,' he said.

'No,' I said. 'I think I can figure that out. You want the file.'

There was a silence as we looked at each other. He smiled then like I hadn't seen him smile before and I decided I preferred him without it.

288

'Cut to the chase, as they say, Johnny,' he said. 'I like that. I don't suppose you have it with you.'

I shook my head.

'Didn't think you would,' he said, and heaved a sigh. 'How much?'

'An eye,' I said.

'Come again?' he said.

'An eye for an eye,' I said. 'Something I learned on my travels.'

He looked at me more cautiously.

'Anyone I know?'

'A Mr Dutch Gaffney,' I said.

The Farmer sat back in his chair.

'If I asked you why, would you tell me?'

I shrugged. 'He killed an old lady I loved dearly. He was looking for the file. Yesterday he sent Mr Mackey to kill me. He's becoming something of a threat.'

McRoarty bared his teeth, narrowed his eyes. 'If what you say is true, Mackey made a balls of it. He had an accident on the Carlow road.'

'That was no accident,' I said.

'You're kidding!'

'No,' I said.

'Well, what do you know? Who was the old lady that was killed?'

'Brett's aunt, the woman he left the file with for me to collect.'

'You are one cool man, Johnny,' McRoarty said. 'That's a big price you're asking.'

'Not for the kind of money you have tied up without the file. Not to mention the money belonging to Mr Lemptke's friends. I'm sure they must be anxious by now.'

He stared at me.

'You're well informed, Johnny.'

'Bert,' I said, leaning forward. 'Please understand me.'

'Oh, I want to, Johnny,' he said. 'I want to be sure I understand you totally.'

289

'I don't care what you and Lemptke are doing. That is none of my business. I had this problem dropped on me by a man I grew up with. It got a lovely lady killed. Because Walter Hartigan is ripping you off, and because that is obvious from the file, he wanted the file and, when he didn't get it, was willing to kill me to stop you getting it. Am I making sense to you?'

He was looking at me as though he would soon fall asleep.

'You sure about that – that the file shows he was ripping me off?'

'Brett saw it when he checked the file the first time. He said Grattan hadn't spotted it. But maybe Grattan is in on it.'

'How do you mean "Brett said"? When were you talking to him?'

'He left me a tape.'

'Does that go with the file?'

'No,' I said. 'That's destroyed as instructed. Besides, it was just personal, family stuff, nothing to do with the file.'

'Did Hartigan kill Brett?'

'I don't know. If you didn't, he did.'

'How do you mean if I didn't?' he asked, a shade indignantly.

'You knew he was to meet Lemptke and Grattan that Sunday night to have the back-dated papers signed. You might have tried for the file yourself.'

'So how come you have it now?'

'Never mind how. I have it and that's all that matters. Do we have a deal?'

'How do I know you'll deliver if you get your eye?'

'I reckon I'd deserve what would happen if I double-crossed you.'

He thought about that.

'You're a smart guy, you wouldn't be doing this unless you had a fall-back.'

'There's a copy,' I said. 'I keep that. Once you can open

290

those accounts you can empty them and after that no one can prove anything and neither the copy nor me are of any further importance. But it could still give you a problem with the Criminal Assets Bureau so I reckon you won't be bothering me. For sure I won't be bothering you. Do we have a deal?'

He levered himself out of his chair and walked about the room. In a while he sat down.

'Deal,' he said, nodding.

'I want my eye as soon as possible. My life and your file are in danger while Dutch Gaffney is on the loose. He's bound to go see that truck driver in the hospital in Kilkenny and find out what happened. After that he's going to come after me.'

'Leave it with me, Johnny,' he said. He stood up. 'I expect to deal with the matter today. Do take care of yourself – I need that file tomorrow at the latest.'

'I'll ring your Mr Carmody as soon as your side of the bargain is complete,' I said.

Paco Ryan was leaning against the Saab in the forecourt. Beyond him, one foot on the paddock rail, Vilmos Lemptke was saying something to the horses. He gave me a lazy look and then turned back to rubbing the strawberry's nose.

'We'll be in touch, Johnny,' McRoarty said, and nodded as I slid behind the wheel.

My back felt soaked in sweat as I drove down the boreen. In my mirror The Farmer stared after me, hands on hips.

I drove to Skerries to look at the sea. I wanted to keep out of the way, stay clear of Dutch Gaffney,

I came back the coast road, drove all around Howth, spent nearly an hour looking out over the bay towards Dalkey.

My phone rang at two. I took it out of the dash compartment.

'Johnny?'

'Who else?' I said.

'A woman has rung here looking for you,' Kate said.

'She give a name?' I asked.

'No. Did you give my number to someone?'

'No.'

'There's something wrong about it, Johnny. I don't like the sound of it. She wanted this number – I said I didn't know it. Where are you?'

'I'm in Athlone,' I said. I hated lying to her but cell phones are tricky things.

'What are you doing in Athlone?'

'Looking at the Shannon.'

'Will I see you later?'

'I'm not sure. This is going to be a busy day.'

'Are you in danger?'

'Not that I'm aware of.'

'You will come back to me.'

'Nothing surer.'

'Please keep in touch. I'm kinda scared. I don't like this woman.'

'Don't worry,' I said and broke the connection.

I put the phone in the dash compartment.

I slept for a bit.


I had a late lunch in an almost empty restaurant in Howth village and went back up on the Head to look at the sea again, waste some time. I wondered what Gaffney was doing, wondered where he was.

I went to a cinema in Sutton and sat through a film. Anytime the door opened I watched to see if I recognised anyone. I was getting jumpy but I knew it wasn't paranoia. They really were out to get me.

I had coffee in a small café outside the cinema at six thirty. No one fired a gun, threw a knife.

Back in the car I checked my phone. There were four messages waiting.

Helen Foley said a woman had phoned the plant. She'd

told Helen it was important she speak to me. Helen had promised to pass on a message but the woman would only leave a mobile number. On a hunch I got out the card Heather Skeehan had given me. It was her number.

The second message was electric. It was Magdalen and she was out of her mind.

'Johnny,' she screamed, 'someone's taken Sean. Oh, Christ! Johnny, they say you have something they want and they'll give him back if they get it. Where are you, Johnny?' There was a pause and then she went on until she ran out of time. The third and fourth calls were also from Magdalen.

I rang Heather Skeehan and she answered on the first ring.

'Hello,' she said, and I could hear a clock sound the three-quarter chime.

'Heather?' I said.

'Johnny, that you?'

'Yeah,' I said. 'Where's the boy?'

'I have nothing to do with it. You got that? Nothing whatsoever to do with it. They forced me to look after him. I don't want to know what's happening so don't tell me. Hartigan wants to see you at the club. Said you were to go there and bring the information with you and everything would go OK for your kid. Do it, Johnny, please. Forget the money. They could harm your son. Go now.' She broke the connection.

I began dialling my home number and Magdalen but stopped halfway through. There was no point when I didn't know where Sean was.

I dug out the number Carmody had left me.

'Yeah?' he said.

'Mr Carmody?'

'Yeah.'

'Constantine. Hartigan has kidnapped my boy. He wants me to bring the information to his club. I'm going there now. I will not be carrying the information. I expect to walk in and out of that club in one piece. If I don't, the Criminal Assets Bureau gets a package. That clear?'

'Yeah,' he said, and there was a long pause. 'Please take a couple of hours to get there. You got that? Two hours at least,' he said.

'Two hours,' I said.

I broke the connection.

I checked my phone every so often. Messages were piling up and I knew Magdalen must be frantic. I waited.

I left for town at eight forty-five. It was well after nine by the time I'd found parking on the quay and walked round the corner into Temple Bar.

The Left Bank it's called these days and there's a hell of a lot more happening there than when I was a lad. There's a great buzz now and plenty of reasonably cheap places to eat. The pubs aren't bad and I wondered if Crotty was around, if he could be in The Duckless Drake.

Some things never change – the streets were pretty crowded with strolling young people looking for some kind of action. Solo guys went sharking through shoals of gum-chewing girls. There was a tension in the air and it looked like a good place to be young.

Doxy Moran's had an old grey brick facade that had been sand blasted and had cleaned up well. The original owner, Moran, had inset his name in yellow brick in the wall and the present owner had avoided having to do something about it by incorporating it into the name of the club.

At ground level a new shop front had been added and painted black and gold. In the window was a half-size cubist sculpture of a rhinoceros. A big man in a tuxedo stood bathed in soft red light just inside the door. He rocked back and forth as he waited for the evening trade.

I went around the corner and got out my mobile but Carmody was unobtainable. I gave it another ten minutes and tried again.

I was on my own.

I toyed with the idea of ringing Crotty but decided I couldn't risk Sean when Gaffney was involved. I squared my shoulders and marched toward Doxy Moran's.

The big man asked if I was a member. I told him I had an appointment with Mr Hartigan. He said Mr Hartigan wasn't there yet, wasn't due until ten at the earliest. I asked for Gaffney and was told he'd be along with Hartigan. He wasn't keen to let me in for some reason. Then I remembered and asked for Patricia Brett or Della Coady. That did it.

Simply Red filled the room at reasonable volume and it looked a nice enough place. The bar was back-lit and the room grew dimmer the farther back you went until you wondered what went on in the booths that were on the periphery. A small square of maple indicated a dancing area but no one was dancing.

Della Coady was stooped over at the sink, her low cut dress offering a fine view of her charms.

Patricia Brett balanced on a bar stool, the hostess with the mostest.

The place seemed empty when I'd walked in, but as my eyes grew accustomed to the darkness I could make out the pale blobs of faces in the booths, the glitter of glasses. I walked over to Patricia.

'Of all the bars in all the world . . . ' I began, but she stopped me.

'Been done so many times I don't even laugh any more,' she said, but smiled. 'What are you doing here? You don't look the roaring forties type.'

'I take that as being meant as a compliment,' I said.

'It sure is,' she said.

'I'm looking for Walter Hartigan.'

'Not here yet,' she said. 'Della, you know when the boss man is due?'

'Ten,' Della said, 'he rang earlier to know if you'd been in, Johnny.'

'Wouldn't have thought you and Hartigan would have

295

much to say to one another now that you have so much in common,' Patricia said, grinning slyly.

'You'd be surprised,' I said, and asked Della for a beer.

Patricia Brett was sex on a stool. Creamy shoulders and alabaster arms blossomed out of something long, tight and slithery – gave the impression she was sloughing a skin. Angelic features managed to convey the barest hint of depravity, of controlled lewdness that created about the woman an intensely sensual aura that promised immediate gratification of all fantasies. The eyes remained aloof from the goods on offer, the cool appraising look intimating there could be a price to be paid for bounty. Walter Hartigan knew a good investment when he saw it. Men would come just to sit near her.

'You planning on keeping this job?' I asked.

'Soon as you come through with the money I'm out of here,' she said, keeping her voice low.

Della arrived with the beer. Patricia declined, said it was too early to start drinking water and laughed.

Two men came in and stood the other side of her. She swivelled on the stool as they called her name. They fell over her, did a lot of bobbing and weaving from the waist, bought drinks and this time she had one. Della didn't look too happy.

I paid and turned to survey the room. In one of the booths a match flared and a pair of glamorous pouter pigeons were momentarily haloed, revealing heavy make-up, glittering predatory eyes.

Ten fifteen they came in.

Walter Hartigan looked very distinguished in evening dress. He walked well, carried himself with a natural assurance. He stopped at a booth to speak to someone who had his back to me and was only a shadow at that distance and in that light.

Dutch Gaffney was the real thing – evil on the hoof. He slid into the room as though he expected knives, tomahawks, slings, arrows, the whole nine yards. He made his

296

way to the bar in an arc – presumably to allow the least exposure of his back. He ended on my right as I leaned my elbows on the bar behind me.

'I owe you for Hocks,' he said, and gave me his best look.

I stared back as coolly as I could. 'Don't owe me a thing,' I said. 'It was a pleasure.'

He started forward, then controlled himself.

'You bring the stuff?'

I sipped my beer and said nothing, waited for Walter Hartigan to finish his conversation and stroll over.

'Evening, Constantine,' he said, and nodded at Patricia. She smiled back tightly before returning to being charming.

'Usual, Della,' he said.

Della Coady put a tulip glass in front of him and poured white wine. She looked warily at Gaffney but he shook his head.

'Did you bring it, Constantine?' Hartigan asked, speaking quickly before turning to survey the room.

'Where's the boy?' I asked.

'All in good time, Constantine, all in good time. Did you bring the information?'

'No,' I said. 'I won't bring it until I know the boy is all right.'

'Oh, but you will, Constantine, you will. Tell him what happens, Dutch, if he doesn't deliver.'

'You're not back here by midnight with the stuff, your kid's going to be pissing blood by morning,' Gaffney said.

'I'll bring it,' I said. 'But you have to bring the boy.'

'You'll get your boy, Constantine. You'll get him safe and sound as soon as you bring the information,' Hartigan said. 'You have my word on that.'

'You'll bring him here?'

'No,' Gaffney said. 'I'll deliver him to your basement car park.'

I stretched my arm to pick up my drink, quickly check the time. It was ten forty.

'Make it two o'clock,' I said. 'It will take me that long to fetch it.'

'One thirty,' Hartigan said, finishing his wine. 'C'mon Dutch. See you at one thirty, Constantine, and don't try anything tricky.'

'Don't let that animal near my child,' I said to Hartigan.

'The remedy is in your hands,' he said.

They walked away from me. At the door Walter stood back and graciously waved in a mixed party of eight. They were already well on, a group of thirty-something revellers. All of them seemed to know Walter, called out boisterous nothings, laughed at his answers.

I remember thinking I had better get to Magdalen before she did what I'd asked and rang Crotty. I needed to talk to her, try to assure her it would be OK, that I'd get Sean back.

I had just moved away from the bar when the champagne corks started popping and I looked about for the party. A woman screamed and went on screaming and I knew then it wasn't anyone's birthday.

Suddenly the room was full of people milling and jostling and trying to reach the door. I pushed and punched my way through. Outside a crowd had gathered in a rough semicircle, the women pale behind the hands they held to their faces.

The bouncer was dead. He looked utterly surprised and there was a hole in his forehead. He must have slid down the door jamb. He sat like a man who'd decided to take a break.

A young man knelt by Walter Hartigan. He had rolled up his jacket and put it beneath Walter's head. Walter was alive. He looked as though he was about to panic and kept licking his lips. Blood was seeping from somewhere and spreading across the blue-whiteness of his shirt. The young man must have undone Walter's bow-tie – it hung lopsidedly around his neck. I remembered something about it being wrong to raise someone's head in a situation like that

298

but I said nothing. Walter kept raising his right hand as though he wanted to draw attention to something.

A man I had never seen before lay crumpled in the middle of the narrow street and looked as though he was trying to reach the automatic that lay close to his right hand. He wore a denim suit and denim shirt. There were two bloody holes in the chest of the shirt. He was dead and people stayed well back from him. He was swarthy and looked as though he hadn't shaved in three days.

There was no sign of Gaffney.

I looked about. Down the street a woman screamed something and the crowd parted and I saw Gaffney walking away, weaving as he went, his arm waving about, a gun at the end of it. I chased after him and as I ran I saw big spots of blood on the cobbles.

I rounded the corner I'd seen him turn in time to see a Range Rover begin to pull out. It tore the rear light from a car parked tightly in front of it before rolling out on to the quays.

I raced for my car but by the time I'd reached it there was no sign of the Range Rover. I drove home, crashing traffic lights at two junctions. I parked in the basement and ran for the lift.

As the lift bell pinged at my floor I realised what had been nagging at the back of my mind. It was the same tone as the three-quarter hour chime I'd heard when Heather Skeehan had answered the phone and I realised where I'd heard it before. It was in the hall of Walter Hartigan's house in Foxrock.

I stepped out of the lift and Magdalen threw herself at me, beating my chest with her fists.

'Bastard, bastard, bastard,' Magdalen screamed. 'Where've you fucking been?'

I pushed her back into the apartment, closed the door with my heel. I held her tightly, waiting for the paroxysm of rage to die down.

'I know where he is,' I said.

Magdalen pushed me away, stared wildly at me.

'Where, tell me where?'

I reached out and caught her, held her again.

'Dutch Gaffney has him.'

Magdalen went rigid in my hands and she stared wide-eyed, open-mouthed.

'Dutch,' she whispered. 'Oh, Jesus Christ! Oh, Mother of God.'

'I know where he is. I'm going to get him now,' I told her. 'You sit tight. I won't be more than a couple of hours.'

She shook her head, picked up a jacket and was working her arms into it as she made for the door ahead of me. 'I'm coming with you.'

I followed. There was no arguing with her.

As I drove up the ramp she was talking, moaning, at times screaming.

'It's all my fault, my own fucking fault. Forgive me, Sean! I should never have used that stupid bitch. I persuaded myself she ran a proper playschool. I was saving money, miserable bitch that I am. Fuck me and my meanness, may I roast in hell for it. A man came earlier than me and told her I'd asked him to collect Sean. Christ! She just handed him over. Just like that! Then the bitch has the cheek to ask me did she do wrong. I rushed back here hoping it was you, but I knew in my heart it couldn't be you.

'A man rang – it wasn't Dutch, I'm sure of that, I'd know that bastard boiled – he said you had something they wanted and I was to tell you to hand it over. I've been waiting for you ever since. Have you got it with you Johnny? I'll give you whatever you want for it.'

Traffic from a concert in The Point hemmed us in, brought us to a standstill. Magdalen reached across and began blowing the horn and I had to wrestle her back to her corner. Eventually I scorched up the wrong side of the road and got away with it. We made the toll bridge and the traffic moved briskly again.

'Walter Hartigan is all shot up and may die,' I told Magdalen. 'Two men are dead. One is the bouncer at Doxy Moran's and I don't know who the other man is, but I'd say he's one of The Farmer's men. Gaffney is wounded. He's leaking blood.'

'Jesus! That makes him even more dangerous,' Magdalen said.

It was a night of few stars. Clouds drifted apart occasionally to expose a drunken half-moon. I turned into Foxrock and slowed for the entrance into Hartigan's cul-de-sac. His gates were open and I wondered if the closed-circuit eye was awake. I cut the lights and went through in first gear.

I crept forward until I could make out the white railing and I hugged it as I crawled on. The sky lightened at one stage and I found the golden mare and her foal moving next to us. They watched our progress intently, like two interested ghosts.

I stopped when the dark bulk of the house came into view. There was light in an upstairs window – not in the room itself, but as though the room door was partly open. I whispered to Magdalen to stay in the car. She nodded and I slipped out my door and pushed it closed behind me until the first click of the lock. I walked on the grass verge and moved quickly along the drive. Somewhere to my right the mare whinnied but I could not make out her shape.

The Range Rover was badly parked, slewed about on the gravel, and part of the rear light of the car Gaffney had damaged was caught up in the bull bars. A silver Opel Corsa was tucked away at the side. I went forward as quietly as I could and hoped there weren't any security beams. I pushed gently on the front door, but it was firmly shut, felt doubly locked. To my right a window was open but I felt I would make too much noise going in that way.

I stepped away and again used the grass margin to walk silently around the house. Light streamed on to the yard at the back of the house and I peered out cautiously. I edged to the lighted window and listened.

I heard a groan and then a woman's apology. The top of the window was open. I chanced a quick peek. Gaffney sat in a chair and Heather Skeehan knelt in front of him, a wash-cloth in her hand.

Gaffney's shirt was covered in blood. His face was a mess. A bullet had torn away a large part of his jaw. To begin with I thought the blood on his shirt was from his jaw, but then saw the black spot and realised he had also been hit high in the chest. Whenever Heather went near his face he drew back with a gurgling groan like a man with pneumonia.

They were intent on one another. Heather Skeehan sounded like someone close to hysteria. Now and then Gaffney raised his right arm and pointed his gun into her face. She would become still then and begin pleading for her life.

'You've got to get to hospital, Dutch,' she kept saying. 'That wound in your chest is terrible. You don't get help soon you're going to bleed to death. Please don't point the gun at me, Dutch, it could go off accidentally.'

'No,' he said, at least that is what I think he tried to say. The sound he made was like someone gargling. Large drops of blood fell from his face as he shook his head.

'We've got to get away from here, Dutch. The police are going to be here soon. We must get away. If they find you like this and the boy upstairs we're done for. Christ! At least let me get away if you won't go yourself. Jesus! I don't want to go to jail. You're going to fucking die if you don't do something, don't you understand that?'

He raised the gun to her face again and shook his head.

Then Magdalen was in the door behind him, her gun in her hand. I had completely forgotten it. Heather saw her, had to see her, but made no move, gave no indication. She kept talking, pleading, as Magdalen came forward slowly.

'Let me go, Dutch, please. I had nothing to do with the kidnapping. Christ! I could go to jail forever. Be reasonable, let me take you to hospital.'

Dutch heard Magdalen at the last moment and began to turn. I had been expecting it and had taken up a large flowerpot. I hurled it through the window and stepped to one side. He got off one shot that went through the upper part of the window before Magdalen brought her gun down full force on his wrist and he dropped his gun with a scream.

Magdalen moved around in front of Gaffney and indicated silently for Heather to stand beside him. Heather protested her innocence but Magdalen wasn't listening. She only had eyes for Gaffney and watched him like a mongoose with a snake.

'Johnny. You out there, Johnny?' she called and I shouted to her as I found the door. It was locked. I returned to the window.

'Open the window, Heather,' I called, but she was terrified, couldn't move.

'Do it,' Magdalen said, 'or I'll kill you now.'

Magdalen was completely in charge, utterly calm. Neither Heather nor I doubted her for a moment.

I climbed over the sill, brushed past Heather and stood next to Magdalen.

'I heard her say Sean is upstairs,' I said, and held out my hand for the gun.

'Find him,' Magdalen said, making it clear she would continue to hold the whiphand.

I hit the switches as I moved through the house, flooded the place with light. I headed for the room with the partly open door and peered in. Sean lay clothed on a small bed, a rug drawn to his waist. For one heart-stopping moment I thought he was dead, but then he sighed and moved his head. He was asleep.

I went downstairs quietly. As I approached the kitchen door I heard Heather plead with Magdalen to let her go, that she'd had nothing to do with it. Magdalen's lips were shut in a grim line, her face bleak.

'Well?' I don't think Magdalen took her eyes off Gaffney

303

as she asked the question.

'He's fast asleep,' I said. 'Didn't think I should be the one to wake him after all he's been through.'

Magdalen looked at me then, her face tense, chalk white.

'What do you mean, after all he's been through? Is he all right?'

'Far as I can see,' I said hastily.

Magdalen swung her gun on to Heather Skeehan.

'Go,' Magdalen said, flicking her gun at the door. 'Fuck off before I change my mind.'

Sobbing, Heather Skeehan raced from the kitchen and in a moment we heard the front door slam and a car start.

Only then did I notice that Magdalen had picked up Gaffney's gun while I was upstairs. She held it in her left hand and I should have known what she intended when I saw she was holding it with a tea-towel. At the time I thought it was because of the blood.

Magdalen squatted in front of Gaffney, her back rigid, both guns held unwaveringly. Red bubbles were forming in the crusted blood around his lips and there were black clots in the messy jaw wound that had begun dripping blood again. His eyelids drooped but the eyes glittered within.

'Can you hear me, Dutch?' Magdalen voice was almost caressing and I became fearful, wondered if I shouldn't tackle her. Try taking the guns away from her. But I was genuinely afraid of her at that moment and I delayed too long.

'This is for Christine, Dutch. This is for my lovely sister,' Magdalen said, speaking very clearly, wanting to be sure Gaffney understood.

At the last moment his eyes came wildly alive and he tried awkwardly to launch himself at her. He was almost out of the chair when she blew him back into it, shot him in the groin. His mouth opened and he screamed or tried to say something. Magdalen never altered her pose, remained squatting in front of him, balanced, detached, almost disinterested, and shot him twice in the stomach. He doubled over, bowed to her it seemed, and she shot him once in the crown of the head.

I was incapable of movement. It was outside anything I had ever experienced. The noise was appalling in the kitchen and the air was full of the smell of burning. The mess was utterly shocking, but Magdalen seemed unaware of it and I remember fatuously thinking that there must be something wrong with Magdalen, the woman who couldn't resist cleaning a kitchen.

Magdalen straightened up, threw his gun on the floor, tossed the tea-towel aside. She put her own gun in her pocket unfired. She turned to me.

'Sean?' she asked.

'Upstairs,' I croaked, foolishly pointing – as though there could be any other direction – and then led the way.

I vaguely remember watching Magdalen pick up her son with unbelievable tenderness, so outrageously at odds with what I'd seen her do in the kitchen. She was so gentle the child never woke. Magdalen led the way downstairs and I followed like a lamb. We left the front door open, the lights on, and returned to the car.

Later that night – almost morning – I asked her for the gun and she handed it to me without question, took it from beneath her pillow as she lay on the bed next to her dreaming child.

There was rain on the wind and hardly anyone about when I went jogging. Looking downriver toward the sea I reckoned there was hope for the day, that it looked as though it could brighten. I dropped the gun in the Liffey by Butt Bridge – one more secret for Anna Livia Plurabella.

I stopped for a pint shandy in Dunphy's, but left half of it when I saw Frankie Quinlan come in – Granny Constantine really had imbued me with her superstitions. I couldn't chance hearing more bad news.

I told Carmody to meet me in Merrion Square Gardens. It's

reasonably secluded and yet public. It's not far from the Enterprise Centre and the plant where I had to go to fetch the diskette. Most of all I had no wish to be in some isolated spot with him.

I sat on a bench where I could see and be seen. The sun had come out and the first of the lunch-hour lovers were strolling hand in hand, the grass still too damp for sprawling about. I had arranged to meet at twelve noon but it was quarter past the hour when I saw Paco Ryan. He walked through on the other side of the garden and hardly looked my way.

Two minutes later Carmody was suddenly by my seat.

'Afternoon Mr Constantine,' he said, smiling, looking to left and right before sitting next to me. 'Isn't it a glorious day?'

He was dressed in a pinstripe blue-grey suit with a navy polka-dot tie and matching handkerchief. The sun glinted on handmade silver cufflinks. From the shine on his shoes I reckoned he must have done time in the army.

'Busy old night you had,' he said, smiling, turning to look after a young woman who'd strolled past.

'Kinda,' I said, and waited.

'Mr McRoarty would like to know if you had assistance other than ours.'

'How do you mean?'

'Come, come, now, Mr Constantine,' he wagged a forefinger. 'Wasn't a little angel that ended Dutch Gaffney.'

'How do you mean?' I asked again, as puzzled as I could.

He looked at me then and his eyes narrowed.

'You wouldn't try kidding me, would you?'

'I do not know what you are talking about,' I said slowly and carefully, and I could see he had a problem with that. He was unsure. 'You and Mr McRoarty have kept your side of the bargain. If you pick up my *Irish Times* you'll find what you're looking for – don't let it fall out now.'

I wondered if Heather Skeehan had been talking to The

306

Farmer. I decided the odds were she had thrown in her lot with Hartigan and was unlikely to try changing horses after what had happened.

He studied me for a bit. 'Who killed Gaffney?' he asked, resting his elbows on his knees, studying his shining toecaps.

'You did,' I said, 'like we agreed. Now I'm keeping my side of the bargain.'

'Where did you go after you left Hartigan's club?' He didn't look at me.

'Home. Where else would I go?'

'What about your kid? He OK? What happened to him?' Still he did not look at me.

'Home before me. He said the woman who was holding him got a phone call. Said she made a couple of calls and then she brought him home. Left him across the road from my apartment block. I reckon someone rang her after the shooting, told her get the hell out. Only explanation I can think of. Any case, I'm not worried. He's home and that's all that matters.'

He sat back and folded his arms as he worked it through. Across the garden Paco Ryan was chatting up some girl on a seat. I said nothing, waited.

'Don't suppose it really matters when you boil it down,' Carmody said, sitting up, his decision made. 'Anything in the paper?' he asked, scooping it up, seeming to read it as he pressed it.

'Full of news this morning,' I said. 'You'll enjoy the Business and Finance section.'

He stood up. He was a handsome man in a cruel way.

'Cheerio for now, Mr Constantine,' he said, smiling his thin-lipped smile. 'Probably won't be seeing you again.'

'I hope not, Mr Carmody,' I said.

I watched him walk away. Across the garden I saw Paco Ryan stand, say something that made the girl laugh. He took out a piece of paper and wrote on it. He glanced across at me and walked in the direction taken by Carmody.

\*

307

'The police rang shortly after midnight,' Kate Hartigan said. 'Julie was gone to bed. I was still up. I was hoping you'd get back. When they said there had been an accident I think my heart stopped. I was sure something had happened to you on the road from Athlone. I was so relieved when they said it was Walter. I think he was a young policeman. He seemed shocked when I told him that it was OK, that everything was fine.'

She was in my arms, in the hallway of her house. Julie came from the kitchen and edged past us saying, 'Oh, God!' We didn't care how Julie felt at that particular moment. The door slammed behind her. We returned to what we'd been doing.

Kate made a salad and we had cold meat and a single glass of white wine each. I said we'd have to go easy or we'd ruin our celebration dinner later on.

'That's what I love about things since you came along,' she said, chewing celery, grinning happily. 'First I didn't know I was being taken out, second I didn't know there was something to celebrate.'

'There's you and the night and the music,' I said. 'What more is needed?'

'I can live with that,' she said. 'You were there when it happened, weren't you?'

She was watching me over the rim of her glass.

'Yeah,' I said, and returned to my lunch. 'Yeah, I was there. Not actually outside when the shooting started. I was in the club when it began. I was talking to Patricia Brett.'

'You weren't in Athlone yesterday, were you?'

I looked at her carefully.

'No, I was hiding out. I was keeping out of the way.'

'Out of whose way?'

'Your husband's man, Gaffney.'

'Did you kill Gaffney?'

'No.'

'Honestly?'

'Scout's honour.'

'Then why did you go to the club? Why were you there at all? I'm terrified you're going to walk out now, tell me it's none of my business. But it is, it is. I'm so tied up with you I have to know the truth.'

'Your husband and his men had kidnapped a little boy. They wanted to trade him for something Paddy Brett left me.'

Kate began clearing the dishes, putting them in the machine. She plugged in the kettle and ground some beans.

'How old is this child?'

'Four.'

She asked her question as she looked out into the garden.

'Is he your child?'

'No.'

Kate moved around the kitchen, put cups on the table. She added two small glasses and a bottle of grappa. She poured a shot of grappa in each glass. She filled the cups with coffee – it smelled good.

'This little boy,' she said, holding the grappa to her lip. 'Is his mother the woman who lives with you?'

'Yes. They've both been living with me for the last week. She owns the apartment downstairs. She's a single parent. She makes a living out of four or five men, I'm not one of them. We're just good friends.'

'Good friends.'

'The best, but not in any other way.'

'Not that way?'

'Definitely not that way,' I said. Then I realised that could be taken out of context. 'But that's by choice, not by desire.'

'Not by desire, huh?'

'She's a good-looking woman.'

'So I'm told. Why were you protecting her?'

'Good question. Last week I thought she needed protection. I've discovered that if I ever need protection Magdalen's the one to go to.'

'Magdalen. Very biblical.'

'Isn't it just.'

'This protection, is it going to continue?'

'No,' I said smiling at her. 'Magdalen is moving out today. Going back downstairs to her own place now that things have quietened down.'

'Are you glad?'

'Ecstatic.'

'Do I get to see this view that Candy says is terrific?'

'Anytime you like. We can go there after our celebration dinner.'

Kate sat back and smiled. 'I'm glad I said all that.'

I finished my coffee and my grappa.

'Friend of yours called here at noon,' Kate said. 'Man called Crotty. Real sexy guy. I must say you have interesting friends.'

'What was Crotty saying?'

'He was talking about Walter. He seemed to know about you and me. Did you tell him?'

'I told him I knew you,' I said carefully, 'because I reckoned Crotty would find out. But I didn't tell him I was sleeping with you if that's what you mean.'

'That's what I meant. I walked into it in that case. When he asked if I knew you I said you were fantastic in bed.'

I was astonished. 'You didn't.'

She grinned. 'Are you ashamed of me then?'

'No,' I said, 'but that was going it a bit. To say that I mean.'

'Course I didn't say that,' she said. 'He really scared me, though, that Crotty. When he told me who he was, first thing I thought was Eddie had given himself up. Then he started asking me about Walter and was I relieved! I think he found my indifference to Walter's condition quite amusing. Walter's going to live, by the way. The bastard!'

'Where is he?'

'Intensive care in the Mater Hospital. Is Crotty married?'

'Not that I know of. Why?'

'Interesting fella. Nice to know where he is if Magdalen ever moves back up again.'

My phone rang on the Merrion Road.

'Johnny, Tom Crotty,' he said. 'Want to have a chat. Where are you?'

'Merrion Road.' It was three fifteen.

'Could you meet me in Scobie's in ten minutes? Won't keep you long, few loose ends is all.'

'On my way,' I said.

I drew into the side and dialled Patricia Brett. Della Coady answered and treated me most abruptly. Patricia was nicer.

'Hiya, Johnny,' she said. 'Hope you're over last night's excitement.'

'Has Detective Crotty been speaking to you?'

'Yes. I told him you came to the club at Mom's request to try to persuade me to give it up and go back to college now that we could afford it. Is that what you wanted to know?'

'You should be running IBM,' I said.

'All offers considered,' she said, and hung up laughing.

'I'll say one thing for you, Johnny,' Crotty said, 'things have a habit of happening near you. Jesus! I wonder if it's safe having a drink with you. Man with an Uzi could walk in at any moment!'

We sat in pubby sunlight at the marble counter. I've always loved pubs at that hour of the day. Willy O'Meara himself was behind the bar, his glasses perched on the end of his nose as he searched through a mess of invoices and ledgers on the bar top. Willy is a small bow-legged man. All his life he's been called Scobie after the great jockey. He told us he was trying to rationalise his Value Added Tax. Every so often he swore. We were the only ones on the other side of the counter.

'Met your lady friend this morning,' Crotty said, smugly.

311

'You must be well in there. She didn't seem to mind her hubby being shot up.'

'Would you if you were married to Walter Hartigan?' I said.

'True for you. Nice-looking woman.'

'I saw her first,' I said, and he was pleased.

'Where'd you go after you left the club last night?'

Typical Crotty – didn't bother asking if I'd been there.

'Home,' I said, looking him in the eye.

'For how long?'

'Until around five when I went jogging.'

'Anyone I know?' Crotty asked.

'Jogging jogging,' I said. 'You don't seriously think I had anything to do with that gunfight at the OK Corral last night?'

'Nah,' he said, sucking froth off his lip. 'You're not fast enough to slap leather with those guys.'

'Who was the dead man in the middle of the road?'

'The foreign-looking fella?'

'Yeah.'

'He's known to us cops as the foreign-looking fella. At fondue parties they used to say "Isn't he very foreign-looking?" Haven't a clue who he was. He had the keys of a rented Nissan, around a thousand in cash. No wallet of credit cards saying "I am Manuel Labour", no passport, no last messages to Dona Maria and the sixteen bambinos. Nothing. You ever in Walter Hartigan's house?'

'Yeah,' I said. 'Fine place, some nice things. He asked me up there once. He thought Paddy Brett might have left some papers with me. That would have been shortly after Paddy Brett died. Why do you ask?'

'Were you up there last night?'

'No.'

'Why did you go to his club?'

'Told it was a place to pull a few birds,' I said, and laughed. 'Joan Callaghan, Brett's wife, asked me to try to

312

talk her daughter into going back to college now that they have the money.'

'What money?'

'Brett's interests in his two practices. Worth nearly a couple of million before tax.

'Nearly go to college myself if I could be in her class.'

'That's your problem,' I said, laughing. 'You're just not in her class.'

'These papers that Hartigan thought you might have – what did he think they were about?'

'Something to do with North East Baltic Bank,' I said, 'Paddy Brett was a director there.'

'And you don't know anything about them?'

'How would I? I don't even bank there.'

'You know a guy called Dutch Gaffney?'

'I met a Mr Gaffney with Walter Hartigan. He the same fella?'

'Yeah.'

'What about him?'

'He died last night as well. He was shot – six times as far as I know. Pathologist might find a few more in him. Funny thing – he was up in good old Walter's house last night. That's where he was found. Popular place, Walter's,' Crotty said.

'I only met him in passing,' I said.

'He's real past now,' Crotty said. 'He was shot in the chest and the jaw outside the club by our foreign friend who was trying to assassinate Walter. In Walter's house he was shot four times, looked as though someone had been torturing him. Anyway, you went home from the club?'

'I had a date,' I said.

I ordered another round, said I'd have to go after it.

'You devil you. That cute little lady that's in your apartment?'

'You've met?' I was surprised. I knew then I should have phoned Magdalen.

'Yeah,' he said. 'I was up at your place a couple of hours

313

ago. Nice, Johnny, very nice. You don't have to worry with friends like that in your corner.'

'What's that supposed to mean?'

'She spilled the beans on you, you rascal. Said you were in the feathers with her all night long. Almost told me all the ways you like it.'

Crotty finished his drink.

'Town's a bit better off without some people,' he said. 'I won't be shedding any tears, but I do like to get things straight. Paddy Brett didn't leave you any papers, Johnny, did he?'

'Nothing,' I said. 'Gospel.'

'And we both know what we think of that,' he said.

He slapped my shoulder and left me at the bar.


It took me the best part of six months to organise the Bretts, get them to do things intelligently. I bought Betty Halpin's house for four hundred thousand and did it up in style, way a house like that deserves to be looked after. An American computer company pays three thousand five hundred a month to rent it for their chief executive.

Betty has moved down the country and drops a line now and then. Someone discovered she's brilliant with mentally handicapped children and she works in some rehabilitation centre. She tells me she's found happiness. Hasn't killed her sense of humour, though, and her letters can be spicy, cheerfully obscene. I wonder if she still does the occasional Lady Godiva.

Joan Callaghan took the big step a few months ago and checked herself into a drying-out station. Before she went in I persuaded her to give me the urn with Paddy's ashes – caught her at a weak moment. She's home now and well on the way to recovery.

Kate and I have her up to dinner at least once a fortnight. Kate is trying to get her fixed up with a fifty-year-old widower who owns a restaurant in town. When we occasionally eat there it's a terrific production. He's a swell guy

314

and I'm all in favour. Patricia and Patrick are trying to hustle her towards it with positively indecent haste.

She says she wants to visit Lourdes, Compostella, Fatima. Henri – her restaurant beau – wants to take her to Rome. We're plugging for Rome.

Patrick is learning to live with his money. He comes to see me now and then and he's always welcome as he usually brings Candy Delamere with him and I could never tire of Candy. I've quite forgiven her for telling Kate about Magdalen living with me.

Patricia's boutique is doing well. The modern miss who wants it known she's really been shopping feels she has to be seen carrying Patricia's sunflower logo. Della Coady came up with the logo design. I passed by their store last week and Della was doing something sexy with a mannequin in the window. She gave me the finger when she saw me but smiled to take some of the harm out of it.

Steady Eddie Delaney still doesn't know what to make of me. I'm sure he must wonder why I haven't turned him in. He seems to have overcome whatever jealousy he feels at my living with Kate Hartigan. Even so, I still walk around him when he has a spade on his shoulder.

Now and then, in various watering holes, I meet Tom Crotty, but he never mentions Paddy Brett or Hartigan. Sometimes he'll joke about Kate – Crotty is always Crotty.

For a while there were two journalists who tried to connect the murder of Paddy Brett with that of Gaffney, but neither ever got anywhere with it.

The Tribunal of Inquiry into offshore funds rolls on and now and then someone mentions North East Baltic Bank in the same breath. Only the lawyers are getting anything out of it.

I saw an article on the bouncer at Doxy Moran's. Seems the poor guy was a mature student trying to make a few bob. He was married with three kids.

Crotty says they are no nearer to identifying the foreign assassin.

315

Magdalen remains my friend and still cleans my kitchen. Kate says she wouldn't trust her as far as she could throw her.

Sean is my best pal.

I'm in love with Kate Hartigan. She likes deserts and mountains and sailing. She adores El Cotillo and we're building a place there with some of the million Paddy Brett left me. She's crazy about Sean and is getting quite broody. Yesterday she told me she hasn't taken the pill for a fortnight. I asked her how she proposed telling Julie and she just laughed.

I spent a lot of time fixing up Aunt Lil's grave.

On a day of soft rain I buried Paddy Brett's ashes under its white marble chippings.

It has dignity. A neat border of Kilkenny marble – 'as black as ink', as it goes in her favourite song, her party piece. For headstone a rough slab of hard limestone from a quarry close by that same city bearing the inscription:

ELIZABETH MEAGHER
AND
HER BELOVED NEPHEW
PATRICK BRETT

Aunt Lil would have wanted her sister's secret to go all the way.